"Careful, your l

"And I was trying so hard to hide it."

"What's the matter, Josh, no new woman in your life?"

"Not in the usual sense, no."

Bridget's throat had gone very dry. "Then in what sense?"

He needed to leave before he did something stupid. And yet he wasn't moving.

And then he was. But he was moving to close the tiny bit of space between them.

The only way she was going to save herself was through bravado, and she knew it.

"You're in my space, Youngblood," Bridget informed him hoarsely, trying to sound annoyed.

"What are you going to do about it?"

He half expected her to shove him back. The one thing he hadn't expected was for Bridget to grab him and press her mouth urgently against his.

And just before she did, he could have sworn that she'd whispered, "Damn you!"

Dear Reader,

Welcome back to the newest branch of the Cavanaughs, the one belonging to Sean, Brian and Andrew's long-lost brother. This time the story is about Sean's oldest daughter, Bridget, who finds herself grappling with what she views as a brand-new identity. This while becoming aware of feelings for her partner of three years, Josh Youngblood, feelings she has been trying to ignore because, after all, the man's relationships have the life expectancy of a fruit fly.

But Josh surprises her by being the one who is there for her while she's trying to sort out how she feels about this new family connection that has suddenly cropped up in her life as well as the lives of her immediate family members. And all this is played out while Bridget and Josh desperately try to bring down The Lady Killer, a serial killer who surfaces every February to kill as many redheaded women between the ages of twenty and thirty as he can in that short month. Interested? Then please keep reading. I promise to try to entertain you as best as I can.

With all my heart I wish you someone to love who loves you back.

Until the next time,

Marie Ferrarella

CAVANAUGH'S BODYGUARD

BY
MARIE FERRARELLA

MILLS & BOON

First published in Great Britain 2012
by Mills & Boon, an imprint of Harlequin (UK) Limited,
Eton House, 18-24 Paradise Road, Richmond, Surrey TW9 1SR

© Marie Rydzynski-Ferrarella 2012

ISBN: 978 0 263 89551 3
ebook ISBN: 978 1 408 97741 5

46-0812

Harlequin (UK) policy is to use papers that are natural, renewable and recyclable products and made from wood grown in sustainable forests. The logging and manufacturing processes conform to the legal environmental regulations of the country of origin.

Printed and bound in Spain
by Blackprint CPI, Barcelona

Marie Ferrarella, a *USA TODAY* bestselling and RITA®
Award-winning author, has written more than two hundred books, some under the name Marie Nicole. Her ro-
mances are beloved by fans worldwide. Visit her website at
www.marieferrarella.com.

To Charlie,
who turned the month of February
into something special
all those years ago.

Chapter 1

Finally.

The thought flashed through Detective Bridget Cavelli's mind at the same time that she glanced up to verify that the movement she'd detected out of the corner of her eye was her partner and no one else. She'd been waiting for her sexier-than-should-be-legally-allowed partner, Detective Joshua Youngblood, to walk into the squad room for the last half hour. This was precisely the amount of time she'd been going over the notes she had taken a year ago this month.

Her partner wasn't late. He was on time. She was the one who was early, but that didn't help to assuage her impatience. She needed to share this with him.

Now.

She struggled to rein in her impatience. It could have been worse. He could have been coming off a forty-eight-hour marathon date and running late rather than coming in right on time.

"He's back," Bridget announced to her partner, raising her voice in order to catch his attention.

Detective Joshua Youngblood said nothing in response as he continued walking to his desk. His green eyes were hidden behind exceptionally dark sunglasses. His measured, rhythmic gait brought him to the desk that had been assigned to him for the last three years.

After setting down the extra large container of ink-black coffee, Josh set himself down as well. His chair groaned. It needed oiling.

Once he was seated opposite her did he even acknowledge that he'd heard what Bridget had said by asking in a monotone voice, "Who's back?"

Bridget, who'd been his partner for as long as he'd been at this desk, leaned back slightly in her chair as she studied his expressionless face. The fact that Josh was still partially hidden behind the sunglasses told her all she needed to know. It was Monday and more likely than not, Josh hadn't amassed enough sleep over the weekend to keep a squirrel bright-eyed and bushy-tailed or even moderately functioning.

Temporarily forgetting the very cold chill that had gone zigzagging down her spine when the new acting lieutenant had told her the news earlier, Bridget asked her zombie-channeling partner a personal question, taking care not to show the slight spike of jealousy she suddenly experienced. "So, what's this one's name?"

For the time being, Josh left his sunglasses on. "I have no idea what you're talking about."

He was focused on removing the lid from the newly purchased, life-affirming black liquid. Josh absolutely *hated* tasting plastic when he drank his coffee and no matter how careful he tried to be, if he left the lid on, he could taste plastic with each sip.

This morning his hands felt like clumsy bear paws. This was what he got for going to bed ninety minutes before he was due in to work, he silently upbraided himself.

With a suppressed sigh, Bridget rose from her desk and made her way around to his. With a flick of her wrist, she made quick work of the coffee lid, tossing it into his waste paper basket. A thin plume of steam rose up from the inky sea.

"So, this one evaporated your brain as well as your energy?" she asked glibly, deliberately sounding chipper as she commented, "Busy little bee."

"I was up with a sick friend," Josh informed her after he had taken an incredibly long sip of his coffee. He could feel it winding through his system. Ever so slowly, he began to feel human again.

"I've never known you to make a woman sick, Josh. A little nauseous maybe, but not sick." Leaning her hip against his desk, Bridget crossed her arms before her and shook her head as she pinned him with a penetrating look. "Don't you think you should start acting your age, Youngblood? Partying and staying out all night all weekend is great when you're in college or in your early twenties, but all that's supposed to be out of your system by the time you start approaching thirty."

Josh appeared not to be paying any attention to her. Then he surprised her by sighing. "If you're going to lecture me—" he began.

She pretended to hang on his every word. "Yes?"

He took in a huge fortifying breath before warning her, "Don't."

A thousand little devils with tiny hammers pounded and danced around in his head. He was in no mood to listen to a lecture or any so-called words of wisdom his overly talkative partner might want to impart. From the first moment he'd seen her, he'd been of the opinion that she was exceptionally easy on the eyes, but definitely not always so easy on the ears.

"I'm just trying to look out for you, Partner," Bridget told him, deliberately smiling brightly at him. "Because whatever you do reflects on me." With that, she removed the black sunglasses from his face and gingerly placed them on his desk next to his computer. She did a quick assessment of his face. The last three days had left their mark. She couldn't remember ever seeing him this exhausted, and that included the time they had pulled a double surveillance shift.

Bridget told herself that it shouldn't bother her that he spent all his free time with women whose bust sizes were higher than their IQs—but it did.

Just sisterly concern, nothing more, she silently insisted.

"I suppose you don't look so bad—for a hungover Peter Pan," she commented.

"I'm not hungover," Josh protested, although without much verve. "For your information, I had the flu this weekend and I'm trying to get over it."

She raised a skeptical eyebrow. That hadn't taken long. She'd caught him in a lie already. "I thought you said you were up with a sick friend."

Josh never hesitated or wavered. "Where do you think I got the flu?"

He sounded almost indignant, but she wasn't buying it, not for a second. She knew him too well. Joshua Youngblood, second-generation cop and handsomer than sin, was a consummate ladies' man from the word *go*. The verb was also his rule of thumb whenever things began to look even remotely serious. The second a woman stopped viewing him less as a good time and more as husband material, Josh was gone. To his credit, he made no secret of it, made no promises that took in a month from now, much less "forever."

"You know," Bridget said glibly, "you might think about becoming a writer. I hear a lot of cops with a gift for fantasy start spinning stories on paper in their free time. Who knows? You might find your name on the binding of a book someday."

A third big gulp came precariously close to draining his container despite its large size. Josh set the cup down and did his best to focus his attention on Bridget. The woman was smart as well as a damn good detective. There was no one who he would rather have watching his back than her, but at times he could easily strangle her as well.

Like now.

All he wanted was to have his coffee in peace and then slowly ease into his day. Hopefully accomplishing both with a minimum of noise and pain until he could focus not just his mind but his eyes.

Didn't look as if that would happen. What he needed to do since he couldn't strangle her—at least not in a building full of cops—was deflect Bridget's attention away from him.

"You said something about someone being back," he reminded her. The coffee, strong enough to be used as a substitute for asphalt in a pinch, was beginning to finally work its magic. All he needed was another half hour or so before last night, Ivy Potter and the now empty bottle of Southern Comfort were all securely behind him.

"Yes, I did."

He sighed. Obviously she was going to make him work for this. "Okay, who's back?" he repeated.

"Who do you think?" Bridget crossed back to her desk and, for the moment, sat down. Or rather, she perched on the edge of her chair, too much tension dancing through her body for her to sit down properly.

"If I knew, I wouldn't be asking, would I?" Josh retorted with more than a trace of irritability in his voice.

As he spoke, he began to go through his drawers, opening one after another and rifling through them. He was searching for a bottle of desperately needed aspirin. If he didn't find it soon, he was damn near certain that the top of his head would come off.

Instead of answering him, Bridget asked, "What month is it?"

Frustrated, Josh raised his eyes to hers for a moment. "More tough questions?" he quipped. When she didn't say anything, he sighed, clearly exasperated as he continued with his up to this point fruitless search.

Damn it, there'd been a huge bottle of aspirin here just the other day. It couldn't have just disappeared. *Where* is *it?* he silently demanded.

"February," Josh bit off. "What does that have to do with—" And then he stopped and raised his eyes to hers again. The answer came crashing back to him. He fervently hoped he was wrong. *Very* fervently. "February," he repeated.

"February," Bridget echoed grimly with a nod of her head.

On her feet again, she went back to his desk. Moving him out of the way, she opened the bottom drawer, which was deeper than the rest, and, reaching in, she pushed aside several folders. Extracting the white and green bottle she knew he was looking for, she placed it on Josh's blotter in front of him without a word. She didn't need to talk. Her meaning was clear. Even though he was a great detective, there were times when the man had trouble finding his face when he was looking into the mirror.

What went unsaid, and she would have gone to her grave denying it, was that the trait was somewhat endearing to her.

Grabbing the bottle the second she'd produced it for him, Josh twisted off the top, shook out two rectangular pills and popped them into his mouth. He downed them with the last few drops of coffee lingering on the bottom of the giant container. Now all he could do was wait for the aspirin to take effect.

With a deep breath, he leaned back in his chair and fixed his partner with an incredulous look. "I was really hoping he was dead."

Bridget nodded. "Weren't we all," she readily agreed.

"You sure it was him?" Josh asked grimly. Before her eyes, he seemed to transform from the exceptionally handsome playboy who thought a long-term relationship meant one that lasted from one weekend to the next, into the razor-sharp investigator with keen instincts she both enjoyed and looked forward to working with.

Bridget answered him by reciting the details she'd

just read of the latest victim's description. "Pretty red-head in her early twenties. Her hands were neatly folded just above her abdomen and she had a big, gaping hole in her chest where her heart used to be. Yeah, I'm sure."

She sighed, shaking her head as she picked up the folder the lieutenant had given her and brought it over to Josh for his examination. After his last spree, the serial killer, whimsically dubbed the Lady Killer by a label-hungry media, had disappeared for almost a year and they had all nursed the hope that this time it was because he was dead and not because he seemed to have a quirk about the month when Cupid was celebrated.

"You know, I'm really beginning to hate Februaries," she told him.

Preoccupied with scanning the report submitted by the initial officer on the scene, Josh read that the policeman had found the body laid out in an alley behind a popular night club. Belatedly, Bridget's words registered in his head.

He glanced up and spared her an amused, knowing look. "I bet you were the little girl in elementary school who always got the most valentines dropped off at her desk on Valentine's Day." Bridget was the kind of woman the label "hot" had been coined for and there were times that he had to stop and remind himself that she was his partner and that he couldn't cross the lines that he ordinarily stepped over without a second thought. There would be consequences and he liked working with her too much to risk them.

"Then you would have lost that bet," Bridget told him matter-of-factly. "I was the girl in elementary school who never got any." She could vividly remember hating the approach of the holiday each year, her feelings of inadequacy ballooning to giant proportions every February fourteenth.

Josh looked up from the folder, surprised. "None?" he questioned suspiciously.

Bridget had to be pulling his leg for some strange reason of her own. Blond, with incredibly vivid blue eyes and a killer figure that not even a burlap sack could disguise, she had to have legions of guys drooling over her since she had first emerged out of her crib.

And, he thought again, he would have been among them if fate hadn't made them partners in the field.

"None," Bridget confirmed with a sharp nod of her head. It was still painful to recall those days and the way she'd felt. There were times now, when she looked into the mirror, that she felt as if that insecure little girl were still alive and well inside her. "I was a real ugly duckling as a kid," she told him. "I absolutely hated Valentine's Day back then. It always made me feel awkward, like everyone was looking at me and knew that I didn't get a single card from anyone. I thought it was a horrible holiday."

"Maybe that's it," Josh said, closing the sparse report and watching her.

Bridget looked at him, curious. She'd obviously missed something. "What's 'it'?"

"Maybe the killer is some psycho getting even," he suggested. As he spoke, it began to make more and more sense to him. "Our guy asked this redheaded goddess out on a date for Valentine's Day and she turned him down, maybe even laughed at him for daring to ask her." As he spoke, Josh's voice grew louder and more resonant. "His pride wounded, he doesn't step aside and lick his wounds like most guys, he gets even. *Really* gets even.

"Now, every February, he's relives that—or maybe relives what he wanted to do but didn't at the time— and takes out his revenge on girls who look like the one who rejected him."

Bridget turned what Josh had just said over in her head, studying it. "So what are you telling me? That you think our killer is Charlie Brown?" she asked him, amused despite the gruesome details of the case.

It seemed almost absurd—except for the fact that it did keep on happening. In the last two years, nine red-heads, their hearts very neatly cut out, had been found in alleys throughout Aurora.

Josh surprised her by explaining why her tongue-in-cheek theory didn't hold. "No, Charlie Brown never got his nerve up to ask the little redheaded girl out, so she couldn't reject him. She's just his eternal dream."

His eternal dream. That was almost poetic, she thought.

Bridget eyed her partner, amazed—and amused. Every time that she was about to write him off as being shallow, there'd be this glimmer of sensitivity that would just pull her back in.

She supposed that was one of the reasons women always flocked to him. That, a small waist and a rock-solid body that showed off his active gym membership.

"My God, Youngblood, I'm impressed," she told him after a beat. "I had no idea that you were so sensitive."

Josh stared at her for a long moment. And then his smile, the one she'd dubbed his "bad boy" smile, which could melt the heart of a statue, curved the corners of his mouth. "There're lot of things about me that you don't know."

Now he was just trying to jockey for leverage and mess with her mind, Bridget thought. There was just one little flaw with his allegation.

"I grew up with four brothers." She loved all of them dearly, but at times, when she'd been growing up, the verbal fights had been brutal. "They'd more than held their own, but I really doubt that there's very much about a living, breathing male that I can't second-guess," she told Josh with a smile.

Before Josh could say anything in response, their acting lieutenant, Jack Howard, came out of his office, saw them and immediately came over. Howard, a rather self-centered man who enjoyed hearing the sound of his own voice, had been the one to hand Bridget the case this morning once he saw that she and Youngblood had worked on it a year ago.

He looked from Bridget to Josh. "You two solve the case yet?" he asked in what appeared to be genuine seriousness.

Bridget knew better than to think he was kidding when he asked the question, but she played along, uncertain where this *was* going. She had a gut feeling that wherever it was, neither she nor Josh were going to like it. There was something very pompous about the man. Added to that, she had a feeling that he resented the fact that she was related to the police department's well-respected hierarchy.

"No, sir, not yet," she answered, allowing her voice to be neither submissive nor combative. She merely gave him the respect that his position was due. It had nothing to do with the man.

She and Josh had originally heard about the case two years ago, after the second body had been discovered. None of the clues at the time had led the investigating detectives anywhere substantial. Four bodies had turned up and then the killer seemed to just vanish into thin air.

Until last February when he surfaced again.

This time, the case became theirs and the killer wound up leaving five women in his wake, five women who were all left in the same pose as this latest one. Hands neatly folded below where their hearts should have been. All in all, it made for a very gruesome picture.

"Then why are you just sitting around?" Howard demanded, his voice no longer friendly. He turned on Bridget. "Just because you suddenly found out that your uncle's the chief of detectives doesn't give you any extra points in my book or cut you any extra slack. Do you understand Cavelli—Cavanaugh?" Flummoxed, he glared at her. "What the hell do you want me to call you?" Howard demanded.

Bridget squared her shoulders like a soldier who had found herself under fire and was making the best of it. She didn't like Howard, and his harping on her recent situation just underscored her negative feelings for the man.

God, would this tempest in a teapot never be resolved? It was bad enough that Josh had teased her about it. But he at least didn't seem jealous of this brand-new status she found herself struggling with, a status she'd never sought out or wanted in the first place.

But here it was, anyway.

Ever since the five-decades-old mix-up in the hospital had come to light, uncovering the fact that her father and some other infant male had accidentally been switched at birth and that her father—and so, consequently affecting all the rest of them—was not Sean Cavelli but Sean Cavanaugh, brother to both the former police chief and the current chief of detectives of the Aurora Police Department, she and her siblings had had no peace.

They were assaulted with questions, innuendos and their share of jealous remarks on a regular basis. They were no longer judged on their own merits but on the fact that they were all part of what was considered by others to be the "royal family" of the police department.

Now that she actually thought about it, it seemed as if there was at least one Cavanaugh in almost every branch of the department. Despite the fact that it was completely without a basis, nepotism and favoritism were words that were constantly being bandied about when it came to talk about their jobs and she for one was sick of it.

She'd gotten here by her own merit long before she'd ever been made aware of her surprising connection to the Cavanaughs.

It was enough to make a woman bitter, Bridget thought, eternally grateful that she at least had a large, thriving optimistic streak coupled with healthy dose of self-esteem—now.

"'Detective' will do fine," Bridget informed the lieutenant with a deliberate, wide smile that might have been called flirtatious under somewhat different circumstances.

Josh wasn't fooled. He knew she'd flashed the smile

on purpose, to throw Howard off and confuse him. If he didn't miss his guess, his partner would have rather eaten dirt than be even remotely coupled with the new lieutenant and the fact that Howard was married had nothing to do with it. He'd only been on the job for a day before it became apparent that Jack Howard had an ego the size of Pittsburgh.

"Well, 'Detective,'" the lieutenant said curtly, giving her a withering glance, "you and your sleepy-looking partner can get off your butts and do some honest police work and catch this son of a bitch before he louses up my record for cleared cases!" Howard snapped.

With that, the lieutenant turned on the heel of his Italian leather, three-hundred-dollar shoes, and marched back into his office, confident that he had made a dramatic impact on not just the two detectives but the rest of the squad room as well.

Josh glanced over toward Bridget and saw the way her hand closed over the stapler on her desk—like she was debating hurling it.

He put his hand over hers, keeping the stapler where it was. "Not worth it, partner," he murmured.

She took a deep breath and nodded, doing her best to ignore the momentary warm feeling that zipped through her and then vanished the second Josh removed his hand from hers.

Chapter 2

"His record," Bridget bit off angrily, struggling not to raise her voice loud enough for the retreating lieutenant to hear her. "That jerk couldn't clear a case if it was lying on the floor and he had a broom in his hands. We're the ones who clear cases," she declared hotly, referring not just to herself and Josh, but to the other detectives who were in their division as well. They were the ones who did all the work, not Howard. He turned up at the press conferences to grab the recognition, but he was never there for the hard work.

"Don't work yourself up," Josh advised mildly. "Like I said, it's not worth it. And, while you're at it," he continued, leaning in so that his voice was even lower than it was a moment ago, "don't raise your voice."

She glared at Josh. How could he remain so calm

around that preening peacock? "It isn't raised," she insisted.

"No," he agreed. Her eyes narrowed into blue slits of suppressed fire that he found arousing. "But it will be," he pointed out. "And this headache is still killing me."

Bridget looked over her shoulder toward Howard's office and at the man inside the glass enclosure. He was watching them. It just made her temper rise to a dangerous level.

"Speaking of killing…"

On his feet, Josh came up behind his partner and placed both hands on her back. With a gentle push, he guided her toward the doorway. "Let's go, Cavelli, before I suddenly find myself having to break in a brand-new partner. You know how much I'd hate that."

Forcing herself to calm down, Bridget spared Josh an amused glance as she doubled back to get her jacket. He really did look out for her, and she appreciated it. He was a hell of a lot more thoughtful than some of the guys she'd dated.

Too bad circumstances weren't different, she mused as she deposited something into her pocket before slipping on her light gray jacket.

"Breaking in a new partner," she echoed. "Who are you kidding?" she asked. "Nobody would be able to put up with you and your quirks for more than a week."

"And I'd find myself missing that unabashed, everflowing flattery of yours," Josh cracked as he led the way to the elevator. "By the way…" He turned toward her. "Exactly where are we supposed to be going?"

She'd stuffed the details of this year's first murder into her jacket and pulled it out now as they waited for the elevator to arrive. Pointing to the pertinent addresses, she held the sheet up for her partner to see.

"We can either go to the scene of the crime or go to break the news to the victim's boyfriend. Take your pick." Folding the sheets again, she slipped them back into her pocket. "I'm guessing that the ME hasn't had a chance to do the autopsy yet, otherwise, *that* would be my first pick."

Josh made his choice. As he saw it, it was the lesser of two evils. "Scene of the crime," he said as they stepped into the elevator. After a beat, he made a confession, which was rare for him. "I absolutely hate breaking that kind of news to people. They're never the same after that."

Bridget laughed shortly. "Haven't found anyone yet who *didn't* mind it, never mind enjoyed it." She clearly remembered each time she'd had to go to a loved one to break the tragic news. The experience never became routine. Her heart hurt every time. "Okay, scene of the crime it is." She leaned forward and pressed for the ground floor. "You realize that putting it off doesn't make telling the boyfriend any easier."

He knew that, but he was hoping for another option. "And nobody else caught this case?" he asked just before the doors opened again on the ground floor.

Bridget made an elaborate show of searching the small aluminum-walled enclosure. "You see anyone else here?"

"Nope," he answered, resigning himself to the fact that they were working the gruesome case solo as they got off. "But that's only because you're so dynamic you make everyone else fade into the background."

Bridget stopped just short of the rear doors that

exited out onto the parking lot. Turning, she looked at Josh quizzically. "What's with you this morning?" she asked.

Wide shoulders rose and fell in a noncommittal shrug. Since she wasn't going through the doors, he did. And then he held them open for her.

"Nothing," he responded dismissively.

Bridget slipped through the doors quickly. She wasn't about to give up that easily.

"Yes, there is," she insisted. They were on the same wavelength, she and Josh. Something was off. She could feel her protective side being roused. "Now spill it. Your latest main squeeze hounding you for a commitment?" she guessed, deliberately keeping her voice upbeat and light. The idea of her partner committing to a single woman was as far-fetched as Prince Charming actually turning out to be a skilled day laborer. And, if she were being utterly honest with herself, she rather liked it that way.

Why should that matter? she silently upbraided herself. *The guy's your partner, not your lover, remember?*

It annoyed her that the word "lover" had even popped into her head in reference to Josh. What was with her lately?

Josh paused, gazing out on the parking lot. He wasn't looking for his car—he knew where that was—he was looking for his patience, which seemed to be in short supply this morning.

"No, not her," he finally said.

Bridget heard things in his voice that he was leaving unsaid.

Not for long, she thought.

"Then who is?" she asked. Josh merely frowned in

response and went down the cement steps, heading toward the vehicle they were using for the day. Bridget followed quickly.

But, getting into the passenger seat, she paused for a second and offered to switch places with him. Whether hungover, coming down with something or disturbed, he wasn't himself today.

"You want me to drive?" she asked.

"Nope." Josh buckled up. "I'm not ready to die today," he told her.

Bridget was quiet for a moment, trying to get to the bottom of what was eating at him. And then it hit her. Belatedly, she finally buckled up.

"It's your mother, isn't it?" she guessed just as he turned the key in the ignition. The car came to life and he slowly backed out of his space.

"It's my mother what?" he asked shortly, straightening out the wheel and then heading out onto the main thoroughfare.

She ignored the shortness of Josh's response. "It's your mother who's hounding you to make a commitment, isn't it?"

Damn it, he thought irritably, the woman was like a pit bull once she latched onto something. She just wouldn't let go. "Not sure how things are done in your world, Cavelli, but in this state, mothers and sons can't get married."

She was right, Bridget thought. She could tell by the set of his jaw. "You know damn well what I'm saying, Youngblood." This wasn't the first time his mother, a really affable woman, had been on his case. "Your mother's after you to settle down, isn't she?"

He gave up trying to get her to back off. "Grandkids," he declared, annoyed. He really loved his mother. They had gotten extremely close after his father had been killed in the line of duty and as far as mothers went, she was rather sharp and with it—except for this one annoying flaw. "She says she wants grandkids. I told her she was too young for that."

"Flattery." She nodded her approval. "Nice. Did it work?"

He laughed shortly and shook his head. "Nope. She says there're a lot of young grandmothers around these days. According to her, she's the only one of her friends whose kid is still single."

"She's lonely," Bridget guessed, feeling for the woman. She'd met Eva Youngblood a number of times and found her to be extremely affable. They got along really well. The woman would make someone a really nice mother-in-law someday. "That's what you get for being an only child."

"Hey, it's not my fault," Josh pointed out. "After my dad died, lots of his buddies on the force came around to make sure we were all right. They took turns bringing me to ball games, coaching my team, helping me study. They did what they could to be there for her, too. I know that more than one of them really wanted to get serious with her."

He frowned, remembering what it was like, hearing his mother cry late at night when she thought he was asleep. It broke his heart and made him promise to himself that he would never love someone so much that he couldn't breathe right without them.

"But Mom swore up and down that Dad had been the love of her life and she was not looking to get married again. Ever. And even if she was, it wouldn't be to another policeman. She said she couldn't go through that kind of pain again. Couldn't stand there and be on the receiving end of a condolence call."

Bridget supposed she could understand that. Once hurt, twice leery. "So, instead of building a second life," she surmised, "your mother is after you to finally build yours."

He sighed. "That's about it."

Parents, she knew, could be exceedingly stubborn when it came to their kids. Her father was laid-back, thank God, but her late mother had been fairly intense. Looking back, she realized it was all out of love, but at the time it had driven her crazy.

"So, what are you going to do?" Bridget asked, slanting a glance in his direction.

He'd already looked into this solution. "I'm going to get her a dog."

Bridget laughed, pretending to study his profile for a moment. "I can see the resemblance, but I really don't think that's what your mother actually has in mind."

Whether she did or not, this was the plan for now. He was stalling for time until something better occurred to him. "I'll tell her it's just a placeholder until I find the girl of my dreams."

Surprised, Bridget shifted in her seat. This was a side of Josh she hadn't expected. In the three years they'd been partnered, Josh had only gotten serious about their work, not about any of the myriad women he'd gone out with in that time.

She caught herself holding her breath as she asked, "You actually have a dream girl?"

"Yeah." Josh spared her a quick, meaningful look.

"One who doesn't ask me any questions or make any demands of me."

For a minute there, she'd thought he was serious. She should have known better. Bridget laughed, shaking her head. Feeling relieved more than she thought she should. "Then I'm afraid that you're doomed to being alone, Youngblood."

"I'm not going to be alone," he told her. They came to a stop at a light. He took the opportunity to turn toward her and flashed a wide, brilliant grin. "I have you."

The very first time she'd seen that smile, it had gotten to her. She hadn't grown immune to its effects, but at this point she knew that he meant nothing by it. He was just charming. And while she caught herself wondering what it would be like to be with Josh, *really* be with Josh, who could have been the living, breathing poster child for the words "drop dead gorgeous," she told herself that she didn't want to ruin a good thing. She and Josh worked well together, anticipated one another and for the most part, thought alike.

At times they wound up completing one another; what one lacked, the other supplied. Partnerships like that were exceedingly rare, not worth sacrificing in order to scratch an itch.

She'd been quiet too long, she realized. To deflect any kind of suspicions or possible questions on Josh's end, she got back to the reason they were out here in the first place. "Yeah, well, if we don't come up with some kind of answers for the narcissistic fool they made our acting lieutenant, Howard might wind up splitting us up out of spite."

He sincerely doubted that would ever happen. When

they had first been paired, all he saw was what one of his late father's friends had described as a "hot babe." It didn't take Bridget very long to set him straight. She might have killer looks, but it was her brain power that he actually found sexy. The fact that she didn't trade on her looks was another plus in her favor.

It also allowed him the freedom to tease her now. "You could always go and complain about Howard to your 'Uncle Brian.'"

Bridget sat up a little straighter as she gave him a withering look. "Hello, possibly we haven't been introduced yet. My name's Bridget Cavelli and I fight my own battles."

"So, you're keeping it?" Josh asked, picking up on the name she'd used. "You're not changing it?"

"Changing what?"

"Your last name. Technically, you are a Cavanaugh, you know. You have no real ties to that moniker you've been sporting around for the last thirty years—"

"Twenty-eight," she corrected tersely. "I'm twenty-eight."

He knew exactly how old she was—knew a great many other things about her as well—but he liked getting under her skin. It helped to keep things light. It also helped him deflect other feelings he was having. Feelings that had no place on the job and would only get in the way of a working relationship.

"And you don't look a day over twenty-seven and a half," he deadpanned.

Bridget sighed and settled back in her seat. It was going to be a very long morning, she thought. She could tell.

* * *

"Andrew, are you all right? You look a little pale," Rose Cavanaugh said to her husband, stopping short.

She'd just walked into the state-of-the-art kitchen to get a glass of juice. This was where the former chief of police and the love of her life spent a great deal of his time each day. He could be found here creating or re-creating meals for any one of a vast number of relatives who had a standing invitation to drop by whenever the occasion allowed, or they were in the neighborhood. She'd never known anyone who loved cooking—and family—as much as Andrew did.

But it was obvious that right now, he had more on his mind than cooking. Like the person he'd just finished talking to.

"Who was on the phone?" she asked him as Andrew hung up the receiver.

He tried to offer his wife a smile, but he was still sorting out the news he'd just received. "That was my father."

The family patriarch, Seamus Cavanaugh, was the first of the family to join the police department and work his way through the ranks, back when Aurora was unincorporated and considered an off-shoot of Sacramento. For the last dozen years or so the retired police chief had been living in Miami Beach, Florida, enjoying the company of some of his old friends from the force who had also migrated there.

Rose smiled fondly. Her father-in-law liked to check in from time to time. He did it in order to keep his sons from worrying, although he insisted that he was perfectly capable of looking after himself.

"What's he up to?" she asked, wondering what had prompted this particular call. If she knew Seamus, the man was probably in love—again—and asking Andrew what he thought about getting a new "mother."

"About thirty thousand feet," Andrew answered matter-of-factly.

Rose cocked her head, trying to make sense out of what her husband was saying. "Come again?"

"He is," Andrew confirmed. "Coming back again." After taking a fresh cup from the cabinet next to the sink, Andrew poured himself some of the coffee he'd just brewed right before the phone had rung. Holding the cup in both hands, he sat down before he attempted to clarify his statement. "Dad's flying back to Aurora right now, even as we're having this conversation."

Sitting down opposite him, Rose placed her hand on top of her husband's in a mute display of unity.

"Is something wrong?" she asked, concerned. They had been trying to get Seamus to come back out for a visit for years now. But he had always been very adamant about not flying. Because of that, the senior Cavanaugh had missed out on a host of weddings and births.

He'd even passed on what Andrew felt had been a major event in his life: finding Rose again after his wife had gone missing and had been presumed by everyone—everyone but him—to be dead. He never gave up working the case, never gave up looking for the mother of his five children. And eventually, his persistence had paid off. The only thing that remotely came close to spoiling the event for him was that his father had sent his hearty congratulations instead of turning up to celebrate with the rest of the family.

"No, nothing's wrong," Andrew told her. "He said he suddenly just got tired of doing nothing with the rest of his life but shooting the breeze with a bunch of old men who were living in the past. He's decided to turn over a new leaf. Part of that involves flying out here. And, I suspect that he's anxious to meet his new son."

Rose smiled. "At his age, Sean can't exactly be called 'new,'" she pointed out, amusement curving the generous corners of her mouth.

He looked at it in another way. "Considering the fact that Dad's never seen him, I think the word 'new' could be applied in this case."

"I suppose you're right." Pushing aside the empty juice glass, Rose got to her feet. "Well, I'd better get myself to the store," she announced. She caught her husband arching his eyebrow in a silent query, which surprised her. "If there's going to be another one of Andrew Cavanaugh's famous parties in the very near future, I've got a lot of grocery shopping to do. Do you have a list ready for me?"

Instead of producing one, Andrew caught her hand and pulled her over to him, stopping his wife from leaving the room.

"No, no list and no famous party," he told her. "I think that this time around, Dad meeting his son for the first time will be a private occasion."

He could have knocked her over with a feather. "Really?" she asked incredulously.

In all the years that she had been part of Andrew's life, she'd found that absolutely *everything* was an excuse for a family get-together and a party. "One for all and all for one" wasn't just a famous phrase written by Alexander Dumas in *The Three Musketeers*, it was a mantra that she strongly suspected her husband believed in and lived by.

"Dad's got a pretty tight rein on his emotions,"

Andrew explained. Friendly and seemingly outgoing, there was still a part of Seamus Cavanaugh that he kept walled in, strictly to himself. That part grieved over loss and mourned over victims who couldn't be saved in time. "But this kind of thing can just blow a man right out of the water. If, once he meets Sean, Dad loses it, he definitely won't appreciate it happening in front of a room full of witnesses."

Rose laughed. "Since when have we *ever* been able to fit all our relatives into just a room?" she asked.

"All right, I stand corrected. A house full of witnesses," Andrew amended. "This is definitely one case of the less people being around for the grand reunion, the better."

Rose pretended to be disappointed—but the hint of a grin gave her away. "And here I was, planning to sell tickets."

"C'mere, woman." Andrew laughed.

He gave her hand a quick tug and swept her onto his lap. He liked having her there just fine. In his mind, because he'd been given a second chance after doggedly searching for her all those years she'd had amnesia and been missing without realizing it, he still felt like a newlywed.

"Anyone ever tell you that you have a fresh mouth?" he asked Rose, doing his best to sound serious.

Rose laced her fingers together behind his neck as she made herself comfortable in her favorite "chair." "Not that I recall," she answered with a straight face. "Why? Do you want to sample it?"

The former chief of police grinned and looked every bit the boy whom she had first fallen in love with in second-period American English all those very many years ago.

"I thought you'd never ask," he said just before he kissed her and rocked her world.

Again.

Chapter 3

The good-looking man behind the bar whose biceps were more impressive than his brain cells frowned as he stared at the photograph Josh had placed on the counter in front of him. It was a photograph of the woman who had been found in the alley behind the club where he worked and even though the more gruesome aspects of the murder weren't detailed, it was obvious that the woman was dead.

Shaking his head, the bartender, who claimed his name was Simon Quest, looked up at the two detectives.

"I'm a lot better with regulars," he protested. "But yeah, I think she was here last night."

My kingdom for a witness who actually witnessed something, Josh thought. The bartender sounded far from convincing. For now, he left the photograph on the bar, hoping that it still might jog Quest's memory.

"Was anyone bothering her?" Josh asked the other man.

Quest shrugged, as if to dismiss the question, but then he stopped abruptly and pulled the photo over to study it.

Josh's hope sank when he shook his head. "Not that I can recall. It was a happy crowd last night."

Bridget glanced at the victim's pale face. "I know at least one of them who didn't stay that way," she commented grimly.

"Can you remember anything at all about this woman?" Josh prodded Quest one last time. "Was she the life of the party? Was she in a corner, drinking by herself? Anything at all?" he stressed.

The bartender thought for a long moment; then his expression brightened. "I saw her talking to the people around her. They acted as if they all knew each other." Pausing, he appeared as if he was trying to remember something.

When the silence went on too long, Bridget urged the man on. "What?"

"There was this one guy," Simon responded slowly, as if he was envisioning the scene again. "He just kept staring at her."

"Did he come up and talk to her?" Bridget asked eagerly.

Quest shook his head helplessly. "Not that I saw. It was big crowd," he explained, then added, "and we were shorthanded last night."

"What else can you remember about this guy?"

Josh asked, hoping they could finally get something to go on.

"Nothing." The bartender went back to drying the shot glasses that were all lined up in front of him like tiny, transparent soldiers. "He left."

Maybe they could get a time frame, Bridget thought. "When?"

Quest set down another glass, then shrugged again. "I dunno. Around midnight. Maybe one o'clock. I remember she was gone when we closed down," he volunteered, then ruined it by adding, "Can't say when, though."

This was getting them nowhere, Bridget thought. "Did she leave with anyone?"

The look on Quest's face said he had no idea if the victim did or not. He lifted his wide shoulders and then let them drop again. "She was just gone."

Ever hopeful, Bridget tried another approach. "This guy, the one who was staring at her, what did he look like?"

Quest exhaled a frustrated breath. It was obvious that he was regretting he'd ever mentioned the starer. "Just an average guy. Looked like he hadn't cracked a smile in a real long time."

Josh tried his hand at getting some kind of useful information out of the vacant-headed bartender. "Was he young, old, fat, skinny, long-haired, bald, white, black—polka dot," he finally bit off in exasperation when the bartender made no indication that *anything* was ringing a bell.

"Just average," Quest repeated. "Maybe he was forty, maybe not. He did have hair," he recalled. "Kinda messy, like he was trying to look cool but he didn't know how. And he was a white guy. He *wasn't* a regular," Simon emphasized proudly. "Or I would've recognized him."

Well, he supposed at least it was *something*, Josh told himself. He took out one of his cards and placed it on the counter, even as he collected the photograph and tucked it back into his inside pocket.

"You think of anything else you forgot to mention, anything comes back to you—" he tapped the card with his finger "—call me."

Quest shifted his glance toward Bridget. "I'd rather call her."

Information was information, Bridget reasoned. Inclining her head in silent assent, she placed her card next to Josh's on the shiny bar.

"Fine. Here's my card. Just remember," she informed the man cheerfully as she stepped back, "we're a set."

"He was trying to hit on you," Josh told her as they walked out of the club three minutes later. The fact that it bothered him was only because he was being protective of his partner. Or so he told himself. Bridget seemed unaware that she had this aura of sexuality about her and it was up to him to make sure no one tried to take advantage of that.

Right, like she can't take care of herself, Josh silently mocked himself.

He blew out a breath. Maybe he needed more aspirins to clear his head a little better.

Bridget headed straight for the car. "He's lucky I didn't hit him back," she retorted, then complained, "I thought bartenders were supposed to have such great memories."

"Sometimes they're paid not to have them," Josh

speculated, aiming his remote at the car. It squawked in response as four side locks sprang up at attention.

Bridget paused beside the vehicle. "You think he knows more than he's saying?"

Josh laughed shortly. He looked at her over the car's roof. "It would be hard for him to know less. Let's talk to her boyfriend and find out if he knows who she was partying with last night."

She nodded. "Maybe one of them remembers something about this guy who was staring at her."

Getting into the front passenger seat, Bridget buckled up and then let out a loud sigh. After Josh pulled out of the area and back onto the road again, she turned toward him and asked, "So, what kind of a dog?" When he didn't answer and just looked at her as if she had lapsed into monosyllabic gibberish, she added, "For your mother. You said you were getting a dog for your mother, remember?"

Now her question made sense. But he'd mentioned the dog over an hour ago, before they had gone in to question the bartender.

"Boy, talk about your long pauses." Josh laughed. "That almost came out of nowhere."

It was all connected in her head. She didn't see why he was having such a hard time with it. "Well, talking about the dog in your mother's future didn't exactly seem appropriate while we were questioning that bartender about a homicide right behind the club where he works," she told Josh, then got back on track. "So? Have you decided what kind you're getting?"

He hadn't gone much beyond the fact that he *was* getting his mother a canine companion sometime in the near future. If she had a pet to take care of, she wouldn't have as much time to nag him about settling down and giving her grandchildren.

"I thought maybe one of those fluffy dogs," he answered.

Off the top of her head, she could think of about twenty breeds that matched that description. "Well, that narrows it down."

She'd managed to stir his curiosity. "Why are you so interested in what kind of dog I'm going to wind up giving to my mother?"

She was just trying to be helpful. "A couple of the Cavanaughs actually *don't* strap on a gun in the morning. One of them is a vet who also works with Aurora's canine division, does their routine checkups, takes care of them if they get hurt, things like that. I think her name's Patience. Anyway, I thought you might want to talk to her, ask her some questions about the best kind of dog for your mother."

That didn't sound like a half-bad idea, he supposed since he didn't really know what he was doing. When he was a kid, he'd never owned a dog, never wanted to get attached to anything after his father's death.

"Maybe I will." He flashed Bridget a grin as he sailed through a yellow light. "When I talk to her, can I tell her that her 'Cousin Bridget' sent me?"

If he was going to use every topic to make another joke about her new family, then she shouldn't have even bothered making the suggestion.

She waved a dismissive hand at her partner. "Forget I said anything."

He was silent for a moment, as if content to let the quiet in the car prevail. But he'd been chewing on something for a while now. This last display of irritation on

Bridget's part told him that his observation over the last two months was probably right. Ever since his partner had learned about the mix-up in the hospital nearly fifty years ago, a mix-up that made her a Cavanaugh instead of a Cavelli, she'd seemed somewhat preoccupied and not quite her usual self.

"This really bothers you, doesn't it?" he asked in a voice devoid of all teasing.

"You getting a dog for your mother instead of growing up and having a meaningful relationship with a woman that lasts longer than a half-time program at the Super Bowl?" she asked glibly, deliberately avoiding his eyes. "No, not really."

She'd used a lot of words to describe a topic that she supposedly didn't care about, but that was a question to explore some other time, Josh thought. Right now, he was more concerned about Bridget's state of mind regarding the recent change in her immediate family. He might get on her case from time to time, but his three-year relationship with Bridget was the longest one he'd ever had with a woman, besides his mother. Beneath the barbs, the quips and the teasing, he really did care about Bridget. Cared about her a great deal. Sometimes more than he should, he told himself. He definitely didn't like seeing her like this.

"You know damn well I'm talking about the fact that your father found out that he'd been switched at birth with another male newborn and that he—and consequently you and those brothers and sisters of yours—are really Cavanaughs."

Bridget blew out a breath as she stared straight ahead at the road. "Yeah, I know what you're talking about, I was just hoping you'd take the hint and back off." She spared him a frown. "I should have known better."

Yeah, she should have, Josh thought. "So why does this bother you so much?" he wanted to know. "I know people in the department who'd give their right arm to wake up one morning and find out that they're related to the Cavanaughs. The very name carries a lot of weight in the department. I mean, think of it, they're an entire family of law enforcement agents and not a dirty one in the lot." He wasn't saying anything that they both didn't already know. "Hell, it's like the city's own personal branch of Camelot."

"So what's your point?" she asked, annoyed.

Driving into the parking lot of an apartment complex, Josh brought the car to a stop in the first empty space he saw.

"My point is, what's the problem you seem to be having with this?" he asked.

He was a guy. She didn't expect him to understand. Hell, she could barely understand all the tangled emotions herself. This unexpected twist made her life seem so confused, so jumbled up. There were times when she didn't know what to think, what to feel.

"The problem, oh insensitive one, is what do I do about my 'old family?' Uncle Adam, Uncle Tony, Aunt Angie, Aunt Anna." She went down the list of the people she'd believed until two months ago were her father's brothers and sisters. "Are they just strangers to me now? What *are* they to me and to the others?" she demanded with frustration. "Not to mention what are they to my dad? How am I supposed to regard them now that I know we're not blood relatives?" she asked, frustrated.

Everything had turned upside down for her. She couldn't be laid-back about the whole thing, the way her older brother Tom was. For her, all this had brought up real questions, real concerns. Moreover, it had left her with a dilemma on her hands that she had no idea how to resolve. Who *was* her family?

Josh still didn't really see what the problem was. Maybe because, in a remote way, he'd found himself in the same sort of position, except that in his case, the positions had been reversed. He'd lost his real father and found himself on the receiving end of a whole handful of generous "fathers."

"Well, speaking for myself, the word 'family' doesn't strictly refer to people with the same blood in their veins as you. After my dad was killed, a lot of his old buddies made it a point to come around to check on my mom and me to see if we were okay. The lot of them took turns looking out for us. After a while, it was like having five surrogate fathers around. They weren't my dad and they couldn't take my dad's place, but they did help to fill the void he left. They were the ones who got my mother through those dark times. I loved the lot of them and I think of all of them as family.

"The uncles and aunts you started out with before all this came to light are still your uncles and aunts in spirit if not in the strict definition of that according to the law. And let's face it, the way you feel about a person is all that counts."

Bridget looked at her partner for a long, silent moment, more impressed than she wanted to let on. "That's pretty profound coming from you. I guess even a stopped clock has to be right twice a day."

He grinned. Now *that* was the Bridget he knew and loved. "I have my moments," he acknowledged.

"Yeah," she agreed with a half smile. "Every twenty years or so, you do."

"Have you thought about talking to your Uncle Adam about how you feel about this? I mean, he is a priest and all and they're supposed to be able to offer guidance when one of their 'flock' has an emotional crisis to deal with." He raised his eyebrows in a unified query. "Right?"

She shook her head, vetoing the idea. "It might feel a little weird for both of us, considering that he's part of that crisis."

"He might surprise you."

"Two surprises in one day? I don't think I could handle that," she said flippantly. "Having you actually make sense is earth-shaking enough for me to try to come to terms with. Going for two might be asking for trouble. Who knows, the next thing that might happen is I'll be hearing the hoofbeats of the four horsemen."

Getting out of the car, he looked around the sprawling, newly upgraded complex. "I'd rather settle for that than what we're about to do next," he murmured under his breath.

They'd arrived at the apartment complex that was listed as Karen Anderson's last known residence. A residence the serial killer's latest victim had shared with her boyfriend.

Remaining beside the car, Josh scanned the area more intently, searching for apartment number 189. He was in no hurry to find it and in less of a hurry to do what he had to do.

His feet felt glued to the asphalt.

"Poor guy doesn't know what's about to hit him," he muttered grimly. Spotting a map of the area posted behind glass and next to the mailboxes, he made his way over to it. Bridget followed. "His girl goes out without him for a night out on the town and comes back dead."

"Ordinarily, if this didn't have the Lady Killer's MO all over it, I would have reminded you that your 'poor guy' would most likely be considered a person of interest. First rule of thumb in a homicide investigation, remember?" she said glibly.

"Thanks," Josh said with a touch of sarcasm. "I didn't know that." And then he grew a little more serious. "He still might be a person of interest, you know," Josh speculated.

That caught her by surprise. "You think this guy's our serial killer?"

"No." He doubted if they would get this lucky this early in this year's cat-and-mouse game with the Lady Killer. "But I think he might have taken advantage of the fact that there was a Valentine serial killer on the loose the last two years, done his homework and done away with his freewheeling girlfriend by copying the serial killer's MO. It's not like that hasn't been done before," he reminded her, "hiding a murder in the middle of a bunch of other murders."

Bridget nodded. The theory did make a lot of sense—as if they needed the extra confusion. "Just when I start to think of you as just another handsome face, you actually have a thought and blow everything out of the water," she pretended to lament.

"I am another handsome face," he acknowledged teasingly, "but I also like keeping you on your toes,

Cavanaugh." The moment the surname had slipped out of his mouth, he slanted a look at her face, waiting to see—or hear—her reaction.

As expected, she frowned—but not as deeply as he thought she might.

"Don't call me that yet," she requested. "Not until I get used to the sound of it. Deal?"

"Deal," he echoed. "Whatever you want." And then he pretended to be feeling her out. "Is it okay to call you Bridget?"

Bridget laughed and shook her head. Leave it to Josh to lighten the moment. It was a quality she really liked in him. "That's not about to change, so yeah, you can call me Bridget."

"The apartment's over in that direction," he announced, pointing to an area to their left. "It's just after the duck pond."

"Duck pond?" she echoed.

"That's what it says on the map. Looks more like a duck puddle if you ask me," he declared as they walked by it. "One way or another, we need to get this over with sooner than later."

She completely agreed. She never liked putting off anything just because she found it unpleasant to deal with. "Man after my own heart."

Leading the way, Josh turned and looked at her over his shoulder and winked. "You should be so lucky."

The wink sent a ripple through her that she deliberately ignored. "Ha! The luck," she fired back, happy to be bantering with him again, "would be all yours." What they did, day in, day out, was dark enough. A little lightness was more than welcome.

He probably would be the lucky one in this, he

thought. If he were in the market for something stable and permanent—

Which he wasn't, he reminded himself firmly before his mind could go wandering.

This wasn't the time.

They stopped in front of the ground-floor garden apartment door with the appropriate numbers affixed on it and rang an anemic-sounding bell.

When no one answered, they rang it again.

Bridget raised her hand to try ringing the bell for a third time when the door suddenly opened.

"Finally decide to come home?" a deep, humorless male voice asked. "What's the matter, lose your key again? Or did you throw it away?"

Both questions came from a semi-wet man wearing a bath towel precariously wrapped around his rather lean hips. He was standing in the doorway and his eyes filled with wonder as he looked at them with surprise. He stopped drying his hair.

His demeanor changed instantly and his expression darkened.

"Hey, I'm not giving to anything or converting to anything so go bother someone else," he said curtly. With that the man grabbed the doorknob and started closing the door.

Josh put his foot in the way and effectively provided an immovable object that stopped the other man from closing the door.

"We're not selling anything," he told the other man. "Are you James King?"

"Yeah," the man answered, his eyes shifting suspiciously from one to the other. "Who are you?"

Bridget took out her badge and ID at the same time that Josh did.

Josh made the introductions. "I'm Detective Youngblood. This is Detective Cavelli." He'd faltered for a second, then decided, in order to avoid any confusion, to state the name that she still had printed on her identification. "We'd like a few words with you. Mind if we come in?"

The man remained standing exactly where he was. The suspicion deepened on his face. "What's this all about?" he demanded.

"Mr. King, really, this will be a lot easier on everyone if we step inside your apartment. You're not going to want to hear this standing out here like this, half naked," Bridget told him, her voice taking on a gentle note.

After a moment, the man took a step into his apartment, opening the door wider so that his unexpected visitors could enter.

Chapter 4

Looking somewhat perturbed and confused about this unexpected invasion, King turned around just as Josh closed the door to the apartment behind them.

"Look, I just got home from the gym and I was taking a shower when you started leaning on my bell," he told them irritably. "You mind if I get dressed first before you ask whatever it is you're here to ask?"

"No. As a matter of fact, I'd highly recommend it," Bridget replied as the man tugged his sagging bath towel back up to his waist.

King looked slightly amused at her answer. For a moment, it seemed as if he forgot he was annoyed and transformed into a player right before her eyes. "Really? Most women don't say that to me."

It was Josh's turn to be annoyed. He didn't particularly like the way the victim's so-called boyfriend was

eyeing Bridget. He moved forward, placing himself between King and his partner. "What are you doing going
to the gym in the middle of the day? Don't you have a
job you're supposed to be at?"

King had already walked into his bedroom to get
dressed. He left the door open; whether it was as an
invitation or just to be able to hear better wasn't clear.

"Not anymore," the man bit off. "My company decided to relocate to Utah last month—without me."
There was a bitter note in his voice. "I've got to do
something to keep myself occupied during the day so
I go to the gym. I've got seven months left on the membership. No sense in letting it go to waste," he retorted
defensively. It was obvious that this wasn't the first time
he'd been asked about his free afternoons.

King walked back into the living room where he'd
left them. He wore a pair of beige slacks and a light
green golf shirt. He was still barefoot and he hadn't
bothered to try to towel dry his wet hair.

"Look, what's this all about, anyway?" he asked,
looking from one to the other. "Is this Karen's idea of
some kind of a joke?"

"Why would you think that?" Bridget asked. It
seemed to her rather an odd thing for the victim's boyfriend to think, especially since they hadn't told him
anything yet. Just what sort of a relationship did King
and the dead woman have?

"I dunno. Maybe she thinks sending over two pretend cops might get me to find a job faster. Well, it
can't. I already told her, there's nothing out there. I've
been looking my butt off and I can't find anything
decent to even apply for," he answered angrily.

Bridget didn't bother pointing out that they weren't

"pretend cops." He would realize they were real soon enough. "You didn't go out with her last night."

She didn't make it sound like a question, but he answered it anyway. "We had a fight."

"About what?" Josh asked.

"Aren't you paying attention?" King demanded, clearly annoyed at the interrogation. "About me not working. She hates it," he complained. "Karen earns a boatload of money at that place she works, but she wants me to be paying all the bills. She thinks that's what a 'real man' is supposed to do." He sneered at the very thought. "Well, the hell with that and the hell with her!"

Josh continued asking questions. He kept his voice mild, as if they were just having a harmless conversation instead of King just possibly painting himself into a corner. "Just how heated did the argument get between you two yesterday?"

King shrugged, as if this was nothing new. "We got a little loud, she threw a few things at me, missed, then stormed out." And then King narrowed his eyes, asking a little uneasily, "Why? Where is Karen?"

"Didn't you wonder that before now?" Bridget asked, curious.

King's temper flared. He was the kind of man who didn't like to be questioned about his behavior. "I thought she crashed at one of her girlfriends' places. Frankly, I liked the peace and quiet for a change."

What a bastard, Bridget thought. This was why she steered clear of relationships. It was all sweetness and fun in the beginning. And then the gloves came off and people started to be themselves—people she could very well live without. Or at least that's the way it had been with the few relationships she'd had. Most of the time, the guys either wanted her to stop being a cop—or they wanted to handcuff her with her own cuffs. Which was why she was currently taking a break from dating altogether.

"That's good," she told him coolly, "because that's something you're going to have to get used to." *Unless the county decides you killed her and then you'll be getting a whole bunch of new roommates.*

"What are you saying?" King demanded, letting his temper flare. "Where is she? Where's Karen? Something happen to Karen?" he asked, the tone of his voice taking on an unsteady lilt.

Bridget exchanged looks with Josh.

One of them would have to tell the annoying man the woman he'd just been ranting about was dead. She decided to spare Josh since he'd just made her realize that it brought back such harsh memories for him of the time he and his mother had been on the receiving end of those awful words.

"Mr. King, I'm sorry to have to be the one to tell you this, but your girlfriend was found dead this morning in the alley behind The Warehouse Crowd," Bridget told him. She assumed the victim's boyfriend was familiar with the club that was predominantly frequented by an under-thirty crowd.

King looked utterly stunned as he stared at her. "Dead?" He repeated the word as if he didn't quite understand what it meant. His breathing grew noticeably more shallow and faster as he asked, "You mean like in a homicide?"

"Exactly like in a homicide," Josh confirmed for King. Dark brown eyes went from one to the other like marbles pushed to and fro by the wind. King still appeared dazed, but anger began to etch its way into his features.

"Who did it?" he asked. "Do you know who did it?" This time, it was a demand.

"Not yet, but that's what we're trying to figure out by piecing things together," Bridget told him, doing her best to sound sympathetic even as she was still trying to make up her mind about King. "Do you know if Karen had any enemies, any old boyfriends who didn't take kindly to being dumped by her?"

"We've been together for three years. There *are* no boyfriends," King said vehemently. "And she didn't have any enemies. Karen could be a pain in the butt sometimes, but then she'd turn around and be this sweet, amazingly thoughtful woman who made you feel glad just to be alive and around her. Everyone liked Karen," he insisted. King suddenly looked stricken, as if what he'd been told was finally sinking in. His voice became audibly quieter as he asked, "She's not coming home?"

Bridget shook her head as sympathy flooded through her. "I'm afraid not."

His knees giving way, King sank down on the cream-colored sofa. He dragged his hands through his hair, distraught. "Last thing I said to her was I didn't want her coming back," he confessed brokenly.

"We can't ever know that the last thing we say to someone is going to be the last thing we ever say to that person," Josh told him. Maybe if people had the ability to have that sort of insight, they'd be a whole lot nicer to one another, he thought.

"Is there anyone you want us to call for you?" Bridget asked him.

King shook his head, struggling to pull himself together and save face. "No, I can call." And then his voice broke again as he asked, "Did she suffer?"

"ME said it was quick," Bridget was fast to assure him. "Can you tell us where Karen worked? We'd like to ask her coworkers some questions."

He gave them the name and address of a firm that handled event planning for the rich and famous called The Times of Your Life. Thanking him, Bridget gave him one of her business cards and asked him to call if he could think of anything else.

"The ME hasn't seen her yet, remember?" Josh said as they left the apartment and walked back to the car. "You said so yourself."

"Yeah, I know," she responded with a dismissive sigh. "But I didn't see the point in burning the image of the killer carving out her heart while she was still alive into his head. Knowing the bloodthirsty media, King'll find out about that soon enough."

Josh looked at her just before he got into the vehicle. "So you believe him?"

She hedged for a moment, wanting to get his take on it first. "Don't you?"

"Actually, yeah, I do. But you're usually the overly suspicious one," Josh reminded her. He found that unusual. In his experience, the softer sex tended to be more trusting. But then, he'd come to learn that there were a lot of amazing, unique things about his partner. She was a woman of substance. "You should have been the one named Thomas in your family, not your brother. As in Doubting Thomas."

Bridget rolled her eyes. "Yes, I'm familiar with that term, thank you," she said briskly. "King looked genuinely broken up when I told him that his girlfriend was dead," she explained as she got in on the passenger side.

Josh didn't know how King had actually felt about the victim in the long run, but he could see why the man had been initially overwhelmed. "It's always harder when the last words you've had with someone were angry or deliberately hurtful."

"You sound like you speak from experience."

"Me?" Her comment caught him off guard. "No," he said with feeling. "That's why I believe in amiable breakups." He started up the car. "Always leaving 'em smiling is my motto."

Leaving being the key word there. The man had trouble written all over him, she thought, not for the first time.

Bridget noted the wide grin on his face as he told her his "motto." Knowing Youngblood, there was only one way to read that. She tried not to dwell on the image of him that raised in her mind. "That's a little bit too much information, Youngblood."

He laughed heartily. "Why, Detective, you have a dirty mind."

"Three years partnered with you will do that to a person," she assured him.

"Can't plant a seed and have it grow where there is no dirt," Josh countered glibly.

"Dirt being the operative word here," Bridget said pointedly.

Josh glanced at the clock on the dashboard. It was getting close to noon. "You want to pass through a drive-through and grab some lunch on the way to this events-planning place?" he asked.

Looking at the dashboard clock herself, Bridget sighed. It was now or who knew when? "What I'd like is to stop someplace and eat lunch slowly at a table like a normal person, but, since that's impossible and in the interest of time, your way's probably better."

"My way's always better," Josh cracked. He gave Bridget a choice of several places that were close by and she picked one. Nodding amiably, he began to drive in that direction. "Why do you think he does it?" he asked as he merged into the left-hand lane. He needed to make a left turn at the next light.

When he plucked conversations out of the air like that, he managed to completely lose her. She could feel her temper growing short.

"Who?" she asked

"The Lady Killer," Josh elaborated. "What do you think his driving force is? Why February? Is he making some kind of a macabre statement about Valentine's Day, or does the guy just hate a really short month?" he ended wryly.

"You mean is he killing women to make some kind of a protest against commercialism?" she asked incredulously.

"I think if that were the case, he could have found a more subtle way to get his point across," she told Josh. "My guess is that someone jilted him, and I mean royally, and unlike a lot of people, he couldn't handle the embarrassment of it." Her mind raced as she fleshed out her theory, trying to find the pieces that fit. "Maybe he's this invisible guy and he got tired of no one really seeing him. This is his way of getting even with the woman."

"And every woman who reminds him of her," Josh speculated.

Bridget nodded, agreeing. But there was a slight problem with that theory. "But why just in February?" she asked Josh. "Why isn't he killing women all year round, every time he sees someone who looks like the woman who broke his heart?"

Josh laughed shortly. The caseload would be absolutely impossible if that were the case. "Whose side are you on?"

"Ours," she told him with feeling. "I'm just trying to get into the guy's head and figure out what motivates him. That way, we can finally get him." She couldn't think of anything she wanted more for Valentine's Day than to get this psycho off the streets of her city.

As he drove to their destination, Josh reviewed what she'd just said when she started using him as a sounding board. Something she'd just thrown out had stuck. "My guess would be that he's doing it in February because that was when she rejected him, during all the hype and commercialism leading up to the 'big day.' Department stores, restaurants, greeting card companies, they're making a big deal of Valentine's Day these days. Subtly or blatantly they make a person feel like there's something wrong with them if they don't have someone special by their side on that day."

He seemed to have a pretty good lock on all the hoopla surrounding the day, Bridget thought. That had her entertaining other questions about her partner. She told herself that she was only being curious about a friend, but even she knew that there was more to it than that. But exactly what she was not about to go into or explore. That would be asking for trouble.

"Speaking of which," she began on a much lighter note, "who's going to be by your side on Valentine's Day? Since your cell phone hasn't rung in, oh, the last two hours, I'm assuming that you and—Linda, was it?—are now officially history." That was the way he operated. Hot and heavy for a few days and then he'd start craving the sweet taste of freedom. She felt truly sorry for any woman who really fell in love with Josh. Luckily that wouldn't be her.

"Don't worry about who I'm going to be with," he told her, flashing his thousand watt-smile. "And you know damn well her name was Linda."

Was. I was right, Bridget thought with a quick flare of satisfaction.

"I'm not worried," she informed him, "just curious. And as for my reaching for a name to your last current squeeze, there've been so many women in and out of your life these last three years that it's hard for me to keep track of their names."

He looked at her pointedly, "No one asked you to keep track."

"You're my partner," she answered matter-of-factly. "If someone finds you strangled and naked in your bed bright and early one morning, I want to know who to go looking for."

Stopping at a light, he took the opportunity to turn toward her and study her for a moment. "You think of me that way a lot?"

"What, strangled?"

He grinned. He knew that *she* knew he wasn't referring to that. "No, naked and in bed."

"No, but I do I think of you strangled a lot." Changing the subject quickly before the color of her complexion changed and gave him something else to tease her about, Bridget nodded toward the drive-through he was approaching. Because it was still the early part of the lunch hour, there were five cars already queued up ahead of them.

"Why don't we just go in and order?" she suggested. She didn't relish the idea of being stuck in a line, idling. "It'll probably be a lot faster and it'll waste less gas."

"Sensible," he agreed. He'd never admit it to her, but it was one of the things he admired about his partner. She didn't just go with the easy answers; she liked to think things through. "How is it that no one's snapped you up yet, Bridget?" he teased.

"Just lucky I guess," she countered dryly as he pulled into an empty parking spot. He put the car into "park" and then turned off the ignition.

"No sense in the two of us going in." Josh opened the door on his side. "I'll go," he volunteered, then paused before getting out. "What do you want?"

"For the Lady Killer to come down with a quick, terminal disease and die before Valentine's Day. But I'll settle for a beef burrito and a diet cola," she concluded philosophically.

"Amen to the first part," Josh responded glibly. "I'll be right back with lunch." With that he got out and shut the door behind him.

Bridget tried to relax for a moment. She leaned the back of her head against the headrest, willing the tension out of her body.

Without realizing it, she watched her partner as he walked toward the restaurant's entrance and mused—

not for the first time—that Josh had a really cute butt for someone who could, at times, be a real pain in the exact same area.

One of life's mysteries, she supposed.

Their long afternoon, spent talking to Karen's co-workers at The Times of Your Life, turned out to be as fruitless as their morning had been before it. They returned to the squad room with nothing more to go on than they already had when they first left. The victim, everyone had sworn, was someone who no one would have wanted to hurt.

Until someone had.

Bridget sat back and stared at her handiwork. The bulletin board was filled with the photographs and names of all of the Lady Killer's previous unfortunate victims. And now Karen Anderson had unwillingly joined their ranks.

What were they missing?

Ten red-haired young women in their twenties all stared back at her, their smiles frozen in time, all silently begging to be avenged and to have their killer stopped and brought to justice.

Who the hell is he and how can he possibly sleep at night? she asked herself.

In the next breath, she silently mocked herself for even asking the question. The Lady Killer undoubtedly slept just fine because he did not operate by the same set of rules that the rest of them did.

As normal people did.

Because he wasn't normal.

That was the big thing she had to remember. The

Lady Killer thought and reacted on a far different plane from that of either she or Josh.

"He got started early this time," Bridget realized, thinking out loud. She could feel Josh watching her, so she elaborated for his benefit. "This is February second. Most likely he killed Karen last night, which was the first day of the month. Last year we didn't find a body until the eighth."

He remembered. The maimed body behind the gas station store. The girl had just turned twenty the week before.

"Didn't mean that there wasn't one," he pointed out grimly.

She didn't agree. "No, this guy likes to show off his handiwork. It's like he's bragging, telling us we can't catch him. That he's smarter than we are." She turned away from the bulletin board and looked at Josh. "Maybe it's someone who washed out from the academy?"

Josh tried to follow her line of thinking. "So he's showing us that he can get away with murder to make us pay for not hiring him?" Saying it out loud made it seem really far-fetched.

She didn't want to let go of the new angle just yet, but it belonged in a different light.

"No, he's reliving getting even with the woman who turned him down—that's his primary driving force. But every which way he turns, he gets rejected. His feelings toward the police department might be no different from what he feels for the woman who turned him down. Thumbing his nose at the efforts of the police to find him might just be a big bonus feature for him."

Josh turned it over in his head. "Worth a shot, I

guess," he agreed. "But if we're going to go through old files," which was what he assumed she was getting at, "we're going to need some extra people and the budget's tight."

He wasn't telling her anything she didn't already know. Lieutenant Howard had made a point of letting them all know that there was no more money for overtime but if extra hours needed to be put in, he expected that to be done—with no extra compensation.

"Don't worry. If Howard says no to putting at least a couple of extra people on this, I know who to ask," she promised. "Someone who can see beyond a dollar sign and fostering his own 'legend.'"

Josh grinned. He didn't have to ask what she was thinking. "That's my girl."

A quick, warm salvo shot through her in response to his words and the way he looked at her as he said it before she had a chance to shut it down.

What the hell was *that* all about? she upbraided herself impatiently.

She didn't have time for this.

Chapter 5

"You think I'm going to endanger my career by going out on a limb and authorizing overtime for you and your little playmate here just so that you can find some dirt to tarnish the police department's good name in the community?" Lieutenant Howard demanded. His voice rose in direct correlation to the pulsating blue vein that snaked its way along his forehead.

It amazed Bridget just how obstinate her new acting supervisor could be. Determined to cross her *t*'s and dot her *i*'s, she had gritted her teeth and deliberately gone through the proper channels—in this case, that would be Howard—to make her request for more manpower. They needed help to plow through the mountain of files she was anticipating—once she and Josh began going over all the academy's rejects from three to five years ago.

The request had momentarily stunned the preening lieutenant into complete silence. He'd come out of his office to ask for a status report on the investigation, apparently expecting to hear that they were closing in on a suspect. Instead, he'd been hit with a request for exactly what he'd already told his squad he had no intentions of allowing.

The vein across his forehead pulsed harder.

The second he'd opened his mouth, the very faint hope that he might actually be reasonable and consider her request went down in flames. Bridget had to admit that it wasn't exactly a surprise.

Well, at least no one could accuse her of going over the man's head without first giving him a chance to work with her.

Still, she felt she had to straighten out Howard's misconception. "No, not overtime. I'm asking for extra people. And it's not to make the department look bad, it's to find out who the department was intuitive enough not to hire in the first place."

Bridget searched the lieutenant's face for some indication that she'd gotten through. There was none. Apparently her words weren't penetrating the force field around his brain.

"The answer's no. You and Youngblood put in whatever time you have to get this guy behind bars, and you do it because you're supposedly good cops, not because you think you're going to line your pockets and your buddies' pockets with extra cash." Drawing himself up to his full five feet ten inches, Howard glared down at her. "Now, did I make myself clear?"

She met his glare without flinching or looking away.

Bridget was not easily intimidated, thanks to growing up with four brothers.

"Perfectly," she bit off.

"Good. Now get this damn case solved and off my desk, and I mean like *yesterday,* you hear me?" Howard ordered. Then, fuming, he turned to go back to his office.

Bridget squared her shoulders, hating the fact that she'd gotten a dressing-down in front of all the other detectives, as well as Josh. The latter was standing beside her and she could literally *feel* his anger. Despite his easygoing manner, she knew that Josh had even less regard for Howard than she did. And, whatever else his faults were, the man was protective of her, as she was of him. It was one of the reasons they worked so well together.

"People on the first floor can hear you," she answered under her breath, but not exactly as quietly as she could have.

Howard's back stiffened and spun around on his heel. Five strides brought him back to her.

"What was that?" he demanded angrily, glaring down at her.

"I said I hear you, Lieutenant," she replied, doing her best to sound calm as she raised her eyes to his.

He appeared to weigh his options as he slanted a glance around the immediate area. She could almost hear what he was thinking. That the squad room was too full for him to say what he wanted to say to her. She had a feeling that he'd save it for another time when he had her alone in his office.

"Damn straight you hear me," he finally bit off curtly. "Just because you found out you have some kind of made-up connection to the chief of detectives, don't think that makes you entitled to any special treatment. It doesn't mean a damn *thing* in my book."

As the lieutenant ranted, she realized that Josh had risen to his feet behind the man and was about to confront him. Bridget got up, moving so that she managed to block her partner with her back, preventing him from easily reaching Howard.

"Now, if you know what's good for you, you'll both get to work!" Howard shouted at her, glared at Josh and then stormed away.

"He shouldn't talk to you like that," Josh growled, frustrated. "Why'd you stop me?" he asked. "That S.O.B. needs to have some sense, not to mention manners, shaken into his head."

"You won't get an argument out of me," she agreed. "But having you put on suspension or brought up on charges of insubordination isn't going to help me or teach that pompous ass anything," she pointed out. The lieutenant's ego made it impossible for him to absorb anything.

Josh shoved his hands into his pockets, fisting them as exasperation rippled through him. "Maybe not, but it sure would have felt good getting things off my chest." Fuming, Josh looked over her head toward Howard's office. The latter had closed the door behind him and now appeared to be staring at his computer.

Or, more likely, he was trying to observe them by pretending to be occupied.

Furious, Josh looked back at Bridget. "How can you be so calm?"

She wasn't calm, not by a long shot. But letting her anger show through wouldn't get her anywhere at this point, so she internalized it. Externally she was the picture of serenity.

"You know that old saying?" she asked innocently. "The one that goes, 'Don't get angry, get even'?" It was obvious that was what she had in mind.

A smile spread across Josh's lips. Just for the briefest of moments, Bridget paused, allowing herself to take in the feeling that his smile generated inside of her.

The next moment, she was aware of what she was doing and quickly tamped everything down.

Everything but her next move.

"What do you have in mind?" Josh prodded. He couldn't think of anything he would have liked better than to take Howard down a few pegs. Well, maybe a few things, but none that he could do here.

Bridget was trying very hard to move past the put-down she'd just received from the acting lieutenant. With any luck, *he* would be a thing of the past soon.

"What I should have done instead of wasting my time talking to Howard and his oversize ego."

Yes! She was finally going to see the chief of detectives, Josh thought. Given the way he knew she felt about getting things done on her own, this was tantamount to a last resort for her. His partner didn't like asking for favors or help. But this wasn't just a minor dustup; this was important. A lot was at stake here and it couldn't be placed in jeopardy just because the acting lieutenant had turned out to be a taller version of Napoleon.

"Want some backup?" he asked her.

Bridget shook her head. She didn't want him being collateral damage. "Thanks for the offer, but if this thing blows up on me, one of us needs to stay with the case to be able to get whoever gets put in my place up to speed."

"Nobody could take your place," Josh told her and although there was a smile on his lips as he said it, his voice was dead serious. She looked at him, somewhat surprised, not quite sure what to make of his tone. Or the corresponding warm feeling his words had created within her.

"Someone might have to. Howard wants my head on a pike," she pointed out.

"Doesn't matter what *he* wants," Josh assured her with conviction. He fell into place beside her as she walked out of the squad room. "I've got your back, just like always."

It wasn't a statement, it was a promise.

She didn't bother trying to talk Josh out of coming with her. Or to point out that he was putting himself out on the same limb. There were things Josh could be kidded out of and things that he couldn't. This was one of those things that fell under the latter heading.

So all she could do was say "Thanks," which she did, and pray that everything would turn out.

She prayed hard.

Chief of Detectives Brian Cavanaugh prided himself on knowing everyone who worked for him not only by sight, but by name as well. He also made it a point to be aware of their records and achievements, both good and bad. He considered them all members of his team. To Brian, they were more than just badge numbers, they were people. *His* people.

It was no small source of pride that his three sons had worked their way high up through the ranks because of their own efforts, not because of anything that he had done for them. They would have never asked him to intervene on their behalf and he would have never interfered in any matter between a detective and his or her superior—unless there was some sort of injustice.

In like manner, Brian was acutely aware of walking a very thin, narrow line every day that he picked up his shield and tucked it into his pocket. And he had sworn to himself that should the day someday come when he, knowingly or unknowingly, stepped off that narrow path, he would turn in that shield and walk away.

He was proud of the fact that, as of yet, that day had not arrived. He was determined that it never would.

Lost now in thought, searching for a word that persisted in eluding him, a noise penetrated through the fog around him. Brian glanced up from his report. The knock on the door seemed designed to give him a reprieve, however minor. He took it gladly.

Rotating his shoulders to alleviate some stiffness, he called out, "Come in."

The next moment, he saw Bridget sticking her head in. She looked at him a little hesitantly.

Brian smiled warmly. He'd taken an interest in her, the way he had in a good many other detectives, when she had first gotten her shield. He'd known her to be a hard worker even before her true identity—like the identities of her siblings—had come to light for all of them. He and Bridget had exchanged a few words since her father's connection to the rest of them had become apparent, but he sensed that she wasn't comfortable in this new role fate had given her.

And now she'd come to him with something that

was obviously bothering her. He found himself growing very curious. He rose to his feet, a habit instilled
in him by his mother.

"Bridget," he said warmly, her very name serving
as a greeting. "Come in."

She remained in the doorway, still uncertain. "Are
you busy?"

"Not for you," he assured her. And then he saw that
she'd brought her partner with her. For backup? he wondered. Or was there another reason they had both come
to him together? He searched his memory quickly, then
remembered that while he was more than satisfied with
the performance of Bridget and Josh's division, the man
who had been placed temporarily in charge left a few
things to be desired—such as actual leadership quali-
ties. He believed in giving people a chance to prove
themselves in new situations, but he had been far too
laid-back when it came to Jack Howard. He suspected
that the man really didn't belong in charge of other
people. For one thing, the lieutenant lacked a very important leadership quality: empathy.

"To what do I owe this unexpected visit?" Brian
asked, sitting down again behind his desk. He gestured
toward the two chairs that faced his desk. "Take a seat,
please."

Both she and Josh immediately did as the chief requested. Bridget placed her hands on the armrests,
giving the impression that she was ready to spring up
to her feet at the slightest provocation. Tension fairly
radiated from her.

"It's not going as fast as we'd like," Bridget said, responding to the chief's question, measuring her words
out slowly in an attempt to make sure that she wouldn't

say the wrong thing. She didn't want the chief of detectives to think that she was some flighty person running to him with a complaint rather than going through proper channels.

Yet here she was, presenting her case. Proper channels were all well and good when there was a great deal of time to spare. But there wasn't. She just couldn't get away from the feeling that they—and the next victim—didn't have a great deal of time left. That their time—like the days in the month of February—was exceedingly limited.

The Lady Killer was out there somewhere, getting ready to strike again. Soon. They needed to find him before he could, they just *had* to. And if that meant ticking off the lieutenant by going over his head after he turned her down, then that was what she had to do if she was ever going to live with her conscience.

Brian leaned forward and folded his hands before him on his desk. "All right, I'm listening," he encouraged patiently.

"The fact is, Chief, we need more bodies. Live ones," she clarified when the grizzly scenario her words suggested echoed back in her head. "This particular serial killer only strikes in the month of February," she pointed out, although she had a feeling that the chief was already quite aware of that. The man was aware of *everything,* to the point that it was almost eerie.

"And if the past is any example," Josh said, picking up the thread from his partner, "with each year, he tries to increase his number of victims. The first year he killed three women, last year he killed five. This year he already killed one woman and there are twenty-seven days left to go."

There was no need to have the dots connected for him. Brian had already had his aide bring him a copy of the file on the Lady Killer. He'd gone over it first thing this morning. His breakfast had weighed heavily on his stomach by the time he'd finished reading.

"Go on," he told the two people sitting before him.

Bridget spoke up first, not because she wanted the attention, but because, if this backfired, she was ready to take the blame. And if word got back to Howard that the request had been made over his head, she didn't want Josh to be the one to take the flak. She was the lead detective on this case. Besides, Josh just might get it into his head to turn in his badge if Howard hassled him, while she would dig her heels in even further.

"We need more people working this case, sir," she stated emphatically.

"I'm in complete agreement," Brian assured her. Something like this, that had gone on for more than a year even if it was only during the length of one month each time, deserved to have the attention of more than just two detectives. The fact that it didn't raised questions. "Why *aren't* there more of you on it?" he asked.

She would have loved to bring a great many issues to his attention. There was the fact that Howard wanted to keep his budget figures reined in while demanding that all his detectives put in extra hours. That would make it appear as if cases were being solved by his division in a minimum of time since only the core hours were logged in.

There was also the fact that since Howard had come in morale had dropped to a dangerously low point. But too many complaints might come across to the chief as her being petulant. The case was too important for her to risk possibly losing the chief's goodwill.

She worded her answer as diplomatically as she could. "I don't think that the lieutenant wants it to appear as if he's exceeding his budget on some momentary whim."

Brian's eyes narrowed at the description. "Taking down a serial killer is hardly a whim in my book," he responded. "It's being a good cop." He looked from his niece to her partner. "Have you found any suspects yet?"

Bridget ran her tongue along her lips that had grown very dry in the last few minutes. "Well, in theory," she began.

"And this theory is?" Brian prodded.

Bridget blew out a breath. *Here goes nothing.* "That whoever the killer is, he might also be trying to get even with the police department, making them regret that they didn't hire him."

That was a new angle. But Brian had learned long ago not to appear surprised by anything while on the job, so, to the two people in his office, he looked as if he took this new information in stride.

His expression gave nothing away as he asked, "You think that the killer is someone who tried to get into the academy?"

"It does seem likely," Josh told him. "The killer never tried to hide any of the bodies of his victims. Instead, he always made sure to leave them out in plain sight, as if he was taunting the police with his kills."

"According to the ME's report," Bridget added, "these women were all killed late at night. Depending on where, that gave the killer plenty of time to either move the bodies where they couldn't be found or get rid of them altogether. But he didn't. It's like he *wants* the police department to see his work."

"He's rubbing our noses in it," Brian summarized.

Enthused because the chief wasn't dismissing their theory out of hand, Bridget laid out her plan. "Exactly. I'd like to go through all the old academy applications from about three, four years ago, limiting the search to strictly the ones who didn't wind up graduating for one reason or another."

Brian nodded, seeing no reason to deny her request. "Do it." He noticed the way Bridget suddenly caught her lower lip between her teeth. The unconscious action reminded him of Janelle. His daughter had the same habit when she debated whether or not to bring something to light. "What?" he asked encouragingly.

"We could certainly use some extra people to make this go faster."

Brian didn't see what the problem was. "Get them," he instructed. "Borrow them from other departments if you have to."

She searched for a way to delicately approach what she was about to say next without making it sound as if she was being disloyal to her department—or the man in charge of it. This being diplomatic was *hard*. As a rule, she liked speaking her mind, not tiptoeing through invisible minefields.

When she paused, Brian read between the lines. His days as a detective were not so far in the past that he couldn't remember what it was like to have to rein himself in and make sure he didn't get ahead of himself and step on toes that were very capable of kicking back.

"I'll inform Lieutenant Howard of my decision to

allot extra manpower for a task force. This case is long overdue for a task force," he added.

Since the unofficial "meeting" appeared to have come to an end, Brian rose to his feet. Bridget and Josh quickly followed suit.

"Thank you for filling me in on the case," Brian said amiably, walking them to the door. "And don't worry," he added conspiratorially, "your names won't come up."

Bridget paused half a second to look at him. For that split second, he wasn't the chief. Instead, for the first time since she'd learned the startling news about her father and who they all actually were, Brian Cavanaugh was her uncle. He was family, family beyond the blue uniform that made them so.

She nodded at his words. "I wasn't worried," Bridget told him.

Brian smiled. There was a great deal about this one that reminded him of the way his daughter, Janelle, had been just a few short years ago. Dedicated and so very intent on hiding any uncertainties and insecurities that she might have. Bridget, apparently, had yet to learn that those insecurities didn't diminish her and surmounting them was what made her the person she was.

"I know," he replied. And then he winked at Josh, as if taking him into his confidence, and told Bridget, "I was talking to your partner."

With that, he closed his door and returned to his desk. Before reaching for the phone to call Howard and inform the man that he wanted a task force set up and was making an allotment in the budget for it, he thought back to the partner he'd had even before he'd gone on to earn his shield.

Best damn partner anyone could ask for, he thought, the corners of his mouth curving fondly. At the time, he couldn't do anything about the way he felt. Both he and his partner, Lila, were married at the time. To other people.

But if something is meant to be, it happens, and every day he thanked God that it had happened to him.

Wouldn't surprise him if Bridget and her partner wound up the same way. They had that look about them, even if they didn't realize it yet.

Brian dialed Howard's extension and sat back in his chair.

Chapter 6

"I'd really watch my step if I were you, Bridget."

The word of warning, uttered in a raspy low voice by Gary Cox, one of three detectives who had been loaned out to her division for the duration of the Lady Killer investigation, had Bridget looking up from her computer uncertainly. Cox had paused by her desk on the pretext of searching for something in the file he was holding.

"What do you mean?" she asked quietly.

His eyes still down, Cox pushed his rimless reading glasses up on the bridge of his nose. It was a losing battle. "I've worked with Jack Howard before the guy was kicked upstairs and made lieutenant. Thinks nothing of throwing people under the bus if that somehow helps elevate him or gets him seen in a better light. I hear you're the reason this task force exists. That can't sit well with him."

"You know better than that, Cox," Josh said mildly, coming up behind his partner and facing the other detective. "Cavelli is a detective, same as you and me. A lowly detective doesn't have the clout to get a task force put together. That kind of authority has to come from on high."

Cox looked at them knowingly. "My point exactly. You went over Jack Howard's head—not that anyone could blame you," he added quickly. "Man's a show-boating jackass. But that doesn't change the fact that he's gonna be watching every move you make."

Bridget nodded, accepting Cox's words for what they were: a friendly warning. "Then I'd better make sure that all my moves are entertaining," she told him with a bright smile.

Cox pushed his glasses up his long, thin nose again. "Yeah," he agreed, an appreciative note in his voice as his eyes quickly gave her frame a once-over. "I don't think that'll be much of a problem for you. Right, Youngblood?" he asked, glancing over to her partner.

Josh wasn't smiling. "Don't you have files to go through?" he asked the older man. "Because if you're done with your share, I've got a ton more for you to review, seeing as how you're so quick and all."

Cox held his hands up in blatant surrender. "I'm going, I'm going," he protested cheerfully. "I meant no offense," were his parting words.

Bridget turned her chair halfway around so that she could get a better look at Josh. The irritated note in his voice was unlike him. She knew if she said that, it would only get her partner's back up, so instead she resorted to a general observation.

"You sound like someone who's in real need of a coffee break."

In response he raised the two tall, covered containers he had brought back with him from the shop across the street. She'd been so preoccupied, she hadn't even noticed he had them, Bridget realized. She needed to relax herself.

"What I need—what *we* need," Josh emphasized, "is a break in the case."

"No argument there." The man was preaching to the choir. "But with all these extra people helping out, we're bound to make headway a lot faster than just on our own."

"We'd better, or else Howard's going to want our blood," Josh said.

Placing Bridget's coffee—extra light, extra sugar; he had no idea why she bothered calling it coffee—container on her desk, he went around to his own desk and planted himself in his chair. He removed the lid and took a long sip of the midnight-black brew. He could feel his pulse speed up even as the dark, hot liquid wound its way down his throat and into his bloodstream.

"My blood," Bridget corrected her partner. "Cox is right. The lieutenant knows that I'm the one who asked the chief for help."

He looked at her over the rim of the large container, wisps of steam rising up into the air like a magical genie that had just been released.

"As I recall," he said pointedly, "there were two of us in the chief's office the other day."

She grinned. At times, the man was downright sweet, although she knew he'd really balk at that description when it was applied to his professional life. But that didn't make it any less true.

"Only because you insisted on tagging along," she reminded him. "I'm the one who made the request to the chief and I'm the one who'll take the fall." Her blue eyes seemed to crinkle as she added, "But thanks for the thought."

"Maybe if you stop grandstanding for a minute, you'll realize that as long as we stick together, Howard'll have a harder time getting back at us."

She leaned back in her chair for a moment and studied her partner. At one time, she might have resented his comment, which implied she couldn't look after herself. That wasn't the case anymore. These days she trusted her instincts—and her partner.

"You really do have a big-brother complex, you know that?"

The way he looked at her in response sent an unexpected warm shiver shimmying down her spine. "Yeah, that's what it is, a big-brother complex," Josh echoed sarcastically.

Unwilling to dissect and examine what she'd just experienced, Bridget lowered her eyes to her monitor and got back to work.

The extra detectives who had been sent over, Joel Langford, Sam Kennedy and Gary Cox, as well as she and Youngblood, had been plowing through a mountain of applications for the last three days. They pulled the ones for the applicants who had washed out or been rejected outright and subjected them to closer scrutiny. Each form dictated a follow-up.

A number of the failed applicants had moved on and had either left the area or the state entirely. They were set aside, reducing the numbers a little. But that still left a fairly large number of would-be police officers to contend with. Each one had to be interviewed, their whereabouts on the nights in question verified. Bridget came in early and stayed late, compiling the list of former academy candidates to interview. Once it was put together, the real work began.

"You get the feeling that this is getting us nowhere?" she asked Josh as the third day saw them wearily walking away from yet another one-time hopeful police academy applicant who ultimately hadn't been able to make the grade.

Finding the former applicants hadn't been easy and talking to them had gotten them nowhere. Many were still resentful at being rejected. Others were suspicious as to why they were being sought out at this date.

All in all, Bridget knew of far more pleasant ways to spend her time.

"It *was* a good idea," Josh told her, too tired to be very convincing despite the fact that he did believe what he was saying. "The odds of us finding the serial killer right off the bat are so astronomically low that I can't even come up with a qualifying number. But just because we haven't found him yet doesn't mean that you were wrong to think he'd washed out of the academy."

If this kept up, she would have to start checking Youngblood's ID periodically. "What's with you lately?" she asked as she got back into the car. "You're not usually this encouraging—not," she quickly added, "that I don't appreciate it."

Josh shrugged, securing his seat belt. "Figure you have enough to deal with right now, what with Howard breathing down your neck and…" His voice suddenly trailed off.

"And?" Bridget repeated, turning to look at him as she waited.

"And that identity crisis thing you said you were having."

Bridget knew he meant well, but she still didn't really want to have the subject brought up. "Never called it an identity crisis."

For a second, he left his key in the ignition and just talked. "Okay, whatever it is that has you wondering who you are."

She took offense at what he was saying. "I know who I am," Bridget protested. "I just don't know what last name I can use in good conscience."

He laughed to himself as a thought occurred to him. His eyes met hers. Hers contained a question. "Why not be like those rock stars who go by one name?" he teased. Then, assuming a deep voice like the one that might be heard making a TV promo, Josh said, "And now, here's *Bridget*." He accompanied the single name with a sweeping gesture of his hands.

Bridget shook her head. "Sorry, it's just not unique enough."

"Maybe not the name," Josh allowed. Then let his voice trail off.

Their eyes met for a moment. Bridget realized she was holding her breath, as if she was waiting for something. Waiting for what? For him to finish his sentence? Or for something else?

She wasn't making any sense, she thought, annoyed with herself. But she did have an excuse. The hours that she'd been putting in ever since the task force was formed had been long and grueling. She was bone weary and consequently, punchy. The mind wandered when you were punchy.

At that moment, as if to further torment her, her cell phone rang.

A half a moment later, so did his.

Josh turned off the ignition he'd just turned on and fished out his phone. "Youngblood," he declared just as Bridget was saying evasively, "This is Bridget," into hers.

As the people on the other end of their respective lines relayed their messages, Bridget raised her eyes to her partner's. The look she saw in his told her that he'd gotten the same message.

There'd been another murder by the serial killer.

She closed her phone and slipped it back into her pocket. "At least we can rule out the last two guys we just talked to," she said grimly. "Although that's not much of a consolation."

"It's a start," Josh said with a resigned sigh as he turned on the ignition again.

The woman who had stumbled across the body lying in an alley behind a strip mall and had subsequently called 911 was still there when they arrived on the scene some fifteen minutes later. Sitting before the open rear doors of an ambulance, it was obvious that the young

woman was very much in shock and fighting the strong
desire to scream.

As they approached, the woman kept running her
hands up and down her arms. Moreover, she was sitting
on the floor of the ambulance, precariously perched and
rocking to and fro in a vain attempt to comfort herself.

The first officer to respond to the call, treading
lightly around the witness, told them that the woman's name was Alyce Jackson and that by some strange
stroke of fate, she and the latest victim, Diana Kellogg,
worked together.

"Diana didn't come in today," Alyce said, pluck-
ing her words out of the middle of her thoughts when
Bridget and Josh asked her to tell them what happened.
She pressed her lips together to keep them from trembling. It wasn't working. The woman was a bundle of
nerves. "Wasn't like her to miss work and not call. She's
usually so good about things like that." She looked from
Bridget to Josh. "She was responsible, you know?"

Josh glanced at Bridget before saying to the distraught woman in a comforting voice, "Yes, I know
the type."

"But I thought, she's young, maybe she met someone and had such a good time, she just lost track. That
happens you know." There was a desperate note in her
voice, as if trying to convince herself, not them.

"Was she meeting someone last night?" Bridget
asked her gently.

Alyce took a deep breath before responding. "Yeah,"
she answered, nodding her head.

They were going to have to be careful, Bridget
thought. The woman was fragile. "You know who?"

The brunette shook her head, tears shining in her

eyes. "I don't think Diana knew who, either. It was one of those dates you get set up for you online. The group was called Romantics-dot-net or dot-com or something," she said, frustrated that the exact name escaped her. "He gave her a description of himself, but said he didn't want to send her a picture. He told her that he wanted to see if she could pick him out since their souls had touched."

"How's that again?" Josh pressed, glancing at his partner uncertainly.

"Those were the words he used," Alyce insisted. "Diana repeated them to me. She thought they were so romantic." Alyce pressed her lips together again, struggling to hold herself together. "The whole thing made me a little uneasy and I offered to go with her, but she said that would really look awkward. She told me she was meeting him at a very crowded place so I shouldn't worry. But I had a feeling, I did," the woman cried, grasping Josh's hand hard with both of hers.

Struggling not to cry, Alyce paused a moment before going on. "Diana just got tired of not having someone in her life, you know?" She looked from one to the other for a sign of understanding. "And what with Valentine's Day coming, she said she was determined not to spend that day alone."

"I take it she didn't have a boyfriend?" Bridget asked the woman.

Alyce shook her head. "Not since she broke up with Alex."

Josh raised an eyebrow. Were they finally catching a break? "Alex? Who's Alex?" Maybe that was an angry ex-lover who didn't like being dumped.

"He was her fiancé." Alyce said, struggling to keep her voice from breaking.

Bridget had her notebook out. "This Alex have a last name?"

A hopeless look came over their witness's face. "Yeah, but I don't know what it is."

Josh mentally crossed his fingers. "Do you know where we can find him?"

"Texas. Dallas. That was what the breakup was all about. He wanted her to come to Dallas with him. She didn't want to leave." Alyce was crying now and didn't seem to realize it yet. "God, but I wish she'd gone with him. She'd still be alive now if she had."

Alyce raised her troubled eyes. "Do I have to look at her again?" she asked, her voice cracking and trembling. "To make an official ID, I mean. I watch procedurals on TV," she explained haltingly. "I really don't think I can handle seeing her again like that."

"No, not right now," Bridget promised, her voice calm, soothing. "Tell me, does Diana have any family or next of kin we need to notify?"

"She's got an older brother somewhere on the East Coast, I think. She never mentioned anyone local." Alyce stopped as her voice hitched. Clearing it, she tried to talk again. "How can anyone do something like that to another human being?" she asked.

"That's what we're trying to figure out," Bridget told her. Looking around, she spotted a female officer working alongside another officer as they both tried to keep the growing crowd from pushing forward and contaminating the crime scene. "Be right back," she told Josh. Hurrying over to the officer, she tapped the other woman on the shoulder. When the latter turned around, Bridget indicated Alyce. "Officer, could you go with Miss Jackson to the hospital and then once she's checked out, see she gets home all right, please?"

"Sure thing." The policewoman, Officer Mahon, seemed happy to be relieved of what she was doing. "Anything to get away from this crime scene. I'm having trouble keeping my lunch down," she confided in a lowered voice.

"We've all been there," Bridget assured the young woman.

The officer followed Bridget back to the waiting ambulance. Bridget made the introduction. "Officer Mahon is going to see to it that you get home all right after they check you out at the hospital, Alyce."

"I didn't get hurt," the woman protested. Her eyes welled up again. "Diana's the one who got hurt. Who got killed," she sobbed.

"You're in shock," Bridget told the woman softly. "We just want to make sure that you're all right," she added. "Here. If you can think of anything else, give me a call. *Anytime,*" Bridget emphasized, handing Alyce one of her cards.

"How come that argument never works with you?" Josh asked as they walked away from the ambulance and the distraught witness.

The paramedic was just getting Alyce to move onto a gurney and preparing to shut the doors so that his partner could drive to the hospital. Officer Mahon would follow them in her squad car.

Bridget looked at her own partner innocently. "What do you mean?"

"That time you were smacked in the head by that idiot who decided he was going to go into training for the L.A. Marathon right then and there, stashes of pot still hanging out of his pockets." He saw that Bridget was deliberately acting as if she didn't remember the incident. The hell she didn't, he thought. "I nearly busted a gut chasing him down. When I cuffed him and dragged him back, you looked like you had all the makings of a nasty concussion, but you utterly refused to go to the local E.R. to get yourself checked out like I kept insisting."

"There was a reason for that," Bridget replied coolly.

"And that is?" he asked, waiting for her to elaborate.

"Because I'm invulnerable," Bridget told him matter-of-factly, ending her statement with a wide, cheerful grin.

Josh sighed and rolled his eyes, then said sarcastically, "Oh yeah, I keep forgetting all about your superpowers."

She merely smiled at him as if they were having a normal, perfectly plausible conversation. "They do make a difference."

"Yeah, especially during a psych exam," Josh muttered.

The lightened mood disappeared as they went back to where the ME was just finishing up her preliminary notes. Directly next to her one of the crime scene investigators was snapping the last of his photographs.

As Bridget drew closer, both the ME and the CSI unit member became only peripheral noise to her. All she could really see or focus on was the woman lying on the ground in the alley. Like the others, her hands were folded below her carved-out chest cavity, as if she were praying.

Maybe she had been, Bridget thought grimly. For

a moment, she said nothing, merely looked. But the longer she looked, the angrier she became.

"I want this guy, Josh," she told her partner, her teeth gritted together.

"You'll have to get in line, Bridget," Josh told her. "There are a lot of relatives who feel the same way you do."

With effort, she tore her eyes away from the young woman who appeared as if she'd had everything to live for—until life was so painfully torn away from her. Bridget raised her eyes to his. "On a slab," she emphasized. "I want this guy on a slab. I want to put him there myself."

"Don't let Howard overhear you say that," Josh warned seriously. "He does, he'll accuse you of carrying on a vendetta."

"Right now," she murmured, more to herself than to her partner, "Howard is the last thing I'm worried about." She struggled not to let her emotions get the better of her. Filled with high hopes, Diana Kellogg had been slaughtered before she'd had a chance to really live.

Just like the ten victims before her.

The bastard who had done that would be made to pay for it.

She silently swore it on her mother's grave.

Chapter 7

Diana Kellogg had lived on the fourth floor of a six-story, thirty-year-old apartment building that had seen better times, not to mention a better neighborhood. While the exterior was fairly well kept up, right down to the recently trimmed juniper bushes that were vigorously growing on either side of the entrance, interior renovations did not seem have interested the landlord.

The moment Bridget and Josh walked inside, they were struck by the amount of fingerprints and smudges of dirt that seemed to litter the hallway walls. In addition, here and there, the paint had begun to peel. The smell of ammonia and disinfectant testified that the ground floor had been recently washed.

What it could really stand, though, in Bridget's opinion, was a complete replacement. Chips, holes and pockmarks seemed to be everywhere on the uninspired, jumbo black-and-white tiles.

"I'd be depressed just coming home every night," Josh commented as they made their way over to the elevator.

Since the elevator appeared to be in use, he pressed the up button and waited. A disgruntled-looking heavyset woman in her late forties came down the staircase to the left of the elevator door.

"It's broken," she told them, visibly disgusted. "Again."

Since the woman was apparently a tenant, Bridget took the opportunity to ask her, "Would you happen to know where the superintendent is?"

A contemptuous expression came over the round face. "Out back, drinking most likely."

"I'd definitely be depressed," Josh affirmed as he led the way out again. Once outside, they circled the perimeter of the building to look for the man who could let them into Diana Kellogg's apartment.

Fifteen minutes later found them inside the tiny one-bedroom apartment where Diana Kellogg had lived until last night. After getting the exceedingly curious superintendent to back out of the apartment and closing the door on him, Josh slowly looked around the living quarters.

Kellogg had done her best to make the three rooms into a home, decorating with bright, cheerful colors and inviting, comfortable furnishings, all of which acted to create a tiny haven for the young woman amid the coldness that existed just outside.

As he took in the apartment, Josh noticed that Bridget was still in the living room. He had expected her to go into the bedroom and begin rummaging through the closet the way she normally did. It was her way of getting more of a feel for the victim, her tastes, lifestyle, and so on.

But this time, she had gone directly to the laptop that had been set up on what was, beneath the pretty light blue tablecloth, a rickety card table. Turning the laptop on, Bridget waited for the computer to go through its various warming up stages until it was finally up and running. The laptop didn't appear to be a new model and the process took longer than she would have liked. The operating system was two upgrades behind the current one on the market, which contributed to the machine's less than lightning speed.

"Find anything?" Josh asked after giving the rooms a quick once-over and finding nothing noteworthy to catch his attention.

"Yeah," Bridget answered with a sigh. "That Diana Kellogg must have been an incredibly patient person. This thing is taking forever to come around," she complained, waving her hand at the laptop. "It's an old operating system."

Josh came up behind her, as if two sets of eyes watching the screen could somehow make it move more quickly.

"That's the problem," he told Bridget. "I never keep mine around for them to get that way. As soon as something new comes along, I always replace the one I have for whatever's new and faster."

"Are you talking about your computer or your love life?" Bridget deadpanned, never taking her eyes off the painfully slow-moving screen.

"Very funny," he responded. Looking closer, he saw that the laptop had finally finished loading and there was now an idyllic rainforest scene on the screen. "Hey, look, you've got a desktop," he congratulated her.

Victory went down in flames. "Yeah, but it's password protected," she observed wearily. The woman lived alone. Who was she protecting her computer from? In all likelihood, it probably only contained recipes and family photos. "We need to have one of the techs take a crack at it." About to shut the laptop down again, Bridget was surprised when her partner elbowed her out of the way. She moved, but never took her eyes off him. It wasn't exactly a hardship from her standpoint. "What are you doing?"

"Giving getting in a shot," he told her, his fingers flying across the keyboard.

"Since when did you become a hacker?"

"I'm not." The way he saw it, that was a title reserved for people who could pull virtual rabbits out of invisible hats and fish out encrypted messages with the ease that a normal person sent out email. "But this girl I dated once could crack passwords like they were so many tiny walnuts."

"Nice to know you're not wasting time just going out with pretty faces," Bridget cracked, moving back to allow him better access.

He gave her a quick, sensual look that would have melted her inner core if she'd bought into it. But she knew that Josh was just practicing his seduction skills on her, skills that he would eventually use on some other lucky young woman.

"They've got more than just pretty faces," he assured her.

"Please, spare me the details," Bridget entreated, rolling her eyes and pretending to be afraid that he was about to begin describing what each of his former girlfriends had going for them.

Focused on the laptop, Josh hit another combination of keys, then suddenly brightened. "She used the numbers of her street address. I'm in," he declared, lifting his arms in the air like a triumphant boxing champion who'd just won the world title.

"I'm sure you say that to all the girls," Bridget muttered under her breath. "Okay," she said in a louder voice, "let me take a look at her messages. Maybe we can find out what this guy's name was."

And then she saw it, the last email that the victim had opened and read before apparently leaving her apartment on her ill-fated date.

"SexyDude," Bridget read out loud. "Sounds like a bad joke."

"Or a disappointment waiting to happen," Josh commented.

"Who knows, maybe he wasn't a disappointment. Maybe he really was a 'sexy dude,'" she theorized, to which her partner simply shook his head. "Okay, why not?" she asked.

"If he actually was sexy, he wouldn't have had to advertise it," Josh said. "It would just be evident the second she met him."

And Josh would be the one to know about that, Bridget caught herself thinking. Annoyed that her thoughts had strayed so far off course, she returned her gaze to the emails that had gone back and forth between the two the last day of Kellogg's life.

"They made plans to meet at The Hideaway." She looked at Josh. "Okay, what is that?"

He laughed. "Oh, Bridget, you *are* really sheltered, aren't you? You need to get out more."

"I get out," she protested heatedly. "Just not to sleazy places."

The lopsided smile on her partner's lips told her that he didn't buy in to her protest. "The Hideaway's a club that caters to the young, single and carefree crowd."

"Maybe that should be young, single and careless crowd instead," she commented.

"Whatever," he countered with a shrug. And then he suddenly realized… "It's not too far away from the place where her body was discovered. Question is, how did SexyDude get from point A to point B without anyone noticing him and his 'extra baggage'?"

"Maybe someone did," Bridget said hopefully. She scrolled quickly through the emails that were either sent to or received from "SexyDude," looking for an attachment. There wasn't any. "Her friend was right, SexyDude didn't send her a picture." She looked up at Josh. "Ten to one SexyDude looks like a troll."

"Not taking that bet," he answered.

She'd gotten as much as she could from the laptop without some serious advanced technical help. "Okay, let's drop this laptop off with the tech department and then talk to the bartender at The Hideaway. Maybe someone remembers seeing Diana with her 'date.'"

"You really are an optimist, aren't you?" Josh commented, leading the way out.

"It's what keeps me going," she answered, shutting the door behind her.

Not only didn't the bartender remember seeing

anyone with the victim, he hadn't seen the victim, either.

The bartender, Raul Lopez, shook his head. "I've got a great eye for faces and hers wasn't here last night," he told them, tapping the photograph that Bridget had placed on the bar.

"Are you sure?" she pressed.

Raul looked as if he thought his integrity was being questioned. "I already told you, I've got an eye for faces. I don't forget them."

"All right," Josh said, placing himself so that the bartender was forced to look at him instead of at Bridget. "Let's run a little test," he proposed. "Describe my partner."

Raul didn't even hesitate. "Five-foot-seven—probably wearing three-inch heels," he guessed. "Straight, golden-blond hair, blue eyes, good skin, great smile. Late twenties. I'd put her at a hundred and ten, hundred fifteen pounds, although that bulky gray jacket she's wearing makes it hard to tell. One thing's for sure," he added, his mouth curving in a seductive grin, "she doesn't look like any police detective I ever knew. You want me to go on?" he asked Josh.

Josh was tempted to ask what else the man thought he could describe but had a feeling that it was prudent to stop here—for Bridget's sake.

"No," Josh said curtly. "You made your point. You're good with descriptions. Thanks for your time."

"Pleasure's all mine." Raul was looking at Bridget as he said it. "Come back anytime," he told her. "First drink's on me."

"Wonder what else he expects to be on him," Josh bit off as they walked out.

Bridget suppressed a grin. If she hadn't known better, she would have said her partner was being jealous. Most likely, he was just being protective. Like one of her brothers.

"So," Bridget concluded, "Kellogg never made it here." She paused as she looked over her shoulder at the club. "I wonder why."

"Maybe 'SexyDude' was waiting outside the club and waylaid her," Josh guessed. Seeing that he had his partner's attention, he continued. "Don't forget, he probably knew what she looked like. She used her real name and she had that social networking page with her photograph on it. It wouldn't have been hard to find it to see what she looked like," he added. "All the guy had to do was look her up on Google."

She kept forgetting it could be that easy. Bridget shook her head as they walked back to the car. "Such a great invention and these jerks have to ruin it by using it to 'virtually' stalk people and kill them."

There was the optimist again, he couldn't help thinking. Bridget was always trying to see the good rather than the bad. It was one of the things he liked about her. That and her mind. It also didn't hurt that she had killer legs.

Josh tamped down the grin that threatened to rise to his lips.

"Happens with everything," he said philosophically. "One of the first uses for the camera was to take what were considered to be pornographic pictures back in Edwardian times." About to get into the car, Bridget gave him a questioning look. "I read a lot," he told her. Getting in on the driver's side, he started to buckle up when he saw her taking out her cell phone. "Who are you calling?"

"Brenda," she answered. "I want to see if she managed to trace back the IP address to SexyDude's home so we can go talk to the creep."

Brenda was Brenda Cavanaugh, the wife of one of the chief of detectives' sons. He'd heard that she was an absolute wizard at what she did, but, as he glanced at his watch, this was pushing it. It had been less than an hour since they'd handed over the laptop.

"Aren't you crowding her a little? I mean, she is still human."

"Only in a very broad, general sense," Bridget deadpanned. "I've been told she's very good at her job." Because the line on the other end was being picked up, Bridget held up her hand, curtailing any further conversation with Josh for the moment.

"Brenda? Hi, this is Bridget—right, Bridget Cavanaugh." She deliberately avoided looking at Josh as she confirmed the other woman's inquiry. "Did you happen to figure out that creep's name and address yet?" The next moment, a huge smile bloomed on her face. "Terrific. I said you were the best. What is it?"

This time Bridget did raise her eyes to Josh, silently indicating that she needed something to write with and a surface to do it on. Turning his body, Josh pulled out a pen, then, because he had nothing to give her to write on, he held up his palm for her. Bridget didn't have the luxury of being choosy, so, bracing his hand with hers, she turned his palm up toward her.

The next moment, she was writing across it with his pen. "Thanks, I owe you one— What? *This* Saturday?" She let go of Josh's hand. "No, I'm not. I'm not busy. I can make it, yes. You're sure? Really? I didn't think I had one of those. Should be interesting. Okay, Josh and I will come by the lab later for anything else you can find. Bye."

Questions crowded his head by the time she got off the phone. "Didn't think you had one of what?" Josh wanted to know.

It took Bridget a second to match his question with something that she'd said previously. "Oh. That. A grandfather," she explained. Why was he asking her that? "Aren't you more interested in this creep's name?"

"Sure, but that doesn't mean I can't ask about this. You looked really surprised—and then kind of pleased—when you were talking to her and it wasn't about the case. Made me curious what could make you look like that."

"Oh, I don't know. Maybe a partner who keeps his mind on his work and hell-bent on catching the bad guy," she retorted.

And then Bridget sighed as she leaned back in the seat. Josh would find a way to wheedle this out of her one way or another and if she got it over quickly, then they could focus on what was important. Bringing that bastard to justice.

"Brenda said that Andrew—*Uncle* Andrew," Bridget amended since the man *was* family, "got a call from his father in Florida. Seems that the patriarch of the family is flying home for the express purpose of meeting this lost branch of the family that has suddenly surfaced and Andrew is spreading the word that he wants everyone to gather together for the old man."

"And the lost branch of the family, that would be you?" Josh guessed.

"Not me specifically," she protested. "It means my whole family."

"Of which you're a part." He was stating the obvious and he knew it, Bridget thought. She'd forgotten how irritating he could be at times. "By the way," Josh continued and she braced herself, "I heard you identify yourself as Bridget Cavanaugh. Does that mean you've made your decision about which last name you want to use?"

It hadn't really been her decision to make, she thought. It had actually been a foregone conclusion from the get-go.

"That means," she told him, "I can't fight City Hall, and if my father was born a Cavanaugh, I guess that makes me one, too."

He found her resigned tone amusing. "It's not exactly a death sentence. you know."

"I know. It just feels weird, that's all." She searched for a way to make him see her point. "It's like all your life, you think of yourself as a duck and suddenly, you find out that you're actually a goose. It takes some getting used to."

He laughed quietly to himself and then told her, "Swan."

She didn't understand. "What?"

"Don't think of yourself as a goose," he told her. "Think of yourself as a swan. It might make the transition easier for you."

Just what was he reading into her words? "I'm not vain—" she protested.

He cut her off before she could get going. "Never said that."

"Besides, swans have bad dispositions." She looked at him pointedly.

Josh shrugged innocently. "Just trying to help," he told her.

"You want to help?" She turned his hand so that he could see his palm with the writing on it. "Drive here," she instructed and then, belatedly, let go of his hand so that he could use it to drive with.

Josh grinned. "Your wish is my command."

"If only," she muttered under her breath. But he heard.

His grin grew wider.

"SexyDude" turned out to be the email name used by George Hammond. Hammond, a rather nondescript, stoop-shouldered man with a seriously receding hairline, worked as a tax form preparer for one of the larger tax consultant firms. They found him with a client and extracted him in order to have "a few words" with him.

Bewildered, Hammond became rather hostile when he realized he was being questioned about the way he'd spent his previous evening. He became even more so when Diana Kellogg's name was brought up.

"I'll tell you how I spent my evening with her," he said angrily. "I didn't. She never showed. I went to that expensive club she picked out—they had a damn cover charge," he complained. "I sat there for two hours, nursing one watered-down drink and watching the door, waiting for her to walk in. But she never showed up." A little of his anger subsided as he looked from one detective to the other. "Why are you asking me about her? Has she done something?" He seemed almost eager to hear something bad in connection with the woman who had stepped on his ego.

"No, not intentionally," Bridget replied solemnly.

"Then what?" Hammond demanded.

"Diana Kellogg was murdered last night," Josh told him. Both he and Bridget watched the man's face.

"Murdered?" Hammond echoed incredulously. Then, rather than display any sense of horror or outrage that someone should wantonly snuff out a life like this, Hammond actually seemed to be smiling. "Well, I guess that if she was murdered, she wasn't really standing me up."

For two cents, she would have wrung the jerk's neck, Bridget thought.

As if reading her mind, Josh placed his hand on her shoulder, anchoring her to her spot. "No, your reputation as a SexyDude is still intact," Josh told the man.

George looked pleased by that.

Idiot! "We might be in touch," Bridget told him. "Don't leave town."

"Can't," Hammond responded, looking at her as if she was simple-minded. "We're heading into my busy season."

"He wasn't affected by her death at all, just relieved that she hadn't actually stood him up. What a jerk." She glanced at Josh as they walked out of the building that housed Hammond's company. "Did you get it?" she asked.

Josh held up his cell phone. It was set to "camera mode." "Got his chinless profile right here," he assured her.

She nodded. "Let's go back and show it to the bartender."

"If he can tear his eyes away from you long enough to look at it," Josh commented.

"You can convince him," she said, giving his shoulder a pat.

Chapter 8

"You guys again?"

It was obvious that the dark-haired bartender at The Hideaway was less than thrilled to see Josh and Bridget making their way over to the bar, especially since it was now during the club's core hours of operation.

"I can see why you have so much repeat business here, what with that winning, outgoing personality of yours and all," Josh commented as they reached the bar. "Excuse us," he said pointedly to two of the patrons as he elbowed them out of the way so that he and Bridget could get closer to the bartender.

"Don't recall you bringing any business the first time around," Raul retorted.

"Now, Raul, play nice," Bridget advised, offering the man a big, bright smile. "We just want to see if you recognize someone." She glanced toward her partner. "Show him the picture, Josh."

Annoyed, Raul reminded her, "I already told you, she wasn't—" And then he curtailed his protest as he saw that the photo on Josh's cell phone wasn't of the dead woman he'd already disavowed. Squinting, Raul took a closer look, then nodded. "Yeah, him I saw."

Straightening, he pointed over to a table on the far side of the bar. "He sat at one of the side tables, holding on to the same damn glass of beer for like two or three hours. He was staring at the door the entire time, like he was expecting someone really fantastic to come through. Could have heard the nerd sighing all the way over here each time the door opened and whoever walked in wasn't who he was waiting for."

"*Did* anyone come over to him?" Josh asked him.

"Nope." Raul shook his head to underscore his point. "It was obvious right away that he'd been stood up. He started to creep out some of the regulars, sitting and staring like that. I was going to go over to talk to him, tell him to go home, when he saved me the trouble. He just got up and left all of a sudden."

"Do you recall what time that was?" Bridget asked, mentally crossing her fingers.

Taking an order from one of the people at the bar, Raul picked up a colorful bottle and poured the drink, then pushed the glass toward the patron.

"I think about eleven," he finally answered. "Why? Does it make a difference?"

She uncrossed her fingers. "Yeah, it makes a difference. It gives him an alibi," Bridget answered, trying to hide her disappointment. She'd really thought they'd found Diana's killer. She should have realized that would have been too easy. With a nod, she stepped away from the bar. "Thanks for your help."

Raul's attention was already elsewhere as orders came flying at him from along the crowded bar.

"He could be lying," Josh told her as they wove their way over to the front door.

"Why would he?" she asked.

Josh laughed shortly and shrugged. Taking out his keys, he pointed them toward the vehicle. "I haven't worked that part out yet."

"There might not be anything *to* work out," she pointed out.

As the car's security system was disarmed, she heard the locks popping up. Bridget opened the passenger door and dropped into her seat. It felt as if all the energy had been temporarily drained out of her.

"We're back to square one, aren't we?" she murmured, dejected.

"Looks that way—unless one of the other detectives came up with the name of a likely candidate from that stack of academy washouts they were going through when we left."

And that, they both knew, would be an exceptionally tall order. Despite the fact that it had been her idea, Bridget didn't hold out much hope that there was anything to be found there.

"It's got to be someone who looks good for all the murders," Bridget reminded him.

She sighed again. Right now, she was feeling pretty damn hopeless about being able to find *anything* worthwhile.

Josh took his cue from the tone of her voice. "It's

getting late. What d'you say we knock off for the night and get an early start in the morning?"

That seemed to snap her out of it, despite the fact that, just for a second, it did sound tempting.

"I say no," she answered flatly. "I mean, you can do whatever you want to, but I'm going back to the squad room."

Damn but the woman could be stubborn. "And what?" he asked. "Beat your head against the bulletin board?"

Maybe he didn't get how determined she was to bring down this psychopath. "If I thought it would help, yeah. But since it probably won't, I thought maybe I'd go back to the first case. This investigation wasn't ours back then," she reminded Josh. Two other detectives had been on the case the first year. One of them had become so frustrated, he'd taken early retirement several months later.

"Maybe we reviewed it too fast," she went on, "missed something the first time around. We were too focused on the latest murders at the time to do justice to number one. Number one would have been where all the mistakes were made," she said, thinking out loud. "The one that was the original crime of passion."

Josh mulled over what she'd said. "If it really was number one."

Did he know something that she didn't? Bridget wondered. "What do you mean?"

Josh was working out his theory as he went along. "Maybe the Lady Killer hid his first murder for exactly the reasons you just mentioned. After he got even with the woman for standing him up, or ditching him, or maybe even not noticing him—whatever he thought her sin was—he discovered, quite by accident, that he *liked* killing. He realized that he got off on the power of it all or maybe it made him feel like some kind of king of the world, or, better yet, a god."

The more he talked, the more he felt his theory was plausible. His voice took on conviction as he continued.

"Whatever the reason, our killer had to have his fix again. Especially when February rolled around. The month just made him feel too miserable, too hopeless and he needed to find a way to crawl out of that hole. His way turned out to be killing his 'lost love' again. And again." Finished, he studied Bridget's face to gauge her reaction and if she agreed. "Is any of this making any sense to you?"

"Yes, actually it does," she admitted. "You realize this means that we're going to have to start digging through old, *unsolved* homicides." She emphasized the word "unsolved" because if the case had been solved, the serial killer wouldn't still be out there.

The proposition sounded daunting, but she didn't see any way around it. Otherwise, they had nothing to work with.

New theory or not, Josh still thought it was a good idea if they went home tonight. "How about I buy you dinner, then we call it a night and come back fresh in the morning?" he suggested. "You look dead on your feet, Bridget," he observed. "Falling asleep at your desk isn't going to help solve this thing."

She wanted at least to get started tonight. That wouldn't happen if Josh didn't start the car, she thought, impatiently. "I'd work on my flattering skills if I were you or you definitely will have trouble landing a woman once this thing is behind us."

"Don't worry about me 'landing a woman,'" Josh told her. "Never had any trouble yet." He inserted his key into the ignition, then left it for a moment as he continued talking. "Besides, in a pinch, I can always turn to you for some female companionship."

He couldn't have surprised her more if he'd tried. "Me?"

He grinned at the look on her face. In a way, he found the trace of innocent surprise enticing. "Yeah, last I checked, you were a female, right?"

Her eyes narrowed. "Just how closely did you check?" she asked.

"I've got eyes, Detective. And you've got a figure that would really look bad on a guy," he informed her, deliberately sounding matter-of-fact. "So, what sounds good to you?"

He did, Bridget found herself thinking. "I don't know," she responded, then added in a whisper as she looked at him, "surprise me."

They had been in and out of the car countless times in the last two days, spending most of them in close proximity, not to mention close quarters whenever they were on the road in the vehicle. As she uttered her last words to him, Josh realized that having her so close stirred him in ways that surprised him. He wasn't quite prepared to deal with it.

His resistance was, admittedly, drastically low. Plus that damn scent she was wearing had been haunting him all day.

That was what he ultimately blamed for what he did next. He wasn't being himself. But whoever he was, he discovered in the seconds that followed that he was *really* enjoying himself in a way he'd never believed possible.

At least, heaven knew, not with Bridget.

Instead of starting up the vehicle and driving to one of the myriad take-out places that catered to those caught up in Aurora's fast pace, he leaned in toward Bridget, framed her face between his hands and kissed her.

And stopped time.

Half a heartbeat before his lips came down on hers, she was about to ask him what the hell he thought he was doing. But then he was doing it and there was no real reason to ask because she *knew* what he thought he was doing.

Unless he'd suddenly been possessed by an alien life form, Joshua Youngblood knew *exactly* what he was doing—and so did she.

He was curling her toes. Not to mention curling other stray body parts as well, including all ten fingers of her hands.

It was a lucky thing she was curling them, Bridget thought, because it kept her from lacing her hands around his neck. That would make it look as if she were compliant with what was happening. She really didn't want him to think that.

Even if it were true.

She wasn't sure she was ready to admit that to him. Or even to herself.

She *would* admit that she now saw what the noise was all about when it came to Josh. And she understood why Josh could get away with being such a player without having been shot yet. A woman could probably forget and forgive a great deal if she thought she might be on the receiving end of this amazing experience again sometime in the near future.

God, but it felt good. *Really* good.

It was becoming harder and harder for her not to thread her arms around his neck, despite the emergency brake that separated them.

She definitely felt as if she were on fire and about to go up in smoke. What's more, she didn't care.

Josh couldn't have really explained what had come over him just then, or what had prompted him to kiss his partner at this particular junction of their working day.

But now that he was doing it, he was glad. Glad that his resistance was down and his thinking had abruptly taken a holiday. Otherwise, he would have never discovered that the woman he'd been partnered with for the last three years, the woman with whom he had shared thoughts and body armor, and to whom, he had to admit, he felt closer than he did to any other human being on the face of the earth, had the ability to fry his brain.

Fried or not, Josh knew one thing to be true. Bridget Cavelli, aka Cavanaugh, was hot. She was also a woman of substance. Who would have thought it?

The desire to deepen the kiss and take it to the next level urgently, insistently, clawed at him, grew stronger by the moment. Any second now, he was certain, it would get to unmanageable proportions and this was neither the time nor the place to allow that.

This should go at a slower pace. He'd just willingly stepped out onto a minefield and one misstep would rend him into tiny smithereens.

He needed to pull back.

No matter how much he didn't want to.

Bridget struggled between desire and a sense that Josh was suddenly drawing away. The world, listing badly on its axis, was only gradually righting itself and coming back into focus.

She blinked, staring at Josh, wondering if she'd somehow slipped into another reality via an invisible vortex. She had no other plausible explanation for what had just happened—or for her reaction to it.

"Surprise," Josh finally said in a soft voice.

He'd drawn away, but not far enough so that she couldn't feel the warmth of his breath. Goose bumps popped up in response.

He was grinning that lopsided grin of his, the one that simultaneously annoyed and enticed her.

"What?" she bit off breathlessly. She decided that her best recourse here was to act as if she was angry and offended despite the fact that she was neither.

"You said to surprise you," he reminded her.

The words she'd uttered an eternity ago, before the world had tipped over, came back to her. Doubling her fist, Bridget took the opportunity to punch him in the shoulder, hard.

"Idiot!" she bit off. "I was talking about food."

His eyes dipped down to look intently at her lips. "Some might say that was food for the soul."

She raised her chin, looking as if she was ready to go fifteen rounds with him, after which she fully expected to be declared the winner. "And some might say that you've just gone off your nut."

For a second, Josh inclined his head, as if agreeing with her. But then he said, "And others might say that it was the smartest thing I'd ever done." His eyes held hers for a second. There was only a trace of humor on his lips. "I had no idea you could kiss like that, Bridget."

The inside of her mouth had gone inexplicably dry. If it had been up to her to spit on a fire to put it out, the fire would have raged out of control. It took effort not to allow her words to stick to the roof of her mouth.

"The subject never came up," she finally replied. Deftly changing the topic before she fell headlong into it—or grabbed him so that he would kiss her again—she abruptly said, "Chinese."

"Chinese?"

"Yes, Chinese. I pick Chinese," she told him impatiently. "Food," she added when he gave no indication that he understood where she was coming from. "Chinese food. Unless you've changed your mind and decided to skip dinner."

"Well," he allowed, squelching the urge to run his thumb along her very alluring lower lip, "some might say that I've already had dessert so maybe I'd better backtrack and have some dinner now," he said philosophically.

She glanced at him, then looked away. "If you know what's good for you."

Bridget was casting her vote on the side of putting all this behind them and just going on as if nothing had happened. But they both knew that you couldn't un-open the floodgates once they'd been raised and the waters were rushing at you.

"Trouble is," Josh said as he finally started up the car, "I think I do."

It was all he said and for once, he didn't elaborate, leaving Bridget to try to figure out if that meant that he wanted to kiss her again, or felt it was safer and more prudent not to.

Had Josh kissed her because of some silent challenge he had issued to himself—or because he actually really wanted to?

Bridget was undecided as to which side she was rooting for. Both were problematic for different reasons So, for now, she pushed the whole incident—fleeting by most standards—behind her.

Or tried to.

"Anything?" Bridget called out to the three detectives they were working with as she and Josh walked into the squad room.

Just about on their way out, the three detectives on loan, Cox, Langford and Kennedy, stopped and looked at what Bridget and Josh had just brought in. Especially Josh, who balanced various white bags in a large cardboard box. Between the two of them there had to be eight white bags, all embossed with the logo of The Sun Dragon, a red dragon exhaling a wall of fire. It was an agreed-upon fact that The Sun Dragon was the best restaurant around Aurora, possibly the county, for Chinese food.

"Is that to bribe us to stay?" Joel Langford, the youngest of the three, asked.

"Well, there's no overtime pay authorized—*yet,*" she emphasized with conviction, sure that once the cases were reviewed—and solved—there would be. "So we thought we could at least feed you. You have to eat, right? And you have to be sitting somewhere while you eat, right? So why not here? And if you continue glancing through the files, what's the harm? A lot of people read while they eat," she said innocently.

Cox exchanged looks with the other two detectives. No one appeared taken in by her innocent expression, but the food did smell tempting.

"When she says it, it sounds so logical," Cox told the other two men. He was already shedding his jacket and putting it on the back of his chair again.

"When you've been around her as long as I have," Josh told the others, "you learn not to waste your breath arguing with Cavanaugh. There's no winning against her so you might as well just say yes, shut up and sit down. Save yourself a lot of grief that way." He placed the bags in a central location and proceeded to take the large containers out of each one.

Kennedy laughed, following Cox's example and making himself comfortable again.

"You sound more like a husband than a partner," he told Josh.

"God forbid." Josh laughed, pulling up a chair.

And that is something you have to remember, Bridget told herself as Josh's words echoed in her head. The man might stir the blood, but he simply wasn't the kind to stick around. Ever. She'd seen him go through enough girlfriends in the last three years to fill up a medium-size theater. No matter what, Josh put his philosophy into play every single time.

The problem was, she could still taste him on her lips. It made her thinking process a little fuzzy.

Determined to erase all physical traces of Josh from her lips, she went for the shrimp in lobster sauce first, relying on the fact that there were always a lot of onions, as well as garlic, in the mix.

That, and a little amnesia, should do the trick, she thought. Or at least she hoped so.

Chapter 9

The Lady Killer's first known victim, a twenty-five-year-old redhead named Phyllis Jones, came complete with a distraught fiancé who, according to Detective McGee's notes in the file, had an alibi for the time of her murder. And while Bridget hated the thought of dredging up her murder again for the man if he actually was innocent, they still needed to interview the man to see if he had alibis for the time of the two most recent murders.

If he didn't, they'd take it from there.

It still wasn't an interview she was particularly looking forward to.

"I'll go with you," Josh volunteered when she announced where she was going and why.

"You don't have to," she told him. "God knows

there's enough work here to keep you busy even if you worked at warp speed—which you don't."

"Yeah, I do 'have to,'" he said stubbornly. "On the outside chance that you turn out to be right," he added.

Pulling her jacket from the back of her chair, Bridget stopped and looked at him. "Are you telling me that you don't think I can take care of myself?"

The edge in her voice did not go unnoticed. "You?" he laughed. "Hell, if you're right, I'm going along to protect the 'suspect.' Given the way you feel about these murders, you're liable to put a bullet between his eyes just as soon as bring him in."

She squared her shoulders as she gave Josh a frosty glance. "I can control myself," she informed him. Her eyes narrowed. "You're the one who can't." With that, she turned on her heel and walked out of the squad room.

"Uh-huh." The word might have indicated he agreed with what she'd just said, but there was very little conviction in it.

For now, Bridget gave up and let him come along. Two opinions were always better than one.

Ryan Roberts, a freelance architect and the first victim's fiancé, was home, working, when they rang his bell forty minutes later. He opened the door a crack, an uncertain expression on his face until Bridget held up her identification. Absently, she noted that was the first time she'd used her new ID since she'd had the name on it changed.

"Detectives Youngblood and Cavanaugh. We're with the Aurora Police Department's homicide division," she told Roberts, putting her wallet back after a beat.

Still wary, Roberts opened the door and stepped back. "Why are you here?" And then he answered his own question with another question. "Did you find him?" he asked, looking from one detective to the other. "Did you find the bastard who killed my Phyllis?"

"No, I'm afraid not," Josh answered with more compassion than he usually employed, Bridget noted.

"Then I don't understand." Average in height and slight in build, the man became reticent again. "Why are you here?"

"We just needed to ask you a few more questions, Mr. Roberts," Bridget told him, slipping into her friendliest tone to put him at his ease.

It didn't work. There was still a look of suspicion on Roberts's face. "I already told the other detectives everything I knew three years ago. They'd grilled me over and over again like they thought I was the one who did it, wasting all that time instead of going after the real killer."

Josh moved in a little closer to the man. "You sound as if you know who that was."

"I don't know his name," Roberts admitted, "but I know what he looks like."

Bridget exchanged looks with Josh. This was something new. There was no mention of another man in the file they had gone over. "How do you know that?" Bridget asked.

"I know because the little creep kept following her around, trying to talk to her, to get her to pay attention to him." A flash of anger was in his dark green eyes. "Phyllis was nice to everyone. Too nice. I guess because she did talk to him, he thought she was interested. He asked her out and she told him that she couldn't go out with him. That she was already engaged to me. He called her a liar, that he didn't see any ring." There was a tortured expression on Ryan's face when he told them, "I was saving up for one. I wanted it to be special, like she was."

A ragged sigh broke free from his lips. After all this time, Roberts was apparently still beating himself up. "I should have given her a cheap one until I could have afforded better. He would have never bothered her if he'd seen the ring. It's my fault she's dead."

Moved, Bridget put her hand on his shoulder. "It is *not* your fault," she insisted. "This man is sick. Chances are he would have still stalked Phyllis and killed her anyway."

A weak attempt at a grateful smile came and went from his lips. "I guess we'll never know, will we?"

"Would you happen to know if this guy asked Phyllis out on Valentine's Day?" Josh asked.

Ryan cocked his head slightly, thinking. "Yeah, he did. That was the day."

"And she never mentioned his name?" Josh pressed, hoping that Roberts might remember a chance reference to the other man.

Roberts shook his head. "No. She just referred to him as 'that sad little man.'"

Josh tried another approach that might lead them to a few answers. "How did she meet him?"

Roberts was silent for a moment. It was obvious he was trying to remember. "I think she said he came into her store—she managed a pet shop that specialized in food for exotic pets. He told her that he had a pet cockatiel that was sickly. He kept coming back with more

questions, most likely just so that he could talk to her."
Roberts's voice trailed off.

This was definitely a possible suspect worth looking into, Bridget thought. "Would you mind if we got
you together with a sketch artist?" she proposed. "See
if we can come up with a picture of this guy?"

"I'll do you one better than that," Roberts countered.
He walked over to the large, tilted desk he had set up
in the living room where he did all his work. "Give me
a few minutes and I'll sketch this guy for you myself."

"That would be great," Bridget told him. She saw the
look on Josh's face and immediately knew what he was
thinking. This was beginning to feel a little too easy.
Maybe Josh had a point. "Oh, by the way, since he was
stalking your fiancée, when did you get a chance to see
this guy? I would have thought that someone like him
would avoid any kind of confrontations with other men."

Roberts explained without a second's hesitation. "I
looked out my window and saw him hanging around
the corner. When I mentioned it to Phyllis she looked
out the window and said that was her not-so-secret ad-
mirer. I wanted to call 911 or at least go down and tell
him to get lost, but she said not to. That he was harmless. I should have realized people like that were never
harmless."

"Like I said, not your fault," Bridget assured him
with conviction. "Now if you don't mind doing that
sketch for us, we'll be out of your hair," she promised.

"Right away," Roberts said. He sat down and started
to sketch.

"You do realize that this looks like every second guy
in the neighborhood," Josh said to her, referring to the

sketch he was holding in his hand as they went back to their vehicle.

"Still, it's something to go on. Cases have been solved on less." Reaching the car, she took a second look at the drawing. It *was* rather unremarkable, she thought. Taking the drawing from Josh, she placed it in the folder on her seat. "Maybe if we show it at that pet shop, one of the employees might recall having seen him. Maybe the guy bought something there and used his credit card."

"Ever the optimist," Josh said.

"Hey," she protested as she got in, "optimists are right sometimes."

Josh buckled up before putting his key in the ignition. "Do you find it a little odd that there was no drawing in the first victim's file?"

"Luke McGee was a really impatient man. Half the time he didn't hear what you were saying because he was busy working out a theory in his head." Bridget felt it only fair to give the man his due. "He was a good detective, but not exactly detail-oriented and he was definitely not the easiest man to work with. He had his own drummer that he marched to."

He looked at her, intrigued. "You sound like you speak from experience."

She shrugged. It wasn't exactly a time she liked to dwell on. "I was partnered with him for a little while." And then she decided that he deserved to know a few more details. "He was hard-nosed and could be very difficult if he wanted to be. I gave serious thought to quitting the department once or twice."

Josh grinned broadly as they drove to the next light. "But then you hit the jackpot."

She laughed at the description. "Not exactly the way I'd put it."

"That's why I said it for you," Josh told her. "I know how shy you are."

He almost laughed out loud as he said the word. If there was *ever* someone who didn't come across as shy, it was Bridget. But even as he thought it, the very word made him think of something else.

"By the way, you are going to that gathering on Saturday, aren't you?" he asked.

For a minute, she'd almost forgotten about that. As much as she was into family, she was still working all of this out in her head, trying to reconcile herself with the fact that her family had suddenly quadrupled.

"Why?" she asked. "Are you volunteering to take my place?"

He grinned, turning left at the light. "I think they'd notice the difference."

"With all those Cavanaughs milling around? They wouldn't even know that I wasn't there," she assured him.

Josh was quiet for a moment, as if he was mulling over what she'd just said. Or perhaps how she had said it.

"You need backup?" he asked her out of the blue.

Bridget laughed. The idea of needing backup attending a so-called family gathering sounded comical, but then, as she turned the thought over in her head, it began to sound more than a little appealing. "Are you trolling for a family?"

"Just kind of curious to watch you in action with yours," he admitted. He thought of what she'd said was the reason for having this party. "Besides, it might be interesting to meet the man who's responsible for this whole 'Cavanaugh dynasty' that's sprung up in the police department. All those policemen who kept visiting my mom and me after my father died were all great guys—and they were almost like family. But the operative word here is 'almost.' It might be interesting to see the real thing."

He'd always struck her as being footloose and fancy-free, not someone who would welcome family ties. Maybe she should reevaluate her view of Youngblood.

"Are you looking to 'borrow' my grandfather?" she asked him, amused.

"I'll let you know once I meet the man and get to know him a little," he answered vaguely. "Besides, you seem less than thrilled about attending. I figure you might feel better about going if someone was in your corner."

She looked at his profile as he continued to drive. That was really thoughtful on his part. He kept surprising her lately. Especially the other day.

She reined in her thoughts, refusing to dwell on what had happened. It would only make her want an encore and that, she instinctively knew, would be a very bad idea.

"I guess you really can be a decent guy every so often," she commented.

His eyes on the road, Josh grinned at her flippant assessment. "It does happen occasionally, but not enough to ruin my reputation," he assured her. "So, what time do you want me to pick you up?"

"You really want to go to this thing, don't you?"

"Andrew Cavanaugh sets a fine table," he reminded her. "I've been to a few of the Christmas parties he throws for everyone. Going with you to this little get-together, I get to eat a great meal and make sure you don't get overwhelmed with all that family. It's a win-win situation as far as I can see."

Although she had to admit, if only to herself, that she did like his company, she didn't like the fact that he thought she might need moral support. It didn't matter that she might, she still didn't like him thinking it. It made her seem vulnerable.

"I don't need a keeper, Youngblood," she informed him.

He took her defensiveness in stride. "How about a friend? Or do you not need one of those, either?" he asked.

He'd found just the right way to get to her. There was no point in protesting any longer. "Two o'clock," she answered, shifting so that she was looking straight ahead rather than at him.

"Two o'clock it is."

She could hear the satisfaction in his voice. "Now can we get back to work?"

"We never stopped," he told her cheerfully.

Without her realizing it, they had arrived at the precinct. Josh pulled up into their spot in the parking lot. Shutting off the engine, he glanced at the folder where she'd tucked in the sketch. She'd mentioned showing it around the place where the first victim had worked, but now he thought of other places as well.

"You know, it might not be a bad idea to show that around to the other victims' relatives or friends, see if any of them remember seeing this guy lurking around somewhere."

She had been thinking the same thing. It amazed her

how in tune they could be sometimes. Bridget nodded. "Worth a shot. Meanwhile, maybe we can have this run through a facial recognition program."

"Better yet, how about the database with the DMV photos?" Josh suggested. "Just the ones from Northern California." Getting out of the vehicle, Bridget took out the sketch. Josh tapped it for emphasis. "I mean, this guy's got to have a driver's license, right? He doesn't ride the bus to the scene of the crime and he doesn't use the bus to transport the bodies."

What Josh said triggered a thought in her head. "Not unless he's a bus driver and uses the bus after hours for his own purposes every so often."

Josh stared at her, amazed at how she kept coming up with these theories. "You've got an answer for everything, don't you?"

She shrugged. "I think we need to look at this thing from all different angles," she told him. "Something's bound to click eventually."

"In the meantime, it can also make you crazy," he pointed out.

"I can't argue with that," she said as they walked up the stairs to the back entrance.

"Sure you can," he assured her with conviction. "You could argue with God about whether or not the sun comes up in the east."

Oddly enough, the comment didn't bother her. Being viewed in that light was a lot better than being thought of as vulnerable.

Once in the building, rather than reporting to Howard the way the lieutenant had insisted they do each time they returned, Bridget and Josh brought Roberts's sketch to Brenda.

They found the woman still busy working with the last victim's laptop.

"What are you looking for?" Bridget asked, puzzled. "You already found the guy from the internet dating site's IP address."

"Yes, but I also found something else," Brenda answered rather proudly. "Totally by accident," she admitted. She waited for a moment, as if to build up the suspense, before telling them that "Somebody hacked into her laptop."

"You mean like someone was trying to steal her identity?" Josh asked Brenda.

"No." Which made it all the more interesting. "From what I can see, this person hacked into her computer so he or she could read her email."

Bridget's mouth dropped open. That was it. That was how the killer knew where to find her. "If he read her email, he'd know that she was meeting the internet dating guy at The Hideaway—and that's why Diana never showed up for her date."

Josh nodded in agreement, picking up the thread. "He could have been waiting just outside the club, identified himself to Diana as her date—remember, she didn't know what the guy was supposed to look like—and say that he knew a better place for them to go."

Brenda was listening to both of them as they talked faster and faster. Raising her hand, she cut into their rhythm. When they both looked at her, waiting, she asked, "Wouldn't that make her suspicious?"

Josh had already thought of that. "Not if he gave her a good reason why he decided that some other club—or restaurant—might be better. Work with me here," Josh urged the women. "This was how he got her to come with him. He knew all about her—"

"Not to mention that she looked just like his first victim," Bridget interjected. The photographs on the bulletin board she'd set up in the squad room had an eerie sameness to them, as if the women could have all belonged to the same family.

"Which he would have known from that social network page," Josh said, looking at Brenda. "Any way to find out if this guy looked at anyone else who looked like our victims?"

"Maybe in a parallel universe, but it's not anything that I can do," Brenda said.

"Can you find the IP address of the hacker?" Bridget asked.

"It's definitely not going to be easy," Brenda warned her. She looked back at the laptop screen uncertainly. "Whoever this guy is, he's really good."

"Yeah, but so are you," Josh told the woman. The smile on his lips was warm and encouraging.

"Flattery will get you somewhere every time," Brenda told him with a laugh. She knew exactly what he was doing, but she also knew what she was capable of if she pushed hard enough. "But when Dax complains that he hasn't seen me in a week, I'm sending him over to you so *you* can explain why I haven't been home."

Josh grinned. "Leave it to me. You track down the hacker for me and I'll personally send the two of you on an all-expenses-paid second honeymoon."

Brenda glanced up, humor glinting in her eyes. "What makes you think we're done with our first one?"

That, Bridget thought as they left the lab a couple of minutes later, was the kind of marriage she wanted. One where the love didn't wear out once the newness of the situation faded away.

But even as she thought it, despite everything she knew about the way Josh operated, she couldn't help glancing at him.

And wondering.

What if…?

Chapter 10

"You clean up good," Josh said when Bridget finally opened the front door.

It was Saturday and two o'clock, the time she'd told him to come by. He'd been all but leaning on her doorbell since she didn't answer the first two times he'd pressed it. When at last the door *did* open, he'd meant to say a few sarcastic things about her taking her sweet time.

But those words completely evaporated in the heat generated of his partner in a gray-blue dress.

The long-sleeved dress only came midway down her thighs, but it lovingly adhered to every curve of her body during that journey even when she wasn't moving.

Josh made the comment to her in self-defense, hoping that the semi-flippant assessment would annoy her enough to draw attention away from the fact that he'd been momentarily stunned into silence by her appearance and had all but swallowed his tongue.

Granted, since he'd already given in once and kissed her, he'd suspected that Bridget was a great deal hotter than their day-to-day relationship would have normally made him believe. But in his wildest dreams, Josh wouldn't have expected that she could look *this* hot.

"You make it sound as if I come in to work looking like something that the cat wouldn't drag in on a bet," Bridget said.

The comical description made him laugh. With a careless shrug he conceded, "Well, maybe not quite that bad."

"But bad?" she pressed incredulously. "You actually think I look bad when I come into work?" She always tried to appear professional and at her best when she came into the squad room in the morning.

"You fishing for a compliment, Cavanaugh?" he asked, raising one probing eyebrow. He made no attempt to hide his amusement. "Okay, I guess I can give you a compliment. You're an attractive woman, partner, we both know that. But to be honest, I really had no idea that you were this hot."

She did her best not to allow a superior, satisfied smile curve the corners of her mouth. No doubt he'd probably have a crack about that, most likely something about her wanting to appeal to him. God forbid he got started on that line of thinking, even though, secretly, his reaction did please her—maybe a little more than it should have.

Even so, she just couldn't pass up the opportunity to make a quip.

"Maybe your radar isn't as good as you think it is,

Youngblood." She tilted her head as she pretended to study him. "Ever think of maybe having it overhauled and updated?"

He'd never really noticed how brilliantly blue her eyes were. Or just how very female she could be.

Or maybe he had, he reasoned, and had gone out of his way to pretend that he hadn't, just like he was trying to block the scent of her perfume now. You couldn't have distracting thoughts about your partner and still operate at maximum efficiency.

But right now, neither one of them was on duty and he was noticing a hell of a lot of things he shouldn't be. Like how enticing her breasts were as they rose and fell with each breath she took.

If he wasn't careful, she'd damn well take *his* breath away.

"Right now," he told her seriously, his voice low, "you wouldn't want to know what I was thinking."

Warning bells went off in Bridget's head. There were a lot of layers to his words and she was wise enough to step back.

"If you've changed your mind about going," she told him, "I can drive myself over."

"I never said that," he pointed out. Seeing her looking like this, Josh wanted to go to the family gathering more than ever. He put his hand on the doorknob. "Ready?" he asked.

Bridget's eyes met his. Something strong undulated through her. If she had an ounce of sense, she'd head straight for the hills.

She didn't.

"Ready," she answered.

He doubted that either one of them really were ready.

* * *

"You're just in time," Brian declared warmly as he opened the front door to admit them. Andrew had asked his younger brother to man the door while he put the finishing touches on something in the kitchen. "The old man just arrived about five minutes ago. He came in the back way and hasn't been out to address everyone yet," the chief told them. He ushered the two of them through the foyer. "Get yourselves a good space to stand in," he advised. "As I recall, my dad could talk the ears off a statue once he got going."

She looked at Josh. "Last chance to back out," she whispered.

But Josh shook his head. "You're not getting rid of me that easily. My ears are glued on tight." Placing his hand to the small of her back, he ushered Bridget into the living room.

As he did, he glanced around. It astounded Josh just how many members of the police department were scattered through the ground floor of the former chief of police's spacious house. It was a matter of record that the Cavanaughs' numbers were not exactly minor. Looking at them now, with their spouses and children around them, Josh found the number to be all but staggering.

Thinking of the precinct, he asked, "Anyone minding the store?" bending close to Bridget's ear so that she could hear him above the not inconsiderable din.

Bridget struggled not to shiver as his breath cascaded down the side of her neck, making it hard to catch her breath.

It took even longer to find her voice. "I'm sure

there're one or two police officers left to defend the good citizens of Aurora."

"I wouldn't count on it," Josh said. He accepted a glass of wine from a woman carrying several on a serving tray. She seemed vaguely familiar. "Thanks," he acknowledged, then finished his sentence. "I see a few non-Cavanaughs here, too. It looks like the whole police department is here."

"Non-Cavanaughs?" she repeated. "You mean like besides you?" Bridget shook her head when the woman—Andrew's daughter, Teri—offered her a glass of wine as well.

"Yeah," he answered. The whole house teemed with police personnel now that he looked closer. Maybe there *wasn't* anyone left patrolling the streets. "You know, if I was an enterprising crook, this would seem like the perfect time to knock off a string of gas stations in Aurora."

Teri Cavanaugh-Hawkins couldn't help overhearing. She didn't bother trying not to laugh. "You call that enterprising?"

"He's had a tough week," Bridget told the woman with a grin. "Cut him some slack."

Teri's eyes danced and she paused, studying Bridget's face. It was obvious that she was trying to remember the other woman's name. "You're… Kendra?" Teri asked, catching her lower lip between her teeth.

"I'm Bridget," Bridget corrected. "Kendra's older sister." Although the difference was only a matter of thirteen months, as children it had been this insurmountable chasm and she'd rubbed Kendra's face in it.

"Sorry." Teri flashed an engaging smile, then promised, "I'll get it right next time."

Josh took a sip of his wine. "You Cavanaughs should come with flash cards," he commented. "At the precinct is one thing." For some reason, he was accustomed to seeing the various members of the clan there and could distinguish between them despite the strong resemblances. "But en masse and in civilian clothes, hell, that's a whole other story."

"Don't worry." Frank, one of the chief's stepsons, came up behind Bridget and Josh and placed a hand on each of their shoulders. "There's not going to be a quiz at the end of the evening."

Zac, Frank's older brother, came in from their other side and joined the growing group. "However, there will be one when you want to get into the precinct come Monday morning. How's it going, Youngblood?" he asked gregariously, picking up a drink from the near empty tray Teri was holding. He and Josh had worked together a couple of times in the past. "Our newest cousin drag you here for the big meet-and-greet?"

"I did not drag him," Bridget protested. "He insisted on tagging along."

"What was the draw?" her older brother, Thomas, asked as he too joined the group. On his arm was a tall, slender, stunning redhead, who was also his fiancée. Kaitlyn Two Feathers, the newest detective to permanently join the department, was a recent transplant from New Mexico. Thomas looked from his sister to the buffet against the far wall. "You or the food?"

"The food," both she and Josh answered at the same time. The grin on her brother's face, Bridget noted, was smug, as if he'd expected them to answer in unison for some reason. She knew better than to question Tom with so many people around. She might hear what she didn't want spread around. So, for now, she ignored both his grin and him.

Instead, she turned to Zac and asked, "Do you know where the chief's father is?"

"You mean our grandfather?" Tom prompted.

It really felt strange hearing someone being referred to as their grandfather, Bridget thought. By the time she was four years old, neither the people her father believed to be his parents, nor her mother's parents, were alive. The idea of having a grandparent was an entirely new sensation for her.

"Yes," she answered. "Our grandfather." She looked toward the chief's stepsons for an answer.

But it was Teri who pointed the man out to her. "He's right over there," she said. "With Dad and Uncle Brian."

Flanked by two of his sons, Andrew and Brian, Seamus Cavanaugh looked more like their older brother than their father. Six feet tall with wide shoulders and a trim waist, his once-jet-black hair was as thick as ever, but it had turned a gunmetal gray. Despite that, his features were still startlingly youthful.

Bridget decided that it was the man's wide smile that made him look younger than his seventy-three years.

It was another several moments before she became aware of the fact that the older man wasn't just walking into the center of the room, he was walking toward someone.

Toward her father.

A large lump came out of nowhere, rising to her throat as she watched Seamus Cavanaugh embrace the son he had inadvertently been separated from almost five decades ago.

Everyone around them burst into spontaneous applause, touched to be part of this reunion, which was to some a miracle in its own right.

Seamus cleared his throat as a host of emotions, led foremost by joy and wrapped tightly in disbelief, fought to gain control over him.

"You look just like your mother," he managed to tell Sean. Then, in a vain attempt to hold back his tears, Seamus said, "I guess you're too big to take for a pony ride."

Laughter erupted after the observation. The family patriarch was referring to something that had become a tradition for him. As each of his sons became old enough, he would take the boy to have his picture taken sitting astride a pony and wearing Western clothes right down to a pair of stitched boots and a cowboy hat.

Brian had copies of the individual pictures on his desk and Andrew had them on the wall of his den. There were three. One of Andrew, one of Brian and one of Mike, the brother who had died in the line of duty. There had never been a fourth one because the brother they believed to be Sean had never lived to see his first birthday. The pictures reflected Seamus's weakness for Westerns.

As the laughter continued, Seamus held his hand up for silence. When it came, he looked around at the members of his family who were gathered around him and observed, "There were a lot less of you when I left."

Smiling, he slowly scanned the area. The faces he remembered had grown older. And there were new faces, some belonging to children who had been born while he was living on the other side of the continent, others belonging to spouses his grandchildren had exchanged vows with.

He'd missed a lot, Seamus thought.

"Maybe I should have come back sooner." Seamus paused for another moment, his steel-gray eyes sweeping over the very crowded room, then coming again to rest on his newfound son. "They say as you get older, life stops surprising you." The corners of his mouth curved again. "They lied."

His heart swelled. Seamus put a strong, firm hand on Sean's shoulder, remembering. And regretting.

"I only wish your mother was still alive so I could tell her that I was sorry and that she was right. She would have loved that." Realizing that some might not understand what he was referring to, he explained, "She swore that the baby we brought home from the hospital wasn't the baby she'd given birth to. I thought she was just stressed out from the ordeal. You were a really *big* baby," he told Sean.

A wave of laughter met his comment.

"I should have never doubted her. Mothers always know," he gladly admitted.

Seamus took in a deep breath and it was obvious that he was struggling to steady his voice and to suppress the emotions threatening to break free.

"We have a lot of catching up to do, you and I, son." He put his arm around Sean's shoulders. "What say we get started?"

"I say great," Sean responded, his deep, resonant voice choked with emotion like his father's.

And for the second time in her life, Bridget saw her father shed tears. But, unlike when her mother died, this time the tears were happy ones.

Tears like her own, Bridget realized belatedly as the dampness on her cheeks registered with her consciousness. She sniffed, doing her best not to draw any attention to herself or the tears she subtly wiped away with her hand.

And then a handkerchief was being silently pressed into her hands. Not by any of her newly discovered relatives, or her brother, who was standing on her other side. To her surprise, the handkerchief came from Josh.

What surprised her most of all was that Josh gave it to her without uttering a single word or comment. Her partner usually teased her about her being emotional, or soft, or something along those lines. Her warmth for Josh grew. The man could really shock her.

Clutching the handkerchief, she wiped her eyes. A moment later, more tears gathered, seeking immediate release. She wouldn't have thought she could get so emotional.

It was obviously a day for surprises.

During the course of the evening, she and her brothers and sisters, as well as Tom's fiancée, were all introduced by their father to their grandfather.

The older man, like his sons Andrew and Brian, had an uncanny ability to make each person feel singled-out and special while he spoke to them. The man really meant it when he said that he wanted to spend time getting to know each one of them. She believed him when he told her that he intended to be a hands-on grandparent from now on.

Andrew, however, eyed his father skeptically. "What about Florida?" he asked.

Sitting on the wide sofa, surrounded by his new grandchildren, Seamus looked over to his firstborn. "What about Florida?"

Andrew had thought, when his father had called to

say that he was finally coming back to Aurora, that he meant on a visit. No mention had been made of staying indefinitely.

"Well, for one thing, your house is there," Andrew pointed out.

Seamus surprised more than a few people who were listening when he shook his shaggy head and told them, "Not anymore. I put the house up for sale." He looked around at dynasty that he had given birth to, marveling at the miracle of it all. "You might as well know, I'm moving back here."

"Back here?" Brian repeated. "But I thought you loved living in Florida, being retired. You called it living the good life."

"Turned out not to be so good," Seamus answered, then elaborated. "A man can only take so much sitting around, doing nothing." He thumped his chest with a closed fist. "I'm still alive so it's high time I started acting that way."

Brian glanced over toward Andrew, who moved his wide shoulders up and then down in a mystified shrug. Neither of them had a clue where their father thought he was going with this.

Brian was the first to put it into words. "Just what does that mean, Dad?"

"It means," Seamus began, then paused impishly for a moment as his gaze swept over the faces of those sitting closest to him, "that Seamus Cavanaugh's getting back in the game."

Andrew and Brian exchanged looks again, this time a little uneasily. That was the way their father had always referred to police work. No one wanted to hurt the old man's feelings, but he had to face the fact that he was just that: an old man.

"Dad," Andrew broached tactfully, "you're a little over the age limit to be talking about rejoining the police department."

"You mean too old," Seamus said bluntly. "Well, in case you haven't noticed, I'm also too old to be taking orders from some wet-behind-the-ears kid young enough to be my grandson—or granddaughter," he tactfully included, nodding toward several of his grandchildren. "Which is why I'm opening up my own detective agency," he announced, ending on a note of fanfare as he gleefully rubbed his hands together.

He let the news sink in before continuing, "And Andrew, if you ever decide you've had enough of standing over a hot stove, feeding this bunch…" He chuckled. "You might think about coming to work for me—or with me," he corrected. Seamus raised his hands and then spread them out wide, as of tracing a large, imaginary sign. "Cavanaugh & Cavanaugh." His eyes twinkled as he looked around the room. "It has a nice ring to it, doesn't it?" Seamus asked with a wide, pleased smile.

"It's official," Bridget heard someone behind her say. "Grandpa's back."

That, too, she couldn't help thinking, had a nice ring to it.

Apparently, Seamus heard the comment from one of his grandchildren. "You bet I'm back," he answered. "And I intend to make up for lost time."

"Take it slow, Dad," Andrew advised.

"Slow?" Seamus's hearty, infectious laugh filled the air. "Are you kidding? I can't take it slow. It's not like I've got another forty years to work with this time around," he reminded his son. "Slow is for young guys like you," he told Andrew. "Whatever I do, I've got to do fast."

"Don't burn yourself out, Dad," Rose, Andrew's wife, warned her father-in-law. "You're going to live to be a hundred."

It was obvious that the older man was pleased by the prediction. "Well, then," he allowed, "I'm going to wind up packing a lot of living into those twenty-seven years," he predicted.

No one in the room doubted it. Not even those who hadn't known the man before today. They were all in agreement that Seamus Cavanaugh was a force of nature and a dynamo, determined to reclaim his place in the world. No one doubted that he would, too.

Chapter 11

"Now that's what I call a family," Josh said, laughing softly to himself.

It was eleven-thirty and while the party was still going on at Andrew's house as they had left, it had grown smaller and consequently more subdued in nature. Approximately half the people who had attended had already said their good-nights and drifted out the door, making their way toward the cars parked along the next two blocks.

Josh had made no indication that he'd wanted to leave. Instead, he left that up to Bridget, waiting for her sign that she was tired or thought that it was time to go. Initially, even though he'd sensed this afternoon that she'd been rather reluctant to come at first, as the evening had worn on, he began to get completely opposite vibrations. It was obvious that his partner was enjoying herself, enjoying watching her father get to know the man who was *his* father.

Eventually, though, Josh noticed her stifling yawns and then, finally, she caught his eye and nodded. Over the course of the last three years, they had developed a sort of shorthand. It was time to go home.

Tired himself, Josh lost no time in taking her at her word. Making the rounds in double time, he and Bridget said their goodbyes. He had her out and in his car in a little more than two heartbeats.

Leaning back against her seat, Bridget laughed in response to his comment now. The Cavanaughs en masse were definitely a force of nature.

"And here I thought I came from a large family." Until this evening, when every single family member had made it a point to show up, she hadn't realized just how huge the family actually was.

Josh slanted a look in her direction, a smile playing on his lips. "You do."

She knew what he meant. Josh was referring to the "small town" they had just left behind them. But thinking of all of them as family would take some getting used to on her part. Yes, they were Cavanaughs and yes, apparently she was, too, but actually *feeling* like one of them would take adjustment.

"No, I'm talking about my core family," she stressed. "My dad, my brothers and my sisters. There's eight of us altogether, counting Dad, and I always thought that was a lot."

He thought back to their entrance and how overwhelming it was to see that her family was taking up every available inch of space in the house. "Not when you compare them to the Cavanaughs."

That was what she was trying to tell him. "My point exactly."

"Still," he went on, mulling the situation over in his head, "it must be nice, knowing that they're there to support you and that they have your back so completely. *Nobody* will mess with you now that you're a Cavanaugh. I hear it's all for one and one for all with that clan."

"I wouldn't go that far yet," she told him. "I mean, they barely know me."

Josh didn't see the problem or why she was hesitating. If it were him, if he had suddenly discovered that he was related to the Cavanaughs, he would have already declared it to the world and opted for a family portrait. Having a family, people with a vested interest in you, appealed to him immensely.

"What's to know? You're a Cavanaugh. That's good enough for them," he assured her. "I never saw a more united bunch of people. It's as if they were all tuned in to one mind."

A smile she couldn't quite fathom played on her partner's lips as he continued talking. Was it wistfulness? Envy?

"Makes me realize what I've missed." Josh said the last words more to himself than to her.

If it was family he wanted, she had more than enough to spare—not to mention that there were times when she would have gladly paid someone to take her brothers off her hands. Things were much better now, but there was a time…

"I've got a few spare brothers I could lend you," she offered. "All slightly used, but they still have a lot of mileage left on them. Just say the word and they're yours."

Turning a corner, Josh laughed and shook his head. "Not that I'm not grateful, partner, but it's not quite the same thing."

Her brothers could still be pretty irritating at times, especially when they thought they were right and she wasn't.

"Trust me, Youngblood, a little while with any of them and you'll be very happy that you're an only child," she promised him.

She sounded sincere, but he had only one question for her. "Would you want to be a loner if you had the chance?"

A flippant answer rose to her lips, but then Bridget saw that he was really serious. If she was going to be honest with him, there was only one answer she could give him.

"No, I wouldn't," she admitted. Because she had a large family, there was always someone to talk to, someone to turn to if she needed a soundboard or a shoulder to cry on. Having a family as large as hers had ultimately given her a great sense of security, a feeling of being safe no matter what.

She wouldn't have traded her life with anyone else's for the world.

Bridget's prolonged silence gave him his answer. "I didn't think so." Her apartment complex was the next right and he took it. "Both of my parents were only children. If my dad had lived, I know they would have had more kids. My mother told me she wanted at least three." Lost in his thoughts, he pulled up into an empty space in the guest parking area. But even as he turned off the ignition, he remained sitting in the car. "After hearing that, I always tried to be three times the son she could have asked for," he confessed with a disparaging laugh. "And probably three times the headache."

Getting out of the vehicle, Bridget pretended to try to envision that. "Wow, three of you would be more than anyone should be forced to put up with," she told him with an exaggerated shiver. "How did your poor mother survive that?"

Josh automatically walked her to her door. "Very funny," he commented.

Coming to her door, Bridget fished out her key and then turned around to face her partner. All things considered, he was a pretty good guy. They were together a minimum of eight hours a day and yet he had volunteered to accompany her to this party, sensing that she needed to have someone with her, a warm body who was on her side. She couldn't deny that she really did appreciate his doing that for her.

"Thanks for having my back, Josh," she said softly, as if saying the words louder would make it seem all too serious.

Her comment caught him by surprise. After a moment, Josh shrugged. "It's not exactly as if we were pinned down at a shoot-out and you were caught in the cross fire," he pointed out.

"Yeah, but I was kind of—uneasy about it." Bridget was going to say "nervous," but that would have been too much of an admission on her part. "I really do appreciate you coming with me."

Josh grinned. "You mean inviting myself along."

Bridget inclined her head and grinned back. "I was trying not to be blunt."

In his experience, his partner had never been what someone might term a shrinking violet. "Blunt" had probably been her middle name at one time or another. "Now that's a first."

Here was the Josh she knew. She was more comfortable reacting to his sarcastic, flippant remarks than to his random act of kindness. The latter put her at a disadvantage.

"You know what? Never mind." She waved her hand at him, dismissing her partner. "Subtleties are wasted on you."

Very slowly, Josh allowed his eyes to drift up and down the length of her, taking in the way her dress still highlighted far more than it hid. Her body was tight, firm, and his knees, he noted, were beginning to feel just a wee bit weak.

"Oh, I don't know about that," he contradicted.

Bridget did her best to ignore her reaction to his languid scrutiny. "You could at least look me in the eyes when you say that."

Josh flashed a full-on sensual grin. The expression in his eyes made her gut tighten twice over. "Not that your eyes aren't pretty, but who knows when I'll get a chance to see you looking like this again?"

Not in a hundred years, she silently vowed. He made her feel vulnerable and that wasn't good. "Careful, your libido is showing."

The grin on his lips only deepened, creating more ripples inside of her. Josh shook his head. "And I was trying so hard to hide it."

If she didn't know any better, she would have said that Youngblood was flirting with her. "What's the matter, Josh, no new woman in your life?"

He watched her for a long, pregnant moment before finally saying, "Not in the usual sense, no."

He'd moved closer, Bridget realized. Somehow, as they stood there, bantering, exchanging words, the air had grown warmer and the distance between them had grown a lot shorter.

Or at least it certainly felt that way.

Her throat went very dry. She swallowed, but it didn't help.

"Then in what sense?" she challenged.

Only when the words were out did she realize that she'd whispered them. She really hoped that he wouldn't notice, but she had a sinking feeling she didn't really have a prayer.

He needed to get going, Josh told himself. To turn on his heel and leave right now before he did something stupid. Something he'd wanted to do since the moment she'd opened the door this afternoon.

It was all very simple, really. He knew how to walk. How to put one foot in front of the other and create space between himself and whatever it was that he was leaving behind.

And yet, there he was. Standing still.

Not moving.

And then he was. But he wasn't moving in the direction he needed to go. Instead, he was moving to close the tiny bit of space that still existed between him and Bridget. Moving until that sliver of space was completely blotted out. Until there wasn't enough space between them for the thinnest sheet of paper to fit in.

The only way she would save herself was through bravado and she knew it.

"You're in my space, Youngblood," Bridget informed him hoarsely, trying to sound annoyed.

"What are you going to do about it?" he asked, well

aware that this could go either way. The way he wanted it to or the way he didn't.

In all honesty, he half expected his feisty partner to place her hands on his chest and shove him back. Hard. The one thing he hadn't expected—admittedly longed for, yes, but really wasn't expecting—was to have Bridget grab hold of the sides of his jacket, raise herself up on her toes and press her mouth urgently against his.

And just before she did, he could have sworn that she'd whispered, "Damn you!"

But he wasn't able to ask her why, because by then her mouth was on his, creating such havoc inside him that all he could think of was kissing her back with the same intensity.

He wanted to rock her foundations the way she was rocking his.

Bridget's heart pounded wildly even as the most remote part of her brain, the part that hadn't been fried to a crisp yet, demanded to know what the hell she was thinking, kissing him at all, let alone like it was the end of the world.

But the simple truth of it was, she wasn't thinking. She was going with gut feelings, with demanding sensations. With a hunger that she would have sworn she wasn't even vaguely acquainted with.

Except that now she was.

Josh had triggered something within her, feeding an untamable hunger inside.

In a velvet haze, Bridget was feeling around along the door behind her, searching for the keyhole. Finding it, she fitted her key into the lock in what could only be the most awkward angle ever assumed by a human being. But she was desperate to get inside her apartment, desperate to drag Josh in with her, and insanely determined not to lose even a moment's contact with him.

Somehow, she managed to unlock the door and get it open.

The next second, they were stumbling inside, lips still very much sealed to one another even as articles of clothing began to fly off.

She felt constricted by what she was wearing, bound, imprisoned. She needed to shed every last stitch so that she could satisfy this overwhelming need to feel Josh against her.

Feel his hands, his torso, his desire.

So even as she shed her spectacular dress as well as its accessories, leaving articles discarded in a tangled, forgotten heap, she was yanking at his clothing as well. She was gratified as she felt him shaking free of his jacket, pulling away his shirt and then stepping out of his jeans, kicking everything aside so that the path was clear for them.

His body was hot as it pressed against hers.

As hot as his mouth, which was no longer sealed to hers but roaming along her throat, her shoulders, her neck, creating chaos and wild, thunderous desire with each pass that he made.

It was a night of revelations.

Just as she was convinced she'd reached the pinnacle of pulsating desire, he managed somehow to bring her up yet another notch.

Caught up in this tango they were dancing, a silent tango composed of throbbing rhythms she could feel within her body, Bridget suddenly stumbled, tripping backward. His arms immediately closed tightly around her, but instead of breaking her fall, Josh went down with her.

Down and twisting so that when they reached the floor a split second later, Bridget found herself on top of him.

The feel of his hardened body excited her, bringing her up to such a high plateau that she could scarcely catch her breath. And all the while, her heart pounded as his mouth continued to roam over the length of her. She could feel herself quivering against him.

Under oath Josh wouldn't have been able to say just how this had come about or what had come over him. Yes, he'd been attracted to Bridget for a long time now and yes, he'd spent the evening keenly aware of her proximity, her scent, her very existence. But he'd always maintained control over himself, known how to keep both his temper and his desires in check under all circumstances.

So what had happened here?

How had this slip of a woman—a strong woman, granted, but still not his match in height and weight by any means—how had she managed to bring him down to his knees, destroying every last shred of his self-control while she was at it?

All Josh could think of was how much he wanted her. How much he needed her.

Desired her.

He knew deep down in his gut that if he didn't try to fill himself with her, he would cease to exist. Cease to be.

It was an absurd thought.

And yet, somehow he knew that it was true. That

if he was to continue living a moment longer on this earth, it would take having her, making love with her, to sustain him.

The fact that Bridget didn't attempt to resist, that she not only welcomed him but had been the one to instigate this crazed, fateful dance, only managed to urge him on further and more quickly.

He'd never kissed anyone who kissed him back with such ardor, such passion before. Never wanted anyone with such intense longing. It was more than a fever of the blood, it was bordering on insanity and as much as he absolutely hated the fact that he was being held prisoner by these feelings, that he had absolutely no free will when it came to his fate, he couldn't seem to break free.

And after a few timeless minutes had faded from existence, he didn't want to.

Didn't want to be free of her or of this need for her. What he wanted, more than life itself—which truthfully scared him to no end—was to have her. To take her now and make her his alone.

Now.

No matter what the consequences.

With one calculated movement, he had Bridget under him.

Balancing his weight on his elbows and knees, the rest of his body so close to hers that boundaries between their two bodies were difficult to define, he framed her face with his hands.

"Look at me," he ordered hoarsely, desire constricting his very throat. When she didn't comply at first, he repeated the instruction more firmly, waiting for her to do it.

Drawing in a shaky breath, Bridget opened her eyes and met his.

There was no anger, no defiance, not even a look of submission in her eyes. Just challenge and desire. She felt the way he did.

It was all he needed to know.

With his eyes on hers Josh drove himself into her, making her his.

Making himself hers.

And then it began, the scrambling journey to the top, to take hold of the wondrous sensation that occurred when all inhibitions disappeared and two, however briefly, became one.

His arms tightened around her and he had to hold himself in check not to cause her any undue pain as the final moment swept them both breathlessly away.

Chapter 12

For several minutes there, as they lay on the floor side by side, Bridget was fairly convinced that she would never catch her breath again, that she would never move normally. Her heart beat so hard that she felt too weak even to get up, much less to walk and talk.

What had he done to her?

What had she *allowed* him to do to her?

Too exhausted to move, Bridget continued to lie there, with the back of her wrist pressed against her eyes, warding off not just the light streaming into her apartment through the kitchen window, courtesy of the full moon, but hopefully the immediate world as well.

Her dazed, chaotic mind searched madly for something coherent for her to say, *anything* that would sound neutral and innocuous so he wouldn't know just how very deeply he'd shaken up her world.

Finally, desperate to bring an end to the silence and the sound of her own irregular breathing, Bridget muttered something, in hindsight, that she considered incredibly inane.

"I didn't turn on the lights."

"Yeah, you did," she heard Josh say. Even without looking at him, she could "hear" the grin on his lips.

What the hell was he talking about? They'd all but fallen into the apartment, never once bothering to turn on any of the lights. At this point, she considered it lucky that they'd closed the door. Passion had completely knocked out any common sense that might have been lying around.

Confused, she lifted her wrist and opened her eyes to glance at him.

"You turned on a whole spectrum of lights," he told her, then lightly tapped the center of his chest with his fisted hand. "Right in here. There were starbursts and even a mesmerizing light show."

Was this actually Josh talking to her like this? Admitting to being moved? Or was he setting her up for some big payoff? Or maybe some big joke?

For as long as she'd known him, Josh had never bragged about his conquests, only about having stellar evenings—or entire weekends—and he'd always end his quick summation with a sensuous, amused grin.

But he never gave her any details—not that she'd ever asked.

She had to admit that she liked that about him, that he kept things like that and what went on behind closed doors between him and his myriad lady friends to himself. It told her that somewhere along the line, someone had made an effort to see that Josh grew up to be a gentleman.

A gentleman who could make the earth move.

Turning her head to look at Josh, and getting an extremely queasy feeling in her stomach as she did so—a good queasy feeling, she thought with an inward smile—Bridget asked, "Should I be checking your garage for a pod?"

"Don't have a garage," he told her, almost drawling. "Have a carport." Like her, he lived in a garden apartment complex.

"Any pod left there would have been moved by the rental office," she speculated, giddy and still far too tired to attempt to move.

And then she became aware that Josh had raised himself up on his elbow and was looking at her. Suddenly, she wasn't so tired anymore. Feeling around on the floor, she searched for an article of clothing, *any* article of clothing larger than a handkerchief so that she could cover herself.

But there was nothing there except for the rug. Frustrated, she reached over her head and pulled down the seat cushion from the sofa and placed that her body. It balanced precariously.

"Looking for a floatation device?" Josh asked, amused. "I don't think the weather bureau predicted any flash flooding for the area." He found her modesty almost sweet. And rather futile. Very gently, he tugged away the cushion. "You realize that's like locking the barn door after the proverbial horses have run off."

He was right, of course, but that didn't keep her from being stubborn. "It's my barn door," Bridget argued. "I can do with it whatever I want."

"That it is," he agreed. "And you can." And then his smile turned from amused to sensual. "All I ask for is squatter's rights."

Bridget could feel warmth spreading throughout her entire body. The kind of warmth that promised to turn her a bright, bright shade of pink from her head to her toes. And he noticed the progression starting.

"Hey, Cavanaugh," he said, calling attention to the color her skin was turning. "You're blushing."

"No, I'm not," she bit off.

He was going to make her pay for this occasion of weakness, wasn't he? This was a mistake, a damn mistake. Why hadn't she stopped herself while she still had a chance?

Because she'd wanted it too much. And now she was going to pay for it, Bridget thought, trying to resign herself to her fate.

"Okay," he allowed, "then you must be lying on something very hot because you're turning a shade of pink I've only seen on preteens and salmon steaks while they're being grilled. The salmon, not the preteens," he added with a widening grin.

He was laughing at her, she thought angrily. Sitting up, Bridget scanned the immediate area, looking for her dress. Why hadn't she been more careful when she'd done her frenzied striptease and taken note where she'd dropped her clothes?

Suddenly spotting her dress, Bridget made a dive for it.

Unfortunately, she had to turn her back on Josh to do it and he found that the view succeeded in arousing him all over again. His partner, he thought not for the first time, was one fine-looking woman.

"If you don't want to turn me on, Cavanaugh, I suggest you find yourself a blanket and wrap yourself up in it *now*." He stressed the last word, conveying a sense of urgency to her. He wasn't about to take advantage of her, but what he did want to do was to seduce her into doing what they'd just done all over again.

Holding the dress, rather than slipping it on and having it reveal more than it hid—since she had no undergarments on—Bridget held it up against her as she turned around again to look at him.

"You're telling me I'm turning you on?" she asked incredulously. The Josh she knew would have *never* admitted to something like that. It completely went against his love-'em-and-leave-'em facade. Just who *was* this man she'd just made love with?

"Right now, Cavanaugh, you could turn on a rock. A petrified rock."

She didn't want him to see how much his words affected her. She wasn't nearly as experienced as he was—who was?—but she wasn't exactly a babe in the woods, either. The last thing she wanted was to hear Josh gloating that she'd been moved by his compliment. She did her best to appear unaffected and blasé.

"Does that line usually work for you?" she asked him, a smirk on her lips.

"Work for me?" he repeated as if he didn't quite follow her.

"Does it get you 'repeat business'?" she stressed. When he still didn't seem to get it, she elaborated even further. "The women you make love with, does saying that line to them have them suddenly desperate to do it all over again?"

"It's not words that they're after," he told her evenly, his meaning clear.

He was telling her the reason the sexual partners he'd had were so eager to make love with him again was because of his technique, not his words. He really had made the earth move, but she would die before ever telling him that.

His eyes seemed full of sensual mischief as he tugged her back down to him. "So, how about those 49ers?" he teased, referring to the San Francisco football team.

"You'll have to ask Logan," she said, bringing up the name of one of her brothers. "He's the resident expert on football."

The sensual smile still very present on his lips, Josh ran his fingertips over her mouth. "And what are you an expert on?"

"I haven't picked an area of expertise yet. When I do, I'll let you know."

Her eyes fluttered shut almost involuntarily as she felt Josh sensually brush his lips—just the slightest point of contact—against her shoulder. Even that fleeting touch sent goose bumps racing up and down her spine.

"I really wish you wouldn't do that, Youngblood," Bridget said. It took effort to squeeze the words out evenly.

He drew his head back a little, as if studying her. "Nope, you don't mean that," he told her simply.

Her back went up. No, she didn't mean that, but he was being just a little too cocky for her taste. "Why? Because you're so damned irresistible?"

Lucky for her he liked feisty women, Josh thought.

The more she resisted, the more she aroused and interested him.

"No," he told her very simply. "Because you're crinkling your nose. You always crinkle your nose when you're lying. It's your 'tell.'"

"You studied my face?" she asked in disbelief, stunned.

"Among other interesting parts," he said, unable to resist giving her a leer. "I like knowing my partner inside and out."

She just bet he did. Bridget raised her chin defiantly. "There's such a thing as too much information, you know."

"Maybe." His smile went straight into her nervous system, causing an instant upheaval. "But not in this case."

Leaning down over her, Josh kissed her. Not passionately the way he had in response to her first kiss earlier, but with small, soft kisses landing gently on her lips like the first spring butterfly delicately perching on a rose petal just before it flew off.

If possible, this had an even greater effect on her than his passionate kiss had. She could feel her very core igniting as desire galloped through her even *more* urgently than the first time. Surrendering, giving up all resistance to this man, she reached for him.

The next moment, he had her in his arms and was abandoning any thought of reining in his feelings. They had this moment and he intended to enjoy it—enjoy her—with every fiber of his being.

Who knew what tomorrow might bring?

Amid the passion and the ardor, the sound of first

one cell phone ringing, then two, took a little time to penetrate.

Bridget wanted nothing more than to ignore it and just absorb the wild feelings shooting through her. But she knew she couldn't pretend her phone wasn't ringing. She was a detective with the Aurora Police Department and that meant that unless she was lying on a table in the operating room and was actively under the knife, she was expected to be on call anytime, anyplace. No matter what.

As was Josh.

Drawing her head back, she looked up at him. His phone was ringing as well.

Resigned, she reluctantly reached for her cell phone. It took her a moment to focus—and then she realized what the call had to be about.

Oh God, please not again.

"Cavanaugh," she declared grimly a second after she unlocked her phone. Her voice blended with Josh's as he announced, "Youngblood."

They were both on the phone and both looking at each other, dreading confirmation that the Lady Killer had struck again.

"He's out of control," the voice on the other end—Langford—told her. Frustration echoed in his deep voice. "The Lady Killer just killed victim number three and it's not even the tenth yet."

"Where?" she asked, sitting up and dragging her hand through her hair. As the detective on the other end of the line spoke, she scanned the room, trying to locate the rest of her clothes. Listening to Langford she was also attempting to make out what Josh was saying at the same time.

He wasn't saying much, but his face had grown grim. "Be right there," he told the detective who'd called him. "No, I've already left the chief's party," he replied to Kennedy's question just before he shut his phone and terminated the call.

There was no reason to state the obvious. The Lady Killer had upped his ante and was on a spree.

"At this rate, he's going to double the number of his total kills by the time he gets to the end of the month," Josh said grimly, standing up.

Bridget suddenly found herself caught in two very different worlds. In one, she was the consummate detective, her mind on the case, in a hurry to get herself together so she could get to the scene of the crime as quickly as possible.

In the other world, she was a woman who'd just been utterly blown away by her partner and was, even now, while in the midst of a tragedy, utterly captivated by Josh. The latter had just stood up, as unencumbered by clothing as the day he was born and completely unself-conscious about the figure he cast.

He had one hell of a magnificent, taut body, she couldn't help admiring. Even her fingertips were tingling.

"Maybe you should get dressed a little faster," she suggested, her throat feeling just the slightest bit tight.

Picking up his clothes from the floor, Josh looked at her quizzically. "Why?"

"Just do it," she snapped, turning her back on him and marching off to her bedroom.

She didn't see Josh grinning at her.

If she was going to be up all night—and this had all the earmarks of an all-nighter—she might as well be comfortable. Going to her closet, she pulled out a pair of jeans and a pale blue turtleneck sweater. She moved quickly, got dressed and hurried out, a pair of boots in her hand.

Almost dressed, Josh was buttoning up his shirt. She sat on the edge of the sofa, pulling on her boots. He gave her a quick once-over.

"Oddly enough, you look just as sexy in that as in the dress you had on tonight. Of course, that might have something to do with the fact that I know what you look like naked," he added with a smoldering, lethal grin.

Glorious as it had been, it was a mistake and she knew it. Most workplace affairs fizzled out quickly, leaving behind a residue of awkwardness if not worse. If that happened, ultimately they would wind up getting different partners, which was a shame because what-ever else went on between them, she and Josh worked extremely well together.

"I'd rather you kept that to yourself," Bridget told him.

Finished buttoning, he tucked in his shirt and then held up his hands.

"No problem," he said. "I wasn't exactly planning on posting it on YouTube."

He was staring at her, she noted. Again. Braced for some kind of punch line or snappy comment at her expense, she told herself she might as well get it over with. "Okay, what?"

"Nothing," he answered noncommittally. "It's just that you think you know a person after interacting with them on a daily basis for over three years and yet there always seems to be some kind of surprise just under-neath the surface."

She had always liked surprises. "I would think that's a good thing."

"Didn't say it wasn't," he replied in his laid-back manner. The same sort of pseudo-country-boy manner that drove her crazy.

Their phones rang again and they exchanged looks. Bridget had a sinking feeling in her stomach.

"Oh God, don't tell me there's another one besides the one they just called about," she groaned. That seemed incredibly macabre, even for the Lady Killer.

"Only one way to find out," Josh said, pulling his phone out of his pocket. "Youngblood." She could have sworn she saw him square his shoulders and snap to attention a beat before he said, "Yes, Chief. No, I wasn't asleep yet."

Her phone began ringing. Why was the chief of detectives calling him, she wondered even as she opened her own phone. This seemed a little beneath the man's level of operation.

"Cavanaugh."

"So, I'm glad to hear you're finally using it," the deep male voice on the other end told her with resonant approval.

"Chief?" she asked uncertainly, looking at Josh. Why was the man they'd left at the party calling both of them on a conference call? Was the man checking on them for some reason?

Had he suspected the way the evening had gone and called to confirm?

Brian Cavanaugh didn't strike her as the type to pass judgment on the personal lives of his people, but then, she wouldn't have guessed that Josh was as good as he was—or as thoughtful—either. Her ability to read people had been temporarily suspended.

"Yes, it's me, Bridget. I've got you both on conference call," Brian told the duo. "Thought it might save a little time that way. I take it the two of you are in the same area."

She took a breath, then said, "Yes, sir," wondering if this was just an innocent question on the chief's part or if, as she feared, the man was putting two and two together. And if he did, would there be a reprimand along with some sort of consequences?

"Okay, then I'll expect to see you both here ASAP. We need to put an end to this. *Now,*" Brian emphasized grimly.

"If the chief's involved," Josh said to her as she terminated the call and closed her cell phone, "that means he's getting a lot of pressure to make an arrest and have a suspect arraigned for this killing spree."

She nodded in agreement. "Certainly looks that way. The chief of D's considers Aurora his city to personally protect." Bridget sighed, shaking her head. "Now all we need is a suspect to arrest," she muttered as they dressed and went over to the front door.

"Yeah," he agreed, setting his jaw grimly. "That would be rather nice, wouldn't it? Well, maybe this time the son of a bitch made a mistake and we can finally latch onto something. C'mon, let's go," he urged, leading the way out.

Locking her door, Bridget hurried to the waiting vehicle.

Chapter 13

She could hear herself breathe.

Josh wasn't saying anything. He hadn't said a single word to her since they'd gotten into the car. It wasn't like him.

One of them had to bring it up before it became the elephant riding in the unmarked car, taking up all the available space, sucking up all the oxygen and growing at a prodigious rate.

If he wasn't going to do it, it was up to her.

"So, what was that back at my place?" Bridget finally asked without any sort of preamble. The silence had gotten just too overbearing and unwieldy for her to tolerate.

"Pretty terrific, I thought," Josh answered with feeling. Sparing her a quick look, he added, "You were good, too."

His breezy tone, as well as the way he'd phrased his answer, told her all she needed to know about how he regarded what had happened between them.

She should have known, Bridget chided herself. What had she expected, anyway? That one encounter with her and he'd magically transform into someone who'd hang around longer than the life expectancy of a fruit fly?

"So, it was just a hookup," she concluded quietly, setting her jaw hard.

It was on the tip of Josh's tongue to confirm her assumption. To say something light and flippant, the way he always did, and to act as if, now that they were back in their clothes, it was just business as usual between them.

But it *wasn't* business as usual. What had happened between Bridget and him earlier had been different. *Really* different. And he knew damn well that he stood the chance of losing something exceedingly special if he fell back on his usual carefree, man-about-town act.

Taking a breath, Josh stepped out on the ledge and then dove off.

"Actually, no, it wasn't 'just a hookup' and I think you already know that," he added quietly.

No, she didn't. If she was being honest with herself, she'd have to admit that she'd hoped, but she really *hadn't* known. Not when it came to Josh, who went through women the way her mother used to go through tissues while watching *An Affair to Remember* for the umpteenth time.

A warm sunspot opened up inside of her. She did her best not to grin like an idiot. "So, what do you want to do?" she asked Josh.

"Truthfully?" He really had only one thought in his head. "Make love to you until I literally come apart at the seams."

It was a real struggle to keep her grin from surfacing. She knew if she came across as eager in any manner, shape or form, Josh would be gone so fast he would make the Road Runner look slow.

So, putting herself in Josh's shoes, she said, "As enticing as that sounds, why don't we take it one step at a time?"

In every other case, that would have worked fine for him. The suggestion would have been right up his alley. It didn't nail down anything, didn't promise anything. No strings, no commitments, which was just the way he liked it.

The operative word here, he realized, was *liked*. As in past tense.

He had never felt uncertain before, never been in this position before. The emotional uneasiness, even if he didn't show it, was a new sensation for him and he didn't much like it.

But to say so would be to lose face. Moreover, it would tell Bridget that when it came to this—whatever "this" that was between them was—she was in the driver's seat and his pride wouldn't allow that.

So instead, he said, "Works for me," and then turned his attention back to what had called them out in the first place. The Lady Killer and his gruesome, growing body count.

"What the hell are we going to do to stop this son of a bitch?" he wondered out loud.

"Until we have a suspect in our sights, nothing,"

she answered, every bit as frustrated as he was. Maybe even more so.

"And once we have a suspect?" he asked. Her tone of voice seemed to indicate that she had a plan in mind after that and he was curious to hear what she was thinking.

He wasn't wrong. "Then we set a trap for him and bring him down."

He couldn't have said exactly why, but there was something about the sound of that that made him uneasy. "What kind of a trap?"

"The simple kind," she answered. "The psychopath obviously likes redheads. If we know who he is, we give him what he likes. I can become a redhead in twenty minutes."

Josh scowled. That was an utterly stupid plan. What the hell was she thinking? "You can become dead in less than that," he snapped.

She looked at him, stunned. He'd never yelled at her before. Never yelled at all to her recollection. "Why, Youngblood, is that concern I hear in your voice?" she teased.

Yes, it was concern. Even if they hadn't just shared an incredible interlude together, she would still be his partner, his friend, and there was no way he was going to let her dangle herself like live bait in front of the cold-blooded shark that was out there.

But again, to tell her that would be leaving too much of himself exposed and vulnerable. He fell back on a standard excuse. "You die, I have to fill out a mountain of paperwork, explaining to HR why I wasn't there to save you."

"The best way around that," she told him cheerfully

as they got closer to the scene of the crime, "is for you to be there like the cavalry, lurking in the shadows." She gazed at his profile. "You're good at lurking, aren't you?"

"Never tried it," he told her seriously. He had already dismissed her suggestion as ridiculous.

"'Lurking' is a little like hiding," she told him, "except more obvious."

Josh didn't want to continue going down this path, or having this discussion. And he definitely did *not* want to contemplate the thought of Bridget risking her life by putting it into the hands of some unpredictable, homicidal maniac.

"Moot point," he said, calling an end to the banter. "We don't have a suspect."

"Yet," Bridget deliberately underscored. "We don't have a suspect *yet*."

He laughed shortly, shaking his head. "You really are a Pollyanna, aren't you?"

As for him, he wasn't nearly as optimistic as his partner was. Granted the police department's record for arrests here in Aurora was better than most, but in general, a lot of killers—serial killers included—were just never caught and brought to justice. He didn't like thinking that way, but it was the simple truth and he couldn't help wondering if the same thing would happen here.

Ordinarily, Bridget bristled at being labeled a Pollyanna, but not this time. And not by him. "Well, after last night, as far as I'm concerned, hell has frozen over and the devils are ice-skating, so anything's possible."

Maybe hell *had* frozen over. In any case, Josh knew

when to leave well enough alone and this was one of those cases.

They talked about other things.

"Another dump job?" Bridget asked the ME the moment she got out of the car and approached the body.

Like the others, this victim was a redhead, probably not even twenty-one years old. Her hands were clasped together, as if in prayer, right below the gaping hole that had been left. The hole where her heart should have been.

The medical examiner, Eliza Stone, a black-eyed, black-haired young woman who had been on the job all of three months, nodded. Because the angle was awkward when it came to conducting a conversation, she rose to her feet before speaking.

"He killed her somewhere else and dumped her body here." Her mouth set grimly, she looked from one detective to the other. "This guy is definitely a professional."

"Yeah, a professional nut job," Josh said disparagingly.

"That, too," the young woman agreed. "But I wish I had his precision. He didn't make a single unnecessary cut or stroke on her skin." Eliza looked back down at the killer's handiwork. "This guy's very skillful. This sort of thing takes training."

"You're obviously not talking about him attending serial killer school." Josh's eyes narrowed. "You're not talking about a—"

"—surgeon, are you?" Bridget asked, finishing her partner's sentence for him as her eyes widened in horror and disbelief. Doctors were supposed to be the good guys, the ones who stitched you up and made you whole, not the ones who stole organs and hollowed you out like some macabre Halloween pumpkin. That just didn't make any sense.

"Actually, I guess I am," the young woman answered in dismay.

Stunned, Bridget turned toward the ME. "Why didn't you say anything about this before?"

The reasons had sounded right in her head at the time. Now, she realized the error she'd made. An error that possibly had cost at least a couple of girls—if not more—their lives.

"Because I didn't want to think that someone who had taken the oath to 'first do no harm' was doing more than just 'harming,' he was slaughtering," the ME admitted. "Besides, until this last one, I wasn't a hundred percent sure that he was a surgeon."

"But now you are?" Josh asked, wanting to pin her down.

"More than before," Eliza allowed, evasive up to the end.

Bridget stepped away from the ME and the body that was still on the ground. Away from the men from the coroner's office who were waiting for the body to be released so that they could transport it to await an autopsy.

"So we should have been looking for a surgeon instead of a police officer wannabe?" Bridget said to Josh, disheartened.

Once the lieutenant caught wind of this, he would have her head on a platter, she thought. She'd gone over his head to secure extra hands to go through the data files, looking for an academy dropout or reject who could have done this. Now, apparently, that very well could turn out to have been a waste of resources, man hours and money.

Head on a platter, big time, Bridget thought, trying to resign herself to that and the fact that the man might even suspend her without pay for this.

"Way I see it, we were covering all possible bases. It could very well have been someone flaunting his kills before the police department," Brian observed, surprising both of them as he walked up behind them.

"Instead of someone who doesn't seem to care if he's caught," Josh speculated.

"Or someone who is trying to *get* caught," Bridget countered.

The medical examiner frowned. "Why would he want to do that?"

"Because he can't stop himself. He needs someone to do it for him," Bridget said. "Someone to stop him. To stop his pain."

"His pain?" the ME echoed, dismissing the theory. She looked back at the latest victim. "Looks to me as if he's the one who's causing the pain."

"There are all kinds of pain," Bridget told the other woman. But she was looking at Josh as she said it.

Josh raised an eyebrow in a silent question, as if to get her to elaborate or explain just what she meant by that, and why she was looking at him so pointedly. But for once, Bridget pretended not to see him.

Turning away from the dead girl, Bridget felt her pocket vibrating. Someone was calling her on her cell. At this hour?

Didn't anyone sleep anymore? she wondered, taking the phone out. "Cavanaugh."

"Cavelli?" the uncertain voice on the other end of the line asked.

Was she going to have to make some kind of a public declaration of the name change? She had been hoping word of mouth would do that for her.

"Yes, it's me," she said, for a moment embracing her previous name. "Who's this?"

"Cox," the voice told her with a touch of surprise that he hadn't been instantly recognized. "When did you change your name?" he asked, momentarily side-tracked.

"Recently," Bridget bit off, then asked with a touch of impatience, "Did you call with something important or are you just updating your yearbook?"

She heard the other detective laugh. "You're going to kiss me when you hear."

At this point, curious, Josh joined her. Angling her hand a little so that the phone was positioned between them, Josh cocked his ear so that he could hear what the other detective was saying.

"We'll see," Bridget said to Cox. "I know I'll kill you if you keep playing games like this," she said in an unflappable voice. "Okay, spill it, Cox. Why are you calling us when we're in the middle of the newest crime scene?"

"Because—wait for it," he announced dramatically, then after a moment, continued, "I think I found our guy, Bridget."

She knew better than to get excited. Disappointment almost always followed. But things were becoming so intense, she couldn't help herself. Excitement pulsed through her veins.

She did her best to sound calm. "What makes you think so?"

The detective on the other end drew out each word. "Because I have found victim zero. The one the Lady Killer killed first, except we didn't know it," he clarified in case Bridget had missed that.

Bridget gripped her cell phone so hard, had it been alive it would have squealed. She exchanged looks with Josh. Almost afraid to breathe, she urged Cox to go on.

The older detective paraphrased what he'd stumbled across. "Three years ago, just before the guy's killing spree took on a more public nature, there was this medical student who was killed leaving the campus late one night. The coroner said that she'd been savagely slashed across her chest."

Now her palms were growing damp. "But her heart was still in her body, right?" Bridget guessed. Otherwise, it would have been flagged by the detectives who had initially worked the cases that first year.

"Yeah, right." Cox's voice grew more intense as he continued. "But reading the report, I got the impression that the killer ran off before he could finish what he started out doing. According to the autopsy, the student was barely dead when the campus security guard found her."

"And he checked out? The guard?" Josh wanted to know, speaking up. "They found him to be innocent?"

"Yup. Like fresh powder on a ski slope," Cox confirmed.

She needed to see that report. "Okay, we're coming in. Don't go anywhere," Bridget instructed. "We'll be right there."

Cox's laugh was hollow. "Where would I go?

This has become my home now," he grumbled good-naturedly. "My wife's probably having an affair with the plumber. We've been getting a lot of bills for repairs lately," he speculated, his voice trailing off.

"Don't let your imagination run away with you," she instructed as she terminated the call.

"You two have a lead?" Brian asked, waiting for Bridget to close her phone and slip it back into her pocket.

Bridget grinned hopefully and held up two crossed fingers over her head. "With any luck, yes. *Finally*," she added with momentarily enthusiasm.

"Then get going," the chief urged. "I don't like this creep running free in my city a minute longer."

Coming from anyone else, the term might have sounded presumptuously possessive, but everyone on the force had come to regard the chief of detectives as a father figure. They knew that he felt that the city was his baby and that he intended to keep it as safe as he could by any means possible.

They slept easier for it.

By the time they reached the squad room, Bridget had picked up her pace and all but burst into the near-empty room.

"We're here," Bridget announced needlessly. Making a beeline for Gary Cox's desk, she asked, "What do you have?" The question came out breathlessly as she all but hovered over the detective's computer.

Cox obliged by punching several keys on his keyboard. Within moments, the case he'd called about was up on his monitor.

But as Bridget leaned in to look, the detective angled

the screen away from her, asking, "What, no bribes? You're supposed to bring bribes." He pretended to pout. "I've been stuck here since the bicentennial, the least you can do is bribe me with a latte."

"The bribes are coming. They've been held up," Josh quipped, turning the screen back so that Bridget could view it. "Now what do you have?"

"Gerald Green gave a statement to the police after they found the woman's body," the other detective recited, summarizing what he'd read. "Said they were engaged to be married. Turns out he was a medical student, too." Looking at the screen, he didn't see Bridget and Josh exchange glances. He had no way of knowing about this latest point that had been raised by the ME about the serial killer. "According to this, Green said they met in one of the classes and 'love blossomed over the cadavers.'"

Josh's jaw all but dropped. "Wow. Is he for real?" he hooted.

Cox nodded. "Apparently."

"We need to do a little follow-up on this Gerald Green guy," Bridget said, doing her best not to get carried away. They'd had leads before only to have them disintegrate right before their eyes. This could be another one of those.

But something in her gut said no, not this time.

"See if he went on to graduate from medical school and just where he is now," she continued. Looking at Josh, she couldn't help saying, "I've got a good feeling about this."

The next moment, she was patting Cox's shoulder. "Nice job, Cox," she told the man with feeling. And then, impulsively, because he'd said that what he had to show her would make her kiss him, Bridget brushed her lips against that man's cheek.

When he looked at her, stunned, his fingers tracing where her lips had just been, Bridget grinned at him. "Thanks."

Recovering, Cox said, "Don't mention it." And then, as mischief entered his dark eyes, the older detective began to ask, "What do I have to do to get you to—"

"Not tell your wife that you were about to make a lewd suggestion?" she finished, raising an eyebrow.

"Never mind," Cox murmured, waving his hand. "I'll let you know if I find anything else."

"You do that," she encouraged. "In the meantime, we need to get hold of Brenda and ask her to do a little digging for us." This she said to Josh as she took out her phone for the umpteenth time.

"My thoughts exactly," Josh agreed. "Except for one little thing. It's Sunday morning."

"She's a Cavanaugh," Bridget answered, scrolling through the list of phone numbers she'd recently input. "They have a code. She'll come in," she told him with confidence.

Being a Cavanaugh definitely had its perks, she thought as she heard the other line being picked up.

Chapter 14

"Thanks again for giving up your Sunday and coming in to help us with this," Bridget said to Brenda as she and Josh came into the computer lab.

Brenda Cavanaugh was already in the lab and working by the time they came down to the precinct's tech lab. Armed with all the information that Bridget had given her when she called, Brenda had immediately started the search for the whereabouts of Gerald Green, the first victim's fiancé.

Brenda brushed off the thanks. "No problem. Hey, it's in all our interest to get this guy off the street as soon as possible." She looked up at them for a moment. "Who's to say that this time around, the animal's going to stop carving up women at the end of the month? According to the reports, he's escalated his kills. Maybe he'll just go on with his spree as well until he runs out of redheads."

"Or gets caught," Josh interjected with a hopeful note.

Brenda smiled at the suggestion. Her fingers seemed to move almost independently, flying across the keyboard at a speed Josh found enviable. Surrounded by technology, he was still a hunt-and-peck kind of guy.

"From your lips to God's ears," Brenda murmured in response.

There was nothing more they could do here for the moment, Bridget thought. "Call me when you get something," she requested, then turned on her heel and retreated.

She and Josh hadn't even gotten halfway across the lab to the door when her cell phone began ringing. Pulling it out of her pocket, Bridget absently glanced down at the tiny screen as she opened the phone. Brenda's image appeared under *Caller ID*.

There had to be some mistake, Bridget thought as she placed the phone to her ear. Was there a glitch in her phone?

"Cavanaugh," she said uncertainly.

"Right back at you," she heard Brenda say.

Turning around to face the woman at the computer, the phone still held against her ear, Bridget looked at Brenda quizzically. Slowly, she hit End and returned the phone to her pocket.

"You're calling me?" she questioned.

Brenda looked at her innocently. "You said to call you when I had something."

"You *have* something?" Josh asked, stunned. The

woman couldn't have been here for very long. Just how fast did she work?

"I wouldn't be calling you if I didn't," Brenda said with a trace of seriousness.

Bridget shook her head in awed disbelief. "You are an amazing woman."

"So I keep telling Dax," Brenda answered with a laugh, as she pulled up the screen for them to look at. "Apparently our grieving fiancé dropped out of medical school when his girlfriend was killed. He disappeared off the grid for almost a year, then surfaced. From the tax forms I pulled up, he bounced around from one menial part-time job to another, never staying very long at any of them."

That could be someone who was heartbroken and couldn't move on emotionally—or someone who was trying not to get caught, Bridget reasoned.

"What's he doing now?" Josh wanted to know.

Brenda went to another screen. "Well, for almost the last two years, he's been working at a nonprofit medical transport service. It's underwritten by the Warner Foundation—" a charitable organization that was run by one of the state's more high-profile billionaires "—and for a nominal fee, the service provides transportation for elderly citizens who don't drive as well as for the handicapped."

"Sounds pretty selfless," Bridget commented. Maybe too selfless, she added silently. She saw the expression on Brenda's face. "I'm sensing that there's a 'but' coming."

"Could be," the other woman allowed. "From what I can see, nobody who was interviewed at the time of the student's murder could remember her actually *being* engaged. This includes her best friend and her parents."

That still didn't make the man a murderer, but it did raise the odds that he had been lying about his where-abouts the night of the murder. Bridget's interest was immediately piqued.

"Oh?"

"Anyone question this guy about where he was the night his so-called fiancée was killed—and why no one knew she *was* his fiancée?" Josh asked. Standing behind Brenda, he looked at the screen, but saw noth-ing there that answered his questions.

Brenda scrolled down the screen before answering him. Reading, she said, "Yes. According to this, the investigating detective did ask. He had an alibi for the time of the murder and it seems that the engagement had just happened. He told the detective that he had just asked her the day before and when she said yes, he gave her his grandmother's engagement ring."

"Let me guess," Bridget said, picking up the thread of events. "When they found the victim, she wasn't wearing an engagement ring."

Brenda nodded. "Give the lady a cigar. *And,*" she added, "there was no telltale line on her ring finger to indicate that she'd been wearing a ring. But then, if he'd just given it to her the day before, there wouldn't have been one formed yet."

"Conveniently," Josh murmured.

He had a feeling that the man had made everything up. Perhaps had even spun an elaborate fantasy for him-self involving him and the girl. When she burst his bubble, he killed her for it.

"We have a picture of this grieving fiancé?" Bridget asked.

"Just his DMV photo," Brenda answered, pulling it up.

Bridget stared at the small picture. For a moment, there was this feeling that she'd seen the man before, but she couldn't nail it down. And then it came to her. "Who does that look like?" she asked Josh eagerly.

Josh took another, closer look. This time, the similarities registered. "The sketch that architect did for us of the creep who'd been stalking his fiancée."

Bridget grinned. "Bingo!" Turing toward Brenda, she requested, "Let me see the address to this transport service." When Brenda pulled it up, Bridget turned the screen toward her, then jotted the address down on her well-worn, dog-eared pad. Finished, she tore off the page and surprised Josh by holding it out to him. "Here, take Langford or Kennedy, whoever you find first, and see what the people running the transport service can tell you about our 'employee of the month.'"

Folding the address, Josh slipped it into his shirt pocket. They all but had the guy. Hanging back like this wasn't Bridget's style. She would have taken the address and run with it. After all, she was the lead on this case and he knew how much catching this guy meant to her.

"You're not coming?" he asked.

But Bridget shook her head. "In case he's currently at the service, I don't want him to see me."

And then he understood. Josh suppressed a wave of anger. He'd thought they'd put this to rest. "You're not still talking about that fool idea of yours, are you?"

Brenda stopped typing. "What fool idea?" she asked.

"Nothing," Bridget answered automatically.

For once, because he was so angry at the very idea of her risking her life, Josh didn't hold his peace and back her up the way he usually did. "She wants to dye her hair red and set herself up as bait for this bastard," he told Brenda.

It was obvious that Brenda didn't like the idea any more than he did. "Maybe you'll get enough on this guy from what his boss says to arrest him."

"And maybe not," Bridget countered. She didn't understand why everyone was so against this. It would make everything so much simpler. They needed proof, and while the sketch was helpful, it wasn't anything they could use in court. It was all circumstantial. "Having him try to add me to his collection of victims would make nailing him for these murders a sure thing."

Josh snapped at her, "It's not worth risking your life for."

The way she saw it, either she did it, or the dirtbag killed someone else. "You'd rather risk another victim's life instead?" she asked.

Josh threw up his hands. Sensing an ally in the woman behind the computer, he deferred to her. "Brenda, you talk some sense into her."

But instead of adding her voice on the side of common sense, Brenda surprised Josh by shaking her head.

"You're a Cavanaugh, all right. No doubt about it." Looking at Josh, she explained, "There's no talking to them when they get like this. They do what they want to, what they believe is right. Trust me," she told Bridget's agitated partner, "I know. Heads like rocks, the whole lot of them."

Josh's eyes narrowed as he regarded the source of his irritation. "I could tie you up," he threatened Bridget.

"We'll talk kinky later," Bridget promised. "Right now, we've got a killer to bring in."

Brenda laughed at Bridget's initial comment, then looked down at the computer screen and pretended to be engrossed in what she saw there.

"I'll let you know if I find anything else," she told them as they left.

Bridget's mind was already racing. "Okay, I'll come with you, but I'll stay in the car, out of sight."

"Good enough." He *knew* she couldn't just hang back. At least this way, he could be sure she wasn't doing something stupid. "If the guy's there," she was saying, "bring him in for questioning."

He didn't like the tone of her voice. She was leaving something unsaid. "And if he's not there?"

She gave him a serene smile. "Then maybe I'll get to find out what I look like as a redhead."

They were going around in circle. "I don't like this," he growled.

The smile faded immediately. Bridget became very serious. "I'm not asking for your permission, Young-blood," she informed him crisply. "If this guy *is* our killer, he's got to be stopped."

"No argument," he agreed. "But why do you have to be the bait?"

"Somebody has to," she said simply, "and I'm not about to ask someone else to do what I'm not willing to do myself." Bridget stopped walking just before they reached the up elevator. No one else was around as far as she could see. For a moment, she allowed herself to get personal. "Don't worry, you're not going to get rid of me that easily." The scowl remained on his face. "I can put it in writing if you'd like," she added when he made no response.

"What I'd like is for you to stop acting like some kind of superhero who thinks she's bulletproof," he said.

"Too late," she told him cheerfully. The elevator arrived and she walked in ahead of him, pressing for the squad room floor. "I'm already taking 'bends steel in her bare hands' classes."

He grabbed hold of her shoulders, then struggled not to shake her. "Damn it, Bridget, this isn't some game or a joke."

"I know that," she answered him quietly, her tone deadly serious. "I've read all the autopsy reports. Besides," she went on, allowing a hint of a smile to return as she tried to lighten the mood for him, "you'll be lurking in the shadows, remember? You won't let anything happen to me."

He only wished he had her confidence.

With the car parked inconspicuously out of the way, Bridget sat in the backseat, listening to Josh and Kennedy talk to the man who managed the transport service. The three were inside the building located several hundred feet away.

They had stopped back at the lab to pick up some equipment—tiny equipment—before heading out to interview the manager of the transport service, Gerald Green's boss. Josh was wearing the same sort of transmitter/receiver that she was, a tiny device that once inserted inside the ear could easily be missed. It allowed her to hear without being seen, just the way she wanted it.

Right now, as she listened to the manager speak, she frowned. Speaking with only a slight foreign accent, the man had nothing but glowing words of praise to say about Gerald Green.

"I wish I had five of him," the man enthused. "All our clients love him. They call to tell me that he's gentle, polite and I guess most important of all, that he listens to them when they talk. The guy's clearly a saint," he went on.

Bridget seriously debated marching into the building to ask what the manager was smoking if he didn't stop heaping all these accolades on the former medical student.

But as she listened, the manager only continued listing Green's virtues.

"He works the odd hours no one else wants, especially the night shifts, and he always returns the rigs looking even cleaner than when he first took them out." It was clear that Green had won the manager's heart with this single act of cleanliness. "I have to keep after the others to make sure they clean up the vans, but not him. Gerald's a self-starter. Why are you asking all these questions about him?" he finally asked.

There was silence for a moment as Josh searched for a way to phrase this without alerting the serial killer's possible unwitting ally.

"We're investigating a cold case," Josh explained. "Gerald Green's fiancée was murdered four years ago and some new evidence has come to light."

"Wow," the manager said, obviously stunned by the information. "I didn't know. He never said anything about having a fiancée or her being killed. But then, he doesn't talk much about himself. His attention is always on the clients he picks up and delivers. That's why he's so popular. Everyone asks for him, even when he's off duty. Like I said, wish I had five of him."

"No, you don't," Bridget muttered to herself.

"Tell me, was he on a run last night?" Josh asked.

The manager didn't even have to check his schedule. It was apparent that he'd already checked his log when he'd come in this morning.

"He was on duty, but no one called in according to the phone log. He left a note saying it was slow and that he was taking the rig to one of those do-it-yourself stalls to give the van a good once-over."

Yeah, I just bet he is, Josh thought. Out loud he asked, "Did anyone see him come back?"

"We just had the one guy on duty at night—Gerald," the manager conformed. "We usually don't get calls, unless someone wants to be taken to the E.R. They call us when it's not really a 911 type of emergency," the man explained.

"Where is Green now?" Bridget heard Kennedy ask the manager.

"He's working a double shift," the manager answered. Pulling up a screen on the office computer, he located the driver. "Said he needed the money. He went out on a run over an hour ago to pick up Mrs. Phelps on Baker Street and bring her over to her daughter's house—we do that sort of thing to pick up some extra money when it's slow," he explained.

And then, frowning slightly, the man glanced at his watch. "But he should have been back by now. We don't have the van wait for our clients. We drop them off, then go back out and pick them up when it's time." He looked again at his watch even though not more than half a minute had gone by. "Don't know what could be keeping him."

The manager laughed to himself. "Unless, of course, he's off somewhere cleaning his van again. He's practically OCD about that," he confided to the detectives. "Hates to see anything out of place or dirty. Takes a lot of pride in keeping his vehicle absolutely spotless. You could probably eat off those floors."

Or kill on them, Josh couldn't help adding silently. "Well, you've been very helpful," he said aloud to the manager. He and Kennedy rose to their feet. "We'd appreciate you giving us a call when Mr. Green gets in," Josh said. He took out one of his business cards and placed it on the manager's desk blotter.

"Sure thing." The manager left the card in the center of his desk. He shook his head again in wonder. "A murdered fiancée. Who would have thought? Just shows you how closed-mouthed the guy could be. If it'd happened to me, I'd tell everybody. Get a little play out of the sympathy something like that would generate, know what I mean?" he asked Josh with a wink.

"Yeah, I do," Josh answered, silently adding, *Unfortunately.* Maybe they should be looking at the manager, too. The man certainly didn't seem upset by the mention of a murder, only that Green had kept it to himself. Takes all kinds, he decided.

"So, what do you think?" Kennedy asked him the moment they walked out of the small, crammed office.

"Compulsively cleaning his van every night before bringing it in?" Josh repeated. "Hell, I think we just found our suspect." He did a quick review of the facts in his head. "Between this and that sketch, I think we've got enough to have the local ADA convince a judge to issue us a search warrant for the man's home and his so-called squeaky clean van."

"Aren't a couple of the Cavanaughs married to judges?" Kennedy asked him. "And the ADA," the older detective suddenly remembered, "she's a Cavanaugh, too, right? The chief of D's daughter, Janelle, as I recall."

Josh nodded. There was no denying it, the Cavanaughs were a very useful family to know.

"Does make things a little easier that way," he admitted. Personally, he couldn't understand why Bridget resisted the association for even a moment. If it had been him, he would have changed his return labels in a heartbeat. It was a win-win situation as far as he could see.

As he and Kennedy drew closer to where they'd left the car, Josh frowned. Quickening his pace, he hurried over to the backseat.

"Hey, where's the fire?" Kennedy called out, then protested, "I can't run, Youngblood. My knees gave out five years ago."

Coming to a stop beside Josh, Kennedy's attention was focused on him. He noted that Josh was scowling. "What's the matter?" Kennedy asked.

Josh gestured toward the backseat. "Notice anything missing?" he bit off, irritated.

The car was exactly where he'd left it. And it was empty, which was *not* exactly as he'd left it.

"Where's Bridget?" Kennedy asked.

"That's the question," Josh verified, fuming as he

looked around the immediate area. He didn't see her—
or anyone—around.

Kennedy was obviously not as disturbed about
Bridget's absence as he was. He shrugged his slightly
bowed shoulders and guessed, "Maybe she had to take
a break, you know, go looking for a ladies' room or
something."

But Josh was shaking his head as he scanned the
immediate area. "The woman's a camel. We were on a
stakeout once and I swear she didn't go once in twenty-
four hours, even though she had like four cups of
coffee." Josh looked around the backseat. There didn't
appear to have been a struggle. She'd left on her own,
he thought. Still, he had a bad, uneasy feeling about
this. "Where the hell did she get to?" he demanded.

"Why don't you call her on her cell and ask her?"
Kennedy suggested.

Annoyed that he hadn't thought of that himself, Josh
pressed the second programmed number on his keypad
and listened to the phone on the other end ring.

Once.

It went straight to voicemail.

"Damn it," he fumed. "When we find her and she's
all right, I'm going to kill her for taking off like that."

"That sounds reasonable," Kennedy quipped.

"'Reasonable' is wasted on that woman," Josh complained. "She thinks she's bulletproof."

"Okay, let's spread out and look for her," Kennedy
proposed. "She's on foot so she couldn't have gotten
very far."

"Yeah," Josh responded with absolutely no conviction in his voice.

The problem was, he thought, that Bridget might not be on foot.

The bad feeling in the pit of his stomach grew to almost unmanageable proportions.

Chapter 15

The same pain that had engulfed her as she was knocked out now yanked her back into consciousness.

The back of her skull throbbed. The pain was almost overwhelming and all but swallowed her up.

A moan rose in her throat, but something—instincts—kept her from allowing the sound to escape her lips.

It took only a few seconds for the fact that she was in motion to register.

Was she in Josh's car?

No, wait, there was something cold against her cheek. Metal, she was lying on some kind of metal floor. And she was being driven somewhere.

Very carefully she opened her eyelids just the tiniest bit, allowing only a hint of light in, not because her eyes were sensitive but because she didn't want anyone to see that she was coming to. *Someone* had hit her in the head and that same person had to be the one who was transporting her somewhere.

Where?

Opening her eyes a little more, Bridget saw that she was in the back of a van, lying facedown on the platform of a hydraulic lift ordinarily used to raise and lower wheelchair-bound travelers.

She realized that she was on the floor of the transport van at the same time that the fact that her wrists were bound with duct tape registered.

Doing her best to rise above the pain pounding along her aching skull, Bridget tried to remember what had happened.

Green.

She'd seen Green pulling up in the van in the rear of the lot. He was driving his transport van. When he got out, he'd started walking toward the main office. But before she could give Josh a heads-up, she saw Green suddenly do a U-turn on his heel. The next moment he was heading straight for his van again.

Apparently whatever he saw—Josh and Kennedy?—had spooked him.

There was no time to wonder what it was. If the transport driver took off, God knew when they'd be able to find him again.

So she'd gotten out of the backseat of the unmarked car and approached him.

"Excuse me," she'd called out just as he was about to get back into the van.

There was suspicion in his eyes when he looked in her direction. "Yeah?"

"My aunt's in a wheelchair and she's very fragile.

I can't get her in and out of my car anymore without risking having her fall. Problem is, she needs to go to a lot of doctors." She nodded toward his van. "Would you know what the company charges for a round trip?"

"Office handles that kind of stuff. You've gotta call them." He'd glanced around, then at her. "Where did you park?" he asked.

To avert any suspicion, she'd half turned to point toward a car across the street that she'd just noticed. That was when she felt as if her skull were being split open.

As the darkness claimed her, she thought that she was going to be the Lady Killer's final victim even though her hair wasn't red.

As she came to, she upbraided herself for turning her back, even slightly, on the man. Just because he was a serial killer didn't mean that he was stupid. Actually, the opposite was probably true. Planning had to go into remaining at large for three years and still carrying out his vendetta against any red-haired female who had the misfortune of crossing his path.

She was a blonde. Was she supposed to be his swan song? Or had he broadened his parameters? Why was she now lying on the floor of the van, her wrists bound? How had she tipped him off?

Her mouth wasn't taped shut. Why?

And then she had her answer. He wasn't growing sloppy, he just hadn't planned on another kill so soon. She saw an empty roll that had held duct tape discarded in the corner. He'd run out.

The van took a sharp turn to the right, then sped up. Glancing toward the door, she thought of the odds of pulling it open and jumping out before he saw she was awake and could stop her.

Not very good, she decided. Besides, they were going awfully fast and she could hear the sound of cars whizzing by.

Were they on the freeway? It sounded like it, but she wasn't sure. If they were, she wouldn't be able to jump clear of the van even if she did manage to open the door. Not with other cars moving so fast. She'd be run over.

Desperate to get her hands free, Bridget tried gnawing on the tape that bound her wrists. Several attempts got her nowhere. This would take too long, and who knew just how long she had?

Maybe she could pull him down from behind. Hoping that the music he was playing—music that made her head throb even more—would muffle any sound she made, Bridget began to inch her way over to him on the floor. She kept her eyes on the back of his head the entire time, praying he wouldn't turn around before she managed to reach him.

She crept toward him, frustrated by her maddeningly slow pace. If she moved faster, he might hear her.

As she debated how to pick her time and not get them both killed, she felt the van stopping. He was pulling up to a light.

They weren't on the freeway after all.

Now or never.

Pushing herself up to her knees, Bridget threw her bound arms forward around Green's throat and pulled back as hard as she could, trying to yank the man out of his seat.

Catching him off guard, Green had toppled backward against her. Horns from the cars around them began blasting, protesting the suddenly immobile van.

Green screamed a curse at her as she unseated him.

"You bitch, you think this is going to save you? You're a dead woman, you hear me? A dead woman."

Because of the angle she'd used, Green had fallen on top of her, pinning her beneath him. She was still pulling against his throat as hard as she could, hoping to render him unconscious even after the air had whooshed out of her lungs.

She had to make him lose consciousness before he could do the same to her!

He was struggling, clawing at her, gasping for air.

And then she felt it. Felt something hard and sharp slash into her side. Felt something akin to fire burst out and engulfing her from the point of contact.

Suddenly, she wasn't able to hold on to him anymore, wasn't able to keep squeezing, robbing his lungs of his air supply. Her arms were just too weak. A darkness was returning for her.

He was free.

She could feel the driver's weight shifting, could feel his body separating from hers.

And then Bridget heard him yell, "Your heart is mine, bitch!"

Fear assaulted her. She was going to die.

As the thought registered in her dimming brain, something that sounded like a crack of thunder exploded inside the van.

Had they been hit by another car?

Had he killed her?

Sheets of flames were closing in around her. And

then, from somewhere in the distance, far, far away, she thought she heard Josh calling to her.

But that wasn't possible. Josh didn't know she was in here.

The next moment, the flames completely smothered her.

And then came oblivion.

"Call a bus, Kennedy. Damn it, call a bus!" Josh yelled, his voice cracking.

He was on his knees in the van, kneeling in Bridget's blood, wanting desperately to hold her to him, afraid to raise her from the floor. There was no longer any doubt that the man they had come after was the serial killer they'd been hunting. Less than a minute before he and Kennedy reached the van and threw the door open, the serial killer had viciously stabbed Bridget.

Josh had shouted out his warning at the same moment he'd discharged his weapon.

The threat was over.

Blood was now flowing from Bridget's side at a frightening rate. Fighting back his panic, Josh pressed the palms of his hands down hard against her side, trying to stop the blood from leaving her body.

Trying to keep her alive.

Terror kept surging through him. "You stay with me, Bridget, you hear me?" he demanded. "You stay with me! I won't let you die. You're not allowed to die. Damn you, anyway, why didn't you wait for us?"

Even in his addled state, Josh knew the answer to that. She hadn't waited because she probably saw the killer taking off. It wasn't in her nature to hang back and wait.

"Stay with me," he repeated, then pleaded again, "Stay with me."

"They're coming," Kennedy told him as he ended his call into the precinct.

She didn't have much time. He could see that. Even with his hands pressed against the wound, she was still losing blood.

"Tell them to come faster!" Josh roared. He tossed his head back, trying to get the tears in his eyes to clear. "I don't know how much longer she's going to be able to hang on."

"You kidding?" Kennedy countered, his own voice throbbing with emotion. Doing his best not to let his thoughts go toward a darker path. "This is Bridget. She's a fighter. She always has been. It'll take more than a stab wound to get her."

"Yeah," Josh agreed.

The word felt like dried straw inside his mouth.

They'd taken her from him.

He had refused to leave her side and had traveled inside the ambulance to the hospital, but once the paramedics reached the hospital, the emergency room surgeons came running out to the gurney and they had taken Bridget from him.

Leaving him to pace and haunt the corridor, feeling helpless and inadequate.

Leaving him to vacillate between beating himself up for keeping Bridget in the car when he knew what she was like and being furious with her for going after the killer herself.

And all the while, Josh kept staring at the operating

room doors, afraid to let himself think what was going on beyond the double doors.

Kennedy had followed the ambulance and arrived just behind it. After that, Josh had lost track of the older detective.

It didn't matter. Nothing mattered except Bridget living.

Leaning against the wall, Josh closed his eyes and prayed for a minute, vaguely remembering a fragment of a prayer from childhood.

He felt ancient.

And scared.

When Josh opened his eyes again a couple of minutes later, a tall, white-haired man with a kindly face was walking toward the O.R. The man was dressed all in black and he was wearing a clerical collar.

A priest.

No! Josh thought frantically. *No!*

As if to deny the man's very presence, to deny the *need* for the man's presence, Josh shifted, placing himself in front of the approaching priest.

As he stood there, a defiant human wall, Josh growled out, "She doesn't need a priest." But if someone inside the O.R. had sent for the man, if she was dying, then he had no right to deny this man access to Bridget.

He felt as if his heart was being ripped out of his chest.

"I'd like to think that everyone needs a priest once in a while," the man answered, his resonant voice sounding oddly comforting. "Bridget's father called me. I live less than a mile away from the hospital, so he knew I could get here before he did," the priest explained. He nodded toward the O.R. "Is Bridget in there?"

The priest's deep blue eyes were kind as they looked at him, Josh thought. He tried to make sense of what he was being told. If no one in the O.R. had called the man, then maybe she would be all right after all.

But then why was he here? And why would Bridget's father have called him?

Feeling lost and confused, it took Josh a moment to realize that the priest was extending his hand to him.

"I'm Bridget's Uncle Adam," he said, introducing himself.

Belatedly, Josh took the hand that was being offered and shook it. The words swam in his head. Her uncle? Oh, yeah, right. Bridget had an uncle who was part of the clergy. He knew that. Or had known that.

Right now, nothing was making sense in his head. All his thoughts were jumbled, as if a force field were keeping the absolutely unthinkable from finding him.

Seeing the confusion on the younger man's face, Adam said kindly, "I'm Sean's older brother. At least that was what we all thought before the hospital mix-up came to light," he said, amused. "For the record, I still consider myself Bridget's uncle. Takes more than blood to make family," he added with a wink.

Josh vaguely remembered saying the same thing to Bridget over an eternity ago, when he found her agonizing over her revised family tree. It felt odd hearing the sentiment echoed back to him.

Father Adam nodded toward the O.R. doors. "How is she doing?" he asked.

The helpless feeling was so oppressive, he was

having trouble breathing. Josh shook his head. "They won't tell me."

The priest took the non-information in stride. "I subscribe to the no-news-is-good-news school of thought," he said with a smile, and then he assured Josh, "Bridget's a fighter."

"So they tell me," Josh replied, hopelessness echoing in his voice.

"In her case, those are not just empty words," Father Adam said. "Let me tell you a little story, Detective. When Bridget was about ten years old, her family rented a cabin in the mountains one winter. She and her younger brother, Logan, snuck out one morning before anyone was up. They were expressly told not to go on the lake because the ice was thin that year." Father Adam's smile was a fond, indulgent one. "So naturally that was where Bridget and her brother went. Long story short, the ice broke right under Logan's feet when they were halfway across, plunging him into the icy lake. Bridget didn't panic, she didn't go running back to the cabin to get her father. She took off her coat, dove into the water and saved her brother. When she pulled him out, she wrapped him up in her coat and somehow managed to carry him back to the cabin. She literally saved his life.

"The downside of the story was Logan came down with the sniffles—and Bridget came down with a really bad case of pneumonia. So bad that she had to be hospitalized. Her parents were afraid that she was going die. Even the doctors were worried, telling them to prepare for the worst."

Listening, Josh nodded. "And she bounced back."

The priest smiled broadly. "That she did."

Josh blew out a breath. "Sounds like Bridget," he agreed, trying desperately to take heart from the story.

Bridget's uncle placed a large, ham-like hand comfortingly on his shoulder. "The point of the story is that Bridget always manages to come out on top no matter what the situation. Don't worry, boy. She's going to be all right."

God, but he wished he had the priest's conviction, Josh thought.

Before he could say anything in response, Josh heard a commotion down the hall. It grew louder. Curious, he took a few steps toward the growing din, thinking to investigate. Looking for a distraction.

The distraction came to him.

The commotion came from what amounted to an army of people. It was headed by the chief of detectives who was walking beside Bridget's father, Sean. Behind them was what appeared to be half the police department. Or, at the very least, half the people who had been at the party the other night to officially welcome Bridget's grandfather.

As they drew closer, the approaching Cavanaughs managed to fill every single space in the corridor, and while the noise they made couldn't exactly be referred to as deafening, it was definitely noticeable.

A couple of moments later, a weary-looking nurse approached the group from another direction. She stopped right beside Josh. It was obvious from the expression on the older woman's face that she recognized at least a large number of the people who now stood in the corridor, shifting back and forth as they made an attempt not to block it.

Sighing, the senior nurse said to no one in particular,

"I knew this was going to happen the minute I saw that last name on the insurance form. You know, between getting shot and giving birth, you Cavanaughs should seriously think about getting your own hospital annex," she said, this time addressing her comment to Brian.

"You make sure our Bridget makes it," Andrew answered, speaking up from the rear, "and we'll see about making that happen."

"Don't toy with me, Andrew Cavanaugh," the nurse fired back, pretending to complain. "I'm a very vulnerable woman."

Andrew laughed at her comment. "I'm counting on that, Virginia."

Even as he answered her, more and more family members arrived, alerted by the others.

Greetings as well as repeated questions filled the air.

The head nurse pointed toward the recently remodeled and greatly expanded waiting room. The facility bore more of a resemblance to an arena than a room.

"The hospital would appreciate at least *some* of you waiting in there." Her features pulled into a faux scowl. "No one can get by with all of you clogging the hallway like this."

"And if we go in there to wait the way you want," Brian bargained, "in exchange, you'll come by and give us regular updates on how my niece is doing?"

"Yes, yes, anything to get you people out of the hallway," Virginia promised.

As she gestured again toward the waiting room, the members of the family slowly began to file by her, taking seats or opting to stand as they all gave one another comfort.

The nurse looked at Josh expectantly. "You, too, young man," she urged.

"He's only one person," Father Adam pointed out. "And her partner. If there's an ounce of mercy in you, I'd let him stay exactly where he is," he advised gently.

After a momentary debate, Virginia begrudgingly nodded. "All right, you can stay," she told Josh, then turned to look at all the others. "But as for the rest of you—"

She didn't need to finish her sentence.

Dutifully, the family members who hadn't retreated into the room yet did so now.

"I am holding you to your promise," Andrew said to the nurse as he followed the last of the combined family into the waiting area.

The nurse nodded. "And I'll keep it," Virginia told him solemnly. Glancing again at the young man leaning against the wall beside the O.R. doors, she withdrew for now. But she would be back and soon, just as she'd promised. Virginia Gibbs knew better than to ignore the former chief of police.

Chapter 16

Seven heavy layers were pressing down on her. Smothering her. Seven layers of hot, searing pain, determined to keep her submerged in a hazy, oppressive, formless world.

Bridget struggled, desperately trying to surface.

Her eyelids felt as if they each weighed a ton apiece. Maybe more. They refused to open.

She refused to give up.

Eventually, an eternity later, she won.

But when she finally opened her eyes, she didn't recognize her surroundings. Only that she'd never been here before.

This wasn't her bed, or her room. And who was that with his head down on the bland blanket that covered the bed and her?

Slowly, the answers came into focus.

This was a hospital room. And her side hurt like hell. Moreover, something must have clearly crawled into her mouth and died there because not only was there a terrible taste inside her mouth, but her lips felt as if they'd been glued together. It hurt to pull them apart.

She did it anyway.

Trying to speak, Bridget wound up moaning instead. Her eyes closed again.

Josh jerked his head up, alert the second he heard the sound. His neck protested the sudden motion, aching because of the position he'd unintentionally assumed when he'd finally fallen asleep. He'd been at her bedside for over two days now, keeping vigil over her. Waiting for Bridget to open her eyes and finally wake up.

"Bridget?" He whispered her name hesitantly, afraid he'd only *thought* he'd heard her. Or maybe he'd only dreamed it and his desire to make it true had propelled him into an awakened state.

Bridget dragged in a ragged breath. "Uh-huh," she managed to push out. With supreme effort, she opened her eyes again.

He'd never seen anything half as beautiful as those blue eyes of hers.

"Oh thank God," Josh cried, grasping her hand in both of his. "I was starting to think that you weren't ever going to open your eyes."

It was still a struggle to keep her eyelids up. And then, it was as if someone had opened a giant door in a cloud. Her memory of the last few minutes that she'd been conscious came flooding back to her. Surrounding her. Josh had found her. Rescued her.

Josh.

"How did you…"

Her energy ebbed away from her before she could finish the question. She tried again, determined to be heard. When she spoke, her voice was a little bit stronger. She peeled each word away from the roof of her mouth.

"How did you find me?"

Josh laughed shortly. As if he would have ever given up looking until he found her.

"Easy," he quipped. "I just asked around for the biggest pain in the butt in the area. It was never any contest," he told her, wanting to take her in his arms and just hold her.

But Bridget was in pain, despite the medication. He could see that and he knew if he followed through on his impulse, he would only be hurting her.

"No, seriously," she pressed hoarsely. "How did you find me?" She had to know why she was so lucky when others hadn't been. How he had tracked her when so many other women before her had fallen victim to the Lady Killer's knife.

"Your earbud," he told her. It was a miracle that it hadn't gotten dislodged and fallen out when she'd been kidnapped. He wasn't about to think what might have happened if she'd lost that tiny piece of electronic equipment.

Bridget blinked, confused. "What?"

"That transmitter you still had in your ear, it was on. I called in and had the lab tech locate the frequency in order to track it. That's how I found you."

He remembered that horrid pain in the pit of his gut when he'd realized that she must have been taken by their suspect. But it was nothing in comparison to the way he had felt when the van had abruptly stopped moving.

Praying she wasn't dead, he'd run, his weapon drawn, to intercept the van. He'd torn opened the back door and had been just in time to keep her from receiving a fatal stab wound from the driver's drawn knife. That was when he'd seen that there was already blood on it. And that there was blood all around Bridget's prone body on the floor.

"Oh," she managed to murmur, then said, "I dreamed you were yelling at me." Each word was a little easier to utter than the last, but her mouth still felt as if she'd had sand for lunch. Sand that had trickled down her throat.

"That wasn't a dream," he told her simply. "I did."

Her eyes drew together. "You yelled at me? But I was just stabbed," she protested.

"And you were also an idiot," he countered, anger suddenly surging through him when he thought of how close he had come to losing her. "*That* was why I was yelling at you."

His tone was accusatory, masking the raw, vulnerable emotion just beneath. If something had happened to her, he wouldn't have ever been able to live with himself.

"Who the hell told you to get into that van and try to take Green down single-handedly?" Josh angrily demanded.

"I didn't get into the van," she protested.

"Then how—"

Bridget wet her lips. They were sticking together again.

"He must have knocked me out and dragged me into

the van." She blinked, trying to remember the order in which everything had to have happened. "I saw him drive up while you and Kennedy were inside the office, taking to the manager. Green must have seen something that tipped him off. I saw him hurrying back to the van. I got out to talk to him. I knew I had to stall him until you came. Otherwise, he could just vanish on us again."

Touching the back of her head, Bridget winced. The pain from that area was unexpected. "He must've hit me when I turned my head to look at something." She closed her eyes for a moment, trying to distance herself from what she remembered. "When I came to, my wrists were duct taped together and I was in the back of the van, on the floor. I knew if I didn't do something, he was going to kill me." As she took another ragged breath, her lungs ached in protest. She would feel like hell for a while, Bridget thought, resigning herself to the fact. "How long have I been out?"

"Three days," he told her.

She'd expected to hear that she'd been unconscious for a few hours, not days. The latter was scary. And then something else occurred to her. She looked at him. The man definitely appeared worn out. "And you've been here the whole time?" she asked in disbelief.

Josh shrugged, trying to make light of it. "Didn't seem to be much of a point to be anywhere else." Because that focused too closely on his own vulnerable state, he changed the subject. "A lot of your family's been by. New and old," he added. "When they heard you'd been hurt, they almost took over the whole damn hospital. They're an impressive group of people," he admitted. He saw a weak smile curving her mouth and found it immensely heartening. "Oh, by the way, I finally got to meet your Uncle Adam. He's a really nice guy. How come you never brought him around?" he asked.

She was going to shrug, but that, it turned out, hurt too so she stopped midmotion. "It never occurred to me. Why? Did you want to make a confession?"

He was still holding her hand, he realized. But he didn't let go. His eyes met hers. "Not to him."

Her sense of protectiveness rose to the fore. "What's wrong with my uncle?"

"Nothing," he answered simply. "But if I was going to confess something, it would be to—" And then he shrugged again. He wanted to pick his time, and this wasn't it. "Never mind."

Pressing the control button beside her, Bridget managed to elevate the back of her bed so that she was in more of a sitting position. "You know I hate it when you do that, start saying something and don't finish it."

Well, if they were going to compare dislikes, his trumped hers, he thought. "And I hate you acting like some superheroine who thinks she's bulletproof."

Where did he get off taking her to task for anything? "You've got a lousy bedside manner, Youngblood, you know that?"

Sometimes she could get him so mad, he could shake her. Did she know what she meant to him? That she was more than just his partner, although that was a pretty big deal in itself. And did she even realize that what she'd done could have cost her her life?

"Maybe that's because I don't want to be standing at a hospital bedside." His expression softened. "I'd rather be standing next to the bed in your apartment—as long as you were in it."

She opened her mouth twice, but retorts didn't come. A third attempt had her saying, "Okay, fair enough." She looked around on either side of her on the bed. "Where's the call button?"

"Why do you want the call button for?" He was on his feet beside her. "Do you need the doctor? Are you in pain?"

"To get the nurse. Not necessarily. And yeah, pretty much," she said, answering all three of his questions in order.

His suspicions raised, Josh eyed her closely as he asked, "Why do you want the nurse?"

Her mouth curved. "To help me get dressed and out of here so I can get back to my apartment and have you stand next to my bed," she told him, her eyes saying a good deal more. "Weren't you paying attention to what you just said?"

Much as he wanted her to himself right now, her place was here until the doctors thought she was strong enough to go home. "You're not going anywhere," he informed her sternly.

Bridget raised her chin, ready for a fight. "You can't boss me around."

"I saved your life," he pointed out. "Technically, it now belongs to me, so yeah, I can boss you around if I want to."

She eyed him for a moment and just when he thought she was going to put up a fight, she quietly asked, "And what do you plan on doing with this extra life you've got on your hands?"

He said the first thing that popped into his head. "What I'd like to do is shove it into a closet to keep it safe."

She laughed softly, relaxing. Suddenly very glad to be alive. And that he had been there to save her. "There are laws against that, you know."

"Yeah, I know. I guess the only other way to keep watch over you and make sure you don't do something else to get yourself killed is to marry you."

After what had just happened in the last few days, she would have thought that she was prepared for anything. Apparently, she wasn't.

Her mouth dropped open and she stared at Josh for a long moment before finally deciding that she was hallucinating again. She had to be. There was no way her carefree, footloose partner had just voluntarily offered to give up his no-strings-attached bachelorhood by proposing to her.

With that thought racing through her head, she felt her eyelids getting heavy again. Before she knew it, she'd nodded off.

"Talk about being cool," Josh murmured, adjusting her blanket. "She falls asleep in the middle of my marriage proposal."

When she opened her eyes again, there was no light shining in through the hospital window.

It was nighttime, she realized.

Her eyelids didn't feel heavy this time, but her eyes did feel gritty. And then, as before, she saw that she wasn't alone.

Seeing him made her smile from the inside out.

"You're still here," she said to Josh in a voice that sounded both surprised and pleased.

Sitting beside her bed, he brightened. He would never tire of seeing her open her eyes, Josh thought.

Each time he saw her do it, it felt like he was experiencing a minor miracle after that awful scare he'd endured.

"Still waiting for an answer," he told her mildly.

She tried to center her thoughts. "What was the question again?"

He phrased it formally now. If there had been any jitters associated with this, they had long since left him. "Bridget Cavelli-Cavanaugh, will you marry me?"

She drew out the moment before answering him. "Aren't you supposed to say something like, 'I love you,' before you ask something like that?"

She was stalling. Why? "You already know I love you."

"No, I don't," she protested. "I'm not a mind reader."

He grinned wickedly. Bridget was back, he thought, loving every second of this. "That wasn't my mind you were staring at the other night."

"Don't try to distract me." She took another deep breath. Mercifully, this one hurt a little less. "I'm waiting."

"I love you," he told her very seriously, then impishly grinned as he asked, "Now will you say yes?"

"You really want to do this?" she asked incredulously. Part of her still believed that there was a punch line somewhere in the offing.

"Yeah," he told her, gently brushing her hair away from her face. "I really want to do this. I know I can't talk you into playing it a little safer and not charging in without thinking it through, but I at least want to be able to fill every moment of my life with you whenever I can for as long as I can."

"Then I better not say no," she concluded.

This had gone easier than he'd anticipated. Bridget could be very perverse at times. "If you do, I'll just have to keep asking you until you finally break down and say yes."

"Then this'll save us both a lot of time," she concluded, tongue in check.

"Saving time. I'm all for that," he agreed

Her eyes told him just how much she loved him. "As long as you're for me, nothing else matters," she whispered.

"Always," he promised.

Bridget cocked her head slightly as she regarded him. "Are you going to keep talking, or are you going to kiss me?"

Josh didn't answer, at least not verbally. Lovingly framing her face with his hands, he went with door number two.

* * * * *

Placing a hand on either side of her head, he drew back and gazed down at her.

He ran his thumb lightly along the fading bruise on her cheek, and she blinked and stared up at him. Her eyes were so dark. They absorbed the light like black velvet. He kissed the corners of her eyelids where tears still clung and he tasted salt.

"We should—" he started, but a loud metallic screech drowned out his words. Without stopping to think, he grabbed Juliana and dove through the open closet door.

He twisted in midair, trying to take the brunt of the impact. His shoulder slammed against the floor.

A deafening crash shook the walls and sent splinters, debris and dust flying. Dawson hunched his shoulders and rolled, putting his back to the destruction. He wrapped his arms around her head and ducked his.

One slight move and she could have been killed. And he still hadn't told her who he really was.

PRIVATE SECURITY

BY
MALLORY KANE

MILLS & BOON

First published in Great Britain 2012
by Mills & Boon, an imprint of Harlequin (UK) Limited,
Eton House, 18-24 Paradise Road, Richmond, Surrey TW9 1SR

© Rickey R. Mallory 2012

ISBN: 978 0 263 89551 3
ebook ISBN: 978 1 408 97742 2

46-0812

Harlequin (UK) policy is to use papers that are natural, renewable and recyclable products and made from wood grown in sustainable forests. The logging and manufacturing processes conform to the legal environmental regulations of the country of origin.

Printed and bound in Spain
by Blackprint CPI, Barcelona

Mallory Kane has two very good reasons for loving reading and writing. Her mother was a librarian, who taught her to love and respect books as a precious resource. Her father could hold listeners spellbound for hours with his stories. He was always her biggest fan.

She loves romance suspense with dangerous heroes and dauntless heroines, and enjoys tossing in a bit of her medical knowledge for an extra dose of intrigue. After twenty-five books published, Mallory is still amazed and thrilled that she actually gets to make up stories for a living.

Mallory lives in Tennessee with her computer-genius husband and three exceptionally intelligent cats. She enjoys hearing from readers. You can write to her at mallory@mallorykane.com.

For Michael, with all my love.

Chapter One

By the time the woman struggled out of the taxi, Dawson knew the color of her panties. They were *pink*.

He swallowed hard and lifted the binoculars to the blue sling that cradled her left arm and hindered her movements. What had happened to her? Three days ago on Monday, when he'd finally spotted her checking the post office box, she'd been fine.

She awkwardly tugged her skirt down, and he lowered the glasses. He hadn't had time to stare at her on Monday. Now he checked out the whole package.

Tall, lithe, knockout legs and finger-tangling black hair. When she bent to pull out three plastic grocery bags, he raised the glasses again. He adjusted the focus for an excellent view of her excellent backside.

Then he noticed something at her waist. Something that glinted in the afternoon sunlight. He adjusted the focus. Under the trim jacket she wore, tucked into her skirt, was a handgun. She was carrying.

"Damn," he muttered. Juliana Caprese was a dealer at the Black Jack Casino in Biloxi. What the hell was she doing with a gun? His gaze lit on the blue sling again. Maybe it had something to do with how she'd injured her arm.

He shrugged and laid the binoculars on the passenger seat beside him. Only one way to find out. He got out of the car and sauntered down the sidewalk, timing his approach so that he'd be in her way when she headed for the stairs to her apartment building.

She hooked all three grocery bags over her right wrist and dug into her jacket pocket. The bags swung back and forth, and even from his distance, Dawson could see the way the plastic handles bit into the skin of her forearm. She wasn't going to make it without dropping something. He sped up slightly.

Juliana Caprese grimaced as the plastic bags dug into her flesh. She fumbled for the bills she'd stuck in her pocket to give the taxi driver. With her left arm out of commission, even the smallest task was a pain. She finally snagged the bills with two fingers and tugged. As she did, she felt one of the plastic straps tear. Her arm jerked as the strap broke and a bag hit the sidewalk. She heard the unmistakable crunch of eggshells breaking.

"Damn it!" she snapped, glaring at the taxi driver, but her effort was wasted. He lounged complacently behind the wheel talking on his microphone in a language she couldn't place.

Before she could lift her right arm to hand the lazy thug his fare, a man stepped right in front of her.

Startled, her instinctive reaction was to run. The last time someone had taken her by surprise she'd ended up with a bruised face, a banged-up knee and a dislocated shoulder.

But there was nowhere for her to go. She was blocked in by the taxi, the man and the spilled groceries.

Then she saw what the man was doing. He thrust two twenties into the driver's face. "I've got your cab number," he said mildly. "Your boss will hear about your lazy butt."

The driver muttered something in a foreign language and sped away.

Juliana crouched to pick up her bag of broken eggs. The man crouched at the same time.

"I got it," he said.

She held out the crumpled bills. "Here."

But he snagged the bag and stood, leaving her at eye level with the front of his jeans.

Oh, boy, she thought, her mouth going dry. The sight of leanly muscled thighs straining against worn denim took her breath away. For an instant, she just stared.

"Need help?" he asked, a definite hint of amusement in his voice. He held out his hand.

She ignored it and rose, wincing when her knee threatened to buckle. "Take this," she snapped, thrusting the money toward him again.

But he didn't even look at it. "Let me help you with those," he said, deftly hooking a finger around the straining plastic straps on her wrist.

"No," she said immediately. "I'm fine."

But he already had them. Apprehension took hold of her again. "Please give me back my groceries."

"I don't think this bag qualifies as groceries any longer," he responded in that same amused voice. "I think your eggs have graduated from groceries to garbage."

Juliana bit her cheek to stop herself from chuckling. She raised her gaze to his and frowned at the look in his very bright blue eyes. He was watching her with a disturbing intensity. "I'll check them when I get upstairs," she said shortly, suddenly feeling vulnerable.

She glanced around. Where had he come from? When the taxi had stopped, there was no one on the street. She knew, because ever since she'd been attacked two days ago, she'd been hypervigilant. And she'd started carrying her gun. She was not about to be caught with no means of self-defense again. *Ever.*

The man's eyes narrowed and his brows lowered dangerously. "What happened to you?" he asked gruffly.

"What?"

"Your face. Your arm."

"Accident," she tossed out. "May I have my bags now?"

"You live here?"

He was starting to scare her. She backed away toward the steps to her building. She glared at him again, avoiding those laser eyes, looking at his mouth instead. But that turned out to be a mistake. His mouth was wide and straight, with a lower lip that she was sure would— *Stop it,* the little voice inside her head said. *You don't know where that mouth has been.*

She glanced over her shoulder and took another step backward. She was nearly at the steps to her building.

"Whoa, hang on," the man said quickly. "You're Juliana Caprese, right?"

Her heart lurched. He knew her name. She half turned, ready to run up the steps. She didn't need those groceries that badly.

"Wait, please. My name's Dawson," he offered. "I guess I'm not handling this well. I don't mean to frighten you. I just want to ask you a question or two. Did you get the business card I left at Kaplan Wright?"

That surprised her. So this was the John Dawson who'd left the card at the architect's office. She paused, but she moved her hand to her side, ready to grab her weapon.

"Hey, I'm not going to hurt you. Like I said, I just want to ask you some questions."

She narrowed her gaze. "Ask me some questions? Well, you're right. You aren't handling it well. Accosting me in the street is not a good way to start." She let her hand drift backward again, wondering how long it would take her to grab her gun.

Too long, the little voice answered.

"Ms. Caprese," he said quickly, "there's no reason for you to be afraid of me. I'm on your side."

"My side?" That shocked her. She clamped her jaw and lifted her chin. She didn't relax her hand. "My side of what?" she asked harshly.

"The collapse of the Sky Walk."

Her heart, already racing, took a header against her chest wall and stole her breath. She sucked in air greedily. Her heel hit the bottom step and she almost stumbled.

"Look Mr.—Dawson," she grated. "I'm—" What was she about to tell him? That she was armed? There was no way she could get her hand on her Smith & Wesson 3913 before he stopped her. He was six inches taller and outweighed her by at least seventy pounds. He could disarm her without breaking an egg, if there were any left whole.

Even so, she was curious. "What do you mean you're on my side?"

The man named John Dawson, whose card was sitting on her desk upstairs, gave her a hint of a smile. "I'm looking into the collapse of the Sky Walk, just like you. We could both benefit from working together."

"Are you a cop?" she snapped, just as the rest of the printing on the card rose in her mind. It said D&D Services, Inc. By Appointment Only.

He allowed his mouth to stretch into a smile that revealed an unexpected dimple in his cheek. "Nope. I'm just a private citizen, looking into this on my own, same as you, but I've got better equipment." He stopped and let his gaze drift over her.

"Well, some of it's better," he amended.

She bristled at the double entendre. She didn't like him. He was too cocky, too friendly—too good-looking. And she had the feeling he hadn't shown up here on a whim. He wasn't the type to act on impulse—his eyes were too sharp, too calculating. She was sure he'd learned everything he could about her before he'd ever decided to approach her.

"Why?" she asked.

"Why what?"

"Why are you interested in the Sky Walk?"

His smile didn't fade, but those blue eyes took on a smoky hue. He shook his head. "Let's just say I have a need to know what happened, too. Look, Juliana—may I call you Juliana?"

"No, you may not. I don't need any help. I'm doing just fine. Now please, give me my bags."

He held them out. One of them was dripping raw, slimy egg. She grabbed on to the straps, touching his hand. She jerked away, but not fast enough to miss that it was warm and large and strong, with long fingers and calluses on his palms. She peered up at his face. He had the looks and the build of an actor or a model, but his hands told her he'd done manual labor. Interesting.

No. No. *No. Not* interesting. "I have to go. I'm not interested in working with you—or anyone else," she said frostily. She started toward the steps to her apartment building, then looked back.

"Thank you for—" She lifted the hand carrying the bags. As she started to climb the first step, he spoke.

"Juliana, who attacked you?"

She whirled. His brows were lowered again in that dangerous expression. She pressed her lips together. For an instant, she felt an overwhelming urge to tell him what had happened. With that fierce glare and those strong, beautiful workman's hands, he could keep her safe from all harm. She was sure of that.

But what if he was lying? What if he worked for the people

who wanted to stop her from looking into her father's death? The people who'd attacked her?

She turned back to the stairs and felt raw egg dripping onto her foot.

DAWSON WAS READY TO GIVE UP—at least for the moment. He stole one more look at her excellent backside and saw her knee give way. She cried out and grabbed for the stair rail. The grocery bags hit the steps and a bag of salad, two cartons of yogurt, a bottle of milk and the last two unbroken eggs went flying.

He dived and managed to catch her before she hit the steps.

They tumbled down the two steps to the sidewalk, him doing his best to break her fall. He landed on his elbow and it screamed with very unfunny pain.

He set her away from him, but not before he got a whiff of fresh, clean, peppermint-scented hair and a demonstration of how fit she was. Her bottom was not just shapely, but it was also firm and toned.

"Hey, Juliana, you all right?" he asked, setting her off him and rising to a crouch beside her, feeling a slimy wetness seeping through the knee of his pants. *Egg.* Damn it.

In answer, she rolled over onto her knees and used one hand to push herself to her feet. Once she was upright, she took her weight off her right knee and a wince crossed her face.

He stood, too, and looked down at the front of her skirt. It had ridden five inches up her thighs, proving that her legs were knockouts. Pink yogurt had spilled down its front and was sliding down her right leg toward the egg yolk.

"Argh!" she growled and tugged at the hem, then glared at him as if it all was his fault.

He spread his hands. "Sorry—" he drawled.

"Don't—" She took a deep breath. "Just don't!" She turned

carefully and started up the stairs. She was favoring her right knee and each time she put her weight on it, she smothered a groan.

"Hey, wait," he said. "You hurt your knee."

She kept going.

"Jules—" He started to grab her arm and stop her, but then he thought better of it. Instead, he picked up a plastic bag and loaded the few intact groceries into it. The eggs were dead, as was the yogurt. But the bag of salad was fine, the quart of milk seemed okay and the French baguette was still whole. He picked up a bunch of asparagus and a package of gnocchi. Then he vaulted up the stairs and stood on the second-floor landing, trying to remember what her apartment number was.

He didn't have to wonder long. A mild curse in a feminine voice came from apartment three.

He knocked on the door. "Jules? I've got your groceries."

After a couple of minutes, the door opened. That haughty glare was in place, and there were tears on her cheeks. She held a wet cloth in her hand and the yogurt on the front of her skirt was smeared.

He held up the bag. "I saved what I could."

She reached for the bag, but he held it out of reach. "Invite me in. I need to wash my hands."

She leaned against the door and shook her head. "I don't know who you are or why you're stalking me, but if you don't leave right now, I'm going to call the police."

"I'm not stalking you. I rescued your butt *and* saved your groceries. Now we can leave the door open, or we can talk outside or I'll buy you a cup of coffee—"

At that she gave him a disgusted look and gestured toward her stained skirt and her yogurt-and-egg-streaked legs.

"Okay. I can wait out here until you clean up, but I'm warning you, I won't leave until we talk. I can promise you that you will thank me afterward."

Her brows rose. "I sincerely doubt that."

He stepped to the side of the door and slid down the wall to a crouch, his forearms resting on his knees.

"Are you kidding me?" she blurted.

Dawson glanced up at her sidelong. "Nope."

"What's your interest in the Sky Walk?" she asked suspiciously.

"I'll tell you," he said, rising, "if you'll invite me in." He waggled his eyebrows. "You know you want to."

She immediately reached behind her for the door handle, so he stopped, his hand up. "Okay. Jules—Ms. Caprese—you want to know who was responsible for your father's death. I want to know the same thing. I have resources that you can't possibly have. Plus I have experience in surveillance. I want to help you."

She stared at him for a long moment. She shrugged, then winced. "I don't—" She stopped. She looked behind her, then back at him, frowning. "You have experience in surveillance?" she asked.

He nodded.

After a few seconds, she inclined her head, begrudgingly inviting him inside.

Her apartment looked like her—trim and elegant and decked out in black and white. The walls were brilliant white. The couch was black and white striped and flanked by a white club chair with large black flowers. The only color was the red rug on the floor and the bookcase, which bulged with hardbacks and paperbacks.

Juliana couldn't believe her eyes. As soon as he stepped through the door, her small apartment changed. She'd decorated it to be elegant and sophisticated. But with him standing there, it suddenly seemed kind of prissy. She closed the door behind him but didn't lock it. "Who *are* you?" she asked.

He reached into his shirt pocket and pulled out a card. He glanced at it, his mouth set, before handing it to her.

Juliana took the card reluctantly by its edge. She didn't want to risk touching him again. It read D&D Services, Inc., Biloxi, Mississippi. John Dawson. It was a duplicate of the one sitting on her desk. There was no street address. Just a phone number and the words *By appointment only.*

She looked up at him, searching his face. "John Dawson," she said, trying out the name.

He raised a brow. "Yep."

John Dawson. An average, run-of-the-mill name for a man who was anything but.

"Okay, Mr. Dawson." She took a deep breath. "You didn't seek me out just so you could help me. What's your game? And how do I know you're not working for the same people who—" She stopped and pressed her lips together.

"Who what?" he said sharply. "Did that to you?" He pointed to her shoulder and then to the scrape on her cheek. "What happened?"

Juliana turned away, trying to figure out why she had such an urge to confide in this stranger. The little voice in the back of her mind that had protected her many times spoke up.

Are we sure we can trust this Dawson? We don't know anything about him except what he's told us. For all we know he could be the person behind your attack.

Chapter Two

To give herself a little space, Juliana walked over to her refrigerator and filled a glass of water. She took a couple of sips, then turned around.

"Would you like some water?" she asked. Only a few feet separated them. And that wasn't nearly enough. He filled up her little apartment with his tall, lanky frame. She'd already been introduced, intimately, to his long legs and lean, powerful thighs and the fact that he was definitely a virile, heterosexual male when she'd fallen on him. Add to that his broad, sinewy shoulders and those really beautiful hands, and the sum was a seriously hot guy.

But there was no way she trusted him. He'd shown up like a good Samaritan just as she dropped her groceries. But unlike a helpful passerby, he knew her name. Had he been following her? Worse, had he been waiting for a chance to worm his way into her apartment?

Suddenly, it didn't matter how hot he was. He was a stranger—a stranger who knew an awful lot about her. Her gaze snapped to her front door.

Big mistake, letting him get between us and the door, her little voice chided her. *We'll never make it before he catches us.*

He looked at her, glanced over his shoulder at the door, then back at her. "Come on. If you're not going to trust me, then I probably should leave. But I'm betting that together we can figure out what happened at the Golden Galaxy Casino and put the person responsible for the Sky Walk's collapse behind bars. I'm not sure either of us can do it alone." He sighed. "So what do you say?"

She leveled a suspicious gaze at him. "How do you know my name?" she asked.

"Because you put an ad in the paper looking for information about the collapse of the Sky Walk."

She set her jaw and shook her head. "My name wasn't on the ad."

"No, it wasn't. I found the post office box and watched it. When you showed up to check it, I got your license plate."

She gasped, trepidation tightening her chest. "You've been following me," she accused, but then a different emotion blossomed in her chest. "Wait a minute, if you were there…did you…did you see who attacked me and stole my letter?"

Dawson frowned. "That's what happened? Someone stole a letter you got through the ad? I can't say I'm surprised. Didn't you realize putting that ad in the paper made you a sitting duck? You're lucky all you've got were a few bruises."

She flushed.

"It didn't take me any time to find you." He'd hung around the post office box for a couple of days, long enough to spot her checking the box. Then he'd had his brother Reilly, a cop for the Chef Voleur Sheriff's Office, run her plates.

Juliana Caprese, the daughter of the casino manager who was killed when the famous Sky Walk at the Golden Galaxy Casino collapsed three months ago, owned the car. That surprised and intrigued him.

"When did it happen?"

"Two days ago—Tuesday. It was a small man in a hoodie. I'd just taken the letter out of the box. It was the first response I'd gotten to the ad. As soon as I walked outside, he knocked me down and grabbed it. That's when—" She gestured toward her shoulder.

"And that bruise on the side of your face?"

"Where he hit me."

"Bastard," Dawson said, not even trying to mask his fury at the scumbag. "Who sent the letter?"

"I didn't open it. It was addressed to the post office box and there was no return address."

"What about the postmark?"

"I didn't look at it that closely. I was late for work. I was going to open it on my break." She made a face. "I should have opened it. There was something inside."

"What do you mean? Something besides paper?"

"It was a regular number 10 envelope, the kind you pay bills in. But there was something besides paper inside it. About two inches long. Kind of flat."

"You couldn't tell what it was? What it felt like?"

"No, I was in a hurry."

"And that's the only response you've gotten?"

"I haven't been back." She indicated her shoulder. "It's a little hard to get around."

"What about the man who attacked you? Did you get a look at his face? Any identifying marks?"

"Yes, he had tattoos on his arms—" She touched her forearm just above her wrist. "At least that far, which was all I saw. Everything happened so fast. But they were colorful."

"What did the police say?"

Juliana's front teeth scraped her lower lip. She looked away. "I didn't call the police."

Dawson's fury morphed into irritation at her. "Why the hell not? Because you decided you'd handle this vigilante-style? Or because you don't have a carry permit for that Ladysmith you've got in your waistband?"

She looked surprised and guilty. "I'm no vigilante, but I did decide I wasn't going to be attacked again."

"Good for you. Question is, do you know how to use that weapon? Because if you don't—"

She nodded. "My dad taught me." Her mouth twisted. "He thought I should be prepared."

Dawson sat back. "Are you any good?"

Her eyes snapped. "You want to go to the pistol range and check me out?"

He shook his head. "I'll wait until your shoulder gets better. Wouldn't want you claiming a handicap." He regarded her solemnly. "Why did you put the ad in the paper?"

Her chin went up. "Because someone out there knows what happened to the Sky Walk."

"You're looking for someone to blame for your father's death."

"No, that's not it, Mr. Dawson," she said.

He held up a hand. "Hey, just Dawson, okay?"

"Fine. Dawson. I'm not looking for someone to blame. I *know* who's to blame. I just need evidence to prove it."

Dawson's eyes narrowed. "You *know?* Who? Who do you *know* caused your father's death?"

"Michael Delancey, the contractor who built the Golden Galaxy. I've talked to the detectives, the crime scene investigators, Mr. Kaplan, the architect who drew up the plans— they all believe that something must have been wrong with the metal framework. Whether it was substandard materials or shoddy workmanship they don't know. But although Mr. Kaplan told me the materials list was marginally up to code, there were definite shortcuts taken. That's what happens when a contractor cuts costs to make a bigger profit."

Dawson kept his expression and his voice even. "From what I hear, the Delanceys are loaded. Why would he bother?"

"Maybe he's in money trouble. Maybe he just wasn't concerned. I don't care why he did it. I just care about getting justice for my dad. He didn't deserve to die like that."

Dawson nodded grimly. "I'm interested in what happened to the Sky Walk, too. For a client who was injured."

Juliana's brows rose. "A client? Who?" Her gaze narrowed. "Just what is D&D Services? Your card is pretty snobbish, with no indication of what your services are."

"I figure if someone needs my services, they'll know."

"Well, assume I don't."

"I own a security agency. I provide bodyguards, security systems, investigative services. My motto is Dedication and Discretion." He made a little gesture. "*D* and *D*."

She gasped, then her eyes widened and to his surprise, her mouth widened in a grin. "You're a private eye?" she asked.

He frowned at her. What the hell was so funny? "Yep, you could say that."

"A *real* private investigator! Wow!" Her dark eyes snapped with interest. "*I'm* going to be a private investigator."

Okay. That shocked him. "You're what?"

"I've always wanted to be a private eye. I got my degree in Administrative Justice. But I can't afford to start my own business, and nobody wants to hire someone with no experience."

"So you're working as a dealer in a casino."

She studied him for a few seconds. "I need to know who your client is."

"Look, Jules—"

Her jaw set again. "Don't call me that. My name is Juliana."

"Fine. Juliana. I have a contractual obligation to my client. I can't tell you anything."

She shook her head. "I see what this is about. You don't want to *work* with me. You just want to get your hands on what I've found out, so you don't have to reinvent the wheel."

She waved a hand. "Just how long have you been following me? Quite a while, I'd guess, because you figured out that I would be going to visit Kaplan Wright Architects, and left your card there. Pretty good detective work. But no, I have no reason to work with you. It could have been your client who stole my letter."

Then a harsh laugh escaped her lips. "You could be working for Michael Delancey, for all I know."

Dawson fought to keep his face from showing any reaction. "I guarantee you I'm interested in the same thing you are."

"Yeah? What thing?"

"Getting to the truth. What's your thing?"

"I told you. I want to know who was behind the collapse of the Sky Walk."

"Didn't you just say you know who it was? Michael Delancey."

Her gaze wavered. "I think it's him. He was the contractor after all, but I need to be sure." She paused. "What about you? Do you think it was Michael Delancey?"

Dawson didn't trust his ability to hold on to his placid expression, so he stood and walked over to the window. "I don't know whose fault it was, but I can tell you this. I will do everything I can to get to the truth."

"No matter who it hurts?" she persisted.

He thought about Michael Delancey, the heir to a vast fortune and a tainted legacy. Infamous Senator Con Delancey's son. Michael had gone into construction rather than pursue politics, wanting to distance himself from his scandalous father.

Once his firstborn son was old enough, he'd brought him into the business. But the son soon grew suspicious of his father's business practices. Then when Michael was indicted for gross negligence and gross misconduct, his son had separated himself from his father. He'd quit the construction business and started his own company.

No matter who it hurts? Juliana Caprese had asked Dawson.

If he pursued the truth, he wouldn't stop until he'd found it. And if the truth led him to Michael Delancey's door, then so be it.

"No matter who it hurts," John Dawson Delancey answered.

At that instant his phone rang. He fished it out of the holder at his belt and checked the display.

Speak of the devil. He grimaced as he killed the connection. "That's a call I've been expecting," he told Juliana. "I have to go. I'll call you later."

"But you don't have my phone—" She stopped when he sent her an amused glance. "Oh." Her eyes sparked with interest. "You used your private eye tricks to get my number, didn't you?"

He shook his head tiredly. But as he headed for the door, she called after him, "You have *got* to tell me how you did that."

He grinned to himself as an image rose in his mind of a gorgeous, long-legged private eye with her left arm in a sling, her right hand brandishing a weapon and her skirt blowing up to reveal pink panties. It would be very interesting to see if Juliana Caprese became a private investigator. Only trouble was, eventually she'd figure out who he was, and once she did, the only thing he'd see of her was that firm butt disappearing from his life. But for now he could enjoy his image of her as a gumshoe. Did they make high-heeled gumshoes?

Dawson climbed into his nondescript Honda Accord and set the phone down in the console. He didn't like driving the boring silver mom car, although it handled well. He much preferred driving his new Corvette, but the Accord was perfect for tailing or surveillance. Its greatest attribute was that it looked like any other car on the street.

As he pulled away from the curb he frowned. He had to call his father back. He hit Redial and listened to the phone ring on his Bluetooth connection. The name on the display read Michael Delancey. He'd removed the word *Dad* years ago.

"Yel-lo." The familiar voice pricked Dawson's chest like a thorn. His dad had finally come out of his melancholy and started answering the phone. For months after he was released from prison, he'd sat in front of the TV, not speaking unless he was forced to.

"It's me," Dawson said shortly. "You called?"

"Hey, son. I was just checking to see if you had any news."

Dawson grimaced. He didn't want Michael Delancey to call him son. "No. I told you, I'd call you when I found out anything. I warned you not to call my cell phone. It's for work only. Leave me a message at my condo or I swear I'll get my number changed."

"Okay. No problem." Michael's voice was almost toneless. Dawson knew he wasn't really listening to him.

"I mean it!" he snapped.

"I get it!" Michael snapped back and Dawson knew he did. "What about that ad? Did you track down who placed it?"

"I'm working on that." He wasn't about to tell his dad that it was Vincent Caprese's daughter who'd offered ten thousand dollars for the name of the person responsible for the Sky Walk's collapse.

"You've been working on it for weeks. Damn it, Dawson, the police have already questioned me three times. I can't go back to prison. I can't!"

"Why do you think they keep coming back? Obviously they don't like something you're telling them. Why don't you give them the straight story for once?" Dawson turned into the parking lot of his waterfront condo overlooking Biloxi's Back Bay.

There was a pause on the other end of the line. "You still think I'm not? Damn it to hell, if I had anything else that would help—" He broke off with a frustrated huff.

There was no mistaking the desperation in his father's voice. Dawson steeled himself against the compassion that he felt rising in his chest—compassion his dad didn't deserve.

"Dawson? You've got to believe me. I didn't have anything to do with the Sky Walk's collapse. If my own son won't believe me, I guess I'm sunk."

The Sky Walk had been a multimillion-dollar two-level suspended walkway that stretched above the main floor of the Golden Galaxy Casino in Waveland, Mississippi, the newest and largest casino on the Mississippi Gulf Coast.

"I've got to go."

"Okay, son. Call your mother later. She's taking a nap now."

Dawson disconnected and looked at his watch. It was three o'clock in the afternoon. His lips thinned. *Taking a nap* was family code for at least one bottle of wine down the chute, if not two. He sighed.

It was hell being the oldest kid—oldest son, he amended. If his sister Rosemary had lived, she'd be thirty-four, two years older than he. But she'd been murdered twelve years before, so she would always be twenty-two.

The twins were older than that now. At the thought of Ryker and Reilly, his identical younger brothers, he gave a gruff snort. They'd gone completely bonkers over the past year—not even thirty and married within six months of each other—right on the heels of a notorious serial-killer case in St. Tammany Parish in Louisiana.

Ryker had married the only woman who'd survived Albert

Moser's obsessive killing spree, and Reilly had married the serial killer's daughter.

Dawson shook his head. He was five years older than them, and he didn't even live in the same hemisphere as marriage. It would be a cold day in hell when he fell into that trap.

It was bizarre. They'd grown up in the same family. As Dawson liked to say, they put the funk in dysfunctional.

Rosemary's death, or to be precise, her disappearance, had begun their mother's fall into discreet, genteel alcoholism. Then, eight years ago, Michael Delancey had gone to prison, his mother had gone into the bottle and Dawson had separated himself from anything having to do with his father.

Inside his condo he tossed keys and jacket onto the kitchen table and laid his shoulder holster beside them. Then he headed for the shower.

As he dropped his egg-and-yogurt-stained shirt and pants into the hamper and stepped under the hot spray, a vision rose in his brain. Juliana Caprese, private eye, with a pink sling to match her pink panties and brandishing a big gun.

Immediately, insistently, something else rose, as well. His buttocks and thighs tightened as the shower's spray changed to caressing fingers. He groaned and raised his face to the hot water, enjoying the feel of it streaming down his neck, across his sensitized nipples, over his abs and down, tickling across the sensitive skin just above his pubis.

He shuddered and contemplated turning off the hot water, but it was way too late for that, so he gave himself up to the fantasy of Juliana Caprese handling *his* weapon.

Chapter Three

Juliana snuggled down under the fake fur throw and wriggled her toes inside her bunny slippers. The slippers didn't have bunny faces on them; they looked like the fluffy fat slippers that Bugs wore when he was relaxing.

On her lap was a stack of building permits, code inspections, material specifications, everything she'd been able to find in public records about the Golden Galaxy Casino. But on her mind was John Dawson.

After he'd left abruptly this afternoon, she'd looked up his website and called every government agency she could think of that might have information—good or bad—about D&D Services, Inc.

There was nothing out there about the company. Apparently what Dawson had told her was true. If people needed his services, they found him.

She remembered what else he'd said. *Dedication and discretion.* She had to hand it to him. He had the *discretion* part down pat. Every search had come up zero. No client list, no reviews, no referrals, no recommendations. Nor had she found anyone who *knew* anyone he'd worked for. In fact, although he had a website, it had hardly more information than his card. Not even the Better Business Bureau or the Attorney General's office had anything on D&D Services. The person she'd talked with at the Attorney General's office told her that no complaints had been filed against the company.

She'd also searched online for a John Dawson. There were dozens of Dawsons in Biloxi, and several John Dawsons. Once the entire Gulf Coast was included, she was looking at scores of possibilities. None of the phone numbers matched, though.

Juliana sighed and picked up her glass of wine. She took a sip, then realized she couldn't open a folder while holding the glass.

She was so sick of trying to do things with one arm. She slipped her left arm out of the sling. It hadn't been broken, just dislocated. The doctor had told her on Tuesday that after a couple of days she could start using it. That was today.

She transferred her wine to her left hand and lifted it to her lips, feeling a pop and a twinge that almost made her drop the glass. The doctor had told her the joint would probably pop for several months. He hadn't told her it would hurt. Still, she got the glass to her lips without spilling any.

Okay. That simplified things. She flipped through the folders in her lap with her right hand. She wanted to look at the note she'd found in her dad's things.

She found the file, neatly labeled in her father's precise hand. Golden Galaxy, Misc. Her heart squeezed, just like it did every time she saw his writing. She opened the folder and took out the plastic bag in which she'd placed a folded piece of lined paper. Inside the baggie, written in deliberate block letters, was the most damning piece of information she had about the construction failure that had killed her father and five other people.

Why hadn't her dad done something? Told somebody? Had the Sky Walk checked? He might be alive today.

She ran her fingers across the baggie, tracing the words.

BE CAREFUL, CAPRESE. THE SKY WALK'S DANGEROUS. DELANCEY SHOULD KNOW. LOOK AT VEGA. HE HOLDS GRUDGES.

There was no signature. Judging by the questions the police had asked her, she was sure her dad hadn't shown it to anyone. The police obviously didn't know about it.

She sure wasn't going to turn it over to them. They had done absolutely nothing about arresting the man responsible for her dad's death. She wasn't letting anybody get their hands on the note, not until she'd done everything she could to identify the sender and find out what he knew about her father's death.

The best clue she had was the name Vega. Compared to her search for D&D Services and John Dawson, finding information about Vega had been a walk in the park. In the Mississippi Gulf Coast area, Vittorio "Tito" Vega was a landmark. She found numerous newspaper articles touting his patronage of the arts and his civic involvement. But there were also op-ed pieces that suggested that he had more money than his real-estate investment business could account for, and that he was rumored to be involved in loan-sharking and bribery.

The day after she'd found the note, she'd placed the ad.

Wanted: Information leading to the conviction of the person(s) responsible for the collapse of the Sky Walk. $10,000 reward. Respond to P.O. Box 7874.

She blew out a frustrated breath. She'd been so pleased with herself, so cocky. Dawson was right. She might as well have painted a bull's-eye on her back. All the guy who'd attacked her had to do was watch the post office box until she received a reply, then snatch it.

Like John Dawson. A disturbing thought occurred to her.

He had admitted he'd watched the box. It could have been him who'd taken the letter. Not personally, she amended. The scumbag had been scrawny, dirty and covered with tattoos. Still, Dawson could have hired him.

She'd been on the verge of trusting the tall, hot private investigator. His assertion that he was working for someone who'd been injured in the Sky Walk's collapse had rung true.

But what if he was playing her? Whether he'd been responsible for stealing her letter, he wanted the information she had about the Sky Walk. And judging by his slick, flirty attitude and his shrewd blue eyes, he wouldn't balk at anything to get it.

DAWSON PUSHED HIS FINGERS through his damp hair and knocked on Juliana's door again. He was pretty sure she was home. After spilling her groceries and hurting her knee, he doubted she'd be going out on the town anytime soon. Besides, the single-serving packaged salad and the small baguette had hinted at a meal at home—for one.

He heard movement behind the door. He stepped back and positioned himself so his bland expression could be seen through the peephole.

He saw a shadow cover the minuscule window and heard a groan. "What do you want?" she called ungraciously.

He held the carton in his hand up to the peephole. "Brought you some eggs."

"Thank you," she called. "You can leave them by the door."

"Ah-ah-ah," he chided. "You don't get them until you let me in. I had to take care of some business earlier, but I still have questions."

"I guess you'll have to live without answers and I'll have to live without eggs." Her voice came through the door, tinged with a note of amusement.

"Have a heart, Caprese. I almost dropped them coming up the stairs. You know how that is."

The door opened slowly. She held out a hand.

"Sorry, you've got to let me in to get the eggs. Just a few minutes, two questions. That's all, I swear."

She shook her head. "Customer support is closed for the day."

Dawson quirked his mouth. "Cute. Now let me in. Like I told you, we can get a lot more done by working together."

"Right, you did say that. Why don't you make me a copy of what you have. I'll look at it and get back to you. You can give me your number—oh, wait. I already have it on your card." She moved to close the door, but he stuck his size-twelve Nike in the way.

She looked down, then back up, her eyes snapping. If they'd been dark lasers, he'd be neatly sliced in two lengthwise. "So that's how you want to play it," she commented. "Hold on a second while I get my gun."

He laughed. "That was your first mistake, rookie. You should have brought it with you."

She drew back, then showed her right hand again—holding the Ladysmith. "Like this?"

"Like that," he said. Neatly and lightning-quick, he caught her wrist, pressed a pressure point and took the gun away from her. He checked the safety. It was on.

"Don't play with firearms, little girl," he growled.

She frowned and her cheeks turned pink. "I wasn't really—"

He pushed past her and set her weapon on the coffee table. "That's the problem. Guns aren't something you fool around with. If you *weren't really,* then you shouldn't have brandished it."

She went around the coffee table and sat, quickly grabbing a folder that lay on the seat cushion beside her and stuffing it in between a stack of similar manila folders. Then she carefully slid her left arm into the sling that dangled from her shoulder and picked up a wineglass. She sipped nonchalantly.

Or tried to. But her cheeks were splotched with pink, and she refused to meet his gaze. She was obviously embarrassed about letting him take her gun.

"If you want to be a private eye," he said drily, "you'd better learn how to handle a gun."

"I know—"

"Don't ever—" he interrupted her "—hold your weapon at arm's length when your target is close enough to grab it." He set the eggs down on the coffee table and picked up her Ladysmith.

He demonstrated. "Stay far enough back that he can't reach it. If you're cornered and you can't step back, hold your weapon close and your arm closer. Press your elbow against your body. It gives you stability. Most importantly, never hold the gun with just one hand, and always check your balance. If the other person gains an advantage over you, you're dead."

She nodded carefully. "Got it," she said solemnly.

"Have you eaten?"

"What?" His abrupt change of subject took her aback.

"Eaten. You know, dinner?"

"I—"

"Great. I know you've got salad and bread. Let's have an omelet."

"I don't—"

But he'd already grabbed the carton of eggs and headed into the kitchen. Checking the refrigerator, he found some Swiss cheese, an open package of cooked bacon, the salad greens and a half-empty bottle of Cardini's Caesar salad dressing. "That should be enough for the two of us."

She craned her neck to look at him over her shoulder. "What are you doing?"

"I assume you like Caesar dressing. I'll just heat the bread, okay?"

"I don't— You don't—"

Dawson turned his back on her, smiling to himself. He had to admit it was fun keeping her off guard. He turned on the oven to preheat for the French bread, then he sniffed the packaged salad. He hated prepackaged greens, but these at least looked fresh. He emptied them into a glass bowl from her cupboard and ran water on them.

"What are you doing?" Her voice surprised him. She'd come into the kitchen under cover of the running water and was peering around him at the sink.

"Rinsing the greens," he said, trying his best to sound calm, although the peppermint scent of her hair brought to mind the erotic pressure of her firm bottom against him when he broke her fall earlier.

"But they're prerinsed."

"Trust me, rookie. Rinsing takes the plastic taste away. It'll be a hundred percent better." He held up a leaf of arugula. "Taste."

She looked up at him, her eyes smoky and filled with doubt, then opened her mouth.

When Juliana's lips parted, Dawson completely forgot about the arugula. His gaze slid along the soft, pink opening of her lips the way his tongue wanted to. His mouth watered at the imagined taste of her lips.

She looked up at him. Her gaze slid down to his neck when he swallowed, then drifted upward again and stopped at his mouth. She rose on tiptoe and leaned toward him.

Just when he'd decided to meet her halfway for a deep, delicious kiss, she plucked the leaf from his fingers and popped it into her mouth.

Then she licked her lips and lifted her chin. If he were a

betting man, he'd bet that she was laughing at him behind those eyes. "Mmm," she drawled. "Good."

It was his turn to be caught off guard. He was left aching with desire and curiosity when she turned on her heel and went back to the couch. What would she have done if he had kissed her?

Most likely thrown him out. He could have lost his best bet for finding out what she knew about the Sky Walk's collapse. He had to be careful. He hadn't met a woman in a long time who interested him as much as Juliana Caprese did. And because he only went to bed with women who interested him beyond the physical, that long time had long since become a very long time.

He broke the eggs into a bowl and added crumbled bacon. He couldn't find a cheese grater, so he chopped the cheese into chunks and tossed it in, then beat the eggs and poured the whole concoction into a heated pan.

But this wasn't even marginally about sex. It couldn't be, even though Juliana Caprese might be the most interesting woman he had ever met. He was here for one reason and one reason only. To find out what she knew about the collapse of the Sky Walk. He needed to know if her father's death was his father's fault.

The odor of toasty French bread filled his nostrils and made him realize he was staring at her black, tumbling hair. He opened the wall oven and grabbed the bread with his bare fingers, then dropped it onto the granite countertop. "Ouch," he muttered.

"Burn yourself?" Juliana asked cheerily, rising.

"Nope. Dinner's ready." He grabbed a plate and slid it under the loaf of bread, then carried it to the kitchen table.

"Burned French bread and watery salad. My favorite," Juliana said, going to the refrigerator and taking out a new bottle of white wine.

Dawson opened a couple of drawers until he found freshly washed dish towels. "Watch this," he said. He unfolded a towel and dumped the greens onto it. Then he caught the corners together and twirled the bundle a few times. When he folded the now-wet towel's corners back, the greens were dry and fresh-looking.

"Impressive," she said. She tucked the wine bottle under her left arm and began to twist the cap with her right hand.

He checked the omelet, flipped it and let it cook on the other side for about a minute. Then he cut it in two and slid the larger portion onto his plate and the smaller one onto hers.

Dinner was ready, but Juliana was still struggling with the bottle. Dawson sat down and crossed his arms, curious about how long it would take her to admit that she couldn't open the wine.

He was beginning to think she might have a stubborn streak.

She took the bottle from under her arm and stuck it between her knees. That didn't work any better. She muttered a colorful curse under her breath.

He chuckled. "Come on, rookie, let me open it for you. How'd you get the first bottle open?"

She sent him a withering look. "It was already open when—" She gingerly shrugged her left shoulder.

"So if I wasn't here, they'd find your skeleton in that chair, with the still-unopened wine bottle clutched in your bony fingers?"

Her mouth twitched. "I'll get it open eventually," she said flatly.

He plucked the bottle from between her knees and gave the cap a quick twist. Then he filled her glass. "Mind if I have some?"

"After all that work you did to open it? You deserve it."

Dawson tore the bread into small pieces so she wouldn't have to struggle with it, and then dug into his salad.

"Rinsing the salad did take the plasticky taste away," she said grudgingly.

He didn't bother answering. He was examining his reaction to sitting in her apartment breaking bread with her. It was a disturbing sensation. After a few minutes of silence, he realized that his discomfort was emanating from her. Despite their outwardly friendly banter, when she thought he wasn't looking, she eyed him with a guarded suspicion.

He finished his salad and dug into the omelet, watching her as he ate. She did pretty well with one arm. She'd take a bite of salad, then a bite of omelet, and set her fork down. She'd pick up a small piece of bread and slide it across the pat of butter on her plate and pop it into her mouth, take a sip of wine, then repeat the process.

He refilled their glasses, buttered another piece of bread and sat back, staring at her. "Your arm's not broken," he said.

She shook her head and considered him narrowly. "Just dislocated. I fell on it when he pushed me down."

"You didn't recognize him?"

"No. Are you relieved?"

Dawson frowned. "What's that supposed to mean?" he snapped.

She raised her brows and shrugged. "You tell me. You already admitted you were following me and watching the post office. Maybe you had someone else watching me, too."

"Come on, rookie," he growled, irritated. "I told you, we're on the same side."

"Yeah, maybe, until you get the information you want from me. You asked me what was in the letter I got. Are you sure you don't already have the answer to that question?"

Dawson stood so abruptly that he almost turned over his chair. He grabbed his plate and hers and tossed them into the sink with a clatter, then he jerked the salad and dressing off the table. In less than a minute he had the food put away. Then he turned on her, his face dark as a storm.

"You're accusing *me* of roughing you up and stealing your damn letter?" he roared, his words splitting the air like a thunderclap.

Chapter Four

Juliana jumped when Dawson yelled at her. Although she should have expected it given the way he'd thrown her dishes around. Then the absurdity hit her.

She chuckled. "Did you seriously just bus the table before stopping to yell at me?" she asked.

Dawson scowled, then looked down at his hands. He still held the dishrag he'd used to wipe the table. He balled it up and fired a line drive into the sink, then scrubbed a palm across his evening stubble. "Chalk it up to a very dysfunctional childhood." He sighed.

He sounded sincere. Juliana resented him for making her want to believe him.

"If you want to be a private eye, you're going to have to get a hell of a lot better at reading people. Because trust me, rookie," Dawson said, fishing the dishrag out of the sink and folding it, "if I had that letter, I'm pretty sure I wouldn't be here begging you for information."

"I thought you told me you had info for me, too," she said, deciding for the moment to trust him.

No, not trust. But she would give him the benefit of the doubt for long enough to find out what he knew.

Then she'd see.

"Well, thank you for fixing dinner and cleaning up the

kitchen," she said, picking up her wineglass and heading back to the couch. She beat him by about two and a half seconds.

She slipped her arm out of the sling and grabbed the stack of folders as she sat. Her left shoulder protested, but at least her research was in her hands and not his.

He sat down beside her. "I see your shoulder's better," he said.

"A little. The doctor told me to keep it immobile and put ice on it for a couple of days, then I could start using it. If I don't move it too far or too fast, it's bearable."

"So what have you got in your lap there, rookie?"

She pressed her right hand down on the top folder as he casually reached for it. "Nothing you get to see until you share with me what you know. And—" she arched a brow at him "—it has to be something I don't already have."

"You don't already know this," he said confidently. He'd gotten it from Reilly, who'd pulled the info from the case files.

She turned toward him. "I guess we'll know soon. So what is it?"

"The initial report from the forensic engineer is that the Sky Walk looked just fine. No code violations, no recorded changes in materials from the submitted plans."

Juliana looked as if he'd slapped her. For a moment she just stared at him. "That can't be true," she finally said, shaking her head. "Mr. Kaplan, the architect, said—"

Dawson shrugged.

"No," Juliana snapped. "Whoever told you that was wrong."

"Sorry. This came from police records."

"But it—" She took a shaky breath. "It couldn't have just *broken*. There had to be something wrong with it. Things don't just break." Her eyes glittered with tears and her hands fisted around the top two manila folders on her lap.

Dawson felt a tug inside him, an urge to give her what she wanted so badly—someone to blame for her father's death. She might say she wanted the truth, might even believe it. But her search was for explanations, not facts. He only had a tiny scrap of hope to give her, but he offered it for what it was worth.

"It's a preliminary finding. But according to my source, the final report won't be ready for at least thirty days." He paused, then said, "Maybe then—"

"Not maybe. There *was* something wrong with the Sky Walk," she said again. "There was." Her fingers were squeezing the folders so tightly that their tips were turning bluish-white.

"Hey," he said, touching her hand. "Relax. If there's something wrong with the materials, the forensic engineer will find it."

She shook her head. "Michael Delancey has plenty of money. He could have paid him off. Somebody like him could cover up anything." Her eyes widened. "There are Delanceys on the police force."

"Whoa, slow down," Dawson said quickly, instinctively steering her away from Michael Delancey as the villain of the Golden Galaxy Casino tragedy. Trouble was, he wasn't sure she was wrong. He decided to press her for more information carefully.

"Why are you so convinced that Michael Delancey is the one responsible for the collapse?"

She looked at him steadily. "Because he built the casino. He was the contractor. Every design, every purchase order, every decision that was made went through him." She stopped and swallowed. "Whatever caused the Sky Walk to collapse and kill my father and five other people was approved by Michael Delancey."

Dawson nodded. Everything she said was true, and her conclusion was rational. He'd reached the same conclusion eight years ago when questions arose about the luxury condominiums his dad had been building in Chef Voleur. At that time Dawson had been working for his dad, but once accusations started flying about inferior materials, Dawson had bailed.

He'd already tired of physical labor anyway, so he'd moved to Biloxi and gone back to school for a Ph.D. in Criminal Justice. He, like his kid brothers, was interested in law enforcement, but unlike Ryker and Reilly, he did not want to work for someone else. So he'd gotten his private investigator license and opened his own business.

By that time, his dad was in prison, so John Dawson Delancey had registered his business under the name John D. Dawson and distanced himself from the infamous Delancey dynasty.

He realized Juliana was talking to him.

"Well?" she said impatiently. "You out there in ya-ya land. Do you want to see it or not?"

Dawson blinked. "Uh, yeah," he said, having no clue what she was referring to. "Sure."

She flipped through the folders and pulled out the flattest one. It couldn't have more than two sheets of paper in it. She opened it carefully and took out a plastic bag that contained a note.

Dawson's pulse hammered. "What's that?" He reached for it, but Juliana held on to it.

"You can look at it, but you can't take it out of the baggie. You can't touch the paper."

"No problem."

She handed him the plastic bag. He quickly scanned the note, written in carefully lettered block print.

BE CAREFUL, CAPRESE. THERE'S PROBLEMS WITH THE SKY WALK. DELANCEY SHOULD KNOW. LOOK AT VEGA. HE HOLDS GRUDGES.

"Where'd you get this?" he demanded sharply.

"It was in Daddy's wallet, under that little hidden flap in the bill compartment."

Dawson held it up to the light, studying it more closely. He turned the baggie over. "Look how creased it is. It must have been folded in your dad's wallet for weeks. See the wear on the creased edges?"

She nodded.

"Are you the one who bagged it?"

She nodded again. "I thought if there were any finger-prints on the paper, I didn't want to take a chance on smudg-ing them."

"How much did you handle it?"

"I took it out of his wallet and unfolded it," she said. "Then when I realized what it was, I used kitchen tongs to slide it into the plastic bag."

"When did you find it?"

"The day before the funeral. I was looking for insurance papers, cards—you know, stuff the funeral home needed."

"And you don't have any idea when he got it?"

"No, he never mentioned it."

"When was the Sky Walk finished? The grand opening of the Golden Galaxy was in May, right?"

"June 1."

"What about the casino? Did your dad talk about it?"

She smiled sadly. "He was so excited about his new job. He'd managed other casinos, but the Golden Galaxy was the largest and the most elaborate. He was so proud of it, and it killed him." By the time she finished, her voice was tight and hoarse, laced with grief and thousands of unshed tears.

He laid his hand over her fist and gently urged her fingers to loosen. She was so rigid, so controlled. Her fingers finally relaxed.

He squeezed her hand reassuringly as he studied the note.

"Is this how you decided that Michael Delancey was responsible for what happened?"

"Yes, it's right there in black and white. *Delancey should know.*"

Dawson had his own opinion of what the three words meant. Was the writer saying that Delancey knew that something was wrong? Or was he saying that Delancey should be told about the note? There was no way to be sure.

"What about this reference to Vega?" He knew who Tito Vega was. He'd heard his dad talk about him for eight years. Michael blamed Vega for framing him and putting him in prison.

"The name sounded vaguely familiar to me, so I looked him up." Juliana flipped awkwardly through the folders in her lap and pulled one out. She opened it and glanced at the pages before she handed it to him. Probably checking to be sure there was nothing in there that she didn't want him to see.

The pages were printouts of webpages, articles and op-eds about Vittorio "Tito" Vega. Dawson skimmed them. She'd done a good job ferreting out information about the high-profile real-estate investor.

Dawson already knew a lot about him. Vega patronized the arts and enjoyed involving himself in local politics. He was an important contributor to both. But like many public figures, rumors abounded that he was involved in other, less laudable ventures. One of the regional newspapers occasionally printed op-ed pieces that suggested that Tito Vega was involved in loan-sharking and even bribery.

"What did Vega have to do with the Golden Galaxy?" he asked, although he already knew from his dad that Vega was somehow involved.

Juliana sat up, pride and excitement giving her cheeks a pretty pink blush. "It took me a long time to find that. He apparently worked very hard to keep his various concerns separate. It was really difficult to track them, but I did it!"

Dawson was impressed. He knew about Vega. He'd done his own investigation into Vega's activities after his dad went to prison. He'd tried to prove that his dad was telling the truth—that Vega had framed him. He'd failed, but he'd ended up with a file drawer full of information and a fairly long list of people who'd been hurt by the real-estate mogul.

"I finally put it all together." She dug out another folder and handed him a sheet of paper. "Take a look at this."

It was a handwritten flowchart. Vega's name was at the top and the Golden Galaxy Casino was at the bottom. Dawson followed the flow of companies down the chart. There were eight of them.

"Wow," he said. He recognized most of the companies, because he'd traced Vega's connection to the Golden Galaxy, too, but if he'd written out a chart like this, his would have had several holes in it. "This is impressive. I was working on something like this, but I didn't find any connection with Meadow Gold and I never heard of Bayside Industries."

Juliana beamed. "That was a hard one. It's actually a company based in Switzerland that makes knives. We export steel to them, then we buy the knives to sell here. It's the only one I'm not a hundred percent sure of. See here? Vittorio Vega, Inc. owns Biloxi Coast Realty and Islandview Condominiums in Bay St. Louis. The corporation manages a number of marinas along the Gulf Coast. It took me a while, but I found a marina in Pascagoula that was owned by Vega, Inc. but was sold a few years ago to Meadow Gold Corporation, which owns the Golden Galaxy."

Dawson was impressed. "You must have dug pretty deep to find that," he said.

She nodded. "Now, here's where it gets really interesting. I couldn't find any figures from the Pascagoula marina, but

Meadow Gold buys a lot of knives from Bayside Industries and sells them to that marina. And the last piece of the puzzle I could find was Avanti Investments. One of their holdings was the tract of land the Golden Galaxy is built on. They went bankrupt after Katrina, and Meadow Gold Corporation picked up the land for a song. Avanti had Bayside Industries in their stock portfolio. And that's how Vega is connected to the Golden Galaxy."

"And you can prove it?"

The triumphant blush left her cheeks and she looked down at her stack of folders. "I don't know. I copied all the public documents I could find, but some of it, like Avanti's stock portfolio, I only found one reference to that, and it was several years ago. So anywhere along the line, the connection could break down." She raised her gaze to his and her dark eyes glistened with tears. "I'm afraid it's not good enough. A lot of paperwork was lost in the storm surge."

She blinked and the dampness that had been clinging to her lower lashes spilled over onto her cheek. Dawson didn't realize he was going to catch it with his thumb until it was too late to stop himself.

Her eyes drifted closed when he brushed the tear away. It would be the easiest thing in the world to kiss her. He leaned forward, mesmerized by the thick dark lashes that threw spiky shadows onto her cheeks. His gaze moved to her mouth. Her lips were slightly parted. A blade of desire sliced through him and he reached for her.

His hand hit the stack of folders.

Her eyes flew open. She grabbed them up and hugged them to her chest.

Dawson pulled back, stunned.

Juliana bit her lip and carefully relaxed her left arm, wincing, but she still hung on to the folders with her right arm.

He stood and stared down at her. "You really think that's

what I was doing? Trying to distract you while I went for your little stack of research?" he asked harshly.

"I—" she looked beyond him, then down "—I didn't know. I mean, you say you're here to help me, but you haven't taken your eyes off the folders since you came in."

Dawson stepped away from the couch and grabbed his jacket. "Yeah, right," he said. He was pissed that she thought he was going to grab her paperwork and run. But he was also embarrassed. His ego was stinging. Not only had he ruined his chances of getting his hands on those folders, but he'd also given in to a stupid impulse and tried to kiss her.

"Look, Dawson, you're charming and—" she gestured toward him "—attractive, and I appreciate the information you gave me, but I'm trying to get justice for my dad. He didn't deserve to die. And the truth is, I don't know what you're trying to do."

Dawson nodded, holding on to his temper with an iron fist. "That's true. You don't." He shrugged into his jacket and stalked toward her front door and opened it. Then he turned back.

"You won't have to worry about me getting close enough to steal your little folders again. But make no mistake, Juliana Caprese, I'm riding your tail until you either find what you're looking for or give up." He opened the door and gave her his parting shot.

"There's no way in hell I'm going to sit by and let you get yourself killed."

Chapter Five

Friday morning Juliana hurried down the steps from her apartment and into the waiting taxi. She wore jeans and low-heeled boots. There was no telling what kind of mess she'd be digging through.

Ten minutes later the driver said, "Here? This is where you wanna go?"

"Yes, right here. And I want you to wait for me," she said as she climbed out.

"No, no, no," he protested, shaking his head. "I'll lose too much money."

"Keep the meter running."

"That don't count for tips."

Juliana sighed. "I'll give you an extra twenty. I'll be out in less than a half hour."

The driver eyed her narrowly. "Fifty."

"Forty. Otherwise forget it."

"Okay, forty," he said, putting the vehicle in Park.

She looked at the expansive gaudy exterior of the Golden Galaxy Casino. It had been billed as the largest casino on the Mississippi Gulf Coast. Now it was the biggest piece of wreckage. The paper had said that demolition was scheduled to begin Monday. And this was Friday. That was why she was here.

Walking past the fountains and reflecting pools that surrounded the main entrance, Juliana saw the crosses and silk flowers families had placed. She hadn't brought one for her dad. She had no desire to memorialize this place that had killed him.

She ducked under the crime scene tape and dug into her pocket for her dad's key ring. There were two keys embossed with the Golden Galaxy logo. Her dad had brought her here before the casino opened to show her the Sky Walk, so she knew what the keys were for. She was worried about opening the electronic doors manually with her injured arm, but when she approached, they easily glided open. The electricity was on.

The interior wasn't as dark as she'd feared it might be. Sunlight shone through the glass doors and the glass-domed roof. The network of structural yet decorative metal beams that crisscrossed below the glass dome cast geometric shadows on the walls. Still, she was going to need more light to see her way through the wreckage and debris to her dad's office.

She glanced around. The electrical closet was to the right. She walked to the door and unlocked it. Inside the small space she couldn't see a thing. She fished her flashlight out of her oversized purse and shone it on the banks of gray metal boxes with black switches.

Squinting, she read the tiny labels. Most of them might as well have been written in Greek. But finally she found a row of labels that made sense. *Offices, Main, Bar, Restaurant 1, Restaurant 2, Sky Walk, Kitchen.* She switched on Offices and Main. Lights flared behind her.

With the lights on, she could see the rows of slot machines. They were all turned off, making them look like silent soldiers guarding the dead. Beyond them, the twisted remains of the Sky Walk glowed with what had to be half of the thirty million minilights that had made it the most spectacular architectural feature on the Gulf Coast.

The massive suspended walkway had stretched from the indoor parking garage on the west side of the casino, over the administrative offices and across the main casino floor. It had hung from the crisscrossed beams above it.

Patrons could walk directly from the garage across to the Milky Way Bar and the Pleiades Restaurant on the east end of the casino.

Tears clogged her throat and her chest tightened until she couldn't breathe. This was the first time she'd seen the wreckage.

But now she had to face it. She stepped up closer to the steel-and-chrome monster that had killed her dad, glass crunching beneath her boots. Reaching in her bag, she pulled out her camera and snapped pictures until tears made it impossible to see clearly enough.

For a few moments, she buried her face in her hands and sobbed quietly. She wasn't used to crying. She'd never experienced this kind of loss. She barely remembered her mother, who'd died when she was a toddler. But she'd had her daddy all her life.

Now she was alone. The emptiness in her chest ached as if her heart had been ripped right out of her.

She blotted her cheeks on her shirt sleeve and followed the line of the wreckage west, until the casino manager's office— her dad's office—came into sight. Her eyes stung again, but she swallowed determinedly and raised the camera.

The view screen brought the extent of the destruction into sharp, raw focus. Obviously, search-and-rescue crews had hauled away much of the shattered glass, wood and drywall in this area.

The tangle of rods and cables that had been the Sky Walk was peeled back like a pile of spaghetti pushed to one side of a plate. She knew that it had taken them several hours and some fancy equipment to get to her dad. He'd been working in his office early that morning.

He hadn't had a chance. According to the autopsy report, he'd died of blunt force trauma to his head when the wreckage collapsed the ceiling of his office. She supposed she should be thankful that he hadn't lingered, trapped there under the tangle of metal and debris.

Juliana blew out a long breath. *We've got to concentrate,* her little voice said. *If we keep crying we'll never get done.*

"I know," she whispered as she stiffened her back, lifted her chin and held the camera steady to snap a photo. Then she heard a sound.

Was that a leather shoe scraping on the marble floor? It had come from beyond her dad's office, from the west, the direction of the parking garage.

She held her breath, waiting for the second step, but it didn't come. Just about the time she'd decided her imagination was playing tricks on her, a solid echoing thump reverberated through the empty darkness, like the slamming of a door.

Her heart pounded in her throat and Dawson's voice echoed in her head.

If you want to be a private eye, you can't let every little noise spook you. Use sound to evaluate your enemy.

She forced herself to think rationally, like Dawson would. A shoe scraping, a door slamming. If that were even what the sounds were, they'd probably been made by some homeless guy. The door had sounded like one of the heavy metal ones that led to the parking garage.

She raised the camera and clicked off one, two, three shots of the Sky Walk. She aimed higher, to the rods that had held it suspended above the casino. Then she carefully maneuvered closer, wanting to include the wreckage of her dad's office in the next shot.

Another sound. This time from the other direction, to the east. She froze, listening, replaying the sound in her head. After a couple of seemingly endless seconds, she figured out what it was. The smooth glide of the glass door at the front entrance. Someone had come inside. Maybe a security guard or the police.

Her first thought was to hide. She could duck behind something and wait until he left. But cowering behind a slot machine or under a blackjack table like a child while the officer shone his light in her face didn't appeal to her. No, she'd face him like a man—a *woman*.

She couldn't see the main entrance from where she stood. She debated heading back that way—toward the sound. But she decided to wait, to see if she heard anything else. She listened, but the cavernous casino was quiet—eerily quiet.

What if it wasn't a guard or a cop? What if someone had followed her here? The same person who'd attacked her at the post office maybe?

She reached for her weapon. Slipping her left arm out of the sling, she used it to steady her right hand. And waited.

Suddenly she heard noises everywhere. From behind her, something scraped. She half turned. Was that another footstep or just a falling bit of debris? A creak echoed over her head. She winced and suppressed the instinctive urge to cower as she thought about the tons of steel above her that hadn't yet fallen.

Then she heard the unmistakable squeak of a sneaker. She whirled, aiming in the direction of the noise. Her heart thudded painfully in her tight chest, this time with fear.

The footsteps were soft, but the sneakers occasionally screeched as they scraped on the marble. Not a cop. Not anyone official.

She didn't move, hardly dared to breathe as she counted, measuring the length of time between steps. The stride told her it was a man, a tall man—a confident, careful man.

The closer he came, the faster her heart pounded. The barrel of the gun wavered visibly in her shaking hands.

If we want to be a private eye, her little voice said, *we can't give in to fear. We need to use the adrenaline to clear our heads.*

"So now you're the expert?" she muttered, then took a deep breath and thumbed the safety off.

The click cracked through the air like a gunshot. The steps paused. Juliana's fingers tightened around the grip.

Don't make me shoot, she begged.

Give me the courage to pull the trigger, she prayed.

Then he, whoever he was, started walking again. A figure came into view, walking with a steady gait. Juliana's mouth went dry.

Backlit by the sunlight through the doors, he was a large, looming silhouette. He spotted her and stopped.

Fight-or-flight response sparked inside her like dozens of matches striking at once. Her finger tightened on the trigger. She gasped for breath. She widened her stance, balancing her weight on the balls of her feet, and aimed at the silhouette.

He started forward again.

"Hold it," she commanded, dismayed at the breathlessness in her voice. "Don't take another step or I'll shoot."

"Son of a bitch, rookie!" a disgustingly familiar voice snapped as long, leanly muscled arms rose. "I thought you had better sense."

Juliana ground her teeth together. It was Dawson. The blood surging through her now carried aggression, not fear. She spoke tersely. "What are *you* doing here?"

"What am I—" Dawson laughed harshly.

The sound shredded her raw nerves.

"Trying to keep your butt alive," he snapped, walking up to her and pushing the barrel of the gun away from his midsection. "Somebody ought to take that thing away from you—permanently."

She could see his face in the glow from the thousands of minilights. His brows were drawn down into a dangerous scowl, made more terrifying by the sharp shadows the tiny lights cast.

"I have a carry permit," she said, hating the lame whine in her voice.

"Now I feel better," he scoffed. "Put the damn thing away, and don't forget to put the safety on or you'll shoot your own butt off."

She meekly flipped on the safety and holstered her gun. "You followed me," she snapped accusingly, while at the same time feeling her face heat up. She should have noticed a car following the taxi.

In fact, she should have paid attention yesterday when he just happened to walk by in time to rescue her groceries. She hadn't even thought about checking out his vehicle. Damn it, she deserved to be called a rookie.

"Yeah, I did. If you want to be a private eye, you need to be able to spot a tail—and lose it."

"What did you do, stake out my apartment?"

"What if it hadn't been me? What if the guy who attacked you had walked in here instead? Did you really think you were going to shoot somebody?"

Embarrassed that he'd sneaked up on her, she snapped, "I was prepared to defend myself. I have that right."

"Not so much when you're the one trespassing," he pointed out. He grabbed her elbow. "Come on, I'm getting you out of here before somebody calls the police."

She jerked away. "No! I have to—" She stopped. "No. I'm fine."

"Still don't trust me, do you?" he said drily. "What did I tell you? If you want to be a private eye, you've got to learn to judge character."

"I'm a good judge of character," she snapped. "I just haven't seen anything to convince me that you're trustworthy."

His mouth tightened. "I gave you that information about the forensic engineer."

"Oh, please," she said. "Like I didn't already know it was going to take time to get that report back."

He gazed at her narrowly. "You didn't know about the preliminary findings."

He was right. Still, that didn't mean he could be trusted.

"What possessed you to come here anyway?" he asked. "What do you think you're going to find that the police haven't?"

"That's not why I'm here. The newspaper said they're going to start demolition Monday. I wanted to look around his office. There are some things of his that I haven't been able to find."

"It's still a crime scene. That's what the bright yellow tape outside means." He gave her a pensive look. "Speaking of which, did you turn on the electricity?"

"The electronic doors worked. I turned on the main casino and office lights. Nobody ever asked me for Daddy's keys."

Dawson nodded. "You should have locked the doors behind you."

"That's true. It would have kept you out." She turned and walked gingerly toward the office. Despite the cleanup, the floor was still littered with glass and chunks of drywall. The massive mahogany desk that sat in the middle of the room had been cracked in the middle, its polished surface scarred and covered with dust. Juliana brushed against a board and felt a nail scrape her calf. Thank goodness she'd worn jeans.

Dawson followed her, taking in the scene. "Look," he said. "That supply closet is still intact."

"Daddy was standing over there," she said, pointing directly opposite the closet. A few of the flat-screen security monitors still lay on the floor. They were smashed beyond repair. "The police told me he must have been looking at them…" Her voice gave out.

"Wow," Dawson whispered. He was craning his neck to follow the mess of steel and chrome that had formed the structure of the Sky Walk. "Look at how the metal is bent back on itself. They must have brought in a couple of Jaws of Life."

Juliana's heart lurched painfully and she squeezed her eyes shut for a moment. "Three," she said, her voice breaking. "The police told me."

"Sorry," Dawson muttered.

Her throat tightened and a small, strangled moan escaped. Dawson's hand squeezed her shoulder. Warmth seeped through her shirt to her skin and flowed all the way through her, warming places inside her that had been cold ever since her dad had died. Tears began to build again.

"Let's go," he said. "Let's get out of here. The police probably have all of your dad's things. I'll take you by the police station."

"No," she said. "I want to look for myself. They might have missed something." She turned to the broken desk, working to suppress the thought of how much more vulnerable a human body was than wood. She picked her way behind it. The large file drawers were on the floor, in pieces.

"Jules, don't do that."

She ignored him, retrieving her flashlight and bending to shine it inside and under the desk. "There's a folder and some papers back there. They must have been stuck behind the drawer."

She reached her right arm in, but the desk was too deep.

"Get out of the way," Dawson said. He took the flashlight from her, gauged the position of the papers, then reached in. He pulled out a torn hanging file folder with a few sheets of paper inside it.

Juliana wanted to sit down and go through them, but Dawson was right. They needed to get out of here. So she stuffed them into her purse.

Turning back to the desk, she tugged on the middle drawer, which was a quarter of the way open, but it wouldn't budge. "Can you get this drawer out for me?" she asked Dawson as he got to his feet.

"Watch out," he said. He pulled on the drawer. It barely gave, so he jerked it. With a loud shriek of wood against wood, it slid halfway and something flew out. Just as the noise faded, a metallic clunk echoed above their heads.

Dawson froze for a few fractions of a second.

"What—" Juliana started.

"Shh." He held up a hand, listening.

Juliana heard a quiet squeak, but that was all. Even though Dawson stood still listening for another few seconds, Juliana didn't hear anything else.

"Something's going on up there," he said grimly. "That's the second time I've heard that."

Juliana looked up. "What do you mean?"

He shrugged. "I don't know, but there's a reason the crime scene tape is still up and they're planning to demo the whole thing. It's dangerous in here."

Juliana was searching around on the floor for whatever had fallen out of the drawer. "Look," she said, picking up a familiar oblong box. "I knew this pen set was here somewhere. I gave it to him." She looked at the initials she'd had engraved into the metal.

"What else is in there?" she muttered, feeling around in

the back of the drawer. She touched something that felt like smooth leather. When she pulled it out she saw that it was a pocket-size photo album she'd given him when she was in high school. She'd had it engraved with his initials. She touched the gold letters and felt tears start in her eyes. Blinking them away, she opened it. The first picture was her school portrait from her sophomore year in high school. She remembered deciding to stop wearing her hair that way as soon as she saw the proofs.

The next one was a picture of her at around age six, judging by her gap-toothed grin. She tried to swallow the anguished moan that rose to her lips, but it slipped out.

Dawson took the album from her and stuffed it into her bag. "You can look at that later," he muttered.

She blinked and looked back at the drawer. She reached inside it and felt all the way to the back. Her fingers touched another smooth rectangle. It was her dad's day planner. He'd always carried one. When she was little, he'd let her doodle on the blank pages in the back. This one had sticky notes tucked inside the back cover, all covered with her dad's handwriting.

"Oh," she whispered wistfully. He'd always used sticky notes to jot down information about his employees. She'd asked him once why he didn't just put the information in his day planner.

These are incidents in an employee's day, he'd told her. *What if he is having a bad day, and by tomorrow he's performing like a pro? Or on the other hand, what if a great employee suddenly changes—becomes surly or lackadaisical?*

Dawson looked up. "What's all that?" he asked.

"Daddy's day planner for this year."

Dawson took it and stuffed it into her bag. "That'll wait until later, too. Ready to go?"

"No," she said as she felt around one last time. Just as she'd decided the drawer was empty, she touched something cold and hard. She pulled it out.

"Oh," she whispered. "It's his wedding ring. I wondered where it was." She slipped the ring onto her thumb and then her middle finger but it was too large. The wedding ring was the last straw. The tears were suddenly falling faster than she could dash them away, her throat ached with grief and she felt sobs gathering in her chest.

She clenched her fist around the ring and lifted her chin. She knew what Dawson was thinking. *P.I.s don't cry.* Well, that was tough. She wasn't a P.I. yet. She was just what he'd called her—a rookie.

Chapter Six

Juliana dashed tears away and waited for Dawson's sarcastic jab. But instead, he laid his hand on her shoulder again, spreading his comforting warmth.

She wanted to act professional, like a private investigator would, but this was where her dad had died. She ducked her head as Dawson took her in his arms.

He didn't say anything. He just held her comfortingly. He rubbed her back, moving his gentle hand up and down, up and down.

As her sobs began to fade, Dawson's hand moved downward, toward the small of her back and the pressure changed. Not much. Hardly enough to notice, but definitely different.

His touch was no longer comforting, she realized. In fact, it was becoming noticeably sensual. His other hand, which had cradled the back of her head, now slid down to the nape of her neck and his thumb lightly caressed the curve of her jaw.

She pulled back slightly and looked up at him. His gaze was soft. A tiny smile, not sarcastic at all, curved his lips.

"How're you doing?" he whispered. His fingers slid across her skin until they rested against the side of her neck and his thumb grazed her lower lip. That unconsciously erotic gesture stoked an awareness deep within her. She felt her body softening, changing. The awareness became a disturbingly sweet heat. She knew what he was about to do and she felt no compulsion to stop him. She was hurting and his touch was dissolving the pain.

She lifted her head and her gaze drifted downward to his mouth. He had a nice mouth, wide and straight. It could set firmly or curve sarcastically, but right now it was soft, like his eyes.

He bent his head. His thumb moved to her chin and pressed gently, urging her head to tilt a fraction higher. Then his lips brushed hers. Matches struck and flared inside her again. But this rush was neither flight or fight. It was desire.

He pulled her closer, molded her body to his as his mouth met hers. Her mouth softened and she parted her lips. She felt the whisper of his breath as he gasped. Then he deepened the kiss, and swept her away from the harsh reality of her dad's death and her single-minded search for an explanation. She was helpless against the confusing mix of feelings gushing through her.

Dawson had done his best not to give in to the hunger that gripped him every time he touched Juliana—hell, every time he laid eyes on her. But he was a sucker for tears, like his dad. That thought nearly killed the desire, but just then her mouth moved sensuously and her tongue touched his and his rational thoughts scattered like shards of an exploding lightbulb.

His libido urged him to lay her down right here in the dust and debris, but his brain warned him of the sheer stupidity of letting his desire do the thinking.

Placing a hand on either side of her head, he drew back and gazed down at her. He ran his thumb lightly along the fading bruise on her cheek and she blinked and stared up at him. Her eyes were so dark. They absorbed the light like black velvet. He kissed the corners of her eyelids where tears still clung and tasted salt.

"We should—" he started, but a loud metallic screech

drowned out his words. Without stopping to think, he grabbed Juliana and dove through the open closet door. He twisted in midair, trying to take the brunt of the impact. His shoulder slammed against the floor.

A deafening crash shook the walls and sent splinters, debris and dust flying. Dawson hunched his shoulders and rolled, putting his back to the destruction. He wrapped his arms around her head and ducked his.

He waited until the last echoing thump died down and the walls stopped quivering before lifting his head and opening his eyes. He looked down at her. He didn't dare move until he was sure she was okay.

She was stiff as a board, her face buried in his shirt. Despite her rigidity, he could feel the fine trembling of her limbs and the hitch in her breathing.

"Jules?" he whispered anxiously.

Her body jerked and she slowly lifted her head. Her eyelids twitched, then fluttered. Relief gushed through him.

"Dawson?" she whispered as she opened her eyes, then blinked. "What happened?"

"Are you okay?" he asked. "Can you move?"

She closed her eyes and gingerly tested her arms and legs. "Ow," she said. "My shoulder hurts, but I think that's all."

He sat up carefully.

"What happened?" she asked, then, "Oh, my God!"

Dawson looked over his shoulder and saw the source of the crash. A two-foot-wide metal I beam lay across what was left of the mahogany desk. Where before it had been broken in two, now it was smashed flat.

"We were—" Juliana gasped.

"Standing right there," he said grimly. He craned his neck and looked up. He knew from the architect drawings his dad had given him that the main floor of the casino with its three-story-high glass-domed roof was flanked on three sides by restaurants, guest rooms, offices and conference rooms and on the fourth side by the enclosed parking garage. The Sky Walk had arced over the main floor, suspended from the grid of beams just like the one in front of them.

He pushed himself to his feet and carefully approached the I beam. It lay parallel to the closet. He shuddered involuntarily as he measured its length with his eyes. If it had swung ninety degrees before crashing, he and Juliana would be dead.

What the hell had made it fall? Pulling out his key ring, he shone his laser light along the metal surface. He leaned in and there it was. What he saw took his breath away.

"Son of a—" He tensed. Instinctively, he held his breath and listened, rocking to the balls of his feet.

His first impulse was to race out and chase down the man who'd sent the beam crashing down on them, but it had been at least twenty seconds, probably thirty, since the beam had fallen. Whoever did it had a half minute's head start. Besides, he couldn't leave Juliana here alone.

He pulled his phone from his pocket to call 9-1-1, but there was no signal.

Behind him, Juliana groaned as she got to her feet. She stepped up close to him and placed her hand on his arm. "Oh, my God, we could have been killed," she whispered.

He didn't answer.

"Dawson, look at those bolts." She pointed. "Shine the light there."

He knew what she'd seen—the same thing he had.

"They've been cut," she gasped.

"Yeah," he said. "Come on, we need to get out of here." He put his hand on the small of her back.

She didn't budge. "I want to get a picture of that."

"Jules, the guy who did this is probably long gone, but I'm not willing to bet our lives on it. We need to be outside." He showed her his phone. "I tried to call the police, but I can't get a signal in here."

"Okay. Just a minute." Juliana was digging in her bag for her camera.

Dawson didn't object. He wanted photos of the beam as badly as she did. Not only to study, but also to show his dad. He figured the cuts had been made by bolt cutters, but he wanted his dad's opinion. Plus, he liked the idea of having proof, if they had been cut.

After she'd snapped several shots, Dawson touched her arm. "Let's go. Now!"

They picked their way past the beam and out onto the main floor of the casino, then headed for the main entrance. Dawson heard the sound of the doors gliding open. Then suddenly, there were two uniformed officers with guns and bright flashlights raised.

"Don't move," the lead officer shouted. "Get your hands up. Higher. Above your heads."

"She can't—" Dawson started, but the officer cut him off.

"Shut up and get those hands up," he shouted. "You, ma'am, take your arm out of that sling."

Juliana glanced toward Dawson, but he didn't want to do anything to antagonize the officers. He nodded.

She eased her arm out of the sling and raised it until her hand was level with her shoulder. He heard her muffled moan.

The officer was apparently satisfied. "Now walk over here. Slowly. And keep those hands up."

A second officer held his gun on Juliana while the first one covered Dawson.

"Who else is in here?" he demanded.

"No one." Dawson knew he wouldn't get anywhere trying to explain what they were doing here until the officers had disarmed them and gotten them out of the building.

The lead officer spoke into his shoulder mic. "I have two intruders at the Golden Galaxy Casino. Meeker and I will walk them out. Have the car ready to take them in for questioning. Send Stewart and Simon to clear the building."

Meeker gestured with his gun for them to pass him and take the lead. "Let's go," he said. "Keep those hands up. Either one of you makes a sudden move and I will shoot you."

JULIANA SAT IN the interrogation room of the Waveland, Mississippi, Police Department, trying not to look at the one-way mirror that covered the upper half of one wall. She'd been fidgeting for over an hour, imagining detectives and assistant district attorneys standing on the other side of the glass, watching her.

Instead, she concentrated on identifying the dingy color on the walls. Did they paint the walls such a vomit-green on purpose? Because between the wall color and the creepy mirror, she was almost ready to confess to anything just to get out of there.

The door opened and a young officer brought in a paper bag from a fast-food restaurant. "Hope you're not a vegetarian," he said with a smile. Juliana managed to get down about half a hamburger and was drinking the watery cola when the door opened again.

A medium-height, pleasant-looking man came in. He looked tired as he sat down and took a small pad out of his inside coat pocket. He had a pen in his hand and he clicked it as he flipped pages.

"I'm Detective Brian Hardy," he said. "You're—"

As soon as she heard his voice, she recognized him. "Juliana Caprese, but you already know that."

He nodded. "I spoke with you on June 20, the day your dad was killed."

She nodded. "You were very nice."

The look he gave her told her he wasn't in the mood to be nice today. He clasped his hands on the table. "Ms. Caprese, what were you doing at the Golden Galaxy?"

Just like the day of her dad's death, he got straight to the point. She felt her face heat up. "I'd rather not say," she said.

Hardy's eyebrows shot up. "Well, I'm afraid you don't have that option. We've looked at the contents of your purse—"

She frowned in surprise. "You can do that?"

Hardy's mouth turned up. "We had probable cause, considering that you were trespassing at an active crime scene. And considering that we found items taken from there—" Hardy flipped more pages. "Specifically an album, a day planner and a hanging file folder."

"How do you—" She clamped her mouth shut, but Hardy grinned.

"How do I know those were the items you took? Okay, well, they appeared to belong to your father." He held up his index finger. "They were in your purse." He held up a second finger. "And they were smeared with drywall dust. Now, I'm going to ask you one more time. What were you doing there?"

Juliana sighed. "I heard that demolition was going to begin Monday. I wanted to see if the police—if you had left any of my father's things there." She shrugged and spread her hands. "I wanted them. I'm sure you saw that the album has pictures in it, and the day planner—it's his writing, his notes and thoughts and the things that made up his day."

Hardy was watching her closely. "So CSI missed those items and you found them."

"I'm his daughter," she said, tears welling in her eyes. "Why are you wasting time with me? Why aren't you finding out who was responsible for his death?"

"We are. In fact, I need to ask you about what happened while you were in the casino."

"You've got the statement I wrote," Juliana said. "Everything that happened is in there." She assessed him. "Did you look at that beam? The bolts were cut. It was obvious. I took photos of the bolts. For evidence. My camera's in my purse."

Hardy's mouth turned up again. "As it happens, our CSI team is taking photos, too. We'll be investigating what happened to cause that beam to fall. Were you aware that you were being followed?"

"Followed?" She figured he wasn't talking about Dawson. "You mean the person who dropped the beam on us? No. Dawson would have known. He'd have told me." Speaking of Dawson, where was he? She glanced toward the door, then back at Detective Hardy. Just as she was about to ask, Hardy spoke.

"What happened to your arm? And your face?" he asked.

She touched her cheek. "I fell," she said shortly.

"You fell," he repeated, raising his brows. "That must have been some fall. What happened?"

Juliana didn't want to tell the detective about her attack. She was afraid he'd order her to stop her investigation, and she wasn't about to do that. "It was an accident," she said, hoping she sounded convincing. "I tripped and fell down the stairs."

"Hmm," Hardy said.

He didn't believe her. She lifted her chin. "I hit my shoulder."

"Juliana, why would someone want to harm you?"

She swallowed and shook her head. "Maybe someone thinks I know who was responsible for the Sky Walk collapsing."

"Do you?"

She hesitated an instant too long and saw Hardy's eyes narrow. "No. How would I know?"

"Now that's a very good question. I'm still interested in how you found those items after CSI missed them."

"It wasn't that hard, Detective. They were in the back of the desk drawer. I found them because I knew they had to be there."

"And the keys to the casino doors and the electrical closet? Where did you just know they had to be?"

Juliana dropped her gaze to her hands. "The doors opened automatically."

"Are you aware that it is a crime to withhold evidence?"

She nodded.

"Well, since these items aren't related to the investigation, we're going to release them to you. But tell me, is there anything else of your father's I should know about?" he asked.

She sent the detective a narrow gaze. "No." She took a deep breath. "Am I going to be charged with something?"

Hardy rose, and his chair screeched on the floor. "Not this time. But Juliana, don't go back there. If you do and you make it out alive, I *will* put you in jail."

Chapter Seven

Dawson shook Detective Hardy's hand. "Thanks, Brian," he said. "I appreciate your helping me out with this."

Hardy gave him a sour look. "I don't like it."

Dawson understood. Detective Brian Hardy had been in Vice when Dawson's dad was indicted eight years ago. It was Hardy's dogged determination that had finally convinced Michael to accept a plea bargain for three years in prison rather than go to trial and risk a much longer sentence.

"Well, you're the one who told me I could call on you any time if I needed a favor."

"I was thinking more along the lines of helping you with a criminal case, not hiding your identity from a beautiful woman whose father just died. I don't like lying to her."

"It's not lying exactly."

"Lying by omission is still lying," Hardy said. "I had to sit there in front of her and deliberately not talk about you. Several times I was sure she was going to ask me why I hadn't mentioned you."

"It's your own fault. If y'all won't put her in protective custody, I'm the only one who can protect her."

"So protect her. I can't do anything until I get confirmation from the Forensics team that the I beam's bolts were cut."

"That beam didn't fall on its own. And before you say

anything, I know she was followed." Dawson grimaced. "I didn't spot the tail."

Hardy assessed him. "Yeah, when I asked her if she knew she'd been followed, she said no. Said you'd have spotted the tail and told her. Are you sure this case isn't getting a little personal for you?"

"Sure it's personal. My dad's under investigation."

"Right. That's not exactly what I'm talking about."

"She's in danger. You saw how banged up she is. She was attacked and a letter was stolen from her."

"She said she tripped on the stairs."

Dawson couldn't suppress a smile. "Well, technically that's true, but as an eyewitness to her fall, I can testify that she had the bruises, the sling and a banged-up knee prior to falling down two steps."

Hardy narrowed his gaze at Dawson. "Tell me about the letter."

Dawson clenched his jaw. Maybe he shouldn't have mentioned it. "She put an ad in the paper."

"That ad was hers? The ten-thousand-dollar reward?"

"I'm surprised you hadn't already figured that out."

"Nope. I was going to put a guy on it, but I had to pull him to work another homicide." He paused for a beat. "What's her angle?"

Dawson rubbed his hand across the back of his neck. He wasn't sure how much he wanted to tell Brian. He sure didn't want him sniffing around his dad's heels again. "I'm in a bind here. She's beginning to trust me. If she finds out I'm a Delancey, she won't let me near her." Dawson shook his head. "I can't let that happen."

"And why is that?"

Dawson almost growled in frustration. Hardy knew the answer to that. He was just giving him a hard time.

"She's out to prove that someone is responsible for the Sky Walk falling. She wants justice for her father's death."

"Let me guess. She thinks it was your dad."

Dawson nodded. "That's right. She's convinced that he skimped on the Sky Walk to make a bigger profit."

"Well, she can join the club. A lot of people think that."

"Including you?"

"I believe in innocent until proven guilty," Hardy hedged, eyeing him closely. "What do you think?"

"I don't know." Dawson heard the defeat and doubt in his voice. "I don't think so."

"You were convinced your dad was guilty eight years ago."

"Yeah, I was a lot younger and I was tired of working for him." Dawson paused for a beat. Then he shrugged. "I have the resources now to do my own investigation. I need to know the truth about my dad. And Juliana has information that I need."

"And that's the only reason you're so hell-bent on sticking to her?" Hardy didn't sound convinced.

Dawson shook his head. "Look at her. She's going to get herself killed. I'll tell you this," he said, lifting a finger toward Hardy. "My dad didn't have her assaulted and he didn't drop that beam."

Hardy scowled. "I told you, even if there is proof that the beam's bolts were cut, I don't have the resources to keep her under guard."

"Which is why I need you to keep my real name out of this. Luckily, I didn't know any of the officers at the scene."

Hardy nodded reluctantly. "Well, they're searching the casino and gathering evidence. I'll let you know if they turn up anything."

"Thanks, Brian." Dawson looked past him toward the interrogation rooms. "When are you going to be finished with her?"

"She should be signing her transcribed statement now. She'll be out any second."

"Mind if I make a phone call?"

"Nope."

Dawson pressed a speed-dial button on his phone and walked a few steps away from Detective Hardy. "Mack, anything on what I gave you to work on last night?" He was being vague deliberately. He didn't want anybody at the police station to pay attention to what he said.

"So I take it you can't talk freely," Mack said. "I got through to the secretary to one of the vice presidents. She's single."

"That's the information you have for me. She's single?" Dawson smiled. Typical Mack.

"There's a method here. I'm thinking I'd have better luck if I went there in person. You know I work best face-to-face."

Dawson chuckled. He definitely knew that. Mack could charm the hairpins out of a spinster's French twist without touching the pins or the spinster. "It's Friday."

"No problem. I've already hinted that I'd like to buy her dinner if she's not busy. And maybe go skiing Sunday."

"I wasn't going to spend that much—" Dawson started when he saw Juliana out of the corner of his eye. She looked tired and sad and bewildered. An odd feeling settled in the middle of his chest. He rubbed it absently.

"What the hell," he continued. "Go ahead, but you'd better pack plenty of charm because I want proof of a connection. Got it?"

"Sure, boss."

Dawson sighed. He had three investigators on his payroll. Two were exceptional. But they ate MacEllis Griffin's dust.

If anyone could connect Tito Vega with Bayside Industries, it was Mack. The question that Dawson couldn't answer was, would that connection help either Juliana or him accomplish their goals? He sure hoped so.

While he talked with Mack, a policewoman had given Juliana a clipboard to sign, then handed over her purse.

She looked around. Her gaze landed on him.

He let his mouth curve slightly in a smile. She didn't smile back. She put the bag over her shoulder and strode toward him. The dust on her jeans and the smudges on her face enhanced, rather than detracted from, the dignified tilt of her head.

She walked straight up to Hardy. "Am I free to go now?" she asked icily.

"For now," Hardy said. "But don't leave town, and remember what I said. I *will* toss you in jail."

She turned to Dawson. "Are you ready?"

"Yes, ma'am," he replied, lifting his hand in a mock salute.

BY THE TIME JULIANA climbed into Dawson's car and glanced at the dashboard clock, it was almost seven o'clock. "I'm so tired. I'm ready to get home and take a shower and go to bed."

Dawson didn't say anything. He just drove.

"Why didn't you tell me my taxi was followed to the casino?" she asked after a couple of minutes of silence.

He glanced at her sidelong. "Because I didn't know."

"I thought you said a private investigator—"

"I missed him, okay? And yes, that kind of mistake can get the client killed." He lifted his chin. "I'm sorry."

"I wasn't after an apology—"

"You deserve one for that. I could have stopped him from nearly killing you."

"Us," she amended, then fell silent. After a couple of minutes, she saw that he wasn't headed toward her apartment.

"Where are we going?" she asked. "I don't feel like—"

"Post office," he told her. "I want to check that box. You've got the key, don't you?"

"Yes." She looked at him. He was driving with one hand on the wheel. He looked relaxed, in total contrast to how she felt. She was dirty, tired, on edge and irritable.

"Aren't you tired?" she asked grumpily.

"I guess," he said. "I know I'm hungry."

"I was hungry several hours ago," she replied. "Now I just feel queasy and exhausted. Where did they keep you?"

He glanced at her sidelong. "Keep me?"

"Were you in an interrogation room, too? That had to be the most depressing room I've ever been in." She shuddered. "I almost confessed just to get out of there."

"Confessed?" Dawson said with a chuckle. "To what?"

"Anything. Everything."

Dawson pulled up to the curb of the post office where she'd rented the box. As he killed the engine, she reached into her bag and pulled out her keys. "I'll be right back," she said, reaching for the door, but Dawson caught her hand and took the keys from her.

"You're not going in there. I'll check the box. Number 7874, right?"

"You think that guy's watching?"

"I just don't want to take any chances." Dawson got out of the car and locked the doors, then disappeared into the building. Within a few seconds he was back out.

"Nothing?" she asked.

"Oh, yeah, there was something," he said, handing her keys back to her. He cranked the car and pulled away.

"What? Another letter?"

"Yep," he said noncommittally.

"Well? Give it to me," Juliana said. "I want to read it. Did you open it?"

He shook his head. "No. It's a federal offense to open someone else's mail."

She laughed nervously. "Let me have it." She reached over and patted his right coat pocket. "Where is it?"

"Stop that," he said, frowning. "I'm trying to drive."

"Then give me the letter."

"We'll look at it together," he said, sending her a quelling glance, "when we get home."

Dawson walked her to her door, still uncharacteristically silent. Once they were inside, she turned to him.

"Let me have my letter."

He shook his head.

"Dawson, isn't withholding mail a federal offense, too?"

"Get some things together. You're going to stay at my apartment for a few days."

"No, I'm not," she said. That would be a bad idea for several reasons.

"Look, Jules," he said, catching her arm. "I asked the detective to put you into protective custody until they could figure out who dropped that beam on our heads, but he said he doesn't have the manpower to guard you. So until they catch the guy, you're staying with me."

"I don't want to stay with you," she protested. "Does this have something to do with that letter?"

"No. Now come on." He stalked past her to the coffee table and picked up the file folders stacked there. "Get some clothes or don't, but you are coming with me."

"Put those down." She glared at him, but he was walking to the door. "Those are mine. You can't—"

"I'll just put them in the car."

"No, wait." She could tell by the look on his face that he was not bluffing. She couldn't let him walk out with her research. Every bit of evidence she had that the Sky Walk was defective was in those folders. Plus, he was holding hostage a response to her ad.

Her little voice protested. *We can't trust him, remember? And we are not capable of rational thought when he gets too close. Are we sure we want to sleep under the same roof?*

We don't know, she answered silently. Then out loud to Dawson, "Please just wait right there. I'll get some clothes."

Within ten minutes, when she came out of her bedroom with a weekender bag, Dawson was still standing at the door with the folders cradled in one arm, looking bored.

"Okay," she said. "I'm ready, but this is only for a day or two, right?"

"We'll see."

She glared at him. "You are such a bully. You think you're always right, so you don't even have to explain yourself. I'm going with you, but only because there's no way I'm letting you steal my research."

"I understand," he said solemnly, but she saw a twinkle in his eye.

She stormed past him, pulling the wheeled bag behind her, and threw the door open. "Bully," she said as she jerked the bag over the threshold.

DAWSON DROVE TO HIS CONDO in silence. Juliana sat in the passenger seat, her arms filled with her precious folders. She wasn't talking, which was fine with him. He had some thinking to do.

The letter he'd pulled from her post office box was burning a hole in the breast pocket of his jacket. The precise, architectural lettering on the envelope was branded on his inner vision. Except for the bars on the *A,* the *H* and the *T,* the words could have been written by any architect in the country. But those crossbars were unique. They slanted upward with a slight curve at the top edge. The envelope in his pocket had been addressed by Michael Delancey, his dad.

What the hell are you doing, Dad? His fist clenched on the steering wheel. He clamped his jaw, quelling the urge to slap the wheel with the heel of his palm.

He turned into the condos and drove around to his unit, opened the garage door, pulled inside and killed the engine.

"Here we are," he said, looking at her armful of folders. "I guess I'll get your bag."

"Fine," she snapped. She shifted the folders into her left arm and reached for the door handle, wincing.

"Hang on," he said on a sigh. He climbed out of the driver's side and went around and opened the door for her. "Can you climb the stairs with that armload?" he asked wryly.

"Yes."

"Good." He pulled her weekender bag out of the backseat and carried it up the stairs that led to his condo. "Come on, let's get cleaned up."

In the kitchen, he shrugged out of his jacket, then pointed toward the hall. "The bathroom is the first door on the right. The guest bedroom is the second. The second door on the left is my room."

She looked at him suspiciously, then headed down the hall, still carrying the folders. He followed with her bag.

"Here you go," he said. "Sorry I don't have a lock for the door."

Glaring at him, she set the folders down on the bed and set her bag down beside them. "Thank you," she said dismissively.

He smiled and backed out of the room. In his bedroom, he shed his own dirty clothes and tossed them onto the floor of the closet.

He heard the bathroom door close and not much later, the shower come on. The vision of Juliana in his shower, naked, using his soap and shampoo, rose before his eyes and he almost gasped as his body reacted immediately and powerfully.

For a few seconds, he closed his eyes and enjoyed that vision. Then he thought about the letter and the erotic daydream died instantly.

He glanced around for a second before he remembered he'd hung his jacket on a chair in the kitchen, like he usually did. The letter was in the pocket.

He opened the door to the hall and listened. The shower was still running. So he dashed up the hall in nothing but boxer shorts and grabbed the jacket. As he did he heard the water go off.

Damn it. He jogged toward his bedroom, figuring she still had to dry off and do stuff to her hair and whatever else women did. But as he passed the bathroom door, it opened and he was cloaked in a cloud of warm steam.

Juliana almost ran into him. "Oh," she said.

He put out a hand to steady her, but she stopped in time.

"What? You're na—" She gulped.

"Yeah," he said, giving her an apologetic shrug. "Sorry." He tried—he really tried—not to notice that she'd belted his terry cloth so tightly that it gaped at the neck. He tried not to look at the stunning view of her damp chest or the tops of her shapely breasts. He dragged his gaze away and looked down.

His turn to gulp. He saw her pink-tipped toes. *Toes.* Pretty sexy toes. A surge of desire nearly knocked him to his knees.

She pulled the collar of the robe together and took a step backward. When he met her gaze, her face and neck turned pink.

"I'll—just—you know, take my shower now," he said, swallowing hard. In about one second he was going to embarrass himself. He held the jacket in front of him as he stepped around her.

"Do you want your robe?"

Yes, his body screamed. *No!* his rational brain interrupted. Without turning around, he shook his head and jerked his thumb toward his room. "I'll get— I'll—manage."

"Please do. Meanwhile, I'm going to drink a gallon of water," she said and turned toward the kitchen.

Relieved that she had her back to him, he ducked into his room. For an instant, he looked at his jacket. Did he dare open the letter? No, not if he wanted her to trust him.

Grabbing a T-shirt and a pair of jeans and fresh underwear, he ducked across the hall into the bathroom and closed the door. It was still steamy from her shower. He climbed into the stall and stood there, letting the wet heat soak into his skin for a minute as his brain taunted him with visions of her.

These visions involved wet, slick, shiny skin and his robe, but instead of being pulled tight around her, it was hanging from her shoulders. Her ripe-peach skin was radiant in contrast to the white cloth.

He took a long shuddering breath, then grimaced and turned on the cold water.

Chapter Eight

When Juliana set her water glass down, it rattled and almost turned over. She was *not* shivering with reaction from seeing Dawson ninety-percent naked. Because those boxers couldn't have covered more than ten percent of his body—his gorgeous naked body.

She'd been shocked when she'd opened the bathroom door and nearly run into him, but not too shocked that her body didn't react. It had taken all her willpower to keep from splaying her fingers across his broad chest.

Thank goodness she'd instinctively stepped backward, away from his hand, because if he'd touched her right then, she might have dropped the robe and her inhibitions onto the hall floor.

The vision of the two of them intertwined, their bodies glistening with steam, rose up before her eyes and a thrill rippled through her, centering itself in her core.

Dawson was strong and smart and protective—everything a girl could ever want, all rolled up into one gorgeous sexy package. And he was a private eye, which for her just made him sexier.

But once in a while, when he wasn't aware of her watching him, she caught a look in his eyes that she couldn't quite define. It was a hooded, shadowy look, like guilt or embarrassment—or deceit.

It worried her because like it or not, she needed him. Not only did he have resources she didn't have, but he was also definitely nice to have around to whisk her out of the way of deadly falling objects.

She just had to make sure she didn't get sidetracked by sex, that was all. At that thought, the thrill within her morphed into yearning.

"Here you are," Dawson said, startling her.

She almost didn't have the courage to turn around. The warm clean scent of hot water and soap wafted toward her. She took a deep breath to fortify herself, but all it fortified was the yearning inside her.

Please be dressed. She turned around. Relief cascaded through her. He had on worn jeans and a black New Orleans Saints T-shirt with a gold fleur-de-lis on the front. His hair was damp and brushed back from his freshly shaved face and—she gulped as she looked down.

He was barefooted.

If there was anything Juliana liked more than long sinewy bodies and beautiful hands, it was bony, sexy bare male feet peeking out from under frayed blue jeans.

"Jules?"

She blinked and looked up at him. He was smiling.

"Don't call me that," she protested weakly.

"Did you want to look at that letter?"

"Yes!" How had she forgotten about the letter? Sadly, she knew how. Because she'd been fantasizing about Dawson naked.

"Yes, definitely. Where is it?"

"It's in my jacket pocket. I'll get it." He headed back down the hall toward his room.

Juliana couldn't take her eyes off him. His skin looked golden under the hall lights. The contours of his back were elegantly masculine, following the curve of his spine down to the low-slung waistband of his jeans.

And those jeans, they cupped his butt perfectly—not too tight and not too loose. *Perfect.* When he appeared in his bedroom doorway and headed back up the hall, Juliana realized she had hardly blinked.

She cleared her throat and turned away, filling her water glass. She turned it up a little too quickly and spilled some down the front of the robe between her breasts. She shivered.

"Okay, here we are." He sat down at the kitchen table.

Juliana swiped away the droplets of water as she sat down next to him and took the letter.

She looked down at it, then up at Dawson. His gaze was on it and that odd, guilty look was shadowing his eyes again.

She slid her finger along the flap and then used two fingers to pull out the single sheet of paper. "It's copy paper. Looks like a regular sheet torn in half, then folded." She unfolded it and read the handwritten note.

YOU'RE ON THE RIGHT TRACK. VEGA'S CAPABLE OF ANYTHING. YOU'LL NEED PROOF, THOUGH. TALK TO KNOBLOCK.

"That's all it says?" Dawson asked, reaching for the paper.

"That's it." Juliana let him take it.

He stared at it for about twenty seconds, much longer than he needed to. He rubbed the paper between his fingers, held it up to the light, turned it over and looked at the back. "Do you know who Knoblock is?" he asked.

She shook her head. "I'm not sure. The name doesn't sound familiar. I was going to ask you. What about the handwriting?" she asked. "That's a peculiar printing style."

He nodded and turned the sheet back over. "Architectural printing."

"Architectural—you mean literally used by architects? Maybe it's the architect who designed the casino."

Dawson didn't answer.

"Or Michael Delancey? Wasn't he an architect before he went to prison?"

Dawson shook his head without looking up. "Good question," he said gruffly. Then he looked at his watch and stood. "I've got an appointment. If you're hungry, there's a frozen pizza in there." He gestured toward the refrigerator.

"You've got an appointment now?" Juliana asked. "But it's after eight o'clock."

"I have to go by my client's schedule." He adjusted his wristwatch.

"Is it about the Sky Walk?" she asked, frowning at him. Why did he suddenly look nervous?

"In a way. So, do you want to fix the pizza or should I bring you something back?"

She shook her head. "I'm not hungry. I ate that hamburger at the police station." She stood. "I want to go with you. I'll get dressed."

Dawson's head jerked as if she'd slapped him. "No!" he snapped, then, "No. How many times do I have to tell you I guarantee my clients' anonymity. If you want to be a private eye—"

"Yeah, yeah," she said, holding up her hands. "I get it. 'If I want to be a private eye, I need to protect my client's identity,'" she said mockingly.

Dawson shot her a look that was tinged with amusement. "That's right," he said.

"Fine. I'm exhausted anyway. I'll probably go to bed pretty soon."

He nodded. "I should be back in a couple of hours. I'll lock the door behind me. Take your cell phone with you. Don't answer the landline and don't open the door for anybody."

Apprehension sent her pulse racing. "Are you expecting someone to come to the door?" she asked.

"No, but—"

"I'll take my gun with me."

Dawson looked pained. "I'm still considering taking that thing away from you. Please try not to shoot yourself or any of my neighbors."

It wasn't until after he was gone that Juliana realized he'd taken the letter with him.

"WHAT THE HELL IS THIS?" Dawson tossed the letter toward his dad's lap. Michael Delancey caught it in midair, then set it on the table beside his chair.

He managed to look scared, desperate, guilty, embarrassed and indignant, all at the same time. "Son—"

"Don't give me excuses," Dawson snapped. "Give me answers for once. Do you have any idea what could have happened if the police had intercepted this letter?"

"The police? How would they get it? And how would they know it came from me?"

Dawson hissed. "Your prints are on file—and your DNA. Did you handle the paper with your bare hands? Did you lick the envelope to seal it?"

His dad squirmed and looked sheepish.

"What the hell did you think this would accomplish?"

Michael Delancey looked up at Dawson. "I *thought* I was giving Caprese's daughter information she might be able to use. I can't get *you* to listen to me."

Dawson paced, hoping to work off the frustration and anger he felt every time he talked to his dad these days. "All I hear is how nothing is your fault, how you've been framed." He stopped and glared at his dad. "Everybody in prison was framed."

Michael stood. He was almost as tall as Dawson and still

in pretty good shape, even though he hadn't done much since he'd gotten out of prison. "Let's go downstairs," he said. "I don't want to wake your mother."

"Right. I doubt a freight train could wake her."

Michael whirled on him, his fist raised. "You watch your mouth."

Dawson feinted and took a defensive stance, doubling his hands into fists. "What? Did I say something that isn't true?"

"You don't disrespect your mother. Not now, not ever. Do you understand?" Michael warned, advancing on him.

Dawson lifted his chin. "Disrespect goes both ways, *Dad*. You—"

"J.D.?"

He froze. So did his dad.

His mother stood in the door to the den. She was in an elegant blue satin dressing gown and her blond hair was mussed as if she'd been asleep. She held a pack of cigarettes and a jeweled lighter. Her eyes were swollen—from sleep or booze? Dawson couldn't tell.

"Mom," he said, resisting an urge to shuffle his feet like a kid.

"Edie," his dad said at the same time.

"What are you doing?" Edina Delancey asked, pushing a strand of hair back from her forehead with the hand that held the lighter.

"Just talking," Michael said. "I thought you were asleep."

She shook her head. "I couldn't sleep. I came downstairs to have a cigarette. Then I heard you two arguing." She gave Dawson an assessing glance. "Aren't you going to give me a kiss?"

Grimacing inwardly, Dawson crossed the room and bent to kiss his mother's cheek, steeling himself against the smell of gin that always clung to her like perfume.

But the only scents that hit his nose were the faint smell

of cigarette smoke and roses, which jarred him with a long-forgotten memory. Rosemary and he sitting with her on the couch while she read to them.

"I'll be downstairs," Michael said.

As his footsteps faded on the stairs, Dawson's mother touched his cheek with a trembling hand. "You shouldn't be so hard on your father, darling. He's hard enough on himself."

"How're you doing, Mom?" he asked, not wanting to get into a conversation with her about Michael.

She smiled and he saw a glint of something in her eyes that he hadn't seen in a long time. Determination. She'd started drinking heavily after his sister, Rosemary, was murdered twelve years ago. By the time Michael had gone to prison eight years ago, she'd been sober for almost a year. But Michael's sentence had been too much for her. She'd relapsed.

"One day at a time," she said, patting his cheek. "One day at a time."

Dawson smiled back at her and kissed her on the forehead before he turned to follow Michael down the stairs to the basement media room.

"J.D.—"

He turned. She'd always called him J.D. She was the only one who did. "Yeah, Mom?"

"Thank you for helping him. He had nothing to do with that tragedy. He needs you to believe in him."

Dawson clenched his jaw, but he gave his mother a small nod. "I'm going to do my best to find out the truth," he said. That was the most he could offer.

Downstairs, Michael had turned on a classical music station. He watched Dawson descend the stairs.

"Mom's sober?" Dawson asked.

Michael's mouth thinned, but he nodded. "Three weeks. She's on medication. I wish she'd quit smoking, but I guess she needs them right now."

The idea that his mom was trying to get sober planted a lump in Dawson's throat. For some reason, it upped the anger at his dad. "What she doesn't need is her husband going back to prison," he bit out.

His dad grimaced. "Son, I know you don't think much of me. I don't think much of myself sometimes, but I'm tired of trying to convince you that I didn't have anything to do with that damned Sky Walk falling."

"Who is Knoblock and why haven't I heard about him before?"

Michael sighed. "Damn it. Do you have any idea how hard it is to talk to a stubborn mule who's already made up his mind that you're guilty?"

"Do you know how hard it is to have an ex-con for a father?"

Michael's face drained of color. The two of them faced off for a brief moment, then Michael shook his head. "You should remember Knoblock. He was the concrete subcontractor on the condos."

"That was Knoblock? Thick glasses? I do remember him, barely." Dawson had worked for his dad as a framer and a roofer. By the time Michael had been indicted, Dawson had already decided that he was through with construction and his dad.

Michael nodded. "I've told you about Tito Vega, the low-life bum who got me put in prison," he said.

Dawson snorted. "Right. I know who Tito Vega is. What about him?"

"Back around the time I was bidding for the contract on the Pearl River Condominiums, I got some information from one of the building inspectors I used that Vega had another inspector in his pocket."

Dawson sat down on his dad's favorite leather couch. He absently rubbed his fingers over the worn leather on the seats.

"Come on, Dad," he said. "I've heard all this before. I've got a stack of files two feet high on Vega, but I didn't find a thing."

Michael looked at him in surprise. "You investigated Vega? For whom?"

Dawson gave him an exasperated look. "The point is, I couldn't find anything linking him to anything illegal."

"Of course you couldn't. The most you'll ever find is an op-ed piece here and there. Vega's a very smart, very careful man. And very influential. He sinks a lot of money into local politics and charities. If you've got that much information on him, you know about his real-estate business. Some of what he does is buy run-down properties, raze the buildings and put up condos or office buildings or what have you. If he has a building inspector in his pocket…" Michael spread his hands.

Dawson nodded. "So you went to the board?"

"I did what I thought was the right thing and it ended up costing me my career, my dignity and a pant load of my money." Michael wiped his face.

"The inspector who came to me knew a sucker when he saw one. He figured I'd go to the board, and he was right. He couldn't—he'd lose his job. But his real fear was Vega. He told me a few stories he'd heard." Michael shook his head. "They sounded like something out of one of Pop's stories. Threats. Dead pets. Broken legs."

Dawson stared at his dad. "How could somebody as high-profile as Vega get away with that kind of thing?" he asked.

Michael rubbed his eyes. "Pop used to say that the nation needed organized crime. He said politics and crime were like love and marriage—you know that old song. *You can't have one without the other.*"

Dawson snorted. "I'm sure that worked—for him. Come on, Dad. Talk about being in somebody's pocket, Con

Delancey was probably in the pockets of every crook in Louisiana, or vice versa."

"Your grandfather had a relationship with the top crime boss on the Gulf Coast back in the day. They were friends. They respected each other's position. Not like today. My point is that Tito Vega's got the same kind of relationship with some of the local elected officials around here. The difference is that he has no integrity. He doesn't care who he hurts. And apparently neither do the politicians."

"Integrity? Con Delancey?"

"I'm just telling you what Pop used to tell me. It was different back then. When I reported Vega for having a building inspector on his payroll, there was a big investigation, sure. But Vega managed to come out smelling like a rose." Michael paced to the sliding glass doors and back across the room to where Dawson was sitting.

"A few weeks after I won the contract for the Pearl River job, a big bald-headed goon in a thousand-dollar suit came to my office. He sat and filed his nails while he told me that I needed to hire Randall Knoblock as a subcontractor." Michael paused. "He had some kind of accent."

He looked down at Dawson. "The inspector who was in Vega's pocket was the one who reported that I'd used inferior materials on the Pearl River Condos. When the state board investigated, sure enough, the reinforced concrete on the stairs was not up to the American Concrete Institute's building code. Knoblock had disappeared, but he'd left behind files with notes that made it look like skimping on the concrete was my idea."

"And you went to prison for a crime you didn't commit," Dawson drawled. "Nice story. How come you never told me all this before?"

His dad shrugged. "You'd already tried me and found me guilty. How come you never asked me my side of it?"

Dawson didn't have an answer for that. He'd idolized his dad from the time he was old enough to understand that there was a big difference between his cousins' family and his. He and his cousin Lucas were about the same age. They and Brad Grayson, Lucas's best friend, had hung out together a lot, but not often at Lucas's house. There was always yelling and throwing things and sometimes hitting at Lucas's house.

"Whatever happened to Knoblock?"

"When I got out of prison, I had to jump through a lot of hoops, but although I couldn't get my architect's license back, I finally got my contractor license restored. I couldn't get any decent jobs, though. My reputation had been destroyed." Michael laughed harshly.

"Then an attorney from some corporation contacted me. The corporation wanted to build a casino in Waveland. They offered me a low-ball figure to take the contract. I managed to get them to raise the offer a little, but not much. I wouldn't make much, but the Golden Galaxy was the biggest casino on the Mississippi Gulf Coast, and was going to feature the Sky Walk, a unique architectural feature that would be famous around the world. I figured if it was half as successful as they were claiming, I'd be back in business."

"The corporation was Meadow Gold," Dawson said. "It belongs to Vega."

"What?" Michael stared at him.

"Juliana figured it out. She showed me a flowchart she put together that connects Meadow Gold to Tito Vega. I haven't verified all her research, but it looks like I might be able to prove he owns Meadow Gold."

Michael's gaze snapped to his. "I'll be damned."

"First, though, I've got to prove a connection between Vega and Bayside Industries. I've got one of my guys checking it out. Ever heard of them?"

Michael shook his head. "I don't think so."

"I hope Mack can find something. So you were talking about Knoblock?" Dawson pressed.

"Yeah. After I signed the contract to build the casino and had started work, I got a call from Vega. He *suggested* I subcontract the Sky Walk to Knoblock. I wanted to build that thing myself. It was going to be spectacular. Besides, Knoblock had screwed me before on the condos."

"Vega called you?"

Michael nodded. "I'm sure he used a throwaway cell. He's too smart to slip up. I told him no. I wouldn't hire Knoblock."

Dawson waited, but Michael stopped pacing and sat down in a club chair near the couch and rubbed his eyes. When he looked up, his cheeks had no color and his eyes looked haunted. He took a deep breath.

"Vega was polite. Said he understood how I felt. But the next day, the goon in the suit came to see me. He did exactly the same thing he'd done before—sat down and filed his nails. He had on an opal ring. He never even looked at me." Michael swallowed. "After he'd sat there—I swear, at least five minutes—he said, 'It's a shame about your wife. I know you'd hate it if she were driving drunk and ran off the road.'"

Chapter Nine

Shock paralyzed Dawson. He tried to speak but his throat had seized. Finally he croaked, "He actually said that?"

He'd guessed his dad was going to tell him Vega had somehow threatened him, but he hadn't expected this.

Michael nodded and rubbed his eyes again.

"What—" Dawson had to work to swallow "—what did you do?"

His dad laughed again, not a pleasant sound. "What the hell do you think I did? Knoblock called me and I hired him."

Dawson stood and walked over to the sliding glass doors. Tito Vega had threatened his mother's life. He slammed his palm against the glass, not caring if it broke. He almost wished it would. The anger and fear were growing so fast inside him that they needed an outlet or he would burst. Anything short of bloodletting would not be enough.

"Son, calm down."

Dawson whirled, his fists clenching. "Calm down? Calm *down?* You *hired* him? You've got two sons who are cops and you just rolled over and let the bastard—" He couldn't even finish the sentence.

Michael leveled a gaze at him. "That's right, I did. Do you think I'd take the smallest chance that your mother might be hurt?"

The question slammed Dawson in the gut. He felt about

two inches high. "No, but you could have come to one of us. You could have come to me."

His father smiled sadly. "I tend to forget how young you are."

"Young? What the hell? Are you saying I couldn't handle Vega?"

"Don't raise your voice at me!" Michael shot back. "This is what I'm talking about. You'd go off half-cocked and probably make things worse."

"At least I'd do something," Dawson shouted. "You're just a—"

"J.D.? Michael?"

It was his mother. Dawson gulped down the words he was about to fling.

Michael shot him a glare and stepped over to the stairs. "It's okay, hon. Sorry if we woke you."

Dawson heard his mother's soft footsteps on the stairs. He looked up to see her blue slippers and the blue satin robe.

"Go on back to bed," his dad said gently. "We were just having a discussion."

Edie Delancey walked down the stairs as if she were making an entrance on a Las Vegas stage. She looked at Dawson, her eyes narrowed, then turned to her husband.

"Michael, you're tired. You go on up to bed. I'll see J.D. out."

"Edie—"

"Go on, Michael."

There was a note in his mother's voice that Dawson hadn't heard in a long, long time. It reminded him that she had been a beautiful, vibrant and strong woman who had reared her children with a gentle, yet firm, hand. She'd rarely raised her voice, but all the kids knew that when they heard that tone, they'd better obey.

He shook his head, trying to rid himself of the conflicting emotions churning inside him.

Once Michael's footsteps got to the top of the stairs and faded away on the hardwood floors, Edie turned to her son.

"Mom," Dawson said in a futile attempt to stave off whatever she was going to say, which he knew would add shame and more guilt to the mix of feelings inside him.

"I know what your father has been telling you."

"Look, Mom, it's just a business thing—"

"No," she said, holding up a slender hand. "No, it's not. I know, J.D.," she said. "I *know*."

"You know?" He tried one more time to pretend he didn't understand her. "About what?"

Her mouth turned up in a small smile, another reminder of what a beautiful woman she was.

"About everything," she said patiently. "The threats. The demands."

He had nothing to say. He couldn't tell her she was wrong. She knew she wasn't. He couldn't tell her the threats were nothing because they weren't nothing. He'd seen in his dad's face, heard in his voice, that the deadly threat was real. If his dad hadn't complied with Vega's demands, his mother might well have died.

"Your father needs you. He needs you to believe in him." She stepped closer to him and laid her hand on his chest, over his heart. "You know, in here, that he wouldn't skimp on materials."

Dawson took an instinctive step backward. His mother was acting too much like her old self and it was messing with his brain. And his heart. She'd always been able to see through him.

"I don't know that," he protested. "Look at Grampa. He screwed people for a living and they still voted for him every election. Look at Uncle Robert. He's like Con reincarnated.

I used to hear him yelling and hitting stuff—sometimes hitting Aunt Bettye or the kids."

His mother's delicate brows lowered. "What are you saying?"

His gaze lit on the glass door. In the dim light he could see his palm print on the glass. "What makes my dad different from his brother or his own father?" He looked down at his palm.

"And what makes me different from any of them?" Hearing the words that he'd never said, even to himself, stunned him.

"You think you're like your grandfather or your uncle? You think your father is like them?" Edie shook her head. "No. Michael is not and you're not."

"Mom, I just nearly put my hand through the glass door over there," Dawson protested, feeling his face heat up. "I don't like knowing I can do that."

"You listen to me, John Dawson Delancey," she said. "Your father went into construction because he wanted to get as far away from politics as he could. He wanted to make his own legacy. He was never more proud than when you went to work with him. Knowing that you believed he was guilty hurt him much more than even going to prison."

Dawson walked over to the glass doors and looked out. It was pitch-black outside, but he couldn't face his mother right then. He swallowed against the huge lump that had grown in his throat. "You believe he was innocent?" he asked, his voice hoarse.

"Of course I do," she said. "I believe in him."

"I can't—" Dawson swallowed again and rubbed his eyes. "I just don't know."

"J.D., look at me."

He looked down at his feet, then took a deep breath and turned around.

"I need you to do something for me."

He grimaced. "Mom—"

"Don't interrupt your mother. Even if you don't believe your father, even if you don't believe me, I need you to do everything you can to prove what really happened to the Sky Walk."

Dawson nodded. "I am, Mom. I'm going to uncover the truth, no matter what it is."

"That's all you can do, darling," she said. "Now, it's late. Why don't you stay here in your old room instead of driving all the way back to your condo?"

Dawson looked at his watch. It was eleven o'clock. "I can't. I've got to get back. Jules is there by herself—" He stopped but not soon enough.

"Jules?" his mother echoed. "Who is Jules? I didn't know you were dating someone."

"Trust me," he said, "I am *not* dating her. She's Juliana Caprese. She's the daughter of the casino manager who was killed when the Sky Walk collapsed."

"Oh, the poor girl. How awful for her."

He nodded. "Yeah. Okay, well, I need to go—"

"If you're not dating, what's she doing at your condo? Is she in some kind of protective custody?"

"No. Well, kind of." He moved toward the stairs.

"J.D.," Edie said, propping her fists on her hips. "What's going on with you and that girl?"

He laughed. "Okay, Mom. First, I'm thirty-two, not sixteen, okay?" He sighed. "Someone's been following her, so she's staying at my place."

"Following her? Why?"

"She's been looking into her father's death," Dawson said. "We're working together to figure out why the Sky Walk fell."

Edie frowned at him. "That seems odd," she said thoughtfully. "If her father was killed when the Sky Walk collapsed, and *your* father is being investigated because it collapsed, why would she want to work with you?"

He felt his face heat up again.

"Oh, my," his mother said. "She doesn't know that you're Michael Delancey's son, does she?"

ALL THE WAY BACK TO HIS CONDO, his mother's words echoed in his ears.

She doesn't know you're Michael Delancey's son. He'd planned it that way, of course, but hearing the words in his mom's disappointed voice made his brilliant idea seem more sleazy than smart.

He saw the lights on in the living room. He really hoped she'd left them on when she went to bed because he didn't feel like facing her with his mom's accusing voice still echoing in his ears.

She was tucked into the corner of his leather couch, with one of her manila folders open on her lap. Beside her was her gun. She looked up. Was that relief on her face? Had she really been scared to stay by herself?

"Hey, I thought you were going to bed," he said. "I smell popcorn."

She nodded toward the coffee table. "There's about half of it left if you want it. It's extra-buttery."

He didn't want popcorn. "I know. I bought it."

She stretched her legs. She had on a pink tank top that said Pink on it and pink-and-gray plaid pajama bottoms that stopped right below her knees. Her calves were smooth and shapely. He could see the edge of a strip bandage on her left knee. It didn't completely cover the scrape from her attack.

When his gaze slid down to her slender ankles and bare feet, his mouth went dry. Those toes. Pink-tipped and sexy. Struggling to swallow, he pulled his gaze back up to her face.

She closed the folder and set it on top of the others on the coffee table, then lifted her gaze to his. She blinked and her tongue flicked out to moisten her lips.

Dawson nearly groaned aloud at the sudden exquisite ache in his groin. If he didn't get a grip she'd soon know exactly how badly he wanted her. Not just for sex. He'd decided a few years ago that sex for sex's sake was an exercise in frustration and boredom. It served its purpose, but he preferred women who could keep up with him other than just between the sheets. And he'd never met anyone as beautiful, as smart or as fascinating as Juliana Caprese. From those dark, snapping eyes to her sexy pink toes, she embodied the perfect woman. As the thought slid through his mind, he saw her breasts tighten under the thin pink top. Adrenaline pumped pure lust through him.

Her eyes narrowed, she lifted her chin and he crashed back into the real world. Which was a good thing, because once she found out who he was, she'd send him crashing to hell if she could.

"How was your appointment?" she said frostily.

"Appointment?" For a split second, he was confused. "Oh, right. It was fine. Lasted longer than I'd hoped it would."

She assessed him for a full three seconds, then nodded and picked up the folders. "Well, if you're going to be a private eye," she said casually as she stood, "you have to be available when your client needs you."

Dawson chuckled.

She wrapped her arms around the folders. Her teeth grazed her lower lip. "What if I need you?" she asked.

Dawson's chuckle dissolved. What the hell? "I'm right here," he said softly. "What do you need?"

She shook her head. "I was scared while you were gone."

He stiffened, looking at her gun on the couch. "Did something happen?"

"No, but—"

He stepped closer until her arms, wrapped around the folders brushed against his shirt. "I thought you said you could handle that weapon."

She shrugged, and Dawson couldn't take his eyes off the bony, sexy curve of her shoulder. Her skin was beautiful, a kind of a ripe-peach color that made his mouth water.

He slid his fingers along the slope of her neck down to her shoulder. He touched the little bump that defined the shoulder socket.

Juliana shivered and raised her gaze to meet Dawson's intense blue eyes. What was it about him that made all rational thought fly out of her head? Silly question. It was everything about him. Starting with his hands. Those large, beautiful hands that she knew would be able to stir her into a frenzy within seconds. Then there were his eyes—no matter how cocky and sarcastic he was, she'd found out that if she was quick enough, she could see a bit of the truth in them. Right now those intense blue lasers were promising her delights that she'd never before experienced.

His mouth was curved, not sarcastically, but gently, sensually. She looked at it, imagining how he would use it. Which was a mistake, because she'd always had a vivid imagination. A tiny moan gathered deep in her throat.

Dawson bent his head and touched her lips with his. At the feel of his mouth, her lips parted and Pandora's box opened deep inside her, releasing a cloud of confusing, conflicting emotions. It had cracked open a little in her dad's office the last time he'd kissed her.

But here there were no deadly beams to crash down on them. Here, the only danger was to her heart. And while he'd been her savior then, now he was the danger.

He wrapped an arm around her and pulled her to him, crushing the folders between them.

She stiffened automatically.

Dawson pulled back and stared down at her. He grabbed the folders and tugged on them. "Still don't trust me, do you?"

"No," she gasped, forcing herself to let go of them. "I mean— I didn't mean to—"

"It's okay," he said, his jaw clenching. "I shouldn't have—"

"Put them down," she said.

"What?" His jaw muscle worked. "Hey, Jules, come on—"

"Put them down—over there." She pointed to the couch. "On the floor, anywhere. I don't care." Then she moved, pressing her body against him, and kissed the line of his jaw. "And relax," she whispered, running a finger along his jawline.

Dawson tossed them onto an end table and pulled her close until she could feel the hardness of his erection against her. He pressed her closer, moving his hips in slow, rhythmic motion as he kissed her.

The pulsing rhythm sent electricity arcing through her as his mouth explored hers. His tongue slid along her lower lip, tickling, teasing, before it delved inside, pushing past her teeth and flirting with her tongue.

Sensation swept her up into a whirlwind. Nothing existed except her body and Dawson's, molded together, heat melding with heat, motion echoing motion.

Somehow, while she was flying inside the whirlwind, they were magically transported to his bed. Her pajamas were gone. He threw off his jeans and shirt and lay down beside her. His body was hot and firm and smooth, and he was engorged—so ready for her that it was a little scary.

But he was in no hurry. His hands explored her body, caressing her, massaging her, delving into secret folds and finding erogenous zones that she had no idea existed.

She did her best to give back as good as she got, but he

was relentless, and she kept forgetting everything except her own pleasure.

That didn't seem to bother him. After he'd brought her to climax with his fingers, he let his mouth do the exploring, and stirred her to a peak even higher than before.

"Dawson," she gasped. "Please." She grasped at his shoulders, pulling him to her. He took his time traveling up her body, stopping to nip and suck at her breasts until she was panting.

He lifted himself above her and kissed her, leaving his own taste in her mouth. Every tendon in her body contracted in an erotic electrical storm as he entered her smoothly and deeply.

Surging and crashing like an ocean wave, she lost all control for the first time in her life. When the waves finally waned, she collapsed, as scattered and still as the sand.

Dawson buried his head in Juliana's neck and waited for his breathing to return to normal. He'd never lost control like that in his life.

He'd planned to stoke her slowly and deliberately, coaxing her to the most explosive orgasm she'd ever had. In fact, if she held on to everything as tightly as she held on to those folders, he wouldn't be surprised if she'd never had one.

But he'd been hoisted by his own petard. Not only had she exploded for the third time as soon as he'd entered her, her explosion had triggered his own. He shuddered as tiny aftershocks sparked and fired through him.

She trailed her fingers down his back, sending goose bumps across his skin. He lifted his head and smiled at her. Her eyes drifted open and she peered at him through thick black lashes. Her teeth scraped across her bottom lip and she smiled back at him.

He felt a twinge deep inside him at the sight of that shy smile. It was oddly painful—and uncomfortably familiar.

Suddenly he needed to separate himself from her. So he bussed the tip of her nose, then rolled away and threw his arm over his eyes.

"Dawson, are you okay?" she asked.

"Sure." He hoped his arm hid his grimace. He wasn't okay, but he didn't want to talk about it. The twinge he'd felt was the same queasy feeling he'd gotten while talking to his mom.

How had all those things he'd never even consciously thought to himself come bubbling out as soon as his dad had left the room? He'd never dwelled on his family's scandalous legacy—other than to joke about it to family and friends. It had surprised him how much he did not want to be like his grandfather or his abusive uncle Robert.

It was admirable that his mother thought his dad was a good man who'd been framed for a crime he hadn't committed. But Dawson wasn't so sure.

Not sure. A week ago he'd been positive his dad was guilty. How had his mom managed to plant doubt in his mind? What had changed?

As soon as the question hit his brain, he knew the answer. *Juliana.* Once he'd met her, everything changed. Listening to her accuse Michael of killing her father had shaken his certainty. Suddenly, he found himself defending his dad.

And now he'd screwed up royally. He'd known before he'd walked in that he didn't want to talk to her tonight. Didn't want to see her. His subconscious, knowing how vulnerable he was after talking with his mom, had been trying to protect him.

It hadn't helped that Juliana had thrown herself at him. *No.* That wasn't fair to her. When she'd said she needed him, all she'd meant was that she'd been afraid to be by herself. He was the one who'd taken it to the next level.

A thrill—half lustful, half fearful—swirled through him.

The next level and the next and the next. He was still stunned by the intensity of his orgasm—of his and hers.

He lowered his arm and when he did, Juliana turned and laid her head on his shoulder. Her breathing turned soft and even. She was asleep.

Dawson shifted into a more comfortable position and closed his eyes. He breathed deeply, filling his head with the scent of peppermint from her hair.

As he drifted off, it occurred to him that this was the first time a woman had slept in his bed since—when?

Since ever.

Chapter Ten

Dawson woke up with a start. Something wasn't right. He opened his eyes and saw a cloud of soft black hair draped across his arm.

Juliana was in his bed with him. It was five-thirty in the morning. Ugh. A part of him wanted to turn over, snuggle up against her naked body and wake her with foreplay. But when he looked at her, peacefully sleeping, trusting him to keep her safe, guilt racked him. He was lying to her. Not just with words, but with everything he did, every move he made. She had no idea who he was.

If—when she found out, she would brand him with the same label he'd used on his grandfather, his uncle and even his dad. And he would deserve it as much as they did—possibly more than his dad did.

He slid out of bed, grabbed a pair of underwear and his favorite around-the-house jeans and slipped out of the bedroom, easing the door closed behind him. He headed to the bathroom, yawning and stretching.

After a fast hot shower, he made coffee and paced in front of his living-room window as he drank it. What was he going to say—what was he going to do—when she woke up?

Would she be battling the same mixed emotions he was? He seriously doubted she slept around. Not as tightly as she held on to those folders.

The folders. He turned and looked at them, stacked on the coffee table. He glanced toward the bedroom and back again. He was dying to look at them. He couldn't imagine that she had much that he didn't already know. But she was sharp and thorough.

He thought about the flowchart she'd put together of the corporations Tito Vega was connected with. The work she'd put into making all those connections was a testament to her determination and focus. It would be interesting to know if any of the city officials and charitable organizations that courted Vega's money for their pet projects knew about all of Vega's involvements.

Glancing at his watch, he wondered what Mack was doing right now. In Zurich it would be—he did the math in his head—around one o'clock today: Saturday. He didn't know what flight Mack had been able to catch. Had he had time to see his little secretary last night? He sighed. He probably wouldn't hear a word until Sunday or even Monday.

He sat down on the couch and set his coffee cup aside. Damn, he wanted to get his hands on those folders—had ever since he'd first seen them.

Did he dare?

If you want to be a private eye, you can't be squeamish about snooping into other people's stuff. He smiled to himself.

He had to admit it was fun to tease Juliana about wanting to be a private investigator. An unexpected and disturbing vision rose in his mind—of the two of them working together, his handling the legwork and her working on the research and paperwork he found so tedious. The disturbing part of his little daydream was that when the day was over, they went home together.

All right, damn it. He rubbed his eyes. What was he going

to do? He glanced toward the bedroom, wondering how late she slept.

He growled. He needed to listen to his own rules about being a private eye. He reached for the top folder, the one she'd been looking at when he'd come in. The tab was labeled Knoblock.

Dawson's pulse sped up. She had information on Knoblock. Hadn't he asked her if she'd heard the name Knoblock? She said she wasn't sure.

She'd lied to him.

He opened the folder. On top of the thin stack of papers was a building permit filed by Randall Knoblock for the Sky Walk inside the Golden Galaxy. He had listed himself as a subcontractor working under Michael Delancey.

Dawson shook his head. He had to admit it wasn't a stretch for Juliana to assume that Michael had not only been responsible for what Knoblock did on the Sky Walk, but that he'd ordered it.

Hell, that's what he'd thought himself—at first.

The sheet under the building permit was a copy of a newspaper article listing indictments. A date, May 23, 1997, was handwritten as was the name of the newspaper, the *Kansas City Star*. The charges listed by Knoblock's name included criminal negligence. Dawson cursed under his breath. Apparently, Knoblock had made a long and obviously successful career of skimping on materials.

How had Jules tracked down all this information? As far as Dawson knew there wasn't a centralized database of crooked contractors. He was impressed.

Dawson set that sheet aside and looked at the next one. It was a copy of a three-line piece that stated that on April 10, 2000, Randall Knoblock was released from prison.

Just as Dawson picked it up, he saw a movement out of the corner of his eye.

"What are you doing?" Juliana stood in the doorway to the living room in her pink pajamas. Her hair was tangled and her eyes were heavy-lidded.

"Jules—" he said defensively, setting the folder down and standing.

"Don't call me that," she snapped. "What are you doing with my folders?"

"I just wanted to take a look at them—" Dawson started.

"You have no right. Those are mine! I did *not* give you permission to look at them."

Her anger was way out of proportion, he thought. "Come on, Jules. I only looked at one folder, Knoblock's. It's not like we haven't already talked about him. Think about my—about the note. *It* mentioned him. In fact, I asked you specifically if you knew the name and you said you weren't sure."

She glared at him and pushed her hands through her hair, pulling it back and twisting it up.

"You shouldn't be snooping," she said, much less vehemently.

"Hey," he said, spreading his hands. "If you want my help, you're going to have to trust me."

The look on her face gave him the answer to the question he'd asked himself earlier. Her cheeks were pink and she wouldn't meet his gaze. Obviously, she'd decided that sex with him had been a mistake. Well, she could join the club.

"Look," he said placatingly, "I can see that you're thinking the same thing I am. So I'll make a promise to you right now. I swear to you that *that*—" he nodded toward the bedroom "—won't happen again. Okay? How's that? Because if we can't trust each other, then neither one of us is going to get what we want."

Her cheeks flamed even brighter than before. "It won't happen again?" she whispered.

Dawson grimaced. He hated that her voice was so small

and tentative. It was a blow to his ego that she regretted making love with him that much.

"No, it won't," he said, but couldn't resist adding, "unless you want it to." He shrugged and smiled.

She didn't smile back. "I have to—" she cocked her head slightly backward "—to take a shower." She turned on her heel and disappeared. He heard the door to the guest room close, then open a few seconds later. Then he heard the bathroom door close.

He blew out a long breath. "Way to go, Delancey," he growled.

JULIANA LIFTED HER FACE to the hot spray, pretending that the wetness on her face was a hundred percent water and zero percent tears, and that the heat was the steam rather than embarrassment and humiliation.

That won't happen again. Dawson's emphatic declaration had sent hurt and embarrassment stabbing through her. She'd woken up in his bed, stretching languidly, satiated after a night of lovemaking that could only be described as mind-blowing, to find that his side of the bed was empty and cold.

Uh-oh, her little voice said. *Are things going to be awkward?* Dawson probably brought women to his apartment all the time. If she judged by his looks, personality and performance in bed, she'd have to conclude that he got a *lot* of practice.

She, on the other hand, did not. She got offers and come-ons, but she was very picky about who she went to bed with. The trail of lovers she'd left in her wake was extremely short—practically nonexistent, in fact. Two hardly qualified as a trail.

She turned around to let the hot water run on her back as she remembered his hot, hard body against hers. She didn't know what made his touch different, but as soon as he'd caressed her, all the careful control she brought to everything had dissolved.

When she thought about how abandoned, maybe even wanton, she'd been, her face burned again. She'd done things, and so had he, that she'd never experienced before.

An aftershock of pleasure centered in her core, turning her knees to jelly. She moaned and steadied herself with a hand against the shower wall as she arched in reaction and tears welled in her eyes. To have a climax, even a tiny one, by just thinking about what they'd done—nothing like that had ever happened to her, either.

And never would again. To her dismay, she was crying again. She had to get a grip. She couldn't let Dawson know how much he'd hurt her. She'd just have to act as though she was as blasé about the sex as he was. It's probably what he was used to—given the type of women she imagined him dating.

She shivered. The shower water was cooling off. She quickly bathed and washed her hair, then grabbed a towel. As she dried off, she thought about him sneaking a look at her folders.

Anger swept through her—at him for snooping. At herself for hanging on to those few pages of information she'd unearthed. She ran her fingers through her wet hair, then dried off the mirror and looked at herself.

Her eyes grew wide and her mouth fell open as a disturbing thought occurred to her. Dawson had come to her. He'd been the one to suggest that they work together. And he'd been eyeing those folders from the beginning.

Juliana didn't like what her brain was telling her, but it made sense. Pitiful sense. She knew that whatever tiny bits of information she'd gleaned needed to be shared with Dawson if they were going to ever figure out what had happened to the Sky Walk. But she'd clung to those folders—not because they contained valuable information she didn't want Dawson to have, but because they *didn't*.

As soon as Dawson realized how little information she had, he'd realize he didn't need her a quarter as much as she needed him. And then he'd be gone.

A brisk knock sounded on the door, startling her. "Jules, I just got a call from Brian—Detective Hardy. They've got a match for the fingerprints they lifted off the beam. The guy's in custody, and they want us down there."

She frowned at herself in the mirror. "But we didn't see anybody."

"Just hurry up," he snapped.

She winced at the tone in his voice. "Do I have time to dry my hair?" she called out, but she heard his footsteps walking away.

She towel dried her hair and rushed to pull on jeans and a top. Obviously, there was no time to put on makeup or fix her hair. So she caught her damp waves up in a ponytail, grabbed her purse and headed to the kitchen.

Dawson was waiting, jingling his car keys. When he saw her his brows drew down for an instant, but he didn't say a word. He just opened the door to the garage and stood back for her to precede him down the stairs.

AT THE POLICE STATION, which was nearly vacant because it was Saturday, Dawson glanced around. He saw Brian Hardy coming out of what must have been the break room, carrying a steaming cup of coffee. He saw them and walked over.

"Morning, Dawson, Ms. Caprese. Coffee?"

Dawson shook his head.

Jules leaned forward and sniffed near Brian's coffee cup. "Yes, please, if it's even half as good as it smells."

Brian smiled at her. "Maybe half as good, if you're lucky. How do you take it?"

"Black is fine."

"I'll be right back."

Once the detective had walked away, Dawson said, "While we're here, I want to ask Brian if he knows anything about Randall Knoblock."

Jules looked at him with a frown. "Go ahead," she said.

He clenched his jaw. "I don't want to step on your toes, seeing how upset you were that I looked at your little folder."

He was being mean and he knew it, but it frustrated the hell out of him that she didn't trust him enough to share with him information that could help to figure out who had caused the Sky Walk to collapse. He wanted to tell her that there was nothing in her precious folders that he couldn't find out on his own, given enough time. He wanted to point out to her that the whole concept of *working together* meant sharing information.

Jules shot him a glare. "Like you said, we'd already talked about Knoblock."

His brows shot up. What was that? A semiapology for being so possessive about her folders?

Brian came back with a second steaming cup of coffee. "The suspect is in the interrogation room. His name is William Maynard. I'm going to take you two into the viewing room, where you can see him through the one-way mirror. See if you recognize him."

"I don't understand," Jules said. "I didn't see anybody and I don't think Dawson did, either."

"I don't remember seeing anyone," Dawson agreed. "But it's amazing what your subconscious notices—someone walking on the street or sitting in a car. It doesn't register at the time, but if you see them again, like this—" he gestured toward the interrogation room "—you might remember."

The detective led the way to the viewing room, which was dark as pitch. He flipped on a light switch, and the glass panel on the wall revealed a skinny guy fidgeting in a wooden chair. He had on a black T-shirt and his arms and neck were covered with tattoos. He was facing the one-way glass. When Brian closed the door, he looked up.

"He can't see us, right? Can he hear us?" Jules whispered.

Dawson shook his head as Brian answered. "Nope. He might have heard the door close, but he can't hear us. This room is soundproof. He sees a mirror. But he's been around enough to know that we're in here watching him."

Jules was staring through the glass with a frown on her face. "His fingerprints were on the beam that fell on us?" she asked.

"Right," Hardy said. "Why? Do you recognize him?"

"No, I don't think so. How could he have dropped that steel beam by himself? It was huge."

"I wondered that myself," Hardy answered. "He's worked construction in the past. In fact, he signed on to work on the Golden Galaxy, but he never got a paycheck. To answer your question, our genius in there dropped the bolt cutters he used to shear the bolts that held the beam. My crime scene investigator found them lying in the office area near the beam."

"Genius is right." Dawson laughed. "What's the charge— assault with intent?"

"He'll probably deal it out, but it should be worth a couple of years."

"So his fingerprints prove he dropped the beam, right?" Juliana asked. "What do you need from me?"

"It would be better if we had an eyewitness who could put him there at the right time."

"I can't do that. I did hear noises, but nothing that would prove anything." She spread her hands in a helpless gesture.

Brian glanced at Dawson. "What about the guy? Any chance you might have seen him somewhere else?"

Jules glanced narrowly from Brian to Dawson. "Somewhere else?"

She looked back at the tattooed man. Dawson followed her gaze. The little skunk was picking his teeth with a fingernail. Both teeth and nails were mottled and broken. *Crack addict.*

Jules said, "You think he's the one who stole my letter, don't you?"

"I didn't say that," Brian replied. "I was just thinking you might have spotted him somewhere if he's been following you."

Jules met Dawson's gaze. Her look said, *I know that's what he means.*

"Well?" he asked. "What do you think? Ever see him before?"

She unconsciously arched her shoulder and put a hand to the fading bruise on her face. She didn't say anything, just stared at the man.

"Talk about what you remember from the attack," Brian suggested. "Try to picture what you saw, what you felt."

She nodded, not taking her eyes off the suspect. "I walked out of the post office. I don't know where he was—not in the building. There was no one else in there." She took a breath. "I hadn't taken three steps on the sidewalk when I was hit from behind." She stopped and shook her head.

"No, not hit. Shoved. He shoved me." She nodded. "I fell on my knee, but for some reason I kept falling. I think he may have shoved me again because I landed on my shoulder—hard." She arched it again, wincing.

Dawson watched her carefully. When she didn't say anything else, he prompted her. "When did he grab the letter?"

She closed her eyes. "I had it in my hand. I don't think I realized right away that someone had hit me. My shoulder was hurting badly, but I tried to get up. That's when he—" She gasped and her eyes flew open.

"Omigosh, that's him!" she cried. "That's him. Look at the tattoos."

"Tell me about them. Why are you so sure this is the guy?" Brian asked, his voice level.

Jules pointed.

Maynard rested his elbows on the table and was playing with a sandwich wrapper. His full sleeves of tattoos were clearly visible. "See the one on his left arm? It looks like a vine—" She paused. "Or is it a snake? Anyhow, it's got all those colors in it. He reached around me and jerked the letter out of my hand and that's what I saw. That—" She made a winding motion with her hand.

Brian set his foam cup on the table. "Great. That gives me probable cause for a warrant to search his house and car for the letter." He glanced at his watch. "I need to call Maura. Maura Presley, the A.D.A. With any luck, she can find us a judge."

"What else do you need from us?" Dawson asked.

"Just a signed statement from you," he told Juliana. "You'll need to go into detail about where and when you saw him, describe exactly what happened, step by step if you can. And state how you're positive he's the man who attacked you." Brian paused. "*If* you are. Please just state the facts. Don't get into conjecture. I need this to be as clean as possible."

Jules nodded. "What will you do? Question him? Will I need to talk to him?"

"No, no," Brian assured her. "I doubt seriously this will go to trial. Our friend in there has priors. He'll be anxious to plead this out. Maybe we can deal with him to give us who-ever sicced him on you."

Jules met Dawson's gaze. He knew exactly what she was thinking. When the slimy little skunk gave up the person who'd sent him to spy on her and steal any answers she got to her newspaper ad, the name would be Michael Delancey.

While Jules wrote out her statement, Dawson talked to Brian about Randall Knoblock and got him to print out a copy of Maynard's mug shot. Then he gave Ryker a call to see if he had time to talk this afternoon. Ryker and his wife, Nicole, were painting the house they'd bought. He gave Dawson the new address.

Ten minutes later he and Jules were back in the car. She settled back against the seat with a sigh. "Did you hear that? He *was* the guy who attacked me."

"I was standing right there," he said with a smile.

"Did you talk to Detective Hardy about Knoblock?"

Dawson nodded. "He knew a little about him, mostly from the information they have on the Golden Galaxy—that he was the subcontractor for the Sky Walk." He glanced at her sidelong. "Interestingly, Hardy didn't have the information from Kansas City."

She lit up at that, just like he knew she would. She'd found something a police detective hadn't found. "Really? Did you tell him what I'd found?"

He shook his head. "I thought I'd wait and make sure you wanted to share that with him."

"Why wouldn't I," she snapped, "if it will help him figure out who's responsible for my dad's death?"

"Hey, calm down. It's Saturday and he's still got to get a warrant to search Maynard's property before some buddy of his goes in and cleans everything up."

"Maynard. He's a creepy-looking guy."

"He's a petty thief, a crack addict, a bully and a skunk. Likes to carry around a billy club."

"A billy club?" Juliana's hand went to her shoulder. "That must be what he hit me with."

"Yeah, no." He laughed harshly. "If he had, your shoulder wouldn't have been dislocated. It would have been crushed. He must have had orders not to hurt you."

"Orders from whom?" she asked with a shiver. "When will Detective Hardy know something?"

"I doubt we'll hear anything until Monday. We'll take him the information about Knoblock in Kansas City and see what he's found out."

"Great. I'm ready for all this to be over."

Dawson glanced at her. Her chin had that little pugnacious lift to it that told him she'd made up her mind about something.

"Take me to my apartment," she said.

"No, you—"

"Dawson, I need clothes. I need to get my mail, and I want my car."

"What about your shoulder?" he asked, knowing he was going to lose this fight.

"It's fine. The worst of the soreness is gone. I probably could have been driving all along."

Dawson racked his brain for a reason to refuse. He didn't want her driving. She'd go running off again and get into trouble or get herself killed. A sinking feeling hit his gut at that thought.

But if he objected, that chin would go even higher. He sighed. "I will if you'll promise me that you won't go running off without me."

She glanced sidelong at him, a veiled look that he couldn't interpret. "Why would I do that?" she asked. "We're working together, right?"

A sense of foreboding settled on Dawson's chest. He wanted to lock her away like Rapunzel or another of those fairy-tale princesses. But the princesses always managed to get into trouble anyway, and he was sure Jules would, too. "Right," he said wryly.

Chapter Eleven

Juliana drove to Dawson's condo after taking care of some chores and washing some clothes. She parked on the street and knocked on the front door.

When he opened it, he was talking on the phone.

"Right," he said as she walked past him. "I'll have to go to the office and check the files. I'll call you from there."

She waited until he hung up, then said, "I still don't see why I can't stay at my own place."

Dawson pocketed his phone and checked his watch before he raised his gaze to hers.

"After two attacks, you're not convinced you're in danger? I'd think you'd be glad I'm keeping an eye on you. I just don't want to be responsible for scraping you up off the floor."

"First, thanks for that image. Second, nobody asked you to be responsible for me. And third, now that Maynard guy is locked up, how am I still in danger?" She walked into the living room while she was talking. The folders on the coffee table were still stacked neatly with the top one slightly crooked, just like she'd left them.

She grimaced to herself. Somehow she had to work up the courage to share her meager information with Dawson. If he took it and ran, wasn't she still better off than if she hadn't confided in him at all? He'd helped her get her dad's things from the casino. He'd saved her life.

"Damn it, Jules. If you're going to be a private eye—hell, if you're going to *survive*—you're going to have to stop being so stubborn and start using your brain for something more than getting the last word." He blew out a breath in frustration. "Why don't you think about it for a few seconds and tell me how you can still be in danger."

Juliana spoke through gritted teeth. "Okay, okay. I know. Because Maynard may be in custody, but whoever hired him is still out there."

"And…"

She frowned. "And…"

"Maynard will make bail before morning."

"They'll give him bail—after he attacked me?"

Dawson sighed. "Don't you watch any of the cop shows on TV?"

"Stop it. You don't have to be so sarcastic all the time." She tossed her purse down on the couch and looked at the folders again, taking a deep breath. "Dawson—"

"Don't worry, Jules, I haven't touched them."

She turned. "I know. I—" She swallowed. Why was this so hard? "If you want, we could look at them together."

Dawson's brows shot up and an unreadable expression crossed his face. He stared at her for an instant, then turned and picked up his keys off the table by the door.

"Maybe later," he said. "Right now there's something I've got to do."

"About the casino? Can I go with you?"

"No. Believe it or not, I have other cases. I'll be back as soon as I can."

"You said you're going to your office. I want to see a real private investigations office."

"It's a security agency, and no." He pointed at her with the hand that held the keys. "Don't leave."

"And keep the door locked," she said mockingly.

That earned her a fierce scowl. His laser-blue eyes nearly scorched her. "If I had half a brain I'd get Brian to put you in jail for your own safety," he growled, then stalked up the hall to the kitchen and out the door to the garage.

Juliana let out a quiet, frustrated scream and stomped her foot. He made her so mad! She balled her fists and punched the air in front of her.

Then she stomped into the guest bedroom and jerked the band out of her hair and pushed her fingers through it. Meeting her own gaze in the mirror over the dresser, she shook her head until her hair stood out like Medusa's snakes. She grabbed a comb and worked out her anger and frustration while she worked the snarls out of her hair.

By the time her hair was smooth, she'd stopped fuming and was thinking relatively rationally.

Before Dawson had driven all reason out of her head last night, before Detective Hardy had called her in to identify Maynard, she'd thought of something she'd wanted to do. What was it?

She walked up the hall to the kitchen to get some water. She brought the glass into the living room and set it on the coffee table next to the stack of folders.

Looking at them stoked her anger again. She'd made what she considered a huge concession, offering to let Dawson look at her stack of research, which contained every bit of information she'd managed to gather about everyone connected with the Sky Walk. But after all his curiosity, all his staring at them, he'd brushed off her offer as if it was nothing. He didn't have time. He had something he had to do. *Another matter.*

Juliana flopped down on the couch. She drank the cool water and tried to clear her brain.

Everyone connected with the Sky Walk. Something—some name—was bothering her. She closed her eyes and tried to concentrate. She picked up her folders and looked at the tabs. *Delancey. Knoblock. Vega. Kaplan.*

A thought tickled the back of her brain, teasing her. Looking at the four names didn't help. Everybody knew the name Delancey. The Delancey family had been prominent in Louisiana politics for years. For that matter, Vega was a well-known name along the coast. The other names weren't familiar.

She stared at the names, trying to make one of them fit her recollection. She couldn't. What name was it that was bothering her? Someone her dad had mentioned? No. The sense she had was of an old memory—school maybe? But when? Where? College? High school? *Grade school?*

Her suitcase was still standing just inside the door. She opened it and dug out her mini-notebook computer. Back on the couch, she looked up her high school. There was no list of alumni on the site. She tried some social networking sites, but although she found several people she knew, not one of their names scratched the itch in the back of her brain.

Nor did she find a complete list of the members of her graduating class anywhere.

She turned off the computer and stood. There was a better way. She grabbed her car keys, then realized she didn't have a key to Dawson's condo. After looking in a few obvious places and coming up empty, she left him a note telling him she had to run out and she'd be at her apartment—*because you didn't leave me a key,* she wrote. She jotted down her cell phone number, then signed it *Juliana* and underlined her name three times.

It took her about ten minutes to drive to her dad's house in Bay St. Louis. Turning into the driveway sent nostalgia rippling through her and caused tears to sting her eyes. Even after she'd moved into her own apartment, she'd visited him a couple of times a week.

Leaves crunched under her feet as she walked up to the porch and unlocked the door. She'd intended to get someone to clean up the yard. She made a mental note to get that done as soon as possible.

Stepping inside, she was overwhelmed by a rush of conflicting feelings. The smell of the house was familiar—she'd lived here all her life. It smelled like wood smoke and dust and the Old Spice aftershave her dad had always used.

Every time she came here, she argued with herself about what she should do about the house. It was paid for, but she couldn't decide whether to sell it or live here. Either way, she'd be set for life.

She wiped her face, trying at the same time to wipe those thoughts from her head. They were for another day. She was here for a specific reason—to find the name that was hovering just out of reach of her conscious mind.

She went directly to her bedroom, where all her yearbooks were stored on a shelf in her closet. She pulled a chair over to the closet and got down an armful of books, tossed them on her bed, then took her boots off and sat against the pillows to page through them.

An hour and a half later, she'd gone through all four years of high school and her freshman year of college. She'd found a Knoblock among the freshmen at the University of Southern Mississippi, but his photo didn't look familiar at all. During her sophomore year in high school, a girl named Sandra Kaplan had joined her class. She'd set the book aside to take with her, but from what she remembered, the girl's father was a pharmacist, not an architect.

She straightened and arched her back, groaning at the stiffness. She was thirsty and beginning to get hungry. She looked up at the closet shelf and grimaced. There were eight years of grade school that she needed to go through before she gave up. Twice as many as she'd already done.

But where to start? Might as well start at the beginning. She pulled down the yearbooks for her first four grades of school. She started with grade one.

And hit the jackpot. The last name listed in the first grade was Anthony Vega. He was a dark-haired boy with a cute grin. She frowned, studying the tiny photo. She'd have never remembered him by his picture. But looking at the printed name below the photo sent a profound relief through her and quieted the bothersome tickle at the back of her brain.

What were the chances he was related to Tito Vega? Not very good, she thought. Why would someone like Vega send his kid to public school?

That thought triggered another. How long had Anthony Vega stayed in her class? He hadn't been in any of the high school photos.

Quickly, she paged through her fourth-grade yearbook and there he was. So she climbed back onto the chair and grabbed her eighth-grade book. No Anthony Vega. So he'd left Bay High School after the fourth grade and before the eighth grade. Staying on the chair, she pulled the seventh-grade yearbook out from the stack. No Anthony Vega.

Sixth grade told a different story. His sixth-grade picture was sullen and seemed vaguely familiar. Maybe he'd been surly more often than cheerful.

In all her research, she hadn't found any information about Tito Vega's family, except for the occasional mention of his wife when they attended a party or a fundraiser. But now she had a connection between herself and Tito Vega. *If* Anthony Vega was Tito Vega's son.

She put her shoes back on, grabbed up the first-, sixth- and seventh-grade books and headed toward the front door, but then she remembered there was one more thing she needed to do.

When she'd pulled the legal papers—deeds, insurance,

will—from the safe in his den, she'd noticed a portfolio with the Golden Galaxy logo on it. But she'd forgotten about it.

She went into the den at the front of the house and turned on the lights. The safe was behind her senior portrait, which hung opposite her dad's office chair. She quickly dialed in the combination—her birthday—opened the door and pulled out the black leather portfolio, leaving the safe empty.

She looked at the clock sitting on his desk. It was after six o'clock and dark outside, and she was hungry and anxious to get back to Dawson's condo.

No, the little voice in her head reminded her. *We're not going to his condo. We're going back to our apartment.* It dismayed her that suddenly she didn't want to be alone. She'd always prided herself on her independence. She'd never been afraid to be out at night.

But then she'd never been attacked before.

Suppressing a shiver, she picked up the yearbooks, set the portfolio on top and started toward the front door.

She felt her phone vibrating before it rang. It was probably Dawson. Her heart fluttered as she dug into the side pocket of her purse. "Hello?" she said.

"This is just a taste of what will happen if you don't stop nosing around," a gruff voice said.

Shock burned Juliana's scalp and raised hairs on the back of her neck. "What? Who is this?"

But the phone went dead.

Juliana stared at the number on her phone's screen, trying to make sense of what the man had said.

Suddenly, all she could see was the tiny screen. She looked up. The lights had gone out. Her heart jumped into her throat and her muscles tensed. She clutched the books tightly and turned toward the study door.

She was ready to run—but where? She set the books down on the edge of the desk and pulled her gun from her purse, thumbing the safety off. Then she eased toward the door. Her throat was clogged with panic and her shoulders and neck ached from tension.

This is just a taste, the voice had said. *This* wasn't just a phone call and lights going out. Something was about to happen.

She put her back against the wall to the left of the door frame and listened. She couldn't hear anything.

Carefully, she rose to the balls of her feet, holding her gun in her right hand and steadying it with her left. She blinked, wishing her night vision would hurry up and kick in. She took a deep breath, then another, and angled around the door and pressed her back against the wall, her weapon leading the way. She whirled left, then right. The hallway was empty.

She stopped again to listen. Everything was quiet—too quiet. It was that odd time after rush hour when most people were home, getting dinner ready or preparing to go out for the evening. There didn't seem to be any traffic. Maybe the voice had just been trying to scare her.

This is just a taste. Then the rumble of a car's engine broke the silence outside. It sounded close, as if it were right in front of her house. But to see out, she'd have to go into the living room.

She held her breath, trying to listen past the engine's rumble. If someone was preparing to break into the house, or was already inside, they might use the noise of the car to mask their movements. Then the engine's noise grew fainter. They were leaving.

A crash hit her ears—breaking glass. Shock paralyzed her for an instant. She almost dropped her gun.

The crash came from the living room. Someone had broken in the big picture window. She held her breath, listening. Were they inside? Every muscle in her body shrieked with tension as she fought the urge to run.

Don't panic. Think.

Then light flickered red and yellow, sending writhing shadows chasing around the walls and floor and she smelled smoke.

Fire. Whatever they'd thrown through the window was burning. She had to get out. She glanced toward the front door. It was about fifteen feet away.

But what if that was their plan? For her to run out the front door right into their clutches.

She slid sideways along the wall toward the kitchen. She could fortify herself there. She'd be ready for anyone who came in through the front and she could guard the back door at the same time.

Halfway up the hall, she froze. She'd left her yearbooks and her dad's portfolio on the desk in the den. But she couldn't go back. It was too dangerous.

She'd have to get them later, if they survived the fire.

The fire's light and shadow beat her to the kitchen. And so had the smoke. And now she recognized the unmistakable smell of gasoline. Molotov cocktail probably. She didn't have much time. The smoke was already burning her throat.

She grabbed her phone from her purse and dialed 9-1-1. Then she called Dawson. By the time his phone rang once, she heard the faint sound of sirens. A second later, the car engine roared and tires screeched.

"Jules?" Dawson's voice in her ear sent relief gushing through her. "Damn it! Where the hell are you? I told you to—"

"I'm at my dad's. It's on fire!" she gasped out as smoke burned her throat.

"Call 9-1-1! Then get out! Stay low and get out! I'm coming!"

"I just— I am! I will." Suddenly, she felt heat buffet her like a giant's breath. "Dawson, hurry!"

She dropped her phone into her purse and ran to the back door. Her eyes were burning as much as her throat, and the air was thick with smoke.

She grabbed the knob and jerked. Then she remembered. Dead bolts. She'd installed them after her dad died to keep out burglars and vandals. She dug down into her purse with her left hand, but she couldn't find the keys. Had she left them in the front door? In her room? In the den?

The roar of the fire battled with the sirens, which were getting louder and louder. The noise was making her dizzy. She closed her eyes and leaned her shoulder against the wall by the door, still rummaging in her purse for her keys.

She took a deep breath and smoke seared her throat, triggering a coughing fit that left her completely out of breath. Gasping, she felt panic clawing its way up her throat. She heard Dawson's voice in her head.

Get out! Stay low!

She crouched down, breathing cautiously. The air near the floor was less thick with smoke, but she was still coughing every breath, and her eyes were pouring tears.

Feeling for the doorknob with her left hand, she pulled herself to her feet, holding her breath. Then she swung the gun's barrel at the panes of glass in the door.

Glass shattered. She swung again—once, twice, three times. Cold, sweet air hit her face. At the same time, a searing wind hit her from behind, nearly throwing her into the door.

The whole sky was ablaze with red blinking lights and the sirens screeched so loud they hurt her ears.

"Help!" she cried, her voice catching on a racking cough. "Help—me!" She fell back to the floor, her whole body spasming with the effort to breathe.

"Daw—son—"

Chapter Twelve

Dawson cut the engine and jumped out of his car, hitting the ground running.

Black smoke and red-and-yellow flames were visible through the house's front windows. Four firefighters wrestled water hoses and two had just battered in the front door.

Dawson sprinted toward the door, but he ran into a stone wall. He blinked and realized the wall was actually a big man in a fire-retardant jacket. "Hold it!" the man shouted.

"She's in there!" Dawson yelled back, fighting to get away.

The man's strong hands gripped his shoulders. "Where?"

"I don't know! She called me!"

Using one hand to trigger his shoulder mic, the man shouted, "Check the back! We may have a female in the house! Call the EMTs."

"On it, Chief. Out."

Dawson barely heard the tinny response over the sirens and fire and the surge of pressurized water.

He wrestled with the fire chief. "Let me go!" he growled, pushing at him without effect. Then he felt the man's grip slacken.

"Not the front!" the chief shouted. "Go that way." He pointed toward the back of the house.

Dawson ran.

By the time he got around back, the door was in splinters

and a firefighter was carrying Juliana's limp form over his shoulder.

"Juliana!" he shouted, rushing forward. She didn't stir and the man carrying her paid no attention to him. He trudged on to the end of the driveway and laid her on a waiting blanket.

Dawson followed, fighting panic and a sick dread. Was she moving? Was she breathing? As soon as the fireman laid her down, he crouched beside her.

"Where's the ambulance?" he demanded as the fireman felt her pulse and listened to her breathing.

Her chest was moving, but barely. Was she getting enough air? At that instant another firefighter set a portable tank down and placed an air mask over her nose and mouth.

He watched with the other men as her chest expanded slightly, then she arched, coughing and sputtering.

Dawson reached for her arm, but the fireman shook his head. So he crouched there, helpless, as the firefighters cared for her.

A new wail pierced the air and red lights came speeding toward them. The ambulance.

Dawson took Jules's limp hand in his. This time the fireman didn't object. But within seconds, two EMTs were out of the ambulance and pushing him and the firemen out of the way. One of them replaced the fireman's air mask with one of their own, while the other listened to her breathing, looked at her eyes and felt her pulse.

Standing, he grabbed a portable gurney out of the back of the ambulance and opened it. Within seconds, they had Jules inside the ambulance and were hooking her up to machines and IVs.

Dawson started to climb in.

"Hey," the lead EMT said, holding up a hand. "Sorry, I can't allow anyone in the ambulance."

"You've got to. I've got to go with her."

"Gulfport Memorial. Meet us there."

The fire chief laid a hand on Dawson's shoulder. "You can meet them in the emergency room. She's in good hands."

Dawson wanted to protest. Actually, he wanted to hit somebody, throw something and force his way onto the ambulance, but he reined in his frustration and anger. He nodded. "Okay. Fine."

"First, son, I need to ask you a few questions."

"But—" Dawson looked at the ambulance, which was pulling away from the curb.

"I told you, she's in good hands. I don't think she's injured. I think it's just smoke inhalation," the chief said. "Come on, I need your help."

Dawson relented. He spent about a half hour giving the fire chief information about Juliana, her dad and the Sky Walk's collapse. He told him that Detective Brian Hardy was handling the case, and described the other two attempts to harm her.

Then he drove to the hospital. An E.R. nurse led him to a cubicle where Jules lay on a hospital bed. Except for her cloud of black hair, she was almost unrecognizable. She had a wet cloth over her eyes and the oxygen mask over her face. She was hooked up to an IV and a whole bunch of monitors. A machine beeped incessantly as a shiny line peaked and fell over and over on a monitor screen.

"Why does she still have that mask on?" he whispered. "Why can't she use the little—" He made a gesture with his fingers at his nose. He had no idea what the thing was called. "It's not breathing for her, is it?"

The nurse shook her head. "No, that's not a ventilator. It's just a full oxygen mask. She inhaled a lot of smoke. It delivers more oxygen," the nurse said. "When the doctor comes back and checks her out, he'll probably change it."

Dawson breathed a sigh of relief, but he was still terrified for Juliana. The part of her face he could see was so white that the yellowing bruise on her cheek stood out in ugly contrast. It hurt his heart to see her like that. "Why isn't she awake?"

"We gave her a sedative and a painkiller. She was coughing and struggling against the mask."

He nodded, not taking his eyes off her. "Can I stay with her?" he asked. "She doesn't have any family."

The nurse smiled at him. "Of course." She checked the monitor, fiddled with the IV for a couple of seconds and headed out of the cubicle.

"Nurse?" he said. "Will they keep her overnight?"

"I don't know. We'll have to wait for the doctor."

"What do you think?" Dawson persisted.

"I think she's suffering from smoke inhalation. She's fairly heavily medicated. But I'm not sure if there's a bed available. We'll see what the doctor says."

"Thanks," Dawson said as she left. He pulled the only chair in the cubicle up to the bed and sat down, but he couldn't stay still, so he kicked it back and stood. He held Jules's hand in his, running his thumb over her knuckles. He bent down to kiss it and smelled the smoke from the fire on her skin.

"Jules," he whispered. "I thought I'd lost you."

She didn't move.

JULIANA WOKE UP with her throat hurting and her eyes burning. She moaned. Did she have the flu? She coughed, but coughing didn't help. It just triggered more coughing.

She felt a warm hand slide behind her back and lift her off the pillows. A pink plastic cup with a big straw appeared in front of her face.

Yes. Thirsty. She reached for the cup, but her right hand felt heavy. She had to make do with her left.

"It's okay, Jules. I'll help you." The voice was low and rumbly and familiar.

"Who—" Her eyes followed the hand up to the elbow and on to the shoulder, neck and finally face. It was Dawson. She smiled. "Dawson," she whispered.

He smiled at her. "It's good to see you, too. Drink." He guided the straw into her mouth and she took a long gulp of cool water.

"Good. When you finish this cup of water the nurse said she'll take the IV out."

"IV?" Juliana looked at him, then down at her hand. It was bandaged and a clear tube ran under a bandage on the back. For an instant, panic seized her, but then the memories rushed back—all of them crowding her brain at once. She couldn't sort them out. All she could do was react.

"Oh, Dawson! Daddy's house! It's on fire!" she cried, pushing the cup away. "I've got to—"

"The fire's over," Dawson said. "Shh. It's all over now. You're in the hospital, in the emergency room—"

"Hospital?" she repeated, the panic clawing its way up her throat again. "Why? What's wrong?"

"Hey, Jules, try to stay calm. Everything's okay. It's Sunday morning. You breathed in a lot of smoke, so they wanted to keep an eye on you." He touched the tip of her nose. "You've got an oxygen tube right there."

She tried to look down at it, earning a soft chuckle from him. "But—"

"They're only going to keep you here until they're sure nothing else is wrong with you. I don't think it will be much longer."

The jumble in her mind was beginning to sort itself out. She blinked. "My eyes burn," she said, then quickly, "not bad. Not bad enough that I need to stay in the hospital."

"I know."

Dawson was acting strange, kind of like an awkward mother hen. He patted her right hand and held the straw up to her mouth. "Drink some more."

She shook her head. "Not now. I'll—" she cleared her throat and winced "—I will in a minute."

"How about some juice? Would you rather have juice? I can call the nurse."

"No," she said, shaking her head. "I'm fine." She needed to think and she was having trouble because Dawson was hovering. He hadn't taken his eyes off her since she'd woken up. Nor had he stopped touching her. His sharp features were softer than she'd ever seen them.

She closed her eyes. She could get used to this—being cared for, hovered over, worried about by Dawson.

But the smell of smoke was still in her nostrils, the sound of the flames still roared in her ears and the hazy, terrifying memories weren't falling into place like they should.

The last thing she remembered was calling Dawson. *No.* The last thing she remembered was breaking the glass in the door and breathing the cold fresh air.

"I tried to get out," she said.

Dawson's jaw clenched. "I know you did," he said. "The fireman said you broke the glass with the barrel of your gun."

She nodded as more memories buffeted her. They were still out of order, like a slideshow that had spilled. "I left my stuff. Dawson, you've got to take me back," she said. "The yearbooks, Daddy's portfolio. They're all in the den."

A thought struck her. "Did the den burn?"

"I don't think so. Jules, when the police get through with the house, we'll see what they'll let you have. One of the firemen gave me your purse, though," he said with a vague gesture behind him. "And your gun."

At that instant the sound of the living-room window shattering hit her brain. She gasped. "They threw a Molotov cocktail!" she cried. "They were trying to burn Daddy's house down. Why?"

Dawson's face went still. He looked past her, then down, then back at her. "I don't think they were trying to burn the house down."

"Well, then what were they trying to do? Kill me?"

Dawson's hand was still on her back. He moved it up to her shoulder and squeezed gently, comfortingly.

"Oh, my God! They were!" Her throat started tickling again and she coughed. That cough triggered others.

Dawson held the cup for her when she was finally able to get her breath. She drank a few swallows.

"But why would they do that? I could have just run out the back."

Dawson's brows drew down in a scowl. "I think they were trying to scare you. Whoever sent them obviously doesn't want you looking into the Sky Walk's collapse. It's probably a good thing that your dead bolt was locked. If you'd rushed outside, if you hadn't called 9-1-1, you might have run right into their trap."

Juliana pushed the cup away again and lay back against the pillows and closed her eyes. She felt drained. "I forgot about the dead bolts," she whispered. "I was so scared."

She felt Dawson's warm firm lips on her cheek. "Why am I so sleepy?"

"They gave you something to relax you and something for pain."

"No kidding," she whispered. "Dawson?"

"Yeah, hon?"

She turned her hand under his and squeezed his fingers. "Don't leave me."

IT WAS NOON BEFORE Dawson got Juliana settled in bed in his guest room. She'd had to make a statement to Brian Hardy.

After she told Brian about the threatening phone call just seconds before the Molotov cocktail was thrown through the window, Dawson had dug her phone out of the sack of her belongings and Brian had taken down the number.

A hundred to one it's a throwaway cell, bought with cash, Brian had remarked. *No way in hell of tracing who bought it.*

"Shouldn't we have gone by the station to sign my statement?" Juliana asked for the third or fourth time.

"No," Dawson said patiently. "Brian said we could do that later. Are you comfortable?"

"I'm fine," she said for the twentieth or thirtieth time. "I'm not sleepy."

"I know," he said, setting a glass of water on the bedside table. "But the nurse said to put you to bed for the rest of the day, until you sleep off all that medication." He pulled the cover up a half inch, then smoothed it.

"I should take a shower," she murmured. Her eyelids were half-shut.

"Yeah, no. That's not happening. Not for a while."

"I smell like smoke," she protested, but there wasn't much resolve behind her words.

"That's true. Smoky peppermint. Very interesting."

She opened her eyes and looked at him. "I could take a bath."

"Not unless you want me to bathe you." Ah, hell, he shouldn't have said that. He'd already had to stand there in the doorway averting his eyes while she got undressed and put on pajamas—blue ones this time. Oddly, they still said Pink on the front.

Now he'd opened his big mouth and joked about bathing her, and planted that image in his head and that stirring in his groin. He huffed and shook his head, but the image wouldn't go away.

He cleared his throat. "Do you need anything?"

She shook her head with a smile. "No, Nurse Dawson." Her eyelids drifted closed. She blinked and opened them. "I guess I will nap for a little while. Don't let me sleep all day."

He nodded agreement, but she'd already drifted off.

He stood beside the bed until her breathing evened out. Then he leaned over and kissed her forehead.

"Sweet dreams, sleeping beauty," he whispered. "I promise you, I'm not going anywhere." He slipped out of the room and eased the door shut.

Then he went into the living room and lay down on the couch. He threw an arm over his face and tried to go to sleep, but images kept flashing through his mind.

Jules trapped in the burning house, screaming for him.

Jules in the bathtub, her rounded breasts glistening with water and soap, beckoning him to join her.

Jules in his arms, abandoning all restraint as he stroked her to climax.

He growled and sat up. He'd been up all night, but there was no way he was going to sleep—not anytime soon. So he took a shower in record time and made a pot of coffee.

Back on the couch, he picked up the folders that Jules had guarded with her life ever since he'd last seen them. She'd said that he could look at them. Okay, to be fair, she'd said they could go over them together, but that was practically the same thing, right?

It took him about two hours to read through every last page in every folder. Once he was done, he knew little more than he had before.

The thickest folder was all about the Delancey family. Dawson had found printouts of webpages, newspaper articles and notes about his dad, his mother, his brothers and himself. But those few pages didn't hold a candle to the printouts about Louisiana senator Con Delancey. Juliana had collected information about all of Con's shady politics, his mistresses,

the bootlegging and illegal gambling that had allegedly sup-
plemented the millions his wife had inherited, and even the
controversy surrounding his death.

He had to hand it to her, she was thorough and she knew
how to ferret out information. She'd covered public records,
newspaper archives, the internet and two books that had been
written about his infamous grandfather. Dawson hadn't seen
one of them. It was by a locally renowned author and titled
Con Delancey: A Controversial Life, a Controversial Death.

He read the inside flap. Sure enough, it sensationalized
Con's politics and his personal life and promised to reveal the
real truth about his death. He sighed and set the book aside.

The real truth was that Con's personal assistant had killed
him. No one, not even Andre Broussard, the assistant, had
disputed Con's proclivity for violent rages. The prosecutor
convinced the jury that Broussard had finally had enough and
snapped. He'd died in prison years ago, still proclaiming his
innocence.

There wasn't nearly as much about Michael, but Juliana
had his school records, including his degree in architectural
design. She had a copy of his contractor's license, as well as
newspaper articles about his indictment, his sentence and his
release from prison after thirty months.

Dawson took a deep breath and shook his head. It was a lot
of damning evidence—circumstantial but still damning. Juliana had done what Dawson himself had done—painted Michael Delancey with the same brush as his infamous father.
And when she found out who he was, she'd do the same with
him.

Dawson leafed back through the pages until he came to the
newspaper article that mentioned Michael Delancey's children. He read it again, clenching his jaw as he looked at the
names. *Three sons, John, Ryker and Reilly, and a daughter,
Rosemary, deceased.*

John. No mention of his middle name. But then, there was no reason the press would know that he went by Dawson. It was his dad and granddad who were locally notorious, not him.

He set the folders back on the coffee table and stared at them. He'd been right about Jules. She'd held on to those folders so vehemently, not because there was valuable information in them, but because they were all she had left now that her dad had been killed. He was no psychologist, but it didn't take one to see that.

He understood. Once he'd decided that his dad was a crook who cared less for people's safety than he did about saving a buck, he'd clung to his independence with every bit as much determination as Jules clung to her research.

But damn it, he wished she wasn't so stubborn. He'd told her not to leave his condo. If she'd paid attention to him, her dad's house wouldn't have been firebombed. She wouldn't have come way too close to death.

How was he going to keep her safe if she wouldn't listen to him?

Chapter Thirteen

Dawson cleared his brain of useless questions—like how to cure Juliana's stubbornness. Checking his watch, he saw that it was after two o'clock.

He'd questioned Hardy about any evidence found on the Molotov cocktail bottle, but Hardy had told him irritably that he'd have to wait until Monday. *Just like me,* he'd said.

Dawson speed-dialed his brother Ryker. No answer. He tried Reilly.

"What's up, Daw?" Reilly said affably.

"Hey, Reilly, where's your brother?"

"I think he and Nicole went to the aquarium. He said he was off duty, so he was turning his cell phone off. What's going on?"

"I need to check out a fire in Bay St. Louis last night. It was started by a Molotov cocktail."

"Something to do with a client?"

"Yeah, you could say that."

"I'm off duty today, too. I could go in and see what I can find if you really need me to, but Christy and I were about to head over to Mom and Dad's. We're going to take them out to dinner this evening."

"No, you guys go on and have fun. Let me know what you think about Mom."

"I can tell you right now. She's doing good. *I* see them about once a week. So does Ryker."

Dawson started to fire back a cutting retort, but he wasn't in the mood. "Say hi for me," he said. "Talk to you later."

As he hung up, he heard the guest-room door open and the bathroom door close. He started to jump up and check on Juliana to see if she needed anything, but he decided to wait. Was she just up for a moment to go to the bathroom? Or was she taking a shower?

He heard the water turn on. She'd slept a couple more hours after sleeping nearly all night in the E.R., so maybe she wasn't too drowsy to take a shower. He stood and paced, straining his ears, hoping he wouldn't miss hearing her if she fell.

Finally he heard the water turn off and about ten minutes later, she appeared in the living-room doorway. She'd dried her hair and it floated around her shoulders, framing her face, which was still pale. She'd put on a long-sleeved pull-over shirt and gray pants and had on pink fuzzy slippers.

Dawson's mouth went dry at the sight of her. It didn't matter that she was fully dressed. He had to clamp his jaw to stop the instant replay of the erotic vision of her all wet and glistening.

"Did you get your nap out?" he asked, wincing when he heard the gruffness in his voice.

A small wrinkle appeared between her brows. "Yes. At least I think so." She yawned. "The hot shower made me feel drowsy again."

And it made me feel horny, Dawson thought. "You want to go back to bed?" he asked.

"Actually, I'm hungry," she said, crossing her arms and walking over to perch on the edge of the couch. "Got anything to eat?"

He shrugged. "I don't know. I don't cook much, but I might have some cheese. I make a mean grilled cheese sandwich."

"That sounds great. I don't even remember when I ate last."

"Me either," he replied. "It takes about ten minutes to make a really great grilled cheese. Get some coffee while I fix them."

Juliana followed him into the kitchen and poured herself a cup of coffee. "Wow!" she exclaimed after taking a sip.

"Too strong?" he asked.

"A little bit," she responded. "Got any cream or milk?"

He shook his head as he dug a skillet out and set it on the stove. "Just canned. In the refrigerator."

She poured some into her coffee and took her mug to the kitchen table and sat.

"How's your throat?" he asked as he put the sandwiches together and put them into the skillet where butter was sizzling.

"Okay," she said, sipping the coffee. "It just feels a little raw. When we finish eating, can we go over to my dad's house? I want to see it, and I need to get those books."

"I told you last night, the police will let us know when you can get in there." Dawson slid the grilled cheese sandwich onto a plate and cut it in half.

"There you go," he said as he set the plate in front of her with a little flourish.

"How long do you think it will be? I need those books."

"Maybe tomorrow." He put the second sandwich in the pan and adjusted the heat.

"Can we just drive by? I want to see how badly the house was burned," she said, then took a bite of sandwich. "This is *good*."

"Told you." Dawson grinned as he served up his own sandwich and sat down across the table from her.

She devoured the sandwich in record time and drained her coffee mug. Dawson finished just a few seconds after her. She stood and took their plates to the sink. "I'll do the dishes."

"No, you won't," he said, standing behind her. "Get out of the way. I'll wash them. You need to go lie down."

She turned on the hot water and squirted dishwashing liquid into the pan.

"Come on," he said, moving next to her and bumping her with his hip. "You'd better take advantage of me while I'm in a good mood."

She turned and plopped a handful of suds on his nose. The handful was too big for just his nose, though, so it got in his mouth. He sputtered, laughing. "What are you doing? You'd better watch out."

She laughed at him and blew on the suds. He felt her breath tickle his lips, and before he even thought about what he was doing, he leaned down and rubbed the soap suds from his face onto hers. Then he kissed her.

She squealed and cried, "Eww," but he didn't stop. He urged her mouth open and thrust his tongue inside, kissing her deeply. Not even the taste of soap killed his desire. He felt her tongue on his, and a spear of lust hit him squarely in the groin. He hardened immediately.

His hands cupped her backside. He pulled her against him. She gasped and rose on her tiptoes, pressing herself closer and returning his kiss with matching passion.

"Damn it, Jules," he whispered hoarsely. "You're killing me."

In answer, she ran her hand down his chest to his belly and farther, finally gripping the button on his jeans. She fumbled with it as she bit his earlobe and teased it with her tongue.

Pushing her hand away, he opened his fly. She slid her thumbs inside his jeans and pushed them down a few inches, then she took him in her hand.

He nearly cried out as his erection pulsed against her palm. "You've got to stop," he begged her, but the only answer he got was a low, throaty chuckle.

So he jerked her sweatpants down, and in one smooth motion, he lifted her and set her down on the kitchen table. Then he touched her, urging her legs apart.

She moaned and thrust toward his hand. "Dawson," she gasped. "Please—"

It was all the invitation he needed. He pulled her to the edge of the table and entered her, smoothly and slowly. She was ready for him. She met him thrust for thrust. She lifted her face to his and kissed him hard and long, the rhythm of their kisses in sync with the rhythm of their lovemaking.

Dawson felt her body change and open. She threw her head back and cried out as he allowed his own climax to overtake him. They came together.

Afterward, Dawson held her in his arms with her head resting against his shoulder. Her hot breath whispered over his skin. When he finally pulled away, Jules looked at him with heavy-lidded eyes.

"Want to take a nap?" she whispered.

He closed his eyes and rubbed his nose against hers. "No," he said softly. "But I would like to go to bed."

JULIANA WOKE WITH A START. *Fire. Dawson.* But she wasn't in her dad's house, breathing smoke. She was with Dawson in his bed. He was beside her, asleep.

Then the real memories came back to her. Memories of Dawson making love to her on his kitchen table, proving to her that their first time hadn't been a fluke. They'd gone to his bedroom and he'd proven it to her again.

She was a believer now. She turned her head and looked across the little mound of white sheets at him. His intense blue eyes were closed and his mouth was relaxed. He looked like he didn't have a care in the world. She propped herself on her elbow and leaned down to kiss his cheek.

He muttered something that she couldn't understand, but he didn't wake up. It occurred to her that while she'd been sedated all night in the emergency room, he'd been awake. He probably had not slept a wink. He'd been watching her.

Watching over her.

Tears filled her eyes. Oh, how wonderful it would be if she could have him to watch over her for the rest of her life. Well, and keep taking her to those incredible heights of pleasure.

She slipped out of bed and pulled on her sweatpants and top. He might be exhausted, but she'd gotten all the sleep she needed. More than enough. She was feeling antsy.

When she stepped into the living room, it was dark outside. If she added it all up, she'd probably slept close to twenty-four hours.

The kitchen clock read after six. And she was hungry. Dawson's grilled cheese sandwich had been good, but it was long gone by now.

She went into the kitchen to look around for something to eat. In the refrigerator was more cheese, the canned milk, half a loaf of bread and some butter. The freezer yielded up little more. There was a pint of ice cream that was over half-empty. A bag of frozen French fries had definitely seen better days.

In the pantry, she found a couple of cans of chili, a big can of peanuts and a bottle of pancake syrup. She shuddered to think about how all that would taste in one dish.

She was considering chili and cheese when she heard Dawson's cell phone ringing. She went looking for it, wondering if she should wake him. It was on the couch where he'd been sitting. She picked it up and looked at the display—and froze.

The name on the display said Michael Delancey. For a couple of seconds, Juliana stared at it, numb with shock. She couldn't move, couldn't breathe. She blinked hard and looked at the display again, but nothing changed.

Why would Michael Delancey call Dawson?

She couldn't think of a reason. Not a good one anyway. Was Michael Delancey his client?

No. She shook her head. Dawson wouldn't do that to her, would he? With a thumb that was shaking so badly she could barely control it, she answered it.

Sirens and car horns screamed through the phone. Before she could draw breath to say hello, a panicked male voice was shouting.

"Dawson, the house is on fire! Your mother and I are all right. Dear God, it's a mess. Dawson?"

Juliana opened her mouth, but nothing came out.

"Dawson! Are you there?"

"Jules?"

She looked at him. He stood in the doorway, his hair tousled and his eyes heavy-lidded with sleep. But as soon as he saw the phone in her hand, he stalked over and took it from her, his fingers touching hers. She jerked them away.

His jaw tensed as he glanced at the display, then held the phone to his ear. "Dad?"

The single syllable stabbed Juliana in the heart. She heard Michael Delancey's voice, and behind it the wail of sirens. "Son, did you hear me?"

"No! Tell me." His eyes were on her, burning like lasers in his dangerously scowling face.

"The house is on fire!"

"Are you okay? Mom?"

"We're fine. I just—"

"Dad, I'll be right there. Don't worry." He hung up and stuck the phone in his jeans pocket. Without a word he whirled and headed to his room.

Juliana couldn't think. Her brain was stuttering like a

scratched CD. Michael Delancey. *Michael—Michael. De— De—De—Delancey.* She pressed her palms against her eyes and shook her head.

Think!

But all her brain would do was replay those words that had cut her heart like a knife. *Son. Dad.*

Dawson came out of his room, talking on the phone. "I'm on my way. Have you talked to Reilly?"

Juliana watched him. It was like watching a car wreck. She couldn't tear her eyes away. He'd thrown on a sweatshirt and run his fingers through his hair.

"Do you know how it started? No? Okay, I'll see you there." He hung up and stuck the phone in his jeans, then looked at her.

"I've got to go," he said. His eyes weren't lasers now. He looked worried and—if she could read him—embarrassed. But she couldn't read him.

Why had she ever thought she'd seen sincerity and honor in this man who had lied to her from the first moment she'd laid eyes on him? She finally managed to tear her gaze away. She nodded once, stiffly.

He headed to the kitchen, then turned back. "Jules, if you're thinking about leaving, don't. This has to be the same people who firebombed your dad's house. It's too dangerous out there."

She lifted her chin.

"Promise me you'll stay here."

"You lied to me. I don't ever want to talk to you again."

"I'll lock you in if you don't promise me."

"I'll stay here," she said, her voice flat. "Just leave."

He studied her for a few seconds, then clenched his jaw, turned and left. She heard the kitchen door slam, heard his car start, heard the garage door open, then shut.

For another minute or so, she just stood there, the image of the phone's display still stuck in her brain.

Michael Delancey.

Then she went into the guest room and started packing. She said the words he'd demanded. *I'll stay here.* But she'd seen in his eyes that he knew she was lying. She had to get out of here.

But his words had frightened her. *The same people. It's too dangerous out there.* She thought of everything that had happened, the attack at the post office, the falling beam, the fire at her dad's house. Was he right?

She shivered. Damn him. This was his fault. She'd come to depend on his being there to protect her.

Why hadn't she listened to her little voice? He had never intended to protect her. Everything he'd done had been to protect his father, Michael Delancey, the man who'd caused her dad's death.

Chapter Fourteen

Dawson sped over to his parents' house in his Corvette, trying to focus on getting there and making sure his parents were all right. But his brain was spinning faster than the wheels of the Vette.

The fire had to be the work of the same people who'd torched Vincent Caprese's house, just like he'd told Jules. He'd tell Ryker, get him to find out what evidence the police had found on the bottle. Had this fire been the result of a Molotov cocktail? Thank God his mom and dad had gotten out without being hurt. Now if Jules would just listen to him and stay put. But he knew she wouldn't. He should have locked her in.

All that swirled in his brain in the thirty minutes it took to get to his parents' house in Chef Voleur.

He spotted the black smoke while he was still several blocks away from his parents' street. As he whipped the Vette around the corner of their street his brain registered two fire trucks. He roared up to the curb, killed the engine and jumped out. As he did, a couple of firemen who were busy wrapping up the water hoses glanced his way.

He spotted his mom right away and ran toward her. "Mom!" he called.

"J.D.," she cried and held out her arms.

He grabbed her and hugged her. She smelled like smoke. "Are you okay? You're not hurt, are you?"

She shook her head. "Look at my house," she said. "Who would do this?"

The flames were out, but smoke still drifted upward from the front door and the broken window. "Where's Dad?"

She pointed. "Over there talking to the fire chief."

The man his dad was talking to was the same man who'd been at Caprese's house the night before. He squeezed his mother's shoulder. "Are you sure you're okay?"

She gave him a wan smile. "I'm fine. You go talk to them. Find out who did this."

At that moment a car roared up and screeched to a halt behind Dawson's. He knew without looking that it was Ryker's BMW. His brother sprinted across the lawn toward them.

Dawson met Ryker's gaze and nodded as his mom turned to her second son and hugged him. Then he headed over to where his dad and the fire chief were standing.

"Dawson," his dad said in greeting. "This is Chief Jeffreys. Chief, my son Dawson."

"Chief," Dawson said, offering his hand. The fire chief took it.

"We've met," the chief said to Michael. "Last night, in fact." He shook his head at Dawson. "How is it you're involved with all this?"

"I'm investigating the collapse of the Sky Walk at the Golden Galaxy Casino," Dawson said. "Apparently, there's somebody out there who doesn't like my nosing around."

The chief nodded. "This is your parents' house? And last night? Your girlfriend?"

Dawson gave a short, unamused laugh. "No, hardly my girlfriend. Vincent Caprese was her dad. He was killed when the Sky Walk collapsed. She's been nosing around, too."

"Maybe you two should stop *nosing* before somebody gets killed."

"There was a fire last night? Involving Vincent Caprese's daughter?" His dad frowned at him. "Why didn't you tell me?"

Dawson sighed. "I've been a little busy, Dad."

The chief glanced at each of them in turn. "I tell you what. The police are on their way. They're going to want to talk to you both about all this. I've got to get my men rounded up and make my report."

Michael held out his hand. "Thanks, Chief. I appreciate it. You and your men did a great job."

Dawson held out his own hand in turn. "That's right. Thanks."

The chief eyed Dawson. "I don't want to see you at another fire," he said.

"Trust me, I'm not planning to be at another one," Dawson replied.

Once the chief walked over to the fire truck, Michael turned to Dawson. "What was going on with your phone? Couldn't you hear me?"

Dawson grimaced. "Not at first," he hedged. "I'm here, though. What happened exactly?"

Ryker walked up, followed by Reilly and their mom. The twins had matching scowls on their faces. After quick hugs and greetings all around, Dawson repeated his question.

Michael wiped a hand down his face. "I was downstairs. Your mother was finishing up the dishes. I heard glass breaking." He reached for his wife's hand. "I thought she'd dropped something, so I started upstairs to check. Then she screamed."

"I heard the big window in the front shatter." She pointed to the hole in the floor-to-ceiling window in the two-story-high foyer. "I ran in there to see what had happened and flames were coming out of a broken bottle."

"A Molotov cocktail," Reilly said.

Dawson nodded.

"I screamed for your father and ran to get some water, but by the time he got up from the basement, the sheer curtains on the side windows were up in flames. We ran out through the garage."

"I called 9-1-1 after we were outside," Michael put in.

Ryker turned to Dawson. "This is all connected to the Sky Walk, isn't it? Who are these people? Do you know?"

Dawson shook his head. "No, but I'm sure as hell going to find out. In fact, I need you to—" He was cut off by the sound of police sirens. Two police vehicles roared up and two officers got out of one, while two young men in casual attire jumped out of the second, carrying cases.

"There's the crime scene unit," Reilly said. "I'm going to go talk to them, see if I can observe."

Ryker started to follow him, but Dawson caught his arm. "I need the evidence from the bottle, plus their findings from Caprese's house last night. This is getting way too close to home."

"You got that right. Why don't you back off and let the police handle this? Your snooping around is just muddying the water, not to mention putting our parents' lives in danger."

Dawson glanced toward the house. "I think I'm getting close to the truth. Why would they target Mom and Dad?"

Ryker took a step toward him. "Maybe they think you're smarter than you are."

"What the hell's that supposed to mean?"

"I'm guessing this is a message to you to back off."

"I'm not backing off. There have already been three attempts to hurt or kill Jules and the police refuse to put her in protective custody."

"Oh, come on, Daw. I know you—you're a maverick. You'd rather work against the police than with them."

"So? I'm getting results."

"Results? You think two deliberate fire assaults are results?"

Dawson scowled at his younger brother. "If I don't figure out what's going on, Dad could go back to jail."

"He can't go back to jail if he's dead," Ryker shot back.

"Look at that," Dawson shouted, gesturing toward the house. "Do you think for one minute that they couldn't have broken in and killed Mom and Dad? The Molotov cocktail was a warning."

"That's what I said! A warning to *you*. Too bad you don't have sense enough to take it!"

"Dawson! Ryker!"

Dawson turned and stared. Michael Delancey's voice sounded stronger and sharper than it had in years.

Ryker took a step backward. "I'm going to talk to the officers," he said shortly and walked away.

"Is Ryker right?" Michael asked Dawson.

"About what?" Dawson growled.

"Are you the one these people are trying to stop?"

"It's Jules—Juliana Caprese—who's being targeted."

His dad studied him for a few seconds. "Until tonight. Now it's your mother and me."

Dawson didn't say anything.

"You listen to me, son. If you're fooling around in Tito Vega's business, you'd better stop. He ruined my life without lifting a finger. If he was behind the Sky Walk's collapse, he won't let you live long enough to expose him."

DAWSON WAITED UNTIL EVERYONE had gone and his mom was packing a bag to go to a hotel to corner his dad.

"I want the truth, Dad. Now!" Dawson growled. They were

standing on the brick entrance to the house, looking at the damage.

"That stained-glass insert is a Tiffany," Michael said. "Your grandmother gave it to us."

Dawson looked up at the colorful circle, the bottom few panes of which were broken. He'd never paid any attention to it. It was just a part of the house he'd grown up in. "Maybe you can get it fixed," he said distractedly, then, "Dad—"

"Don't start with me. This has been a horrible night. I don't want Edie to come out and hear us arguing again. She can't handle all this stress right now."

Dawson clenched his fists as he thought of his mother struggling to stay sober. "Then why didn't you think about her when you were getting yourself thrown in prison?"

A pained expression crossed Michael's face. "What's it going to take to make you believe I didn't deserve to go to jail? I've never done a dishonest day's work in my life."

"You want to know what it's going to take to make me believe you? How about the whole truth? How about telling me everything you know about the Sky Walk, who worked on it, who was responsible for it falling if it's not you." Dawson blew out a frustrated breath. "Tell me now, before someone else gets hurt."

To his surprise, his dad nodded. "Okay." He sighed. "I did hire Knoblock after the guy in the suit threatened your mother. I knew he'd been sent by Vega, although he never said. So, yes, even though I knew exactly why Vega wanted Knoblock on the project, I hired him and let him handle the Sky Walk." Michael shook his head and sat down on one of the brick steps.

"He was a nervous wreck the whole time. Always looking over his shoulder, snapping at the workers. One day I was there after hours, around eight o'clock, just taking a look at everything, and I heard him on his phone. He obviously didn't think anyone was around. He was angry." Michael leaned his forearms on his knees.

"Best I can remember, his exact words were 'revenge for your son is between you and him. I've taken care of everything you asked for. We're square now. My men and I will be out of here by tomorrow.'" Michael paused for a second. "Whoever was on the other end of the phone said something. Then Knoblock said, 'Fine. You keep your blood money. It'll be worth it to me if I never hear from you again.'"

Dawson frowned. "*Revenge for your son.* Who was he talking to?"

Michael shook his head. "I have no idea."

"Have you told this to the police?"

"No! And I'm not going to. If that was Vega on the phone and it gets out that I heard the conversation, he'll make good on his promise. He'll kill your mother."

"Are you sure it was Vega?" Dawson asked.

"No, I'm not sure of anything. But Vega wanted Knoblock to build the Sky Walk."

"Where's Knoblock now? I'll get him pulled in for questioning and get a warrant for his phone records."

"No idea. He came in the next day, reported to me that the job was finished, and I never saw him again. He didn't even wait for me to pay him."

"Damn it, Dad! If I'd known this, I could have had the police looking for him all this time. I saw where he'd been indicted for a bridge collapse in Kansas City. Maybe he went back there. I'll get the police to check on that."

"Don't do that, Dawson. If you do, Vega will hear. He'll know. You'll get your mother killed."

"How do you think he's going to find out?"

Michael stood and paced. "Are you kidding me? Look at the man. He's right up there with all the big-city officials and politicians. How do you think he's managed never to get caught in all this time?"

Dawson spread his hands. "I'll tell you how. Because people like you are too chicken to come forward." He stepped up to his dad. "Well, that ends right here, right now. You—" he poked a finger at his dad's chest "—are going to the police and telling them everything."

Michael lifted his chin and stared Dawson down. "I will not. I can't risk your mother's life!"

"We can get both of you into protective custody. Hell, *I'll* get a couple of my men to guard you." He turned and paced, taking the same path Michael had. "I just wish we had some proof."

He pushed his fingers through his hair. *Proof.* The police weren't going to be very impressed with a couple of notes, especially considering that Michael Delancey wrote one of them. He turned back to his dad. "Are you sure there's not—"

Michael was staring at the ground, an odd look on his face.

"There's something else, isn't there?"

The older man kept staring at the ground for several more seconds. Then he looked up at Dawson.

"Dad?"

"Can you promise me you can protect your mother? She's so—fragile right now. Her nerves are nearly shot from trying to quit drinking."

Dawson stared at his dad. "What are you saying? I can keep both of you safe, but— What are you thinking?"

"I've got proof—proof at least that the design for the Sky Walk was altered. It implicates Knoblock. It's not going to give you Vega."

Dawson's pulse raced. "You've got proof? Why didn't you tell me? Where is it? *What* is it? Is it here, in the house?"

Michael nodded. "In my safe." They went into the house and met Edie coming from the bedroom with her suitcase.

"Here, Mom, let me get that," Dawson said.

"Ready to go?" Michael asked Edie. "I'll get the papers while you put the suitcase in the car," he told Dawson, tossing him his keys.

By the time Dawson got the suitcase into the trunk of their Lexus and his mother settled in the passenger seat, Michael was there with a large envelope. He gave it to Dawson.

"That's the altered plans. You'll see Knoblock's notes about the changes." Michael shook his head. "The only thing it proves is that he compromised the structural integrity of the Sky Walk. Not who ordered it."

"Where did you get these?"

"They were in a locker in a dressing room the construction workers used. I knew Knoblock had stored some things there, but I figured he'd cleaned out his locker before he left. It was a long shot."

Dawson peered inside the envelope. The sheets of paper he saw were stained and wrinkled. "What happened to them?"

"The lockers were under the Sky Walk. Everything in them spilled out onto the floor."

"You went in there and found these *after* the collapse?"

Michael nodded. "I was hoping I could find something that proved that Knoblock was responsible." He shrugged. "That does, but it doesn't prove I'm innocent."

"What do you want me to do with them?"

"I'd bet money that Knoblock's dead. Vega wouldn't leave a loose end like that hanging. Especially not after what I overheard. But on the off chance he's managed to stay alive, maybe you can find him."

Dawson was afraid his dad was right. If Vega was behind all this, and he was on the other end of Knoblock's phone call, he might very well be dead. "I'll see what I can find."

He walked over and leaned down to speak to his mother

through the passenger window. "Mom, get some rest, and don't worry about the house, okay?"

She shook her head with a wry smile. "I'm not worried about the house, dear. I'm worried about my men." She patted his hand. "Please be careful. And don't forget what I told you about your father."

"I won't," he replied. "I'll call you tomorrow." He straightened as his dad opened the driver's-side door. "I'll call you, too, Dad."

Michael got in the car and pulled away.

Dawson watched the taillights until they disappeared around a corner, then he turned and looked at the house. Ryker was right. He'd put his parents in danger, and for what? He looked at the envelope in his hand. It might be the only solid piece of evidence he had that Knoblock changed the plans for the Sky Walk. But was it enough to clear his dad?

Sighing, he pulled out his phone and called Grey Reed, his best investigator after Mack. "Grey, you're not on assignment right now, are you?"

"Nope. I turned in the final report on the Barber case Friday."

"I need you to bodyguard my parents." He gave Grey a synopsis of what had happened and told him where they were staying. As he got into his car, he called his dad to tell him what he'd arranged. Then finally, he headed back to his apartment.

His apartment. Jules. Yeah, no chance she'd still be there, not now that she knew he was Michael Delancey's son.

Chapter Fifteen

Juliana breathed a sigh of relief as she shifted the plastic bag of books to her left hand to unlock the door to her apartment. She'd made it. It was after ten o'clock, but she was finally home.

She dropped the books and her purse onto the couch and trudged into the bedroom. Without doing anything except kick off her boots, she fell onto the bed and pulled the throw over her.

She closed her eyes and waited to fall asleep. It couldn't take more than a few seconds—she was that tired. But now that she'd made it safely back here, sleep evaded her.

She turned over and pulled the throw over her head. She took a deep breath that ended at the top with a yawn, then let it out, coaxing her limbs to settle onto the mattress as her lungs deflated.

There. Relax and go to sleep.

But no. Her brain was on fast-forward. Everything that had happened in the past thirty-six hours or so was flashing before her closed lids like a slide show out of control.

The fire, the hospital, Dawson taking such gentle care of her, then making love to her over and over again.

And then—that phone call.

She threw off the throw and sat up. She couldn't sleep. Tossing her clothes on the floor of her closet, she headed into the bathroom and took a hot shower. It made her feel better but it didn't stop the images from spinning in her head.

As she towel dried her hair, the image of Dawson as he'd looked standing in the living-room doorway rose in her mind. He'd looked horrified, chagrined, embarrassed. As well he should have.

But no matter how horrified he was that she was holding his cell phone, staring at the display, his horror hadn't held a candle to hers.

Dawson was Michael Delancey's son.

How could she have been so naive, so stupid? She'd been suspicious of him from the first moment he'd stepped in front of her to pay the taxi driver. She should have checked him out further. Somewhere on the internet was a mention of his full name, she was sure. He was John Dawson Delancey.

She tossed the towel onto the floor and threw on her terry cloth robe, then headed into the kitchen to see what she had in her freezer. She knew that whatever was in the refrigerator was probably growing green mold by now.

Ice cream. Perfect. She'd give herself brain freeze. That would stop the slide show. But did she have any chocolate syrup? She opened the refrigerator door, ignoring the green stuff, and found it. Squeezing an ignominious amount onto her two scoops of ice cream, she went into the living room and plopped down on the couch.

She took a big bite of vanilla ice cream swimming in chocolate syrup and closed her eyes as the dark sweetness and icy cold stung the roof of her mouth. She took another bite. It was necessary to eat fast to get brain freeze. Then she reached for the remote control—silly sitcoms went well with brain freeze—but instead she found herself reaching into the bag of books she'd retrieved from her dad's den.

As soon as Dawson left to check on his parents—the Delanceys—she'd called a cab to take her to her dad's. The house might be a crime scene, but she still had keys, so she'd gone inside. She'd studiously ignored the damage and headed directly to the den and grabbed the yearbooks and portfolio she'd left there.

She had no idea what was in the portfolio. When she'd glanced inside, all she'd seen were small, black bound notebooks, like day planners.

She emptied them onto the couch beside her. Picking up the notebooks one by one, she saw that they actually were day planners—eleven of them, one for each of the past eleven years, except for this current year. She flipped through a couple of them. Her dad had kept a record of his life, measured out in pages divided into hours and half hours. And in the back of the recent ones were a pile of sticky notes.

Her throat closed and her eyes grew damp, looking at the pages of her father's life. She had vague recollections of his reaching into his shirt pocket for a black book and jotting notes into it, but it had never occurred to her that one day he would be gone and she would be reading the events of his life in his own handwriting, hoping to find a clue to why he'd died.

But where was this year's planner? Then she remembered—she'd found it in his desk at the casino. Dawson had put it in her purse, along with the other things she'd found there.

She grabbed her purse and dug inside until she found the day planner. She stared at its cover for a long while.

She didn't think she wanted to read the entries for the last day of his life. She wasn't sure she wanted to read any of them. But she'd never forgive herself if the answer to why he'd died was on one of those pages and she didn't even try to find it.

She finished the ice cream while she paged through, starting at January 1. Her dad had been semiretired before he got the job at the Golden Galaxy Casino, so the pages were filled with notes about fly-tying or woodworking projects, dates for coffee or golf with friends, and notes about her. Several times she had to stop and dry her eyes as she read things he'd written about her.

Then, on April 20, next to the 2:00 p.m. line, a name jumped out at her as if it were printed in flashing red ink.

Vega, written in her dad's neat, precise hand. Her heart thudded against her chest so hard that she put her hand over it.

Vega came through. Surprise! Got call from Meadow Gold Corp. Golden Galaxy, here I come! Opening June 1. Short notice...

It was the connection she'd been looking for. *Vega came through.* There was only one way to interpret that. He'd gotten her dad the job as manager at the Golden Galaxy. The mention of Meadow Gold Corporation implied that Vega was connected with the business.

She looked at the next page and the next. There were a number of meetings scheduled with the corporation, with the Gaming Commission, with other employees who had already been hired, but nothing else about Tito Vega.

She picked up the other notebooks and shuffled through them looking for last year's. Her dad had said *Vega came through.* That meant he'd talked to him previously, didn't it? But when?

She knew it wasn't after January 1, so she started at December 31 of the previous year and worked backward.

Then on the page for August 23, she found Vega's name.

Tito Vega—underlined three times—*called. re: me as Mgr Golden Galaxy Casino? Waveland. What's his angle? Prob. 6 mo.- 1 yr. Not holding breath.*

Tito Vega had gotten her dad the job at the Golden Galaxy,

but why? And what, if anything, did this have to do with her father's death?

Juliana laid the two day planners on the coffee table, open to the notes about Vega. Then she opened the yearbooks to her class's pictures. She stared at her dad's notes, then at the tiny photo of Anthony Vega in her sixth-grade yearbook.

What did it mean that she went to school with Anthony Vega? If anything. She didn't even know if Anthony was kin to Tito Vega. She picked up her folder with information she'd gathered about Vega and paged through it. There were mentions of his wife and children, but not many. His prominence along the Gulf Coast had developed over the last twenty years or so.

Anthony Vega was in her sixth-grade class but not seventh. She was eleven in the sixth grade, eighteen years ago. Maybe Tito Vega had sent his son to public school until his growing wealth made him able to afford private schools.

But even if that were true, what did it mean? Anything at all? Or was it just coincidence?

She stared at the pages, frowning, concentrating, but no flashes of inspiration came to her.

She wiped her face, then plunged her fingers into her hair. This was so frustrating. She had something here—she knew it! But she couldn't figure out what she had or what she should do with it. There was a piece of the puzzle missing. Trouble was, not only didn't she know which piece it was, but she also didn't even know where in the puzzle it fit.

She needed help. She was out of her league.

Damn it. She needed Dawson.

JULIANA WOKE UP with a cramp in her leg. Sitting up, she realized she'd fallen asleep on the couch, wrapped in her terry cloth robe. The pages were still spread out on the coffee table, next to her empty chocolate-smeared ice-cream bowl.

She pushed her hair out of her eyes. It had air dried into tangled waves. As she finger combed it, she studied the array of information she'd gathered about Tito Vega. It made no more sense this morning than it had last night.

She blew out an exasperated breath. What she'd realized last night hadn't changed. She needed Dawson's help to solve the mystery of how and why Tito Vega was involved in the collapse of the Sky Walk.

She looked at her watch. It was seven-thirty. Too early to call him? He'd probably been up late, talking to the authorities about the fire at his parents' house.

Tough. She needed her research, which she'd left at his apartment, and she needed to talk to him.

A flutter of apprehension whispered in her chest. She didn't want to talk to him. He'd lied to her—taken advantage of her. *Hurt her.*

She reached for her cell phone. Her hand hovered over it. What was she going to say? She needed to sound detached, businesslike. She couldn't let him know how much he'd hurt her.

She clasped her fingers together. Okay, here goes.

Dawson, I need to see you. I have information that links my father with Tito Vega. Yes, that would work.

She cleared her throat. "Dawson, I need to—" Her hand went to her neck. She sounded like a strangled frog. She got up and went to the kitchen for a glass of water. Her throat felt like the frog had taken up residence there. Taking a sip, she swallowed carefully, then tried again.

"Dawson, I need to see you." That was better.

Back in the living room, she picked up the phone and dialed Dawson's number. Taking a deep breath, she blew it out slowly as she listened to the ring.

"Yeah?" Dawson's voice sounded sleepy, gruff, sexy.

"Dawson, I need—" And then suddenly the frog was back. She swallowed with difficulty.

"Jules? Where are you? Are you all right?"

"I'm fine," she said quickly and cleared her throat, but before she could say anything, he lit into her.

"You told me you'd stay put."

Her temper flared. "You told me that we were on the same side."

"We are! We both want the truth."

"You don't want the truth! You want to keep your *dad* out of prison."

He was quiet again. "What do you want, Jules?"

She bit her tongue. No matter whose side he was on, he was the only person she could trust to help her put the puzzle pieces together.

"I need to talk to you. I've—I've found proof that Vega hired my dad to work at the Golden Galaxy Casino."

"Vega hired— I don't understand."

"I know. Me, either. Somehow all this is connected, but I can't put it together on my own. And I need my folders."

He was silent for a beat. "Is that what this is about? You want your little folders back?" he asked. "Well, I'm guessing you must have picked up your car last night, so why don't you just drive on over here and get them. I'm going to be gone anyway."

Juliana scraped her teeth across her lower lip. He sounded so harsh. If she didn't know better, she might think he sounded hurt. But she did know better. She blew out a frustrated breath.

"I wonder if you could make some time for me. I'd appreciate it."

She heard his sigh through the phone. "Fine, but I'm busy this morning. I've got to go with Mom and Dad to sign their statements about the fire and see if the police found any evidence on the bottle or in the driveway."

Juliana's heart sank. She'd expected him to sound defensive, even chagrined. But he sounded angry. *She* was the one who had a right to be angry, not him. How dare he make her feel defensive?

But she was also the one who needed him. So she'd take what she could get. "All right. This afternoon, then? Two o'clock?"

There was a brief silence on the other end of the phone. "I'll call you. I'm not sure when I'll be done."

Later than two o'clock? She couldn't sit here that long without losing her mind. She took a deep breath, prepared to yell at him that this was the first piece of real evidence they had. That it had to be Vega who was behind the Molotov cocktails. But she bit her tongue, stopping the retort. If she antagonized him, he might not agree to see her at all. After all, she'd practically thrown him out of his own apartment.

"Okay," she said, trying to mask her disappointment. "Please call me as soon as you can. This is important."

"Yeah," Dawson said, but she could tell he'd already stopped listening to her.

"Bye," she said, but he'd already broken the connection.

She set the phone on the coffee table and stared at it. It wasn't quite eight o'clock in the morning and Dawson had just ruined her entire day. She was going to have to sit here until after two o'clock, when he decided he had time to talk to her.

She looked at the sheets of paper spread out on her coffee table and shook her head. She couldn't even think. She needed a cup of coffee. She sighed and rubbed her eyes, then picked up the remote control.

She turned on the TV to the local news and listened as she headed into the kitchen to put on a pot of coffee. By the time she'd poured herself a cup, she heard the news anchor mention the Golden Galaxy. She hurried back into her living room and turned up the volume.

"Planned to begin today. The mayor of Waveland said that he hoped the rain would be gone by tomorrow, so that the demolition could begin. He stated his belief that cleaning up the debris from the collapsed Sky Walk would not only remove an eyesore and a dangerous temptation for children from the town, but it would also help the families of the six people killed in the tragic accident to heal."

Today was Monday! With everything that had happened, Juliana had lost track of the days. Today was the day that demolition was supposed to begin on the Sky Walk. She walked to the window and opened the blinds. Rain was pouring down in sheets. No wonder it was delayed.

She picked up her coffee cup and sipped as she changed stations, looking for more local news, but the morning programs had started. She'd probably have to wait until noon to hear anything else about the schedule for tearing down the casino.

She sat back against the couch cushions, drinking her coffee and thinking about the casino. Soon the mass of cables and steel beams that had killed her father would be gone. Thank goodness she'd gotten his things.

His things. Everything but the day planner was still in her purse. Had it only been three days ago—Friday—that she'd gone to the casino to get them? She shuddered as she thought of the steel beam that had almost hit them.

She set her coffee cup down and dug into her purse again. There was the photo album and the few sheets of paper Dawson had found stuck behind the file drawer. She set them aside and continued digging. Where were the pen set and the ring?

A little more digging turned up the pen set, but she

couldn't find the ring. She felt along the bottom of the purse but it didn't seem to be there. She started to turn her purse upside down. Then she remembered. She'd been holding it when Dawson had grabbed her and flung her to the floor inside the supply closet. She must have dropped it.

Still, just to be sure, she dumped her purse and sifted through everything. No ring.

It had to still be on the floor of the office. She walked over to the window again and peered out. Still raining, though not as hard as before. She looked at her watch. It wasn't even eleven o'clock. Dawson wouldn't call her until after two. She had more than three hours to kill.

She loaded all her stuff back into her purse and grabbed her raincoat. She had to find her dad's wedding ring. If she didn't do it today, it might be lost forever.

Chapter Sixteen

Dawson looked at his watch again as he turned into the parking lot at Juliana's apartment complex. He'd tried to call her a couple of times already, to let her know that he'd finished with his parents early, but she hadn't answered her phone.

He drove slowly up and down the rows of cars, listening to the slap-slap of his windshield wipers and squinting against the colorless haze created by the falling rain. He didn't see her car anywhere. He activated his Bluetooth.

"Dial name," he said as he circled around and pulled into a parking space close to the front door of her apartment building.

"Please say the name," the annoyingly patient, yet cheerful, voice begged him.

"Jules."

"Dialing Jules."

Her cell phone rang seven times before it went to voice mail. "Jules, it's one-thirty. Call me," he said before cutting the connection and turning off the car. It was the third message he'd left.

Why wasn't she answering? The phone wasn't going directly to voice mail, so it wasn't turned off or out of juice.

Then his phone rang. He looked at the display. Not Jules. Mack.

"Mack," he said. "What you got for me?"

"You've got to give me a raise for this."

"For what?"

"The secretary I just spent a great mini-vacation with? The secretary to the vice president for *finance*."

"Yeah?" Dawson pushed. He didn't have time to hear about Mack's escapades. "Give me the short version. I've got a situation here."

"Right," Mack replied, suddenly all business. "One of Heidi's jobs is payroll."

"Heidi," Dawson broke in. "Seriously?"

"Yeah. Heidi. Anyway, the checks for Bayside Industries are drawn on a bank in the Caymans."

"They're in Switzerland, and their payroll comes from the Caymans?" Dawson asked.

"Yeah, but that's not all. She got the wrong checks once. They were for a corporation based in Waveland, Mississippi."

Dawson straightened in his seat. Anticipation burned along his nerve endings. "What corporation?"

Mack paused for effect. "Meadow Gold."

A chill ran down Dawson's spine. "You're telling me that Meadow Gold and Bayside Industries use the same bank in the Caymans?"

"Not just the same bank, boss. The same account."

Dawson was afraid to breathe. He didn't want to ask the next question. Didn't want the answer to be no. "Do you have proof?"

"You'd better believe it. I have photocopies in my hot little hands."

"Photocopies?"

"When it happened, Heidi got worried that if the bank could make that kind of mistake, something might happen one day that might implicate her. She never wanted to handle payroll in the first place. So when the checks came in, she photocopied all of them plus the envelope and put them in a personal safe-deposit box, along with photocopies of Bayside Industries checks and their envelope. She also wrote out a statement about what happened and had it notarized."

"You've got copies of all of that?"

"Yep. And I should be back there by tomorrow morning."

"Call me when you touch down."

He hung up. He had the connection between Meadow Gold and Bayside Industries. The missing piece that connected Tito Vega with Meadow Gold, the company that funded the Golden Galaxy Casino. Was he one step closer to proving that Vega ordered Knoblock to skimp on the Sky Walk? He didn't know. But the papers Mack was bringing back should be enough to get a court order to open those Cayman Island bank records.

He'd parked while talking to Mack. Now he vaulted up the steps to her apartment two at a time and banged on her door. "Jules?" he called. "Juliana? Open up. It's me. I've been trying to call you."

Nothing. He held his breath and listened. He could hear the TV. She must be home. Why wasn't she answering? With worry twisting his insides, he took his phone out and dialed her number. Within a second, he heard it ringing—from inside the apartment. If she was in there, something was wrong.

"Jules!" he shouted, banging on the door.

"Hey!" a man said from behind him. Dawson whirled. A middle-aged unshaven man in a white sleeveless undershirt stuck his nose out from the apartment directly opposite Juliana's. "Shut up out here. I'm trying to sleep."

Inclining his head a fraction of an inch, Dawson turned back to Juliana's door. The man cursed and slammed his door.

He held up his key chain and chose the brightest, newest key. Thank God he'd ducked out and had a copy of Juliana's key made while she was in the hospital. If he kicked the door in, the neighbor would probably call the police. He inserted the key into the lock and turned the knob. Stepping into her living room, he closed the door behind him. "Jules?" he called, but he knew without checking that she wasn't there. The apartment felt empty.

He looked around for the remote, prepared to turn the TV off, but if Juliana—budding private investigator—came home and didn't hear it, she might think someone had broken into her apartment. So he left it on.

He surveyed the living room. School yearbooks and loose papers were spread out on the coffee table, along with a pile of small notebooks. A coffee cup was sitting precariously on the edge of the table. He picked it up. It was cold. He frowned and hit redial on his phone. When he heard her ring, he followed the sound and found her phone stuck between two couch cushions. He picked it up and pocketed it.

Damn it. She knew better than to leave without checking that she had her phone. Wherever she was, she didn't have a way to call for help. He didn't like that one bit.

Hoping that leaving the TV on meant she was on a quick errand and would be back in a few minutes, he sat down on the couch. Until she came back or he figured out where she was, he might as well do something productive. He did his best to ignore his instinct, which was telling him that she'd taken off on her own to check out whatever she'd called him about.

He looked at the books and papers spread out on the coffee table. The proof she'd mentioned that Tito Vega and her father were connected?

Without moving them, a habit he'd cultivated for his job, he studied the open books. As he'd first thought, they were yearbooks—old ones. The first one was open to the first-grade class photos. His eyes automatically skimmed the names until he came to the *C*s. There she was. Caprese.

"I'll be damned," he whispered. Juliana was skinny and had her hair pulled back in a ponytail. A huge gap-toothed grin stretched her mouth and her dark eyes danced with mischief. Dawson smiled and touched the picture. Then he shook his head and turned to the second yearbook.

It was open to the sixth-grade class photos. There was Juliana again. Her smile wasn't as natural or as mischievous, and her hair hung down to her shoulders. She had on eye makeup and lipstick and she looked like what she was—a little girl playing dress-up. He remembered her telling him that her mother had died when she was a toddler and her father had raised her.

Somewhere between sixth grade and now, she'd figured out how strikingly beautiful she was, and had learned how to make the most of her many assets.

Dawson blinked and realized the sixth-grade picture was a blur. He'd drifted off into a daydream about Juliana's long black hair and snapping dark eyes.

He rubbed a hand down his face, then slid the third yearbook out from under the second one. He compared the dates. This was Juliana's seventh-grade yearbook.

He paged through it until he found the seventh-grade class photos and there she was. Her eye makeup—if she had any on—was subtly applied and she didn't have on lipstick. *Much better,* he thought.

He sat back against the couch cushions and regarded the three books. Why had she been so adamant about retrieving them from her dad's house? What was so important about those three pages? He didn't have a clue.

He turned his attention to the small leather notebooks lying open, facedown on the table. He picked up the top one, the 2006 one, and quickly scanned the two facing pages. The dates were April 19 and 20 of this year. Then, even though he already knew who the pocket calendar belonged to, he flipped to the inside front page.

Sure enough, printed in a neat, precise hand, was the name Vincent Caprese. He went back to the page for April 20.

On the 2:00 p.m. line, he saw what Juliana had seen. A note her father wrote about Vega.

Vega came through. Surprise! Got call from Meadow Gold Corp. Golden Galaxy, here I come! Opening June 1. Short notice...

That's what Juliana had told him on the phone. Vega had hired her father to manage the Golden Galaxy Casino. It was another piece of information that linked Vega to Meadow Gold Corporation.

He remembered what else she'd said. *Somehow all this is connected, but I can't put it together on my own.* That's why she'd called him.

As angry as she'd been at him for lying to her about who he was, she'd turned to him first when she needed help. And he'd blown her off. He blew out an exasperated breath. His parents had been grateful that he'd gone with them to review and sign their statements, but they'd have understood if he'd told them that he had to follow up a lead on the vandals who'd thrown the Molotov cocktail.

He could have been here for Jules. He *should* have.

He frowned at the yearbooks, trying to think the way she would. Why had she pulled out old grade-school yearbooks? What could be in them that could help her with her case?

He did not have a clue, but because she'd thought they were important, he decided to go over each page thoroughly. By the time he'd gotten to the last row of names, he was more confused than ever.

Then he zeroed in on the last name and the last picture. *Anthony Vega.* Dawson knew from his own research that Vega had two children—a daughter and a son. He didn't remember their names, but there was something about the son. Hadn't he gone to prison?

Dawson looked at Juliana's sixth-grade class photos. There Anthony Vega was again. But he wasn't in the seventh-grade yearbook. So Tito Vega's son had gone to school with Juliana from first to sixth grades.

So what?

Now he understood what she'd meant when she'd said that she was sure all this was connected, but that she couldn't figure it out. He felt the same way. There was something important here, if he could just put it together.

Tito Vega got Vincent Caprese the position of casino manager with Meadow Gold Corporation, who owned the Golden Galaxy Casino. Vega's son went to grade school with Caprese's daughter. Michael Delancey was convinced that Vega was behind the collapse of the Sky Walk. What was the missing link?

He pulled out his phone. It was a smartphone but he'd rarely used all the features. But now he wanted to see what the story was with Vega's son. With a few clicks, he was on his browser, searching for Vittorio Vega. There wasn't much. At the top of Vega's bio on his real-estate webpage was a family portrait, but there was no mention of the children's names.

Dawson searched the name Anthony Vega. He got over a hundred thousand hits. He added Mississippi to the search. That brought the number down a bit. When he added the word *prison,* he finally found a small archived Mississippi newspaper article that mentioned Anthony Vega. He'd been indicted and convicted of extortion in 2008. Dawson searched further, but nothing else came up.

There was only one thing to do. He called Ryker. "What's up?" he asked when his brother answered.

"Me," Ryker said disgustedly, "to my neck in paperwork. Did Mom and Dad get their statements signed?"

"Yep. They're back at the hotel fretting about when they can go home. I need you to do something for me."

"As long as it's legal."

"Anthony Vega. What do you know about him?" While he talked, Dawson flipped through Caprese's day planner for 2006, skimming the entries. Luckily, Caprese's handwriting was neat and easy to read.

"Tito's kid? I believe he got a nickel for extortion, despite his daddy's best efforts. He was a floor manager at a casino and was hitting up players who weren't there with their wives. Seems to me he was killed in prison. Some kind of scuffle or lover's quarrel."

"That's what I thought. Got any idea when that was?"

"Hang on."

Dawson heard the soft stutter of fingers on a keyboard.

"Here it is," Ryker said. "He went to prison in 2008. He was killed sixteen months later."

"What about the name of the casino?" Dawson asked.

"It's right here—yeah. The Beachview Casino in Gulfport."

At that exact moment Dawson's gaze lit on Anthony Vega's name, printed in Caprese's neat handwriting. "Great. Thanks," he said.

"What are you up to, Daw? You're not going to tangle with Tito Vega, are you?"

"I've got a theory. If it's right, then I may know who killed Vincent Caprese and five other innocent people."

"Do me a favor, maverick. Call the police. Don't go up against Vega by yourself."

"Do *me* a favor and tell me why nobody has put him away before now."

Ryker sighed. "You know what Con Delancey always said. *Politics and crime are like love and marriage.*"

"Right," Dawson put in sarcastically. "You can't have one without the other. Tell that to Aunt Bettye."

"It's just a saying, Daw."

"Don't tell me you buy into that?"

"Luckily, I don't have to worry about Vega. His influence doesn't reach as far as Chef Voleur. He concentrates on the Mississippi Gulf Coast."

"Lucky you."

"Just watch out, Daw. You mess with Vega and somebody's going to get hurt."

"You know, nobody has messed with Vega so far, and it looks like a lot of people are getting hurt." Dawson thought about the threat Vega had sent his dad. "Dad ever mention anything about Vega to you?"

"Dad? No. Why?"

Dawson didn't want to go into it. If Michael had thought Ryker or Reilly could do anything, he'd have told them about the threat on his wife's life. "Nothing. Something I was thinking about. I've got to go," he said. "Talk to you later."

"Daw, be careful."

"Always am," Dawson tossed back, then hung up. He read Caprese's note written on April 6, in his 2006 day planner.

Anthony Vega. Flr mgr hired 01/2006. Q re: blackmail! Davis interviewing complainants.

Anthony Vega worked for Caprese in 2006! He turned to the front of the day planner. On the inside front cover Caprese had printed his name and his position. *General manager, Beachview Casino, 3700 Beach Blvd, Gulfport, Mississippi.*

This was the missing piece of information that Jules was working on. Vincent Caprese had hired Anthony Vega as a floor manager at the Beachview Casino. Dawson glanced at the yearbooks. Maybe because Vega had claimed to be a friend of Juliana?

He flipped through the pages and found more notes about Anthony Vega's illegal activities. Finally on September 10, 2006, Vincent Caprese had Anthony Vega arrested for extortion.

It was motive for Tito Vega. Caprese had sent his son to prison and the son had died there. Dawson stuck the day planner in his pocket to give to Detective Hardy. This really could be the missing piece that could end up linking Vega to Juliana's father's death.

Dawson looked at his watch. "Damn it," he muttered. "Where are you, Jules?" The clock in his phone read three-fifteen. He'd been here over an hour, and she knew he was going to call her after two o'clock. Hadn't she realized she didn't have her phone with her?

He'd go after her—if he had a clue where she'd gone. He looked at the rest of the items on the coffee table. It appeared she'd left in a hurry. What had she been looking at besides the yearbooks and day planners?

Among the items on the coffee table were the things she'd pulled out of her dad's desk at the casino. The loose paper and torn file folder he'd pulled from the back of the desk, the pen set and the photograph album. He skimmed the loose pages. They were an original and a copy of a routine memo to the Golden Galaxy administrative staff. No help there.

He dismissed the pen set Jules had found in Caprese's desk drawer, and although he wanted to look at them, he also dismissed the collection of photos in the leather pocket-size photo album.

Wasn't there something else she'd found? She'd felt around the back of the drawers, searching for anything of her father's.

Then he remembered. The last thing she'd found was the

wedding ring. She'd had it in her fist when the beam had come crashing down. Only Dawson's quick instinctive reaction had saved them.

Oh, crap. It wasn't here with the rest of the things she'd brought with her from her dad's office. Had she dropped it when the beam fell?

Something from the TV drew his attention. He looked up. The news anchor was announcing the top stories of the day. With a still photo from the Golden Galaxy Casino pictured behind her, she announced that because of the rain, demolition and cleanup from the collapse of the Sky Walk would be delayed until the next day, Tuesday.

"Ah, hell, Jules," Dawson muttered. She'd gone there. He knew it as surely as he knew his own name. She'd gone back to the site of her dad's death and her own near-death experience to retrieve her dad's ring.

JULIANA SNEEZED into the crook of her arm. Her eyes itched and her throat was getting scratchy from the dust and debris. She was never going to find her dad's ring. It was after three-thirty and the sun was low enough that her dad's office was cloaked in shadow. She continued her methodical search of the supply closet, thankful the beam that had nearly hit them had been removed.

She blinked. Was that a glint of metal? It was, but she'd unearthed a pile of nails and screws that had reflected the beam of her flashlight. This was probably another one.

Crouching down, she held the light steady, moving it a fraction of an inch at a time, as she tried to catch the metallic glint again. There it was. She reached out, but it was just a tiny piece of aluminum foil—a candy wrapper?

She was about ready to give up and get out of the dark deserted building. From the moment she'd come in through the main entrance and discovered that the electricity was off, she'd felt like ghosts were breathing down her neck. As she'd made her way past the silent slot machines, she remembered the first time she'd sneaked in here on Friday, three days ago, looking for her dad's things. The machines had lined up in front of her like grim soldiers guarding the dead, their pull levers sticking up like rifles. And that had been with lights on.

Today they were much more ominous. She'd cringed as she'd hurried past them, the beam of her flashlight sending shadows dancing and her imagination spinning out of control. Every glass screen looked like a monster's face in the stark flashlight's glow. Sometimes from the corner of her eye, she thought she'd seen them move.

She'd been practically running by the time she'd reached the office. It hadn't helped that for every step she'd taken, she'd been sure she heard footsteps behind her.

Even now, creaks and rattles and rustling noises plagued her ears. Were other precarious beams working loose from their bolts? Rats and cockroaches? Ghosts?

Another creepy sound swirled around her. She hoped it was the wind, but it sounded like people whispering. The susurrous mutterings rose then faded, rose then faded. It had to be the wind, didn't it? Human beings' whispers wouldn't fade in and out. Juliana shivered and ran a hand across the back of her neck where she could swear she felt a cold breath.

We know there's nobody there, her little voice assured her. *Do we?* she countered. She set her jaw and concentrated on searching the dirty floor.

The flashlight's beam glinted again. This time the flash was definitely yellow rather than silver. Carefully, she slid her hand down the beam of light, and patted the small circle of illumination on the floor.

She felt something. Swallowing the hope that sprang up to clog her throat, she closed her fingers around the hard, circular object and stood. Without daring to breathe, she shone the light on her fist and slowly opened her fingers.

She'd found it. Her dad's ring! The wedding band he'd worn for years until it became too small. She held it up and blew the dust off it, then shone the light on the engraving inside the gold band.

Love forever, J.

Her dad had told her the story of their wedding many times. Her mother, Julia Mills Caprese, had placed it on her dad's finger the day they were married. Her dad had given Juliana her mother's ring when she'd graduated from high school. It was in her safe-deposit box. She carefully tucked her dad's ring into the pocket of her jeans.

As she turned to look at the wreck of her dad's office, where he'd drawn his last breath, more creaks and thuds echoed through the main floor of the casino. She needed to get out of here before the sun went down and left the casino pitch-dark.

Her flashlight had fresh batteries, but the place was giving her the creeps.

She picked her way back to the door of the office and turned toward the main entrance. The day was cloudy, but a dull gray light shown in from the glass doors. The dim glow reflecting off the slot machines played tricks on her vision. She was sure she could see them moving, marching in sync, guarding the doors. She shivered. If only they were guards, keeping her safe.

Then she saw a different movement, a paler, slimmer shadow among the one-armed bandits. She blinked and looked again, but it was still there.

Suddenly, a light flashed. Her heart jumped into her throat and lodged there, interfering with her breathing. She gasped and gasped again, her breaths sawing loudly.

Get a grip! she commanded herself. *Breathe slowly, evenly, silently.*

The light was still there, glaring in her eyes. She squinted and saw the pale halo around the bright circle of light. It was a flashlight. Her heart jumped again, thudding against her chest wall and pounding in her ears.

Who was it? The beam flared as the person swung it from side to side. He was just inside the main entrance, probably sixty or more feet away from her.

Then the pattern of light changed. He was coming toward her. Her hand went to her throat and she could feel her pulse throbbing rapidly. She squinted again, but whoever it was, he'd walked out of the light from the glass doors and all she could see was the flashlight's beam.

Maybe it was Dawson, she told herself. But she knew it wasn't. That pale shadow looked nothing like his long, lean body. Plus, he would have already identified himself to her. In fact, he'd already be berating her, telling her that if she wanted to be a private investigator, she needed to learn how to hide in plain sight.

The police, she thought. It had to be the police. She sniffed in irritation. Were they watching the abandoned casino 24/7? But as the light came closer and she had to strain to hear the almost-silent pad of footsteps, she knew it wasn't the police, either. They wouldn't be sneaking up on her. They'd have their high-intensity flashlights next to their raised weapons and be shouting at her to put her hands up and freeze.

Whoever was behind that beam of light had no more business being in the abandoned casino than she did. Had they come here to find something they'd lost, like she had?

Or were they here for her?

Chapter Seventeen

Juliana reached into her purse for her phone, but it wasn't in the pocket where she usually kept it. She felt frantically around the bottom where things tended to collect, but no luck. Then she remembered calling Dawson on it. She'd set it down on the coffee table or on the couch. How stupid of her to leave without checking that she had it.

She was on her own. Her pulse throbbed in her throat—those footsteps were coming for her. She could hear Dawson's voice in her head. *I told you to stay put.*

Damn it, Dawson. If you'd made time for me, I might not be here with faceless people coming at me in the dark. Her hand went to the small of her back, to her weapon tucked into the waistband of her jeans.

Put that gun away. If you want to be a private investigator, you've got to know when to attack and when to hide, Dawson's voice told her.

Fine. This was definitely the time to hide. If she turned off her flashlight and didn't run into anything, she might be able to slip out through the west side fire door before her pursuer could get to her.

She pressed the off switch. The click was alarmingly loud in the suddenly pitch-black silence. The only thing she could see was the flashlight beam approaching. It stopped and wavered, then the person holding it lifted it and swung it in a wide arc, as if trying to find her.

She shrank back against the wall. Without her flashlight, she felt disoriented. Without the wall, she'd certainly lose her balance and fall. It was an awful feeling. She blinked hard, as if blinking would help her eyes to adapt. The sun peeking through the windows barely spread a dusty sheen over the wreckage. Rather than helping, the dim glow actually hurt. The shadows seemed blacker, and the light kept her eyes from adjusting.

The flashlight kept coming. She needed to get to the fire exit. That was her only chance of escape. It was to the left of her dad's office door. If she worked her way to her left while hugging the left wall, maybe she could make it without tripping over anything.

She inched her way along the wall, which had survived most of the damage when the Sky Walk collapsed. Shuffling, sliding her sneaker-clad feet carefully along the Italian tiles, she moved slowly, feeling for objects or debris that might trip her up. She kept her eyes on the flashlight beam coming toward her.

He had slowed down. Why? Whoever he was, he'd had plenty of time to get to her by now. She clung to the wall, her left hand feeling the way ahead of her.

Her hand hit something cold and hard with a dull thud that to her ears sounded like a gong. She felt it—it was a fire extinguisher. She must be close to the door. She blew out a breath she hadn't realized she'd been holding. Her stuttering pulse slowed.

The flashlight's beam swept across the floor, pulling her gaze to it. She measured the near edge of the ellipse with her eyes. He was close and he was still coming.

Then a muffled sound reverberated through the building.

Panic gripped her again and she froze. Her fingers tingled and her stomach sank.

The sound was unmistakable, wasn't it? It sounded like a heavy door closing, she thought. But where? In front of her?

The echo bounced from wall to wall, from ceiling to floor, all around her. Why did sounds that were ordinary in the daytime become magnified and distorted in the dark?

Taking a deep breath and blowing it out eased her shivering panic a bit. *Concentrate. Listen.*

Who had slammed the door, if it was a door slamming? It could have been a piece of debris falling, she supposed. Did the guy with the flashlight have a partner? A dreaded certainty weighed her down. Even if the sound she'd heard had come from the fire exit, she still had only one choice. She had to get to the door. She didn't know how far the nearest exit was and she'd never find it in the dark.

With her tense muscles beginning to ache and her confidence draining away, she slid farther along the wall.

Her toe bumped something. It rolled noisily. She stiffened, her arms and legs quivering in reaction. Her first instinct was to reach for it, to quiet it, but she suppressed the urge. The man with the flashlight knew where she was anyway.

We've got to keep going. Get outside where we can see. It sounded so easy, but what if she opened the door to an ambush?

A chill crawled up her spine, raising the hairs on her nape. Her body was betraying her—giving in to fear. She was close to the breaking point.

Suddenly, she was surrounded by sound. Rustling, whispering. The nearly silent footsteps were getting louder. The flashlight's beam was brighter—blinding. And the sound of that door still resonated through the walls.

Forcing herself to ignore her imagination, she patted the wall with her left hand and stretched to feel as far in front of her as possible. Where was the damn fire door? Shouldn't she have reached it long before now?

She kept moving, her hand kept sliding until finally her fingers hit a door frame. Thank God!

At the same time, the flashlight beam reached her boots. This was it. She pulled her weapon from the waistband of her jeans, thumbed off the safety and gripped it two-handed.

She took a deep breath and pushed against the metal panic bar with her elbow, preparing to lead with her gun. Maybe they wouldn't expect her to have a weapon.

The door slammed open. Light blinded her. Her grip tightened on her gun. Then she felt a rough hand on her arm and pain exploded behind her eyes.

JULIANA'S HEAD FELT LIKE somebody had stomped on it. She curled her fingers and they scraped across rough, cold concrete. She decided that before she moved, she needed to do an inventory—see if she was all in one piece. She knew her head was attached to her neck because both of them throbbed with pain.

Her shoulders hurt, too, especially the left one. She flexed her fingers against the concrete. All ten present and accounted for. She felt vaguely nauseated and her left hip ached. Apparently, she was still intact.

She tried lifting her head. The throbbing pain turned to screaming agony.

"All right, then. Stop whimpering and sit up slowly."

She jerked in surprise and pain stabbed into her brain. Carefully maneuvering her hands under her to lift her leaden head, she grimaced and pulled herself to her hands and knees.

"Oh!" she grunted as she rolled into a sitting position. As soon as her hands were free, she gripped either side of her head. Her fingers touched thick, sticky wetness on the left side of her head. Blood. "Ow," she groaned.

"I said, enough whining."

She raised her head a millimeter at a time. Highly polished black shoes came into her line of vision, as did two exquisitely tailored pant legs. She almost chuckled. Her brain seemed to be on autopilot. She couldn't make it assess the situation or scope out her surroundings for a possible escape. In fact, it hurt her head to even think about not thinking.

She winced and that hurt her head a lot. So she just let her thoughts go and listened to them. The tailored pant legs were a dark charcoal-gray with a pinstripe that she would swear was pink. The coat was a match for the pants. The shirt, which had to be silk, was white and the tie was an abstract pattern of gray, black, white and pink.

Then she noticed that the suit was big—very big. It had to be to fit that body into it. Those were the hands that had grabbed her—huge and beefy. He wore a large opal ring on the left pinkie and his nails were buffed.

"Feeling better?" the man asked, as he shrugged out of his suit jacket and tie and rolled up his shirt sleeves. He carefully folded the jacket and tie and set them on the loading dock.

Juliana noticed something odd about his voice. No, not his voice, his words. He had some kind of accent. She filed that information away to think about later, when her head didn't hurt so much.

She focused on his head and wished upon him the pain she was feeling in hers. He was bald—shaved-head bald, not genetically bald. His head was shaped like an egg, but he didn't look silly. He looked ominous. His eyebrows were bushy and slanted downward toward his nose, giving him a perpetual scowl. The nose looked as though it had been broken more than once. His lips were full. His mouth had an odd slant that transformed the frown into a smirk.

She shivered. He looked as though he could kill her with one hand and not even chip a nail.

"Who are you?" she demanded. Her voice gave her away, though. It was high-pitched and timid.

"Ah, the usual question. I'll take that as a yes, that you are feeling better. Shall we get down to business, then?"

She was beginning to notice things around her, although the connection between her eyes and her brain was still a bit hazy. They were right outside the west fire exit, on a concrete loading dock. Somewhere—she couldn't remember which side—there was a ramp for rolling dollies and carts. If she could get to it—

A noise behind her made her jump. The throbbing in her head made her teeth ache as she squinted at the man behind her. She recognized his skinny frame and the ridiculous tattoos he had all over his arms. He was holding a flashlight that had blood smeared on the edge of it.

"You're that guy!" she cried. "You stole my letter!" She couldn't come up with his name, but she knew it was him. She recognized the colorful snake tattoo, as well as his narrow face and bad teeth.

"Get her up," the big man said.

"Maynard," she said. "Your name's Maynard."

"She's—" Maynard started.

"Shut up! Get her on her feet."

Maynard reached for her. She cringed away and held up her hands. "Don't touch me. I'll get up." She tried to get her feet under her, but her head began to swim.

Maynard grabbed her under her arms and jerked her upright.

Nausea gripped her. For a couple of seconds she clung to Maynard as she struggled to stand on her own.

"Very good, Ms. Caprese. Now to business."

"What—business?" Juliana rasped. She let go of Maynard's ratty T-shirt and wiped her hands on her jeans. Getting away from him cured a lot of the queasiness. "Who are you?"

"It doesn't matter who I am. Not to you. What matters is why we're here like this. You're meddling in things that are none of your business."

"None of my—" Sharp, searing anger burned away her queasiness. "I am trying to find out who caused my father's death. It *is* my business!"

The bald man shook his head. He reached into the inside pocket of his coat and brought out a fingernail file. He looked at his nails, then ran the file across one. "You're annoying Mr. Vega. That's never a good thing."

"I *knew* it! Vega's behind all this, isn't he? You—" She jabbed a finger in Maynard's direction. "Vega ordered you to attack me, didn't he?"

"Please, Ms. Caprese," the bald man said, lifting the hand with the file in it. "Calm down. I'm sure you can understand that accidents happen."

Juliana's scalp burned; she was so angry. "The Sky Walk's collapse was *no* accident. It was negligence at the very least."

The man shook his head, his expression showing regret. "As I said, accidents happen. It would be a tragedy if you were to fall from the cross beams of the casino's ceiling while trying to find proof for your theory about the Sky Walk."

"What?" His words made no sense at first. *Casino's ceiling?* Her head was still pounding. Then it hit her: he was threatening her.

"Oh, no," she said, shaking her head. "You'll never get me up there. If you want me dead, you'll have to shoot me. I'm not going anywhere."

"Trust me, you will. Maynard—"

Juliana reached for her gun but slapped at her empty waistband. Maynard's skinny arm hooked around her neck with surprising strength. She instinctively grabbed his tattooed forearm and tried to stomp on his feet, but he was as quick and agile as he was strong.

The bald man approached her. He still held something in his hand, but it was no longer the fingernail file. It was a syringe.

"No!" she cried, then filled her lungs to scream, but he punched her in the stomach.

Her breath whooshed out and pain cramped her insides. Before she could draw in another, she felt a pinprick on the side of her neck and everything went black.

THE CORVETTE'S TIRES screeched as Dawson turned in to the large driveway on the west end of the Golden Galaxy Casino. He had no plan except to storm the casino and find Jules. He headed toward the main entrance, but as he passed the loading dock, he caught a glimpse of a white face and a cloud of black hair.

Jules! He slammed on the brakes. Threw the stick into Reverse. Replayed the snapshot his brain had just taken.

A man held Jules's limp body as a smaller figure opened the fire door.

Dawson laid rubber as he backed around the massive concrete corner of the loading platform. Screeching to a halt and killing the engine, he jumped out just as the smaller man whirled around in the doorway to look at him. It was Maynard, the skinny tattooed skunk who'd attacked Jules and stolen her letter.

The skunk's close-set eyes widened. He yelled something. Then he backed through the door and manually jerked it shut.

Dawson took a running start and leaped up onto the dock. He lunged for the door. Pulling his weapon with one hand, he yanked the door open with the other.

He forced himself to enter cautiously. One or both men might be on the other side, waiting to shoot him. Standing in the doorway, he was painfully aware that his form was clearly outlined by the waning daylight. But he needed the light, too. He'd be totally blind in the dark until his eyes adapted—a sitting duck.

He didn't see anyone, but he heard footsteps—the sound of leather-soled shoes on hollow metal—the sound moving upward. Could that be what it sounded like? A ladder? He hadn't noticed a metal ladder in the casino. It had to be a service ladder, leading up to the network of beams that formed the framework of the huge glass dome. Was the bald goon climbing up to the rafter beams? With Jules?

Dawson gripped his weapon two-handed and swept the area in front of him with his gaze, then he let the fire door close.

When the sound of the latch slipping into place echoed through the dark building, he blinked several times. *Come on. I need to see.*

He heard the bullet whiz past him at the same time as the report. He ducked, too late to dodge that bullet. But he had to shield himself from the next.

Maynard had to be as blinded by the darkness as he. If so, he'd lucked out with a damn close shot. But just in case the skunk could see better than he could, he stayed low, studying the shadows, trying to judge what was where by the different shades of black.

He remembered that the poker room was on this end of the casino, near Caprese's office. Now the varied shadows made a little more sense. They were oval tables and straight chairs and small beverage carts. Plenty of cover. Or they would be once he figured out where Maynard was. He had an inkling from that first shot, but if the little skunk was smarter than Dawson thought he was, he'd have moved after he fired.

Crouched against the wall, Dawson yanked out his phone. He dialed 9-1-1.

"This is 9-1-1. What is the nature of your emergency?" the detached voice asked.

"Golden Galaxy Casino, Waveland," he said quietly but distinctly. "Shots fired. Two armed males holding female hostage."

"Sir, can you—"

A shot rang out.

"Send the police now! Golden Galaxy!" he commanded and hung up. He stuck the phone back in his pocket.

"Maynard!" he shouted. "Give it up. You know I'll get you."

No response. Would Maynard figure out Dawson was baiting him? Dawson was betting he wouldn't.

"I'd hate to have to kill you, Maynard. Give yourself up and I'll put in a good word for you."

"Screw you!" Maynard shouted in his tinny voice.

Dawson pinpointed the direction. For a split second, he hesitated. How much was he willing to bet that the big man had carried Jules up to the metal beams? How much was he willing to bet that she wasn't there with Maynard?

Was he willing to bet her life?

"Jules!" he shouted, but there was no answer. He shook his head. He had to. It was the only chance he had to save her. If he was wrong and his bullet found her— He shuddered. He took a long breath, rose and fired a shot.

Maynard yelped, cursed, then returned fire—three shots.

He doubted he'd hit the skinny skunk. The yelp was more likely surprise. He held his fire and crawled out onto the floor, away from the wall.

Another shot rang out. He dived instinctively and slammed into the leg of a table. He rubbed his stinging arm, feeling the unmistakable thick warmth of blood. The damn thing had cut him. It was metal, and that was a good thing. He was glad to sacrifice a little blood to find out that the tables would shield him from bullets. Now if he could just get Maynard to empty his gun. So far he'd fired four rounds.

"Maynard, you're going to run out of bullets," he shouted, hoping the skunk wouldn't be able to keep from bragging if he had another magazine.

No answer.

Dawson wasted another bullet, hoping to draw Maynard's fire. Sure enough, two more shots rang out.

Then, just as the echo of the second shot was fading, Dawson heard a sound that chilled him to the bone.

Jules screaming—or trying to.

Chapter Eighteen

Juliana had tried to scream, but her voice sounded so weak that it broke and ended with a fading moan.

"Jules!" he cried, unable to help himself. Where was she? The sound had echoed through the silent casino, but Dawson was pretty sure it had originated from over his head. That bald goon *had* carried her up to the ceiling. But why?

Bald goon. Damn! It was the same man who'd threatened his dad, who'd threatened his mom's life. He worked for Tito Vega!

So it was Vega who'd had her followed, who was determined to stop her from digging into the collapse of the Sky Walk.

"Daw—" Jules started, but Dawson heard a sharp slap and she cried out. The bastard had hit her. Anger burned in him.

Stop, he ordered himself. *Focus.* What was Vega up to?

Then he knew. Oh, God! He knew without a doubt exactly what the plan was. The goon had taken her up to the metal framework that had held the Sky Walk suspended over the casino.

It was brilliant. He had to give Vega that. *Poor Juliana had become obsessed with finding someone to blame for her father's death. She'd climbed up there to see for herself if the Sky Walk had failed or had been tampered with. She'd slipped and fallen to her death on the floor of the casino.*

Dawson shook off that image and tamped down the fear and sudden grief that came with it. He couldn't let emotions get in the way if he was going to have any chance to save her.

Tomorrow when demolition started, if the work crew didn't find her broken body in the wreckage, they'd plow her under the twisted wires and debris.

"Hey, Maynard, why did your fat, ugly partner leave you down here to get shot? Because if you don't give up now and make a deal, I *am* going to shoot you. And because you hurt her, I'm going to make it count. How'd you like to get gut shot? You'll have to carry your bathroom around strapped to a hole in your belly for the rest of your life. How much fun do you think that'll be in prison?"

"Shut up!" Maynard shrieked.

At the same time, the bald goon yelled, "Maynard, he's trying to rattle you! Kill him and get up here!"

Dawson rose up enough to get off a shot, then he scrambled toward the stage. He was gambling that the service ladder was hidden behind the stage.

Maynard shot three more times. Hell, that was nine shots. How big a magazine did he have? Must be a fifteen or a twenty-five round.

Dawson craned his neck, trying to get a glimpse of Jules and the goon. The sun was long gone and he could see the dark sky through the glass dome above him.

"Hey, Baldy," he shouted, squinting, searching for a human shape.

There! He saw a movement. Then he could make out Jules's pale oval face and the goon's shiny head. "You're not leaving here alive, you know."

"Don't worry about me," the man yelled. "Worry about yourself and your young woman. You are the ones who won't leave here alive."

"How're you going to get out? The police are on their way,

and of course I'm here, just waiting for you to climb down those stairs." Dawson heard a noise behind him and ducked. He felt the heat from the bullet as it whizzed past his neck. Way too close for comfort.

Maynard had decided to go on the offensive. He'd picked up a piece of plastic from the front of a slot machine and was using it as a shield as he walked toward Dawson. He fired again. *Twelve.* Did he have three more bullets or thirteen?

Dawson hit the floor and rolled under one of the game tables. He tipped it over. Maynard put three bullets into the tabletop.

"Enough of this," Dawson muttered. He didn't care if Maynard had ten bullets left. Rising from behind the table, Dawson took aim and shot Maynard, right through the plastic shield. He hit him in the gut, just like he'd promised.

Maynard screamed.

Dawson quickly went over and grabbed Maynard's gun. "You pitiful idiot," he said. "Your damn shield was plastic, you imbecile."

Maynard was sobbing and moaning. "D-deal—" he gasped.

"Not now." Dawson turned his back on Maynard and maneuvered between tables until he was less than six feet away from the ladder. He shone his flashlight up and found them.

The goon had his forearm around her neck. It looked like her feet were barely touching the ground. Whenever he wanted to, Baldy could let go and with no more than a nudge, could send Jules crashing to the casino floor. And there was nothing Dawson could do. The most he could hope for would be to put himself under her, hoping to break her fall. But from fifty feet, he doubted either one of them would survive.

He racked his brain but couldn't think of a way to save her. He'd promised to protect her. He could hear her now.

I can take care of myself. His mouth turned up in a smile, then it hit him.

She could save herself. She might end up falling anyway, or Baldy could toss her over. But it was her only chance to live.

"Jules, listen to me," he shouted. "Grab hold of him. His arm, his neck, his belt. Anything you can grab. You've got only one chance, so make it good. Hold on and don't let go. No matter what! Then kick him, bite him. But *don't let go.* If you do, you'll fall. I'm coming up." He headed for the metal ladder. He had to hand it to Baldy. He'd climbed up here one-handed, carrying Jules. While she was slender, she was tall and shapely—certainly not tiny. The man must be strong.

"Maynard! You stupid—" Baldy broke off and growled.

Dawson could barely see the two of them, but he could hear Jules grunting and Baldy growling and cursing. He almost lost his grip—his hands were trembling so. *Don't fall, Jules. I can't lose you.*

"Maynard, shoot him!"

Dawson laughed out loud. "Maynard can't shoot, Baldy. Why don't you do your own dirty work?" The thought had barely popped into his head before he'd said it. He was sure Baldy had a gun. Maybe he'd pull it and try to shoot Dawson. If Dawson could make him do that, it would make it even harder for him to hold on to Jules.

"Ah!" Jules shrieked.

Dawson's heart nearly exploded with panic. He was almost at the top of the stairs, but he'd had to use both hands to climb. He paused to pull his gun out of his waistband.

Baldy was turning in place, trying to maintain his balance while kicking and swinging at Jules. Somehow she'd managed to grab on to the back of his belt. Her legs were wrapped around his knees. She was desperately holding on as Baldy whirled and grabbed at her clothes, her hair, anything he could reach.

He snagged her hair and pulled. Jules shrieked and almost lost her grip.

"Freeze, Baldy," Dawson shouted as he stepped onto the two-foot-wide beam from the ladder. It was amazing that the man could stay on these beams, as big as he was.

The bald goon cursed and spat, then he let go of Jules's hair and reached inside his coat.

"Don't do it!" Dawson warned.

Baldy ignored him. His hand came out holding his weapon, a big 9 mm. But instead of aiming it at Dawson, he put the barrel of the gun against Jules's thigh.

Dawson's pulse burned through his veins like jet fuel. Had he blown Jules's only chance? "Wait!" he yelled. "What do you want?"

Baldy smiled. "You are smarter than I thought. That's good. I want out of here, free and clear, of course."

"Can't do that," Dawson said, trying to keep the fear out of his voice. "But I can let you out alive. If you shoot her, I swear I'll make you a quadriplegic."

Baldy shook his head. "You're not going to risk shooting me. If I go down, so does your girlfriend."

"I can get you a deal. I've got influence," Dawson pressed.

"Not good enough." Baldy had the barrel of the gun pressed against the top of Jules's right thigh, which was wrapped around his knees. His elbow was bent and he held the barrel straight, to keep from accidentally hitting himself with the bullet. "Try again."

Dawson saw Jules bow her head. Was she losing her grip on Baldy? Were her arms and legs getting tired? *Don't give up.*

"Come on, man. Vega would give you up in a heartbeat.

Give me Vega and I'm betting you could skate by with five years, no more."

"I can't be in prison," Baldy protested. "I might as well die right here." He looked down at his gun, as if contemplating taking his life.

At that instant, Jules leaned farther over, let go of Baldy's belt with her right hand. In one fluid motion she grabbed his shirt sleeve, opened her mouth and bit down on the skin of his elbow with all her might.

Baldy bellowed, jerked sharply and nearly dropped his gun. He teetered for a second or two, and nearly fell when Jules let go of his belt and scrambled away. But he finally managed to grab hold of a strut.

"Careful, Jules!" Dawson shouted as he dived toward her across the metal latticework.

Baldy touched his elbow. His hand came away covered in blood. He roared in rage. "You—" he growled at Jules. He lifted his arm and aimed at her.

"Jules!" Dawson yelled. He threw himself in front of her, grabbing a wire to steady himself and, in the same motion, he raised his gun to shoot.

Something struck him right below his ribs. The impact knocked him backward. The wire cut into his hand. He fired at Baldy one-handed, too off-balance to aim.

He heard the man grunt, heard his leather-soled shoes slipping on the metal.

Don't fall, man! Don't die. They needed his testimony.

"Police," a commanding voice rang out from below them. "You up there, drop the gun."

Dawson was shocked. He hadn't heard sirens. He'd decided the 9-1-1 operator had written him off as a crank call, and he hadn't had a chance to call back. He blew out a breath of relief, which hurt—a lot.

He touched the place where it hurt and his hand came

away all bloody. Had he been shot? It didn't matter. Everything was okay now. The cavalry had arrived. He kept Baldy in his sights, just to be sure he obeyed the officer.

"I said drop it," the officer yelled. "I *will* shoot you." Dawson had no doubt he would. His determination resounded in his voice.

Baldy looked at the gun and Dawson's heart rate tripled. His mouth had lost its perpetual sneer. He looked like—like he was considering suicide. Dawson took a breath to try to reason with him.

Then Baldy met his gaze. "Deal?" he said.

Dawson nodded. "Deal."

"This is your last warning, mister," the officer shouted.

"Don't shoot. I'm dropping the gun," Baldy yelled. "Here it comes." He let go of the weapon. It hit the marble floor with a sharp clatter.

Then two officers were scrambling up the metal ladder and heading straight for Baldy. They warned him to stand still while they patted him down and cautioned him to walk carefully on the beams and not make any sudden moves.

"You go down the ladder first," one officer told him. "Sergeant Flynn has you covered. Flynn, coming down," he shouted.

As Baldy climbed down, Dawson could hear Flynn reciting his Miranda rights.

The officer turned toward him. "You all right? Any injuries?"

Dawson shifted and grimaced. "I've got a flesh wound, but—"

"Ma'am, are you okay?" the officer called to Jules.

She didn't answer.

"Jules?" Dawson whirled in place. She was lying still—too still. Her eyes were closed.

"Jules, answer me!" He touched her shoulder but she didn't

move. He reached out to push a strand of hair away from her face and his fingers came away wet. He stared at them, uncomprehendingly at first. Then he knew.

It was blood—her blood.

JULIANA WOKE UP but she wished she hadn't. The lights were too bright and something was buzzing around her head. She lay there without moving, hoping she could go back to sleep. And maybe she could, if her head weren't hurting so badly.

The buzzing wasn't helping, either. She tried to block it out, but it just got louder and more annoying.

...still not talking...

...if he'll give up Vega or not...

Those were words, mixed in with the buzzing. Giving up on the possibility of any more sleep, Juliana lay there listening. She'd recognized some of the words, so maybe if she lay very still, she'd be able to make sense of all of them.

...when she wakes up enough to...

That was Dawson. "Daw—" She opened her eyes, blinked and looked around. Moving her eyes made her head hurt, so she closed them again.

"She's awake."

"Ms. Caprese, I just need to—"

"Hey, Brian!" Dawson's voice again, sharp and commanding. "Get out. I promise you'll get to talk to her, but not now. Go put the screws to your Mr. Schumer again."

Juliana left her eyes closed. She listened to the people leaving. After the footsteps faded, she heard a door close, then Dawson took her hand in his.

She squinted at him.

"How're you feeling?" he asked.

She narrowed her gaze. Why was he being so nice? A knife blade of fear tore through her and she gasped.

"What is it?" he asked, squeezing her hand more tightly. "Are you hurting?"

"What happened?" she asked. "I can't remember—"

"You were at the Golden Galaxy and two men grabbed you. One was—"

Juliana didn't hear anything else Dawson said. Memories pelted her like machine gun fire, rat-tat-tatting too fast to process. All she could do was let them blast the inside of her eyelids.

The dark casino. The slot machines. The eerie sounds. Flashlight beam. Whisperings. Bald man. Syringe. Dizziness. Gunshots. Grasping. Holding on. Blood. Pain. Silence.

She pressed her palms against the side of her head. Her fingers touched a bandage. She explored it gingerly as she waited for her head to stop spinning.

"What's wrong, Jules? Is it your head? Should I call a nurse?" He reached for the call button. "Yeah, let me get a nurse."

"No!" she snapped. "Stop. Nobody else." She cautiously lowered her hands, testing to see if the machine gun fire had stopped. It had—at least for the moment.

"Tell me what happened," she ordered him.

He gave her a hard glance, then stood.

She gasped. Under the blue scrub shirt he had on, she saw the bulge of a bandage. "What's that?" she asked, pointing. "You're hurt."

He looked down and gingerly touched the bandage. "This, nothing. It's nothing."

She frowned at him. "Dawson—"

"Okay, I'll give you the abridged version for now. You apparently went to the casino to find the ring you'd dropped when the beam fell."

"How—"

He held up a hand. "Let me finish, then you can ask questions. Somehow, Maynard and Schumer cornered you and knocked you out with something—we found the syringe and it's being analyzed. Schumer carried—"

"Wait," she said, holding up a hand. "Schumer?"

"The bald goon. He carried you up to the ceiling framework. We think he was planning to push you, making it look like you'd climbed up there and lost your balance. It would have been a tragic accident and your suspicions and your proof would die with you."

"But you followed me."

Dawson shook his head. "No. You didn't wait for me, so I had to try and *guess* where you'd gone. If I'd been a few seconds later, you'd be dead."

Did she imagine it or did Dawson's voice break? "He shot you, didn't he?" she snapped. "That's a gunshot wound."

"He did." Dawson walked over to the bed and touched the bandage on her temple. "But what I didn't know, and what scared me to death, was that the bullet went through me and grazed your temple." He paused. "God, Jules, I thought—"

"Then why aren't you in bed like me? If the bullet went through you—"

A nurse who'd come in holding a clipboard interrupted. "I'll tell you why, Ms. Caprese. He's gone AMA—against medical advice. He wouldn't stay in bed. Had to get in here to see you." The nurse leveled a hard stare at Dawson, then turned back to her.

"You're being discharged. Do you have someone who can drive you home and stay with you for a couple of days?"

"She does," Dawson said quickly.

"Good. Now if you'll just sign these—" The nurse thrust the clipboard into Juliana's lap and handed her a pen. "We'll get you out of here. That first sheet is yours. It's wound care instructions. Although your little scratch won't be a problem.

Put some antibiotic ointment on it and keep it bandaged for a couple of days."

Juliana signed where she was supposed to and handed the clipboard back to the nurse. While she was signing, Dawson's phone rang. He stepped out of the room to answer it.

By the time he was done, the nurse had brought a wheelchair. While she wheeled Juliana downstairs, Dawson went ahead to bring the car around. He got her situated in the passenger seat and headed east.

"I'm taking you to my condo. You can rest while I go meet Brian Hardy. Schumer's finally decided to talk."

"No, I'm going with you," Juliana said. She was not going to miss this. The bald man's confession could be the last missing piece of the puzzle. She might finally know just exactly what happened to the Sky Walk and why.

"I don't think—"

"If you can go with that hole in your side, I can. Mine is just a 'little scratch.'"

Dawson shot her a glare. "The nurse said you should take it easy for a few days."

"Oh, yeah? Well, she said you were going against medical advice."

"Jules, you've been through a lot."

"And you haven't?" Juliana rubbed her head. "I barely remember what happened. Did I bite somebody?"

He smiled. "You bit Baldy—Schumer. You were hanging on to his belt. You did good."

"Whatever he gave me, every bit of that seems like a dream. Was I really way up above the casino?"

"Yeah. It's probably better if you don't remember it. So I'll put you to bed and then—"

"I have to give a statement anyway. I can do that while I'm there."

He sent her a disgusted glance but he didn't argue. He turned toward the Waveland police station.

When they got there, Detective Hardy greeted them. He peered at the strip bandage on her temple. "Juliana, I wasn't expecting to see you for a day or two. It looks like you're doing pretty good."

"Thank you. Where's the bald man?"

Hardy looked at Dawson, who shrugged. She chose to ignore them. "He's in the interrogation room with his lawyer. The assistant district attorney, Maura Presley, just left. She's giving him a few minutes to talk with his lawyer about her offer of a deal."

"What did she offer him?" Dawson asked.

"Well, I told her what we have on him—aggravated assault on Juliana."

"Assault? Don't you mean *attempted murder?* He was going to throw her fifty feet to the casino floor. He took her up there to murder her."

Juliana knew that—in her head, but hearing Dawson say it sent icy fear up her spine. The memory of being fifty feet above the casino on a maze of two-foot-wide beams was unreal. It seemed like a nightmare.

Hardy looked exasperated. "I thought you were the one who wanted a super-deal for him, so he'd talk."

Dawson's jaw flexed. "So what is Maura offering him?"

"Ten years—eight suspended, plus two years of supervised probation, if he testifies against Vega."

"Vega? He's going to testify against Vega? That's what the deal is for?" Juliana asked. Her heart fluttered like a panicked butterfly. Was Vega finally going to be exposed for what he really was? Then a memory that had gotten buried under the terror of her ordeal surfaced.

"Vega!" She grabbed Dawson's arm. "Dawson, I think

Vega was targeting my dad! It was something to do with his son."

Dawson nodded and jerked a thumb toward Hardy. "I've already told Brian. Your dad gave Anthony Vega a job at the Beachview Casino in Gulfport, but before long he found out Anthony was shaking down customers. Your dad had him arrested and despite Tito's influence, Anthony went to prison and was killed."

Juliana broken in. "I knew it! I knew there had to be a connection. So he blamed my dad for his son's death? That proves it, doesn't it?"

"Listen, Juliana," Detective Hardy said. "Even if we could prove that the Sky Walk was brought down deliberately at a specific time when your father was in his office, linking it to Tito Vega will be a crapshoot at best. He has friends in places so high you need an air mask. Plus, he could drag a lot of prominent people down with him—politicians, businessmen, community leaders. It's liable to be a bloodbath."

"He murdered my father. What are you saying? That you can't do it? Or that you won't?"

Chapter Nineteen

Hardy ran a hand down his face. "We can't prove it. Our best bet is sitting right in there." He nodded toward the interrogation room. "But right now we're at a standoff. Schumer won't share what he's got until he has a deal and Maura won't offer a deal until she knows what she has to work with." Hardy gestured with his head. "There's Maura." He motioned her over.

"Maura Presley, this is Juliana Caprese and Dawson Delancey."

Maura was a tall blonde whose black-rimmed glasses couldn't hide her beauty. She was dressed conservatively, in a black suit with a no-nonsense white shirt. Her briefcase was Coach and her pumps were Alexander McQueen. She held out her hand to Juliana and then to Dawson.

"So are you about to go back in?" Hardy asked her.

"We've taken it this far. Let's go see what Schumer has to say."

"Maura, before you go in, I've got something on Vega," Dawson said. "Or I will have by early in the morning. It just might link Vega with money laundering, maybe even worse."

Maura Presley eyed him narrowly. "Might?" She sounded interested but skeptical.

He nodded. "That's why I want to hear what Schumer's got."

The three of them slipped into the viewing room as Maura

entered the interrogation room. The big bald goon sat at the table. His shirt was wrinkled and the right elbow was soaked in blood. His mouth no longer curled up in a sneer. Maura walked in, set the tape recorder on the table and flipped the switch. Schumer wiped a beefy hand down his face.

"Well, Mr. Schumer, have you had a chance to think about my offer?"

He regarded her silently and a ghost of the sneer briefly crossed his face. "What I've got is good enough to put Vega away. But if he knows that I have done this, I will not survive two months, much less two years behind bars. His fingers reach far."

Hardy whistled and Dawson slammed a fist into his palm.

"What?" Juliana asked.

"He's never mentioned Vega's name before," Hardy said, glancing at Dawson. "This could work."

Maura sat back and folded her arms. "I can put you into a maximum security federal facility in another state, *if* what you have is good enough—"

"It is!"

Maura held up her hand. "*If* it's good enough to stick," she emphasized. "If Vega walks, you go to the Mississippi State Penitentiary."

Schumer's face blanched. "I won't last a day at Parchman. Vega can snap his fingers and have me killed."

"Then you'd better hope your information is good."

The bald man nodded. "I swear it is."

Juliana touched Hardy's arm. "Do you know what he's got?"

Hardy exchanged another look with Dawson. "Let's get out of here."

He led them out of the viewing room and to his desk. He sat behind it. Dawson gestured to her to sit in the single straight-backed chair, and he stood behind her.

Hardy said, "We informed Schumer that Maynard copped to stealing the letter and that he told us Schumer had it. Schumer finally admitted it. He claims it was written by Randall Knoblock and that Knoblock enclosed a flash drive that held a recording of a telephone conversation he had with Vega."

"Of course! That was the rectangular object I felt in the envelope," Juliana said.

"Did he say what the phone conversation was?" Dawson asked.

"He said it proves Vega was the one who ordered the changes in the Sky Walk. Said Knoblock told Vega he was done with him."

"What about Knoblock. Can we find him? Will he testify?" Dawson asked.

Brian shook his head. "I've had a man checking on him. Knoblock's dead. He was killed in a car crash—hit-and-run—about a week after the letter was stolen."

"That's what my dad was afraid of. He told me Vega would never leave a loose end like Knoblock alive," Dawson said.

"Vega killed him," Juliana gasped.

"I doubt we can prove that," Brian said.

"So what about the letter and the flash drive?" Dawson continued.

"If Maura can talk Schumer into taking her deal, he'll produce the evidence. She'll have to decide if it's substantial enough, If it is, she'll send Schumer to the facility she mentioned, and take the evidence to the grand jury. This is going to be a long process at best. And I doubt seriously there's a judge in the country who will remand Vega."

"So Jules could still be in danger."

"Vega will be under a microscope once all this comes out. My guess is that with you to protect her, Juliana will be safe as houses."

She felt Dawson stiffen beside her and she knew exactly what he was thinking. After the way she'd acted when she'd seen Michael Delancey's name in his phone, he wanted nothing more than to be rid of her.

A WEEK LATER Juliana stood in the living room of her father's house and waved goodbye to a real-estate agent. The woman had given her the name of a handyman to replace the picture window and rip out the carpet. She needed to have the whole house professionally cleaned to get rid of the odors of smoke and gasoline before she had new carpet and drapes installed.

The agent had suggested that she update the kitchen with new appliances and new cabinets. Juliana told her that if she were keeping the house, she'd do a total kitchen remodel, but because she was selling it, she'd just throw in an appliance allowance for the buyers.

She felt good about the asking price. A wistful pang brought sudden tears to her eyes. She loved this house and would love to live here, but it wasn't practical. It was much too big for a single woman, and selling it would secure her future.

Several years ago, when he decided to retire, her dad had added the den and made the carport into a combination media and craft room where he tied fishing flies and tinkered with small wood projects. Then he'd added a two-car garage. Altogether, he'd increased the size of the house from 2,100 to 3,200 square feet.

She swallowed against a lump in her throat. She'd give every last penny to have her dad back. But at least Vega would pay for his part in her dad's death.

Don't get your hopes too high, Dawson had warned her. *If Vega draws a judge who owes him or one he's got dirt on, things might not go your way. One big thing in our favor, though, is that bank records from the Cayman Islands prove that Vega may have been laundering money through his various corporations for years.*

Our favor. The only reason he'd said that was because the evidence not only connected Vega with the Sky Walk, but it also helped to prove his dad wasn't responsible for the collapse.

"Get out of my head, Dawson," she muttered as she picked up the real-estate agent's card and headed for the kitchen to stick it in her purse.

"Somebody taking my name in vain?" a familiar sexy-as-sin voice said.

Juliana whirled. Dawson was standing in the doorway, looking like everything she'd ever dreamed of. He had on creased khaki pants and a crisp white shirt with the sleeves rolled up.

She frowned, reminding herself that he was done with her. "What are you doing here?"

He stepped inside and frowned back at her. "Was that a real-estate agent's car I saw leaving?"

She nodded. "I'm going to sell it, after I get the repairs done."

"Hmm."

"What?"

"Nothing," Dawson replied, looking around the living room. "The damage isn't too bad in here."

What was he doing here, acting all normal? "Do you have news about Vega?" she asked.

He walked over to the hall door and checked out the hall. Then he turned back to her. "Hardy told me what Knoblock's letter said. He claimed Vega ordered him to use materials that would guarantee the Sky Walk would collapse."

She tried to process that. "I don't understand. I mean, I'm glad if it's enough to put Vega away, but why would he do something that would kill innocent people?"

"Remember I told you that your dad had made notes in his day planner about Vega's son? He told your dad he'd been a friend of yours in school. Once your dad figured out that Anthony was blackmailing wealthy gamblers who were running around on their wives or cheating or whatever else he could dig up on them, your dad called the police. Anthony was arrested for extortion and blackmail."

Juliana nodded. "You gave the day planners to the assistant district attorney."

"Vega had already begun plans to build the Golden Galaxy. He was going to give it to Anthony to run. But then Anthony was killed. Vega was devastated by the death of his only son, but he went ahead with his plans to have the casino built."

"So he hired Daddy to manage it—"

"Because he blamed him for Anthony's death. It was your dad who'd put Anthony in prison. Vega wanted your dad ruined. The Sky Walk would collapse. Vega would make sure your dad never worked again. He probably didn't plan to kill him. Who knows if he thought innocent people would die. But he made sure the Sky Walk would break. It was his idea of vengeance."

"All that for vengeance against my father."

"That's the way Knoblock outlined it in his letter. The recorded phone conversation, plus my dad's testimony, should clinch it."

"Your dad?"

"My dad overheard that same telephone conversation with Knoblock. He had no idea what it meant because he only heard Knoblock's side of it. His statement to the police is almost word for word what Knoblock said on the phone."

Juliana squeezed her eyes shut. "I think I'm still very confused."

"Hey, you're the one who got all this started by figuring

out the connections between Vega and all those corporations. Because of your flowchart, I sent an investigator to Switzerland to check out Bayside Industries. What he brought back was solid gold—a connection between Bayside Industries and Meadow Gold and a bank in the Caymans. It was your research, your flowchart, that will convict Vega of money laundering."

"So Vega is facing money laundering charges? What else?"

"Probably reckless endangerment is the most they can get him on for the Sky Walk's collapse. But he's also being investigated for extortion and possible murder charges, if anything comes of Knoblock's death."

Juliana felt overwhelmed. "I don't know if I'm glad he's going to be punished or furious that he won't be serving consecutive life sentences for six murders."

"Hey," Dawson said, reaching out an arm toward her, but then hesitating. "In all these years nobody has been able to bring Vega down. You did it."

"Not by myself. And I don't really feel triumphant. Just sad."

He nodded, then turned back toward the hall door. "What's through here?" he asked, walking into the hall and across to the den. "Wow, nice den. It would make a great office."

"Haven't you seen it before?"

"No, I never made it inside the house." He turned and gave her a small smile. "I'd like to say I rescued you from the fire, but a fireman was bringing you out by the time I got here." He went to the next door off the hall.

"What's through there?" He headed toward it without waiting for her to answer.

"Dawson," she started, but he was through the door and turning on the light. She had no choice but to follow.

"What a cool room. Big-screen TV, surround sound. Why're you selling? You ought to move back here." He looked around. "A refrigerator. Your dad sure knew how to live." As soon as the words left his mouth, he grimaced. "Sorry."

She smiled. "It's okay," she said, and realized it really was. "He did know how to live. He loved football and basketball. I was stunned when he added all this, but he told me he was—" She had to stop. That lump was back. She swallowed, then continued. "He said he wanted plenty of room for—for grandkids."

Dawson had his arms around her before she was aware that he'd moved. She stiffened. She couldn't bear to have him hold her and then walk away.

He obviously felt her go still because he let go of her, but not before planting a gentle kiss on her forehead. "I'm sorry, Jules. I know you miss him."

"So you came here to tell me about Vega? I'm glad he's going to pay for what he did. But—" she gestured vaguely in the direction of the living room "—I was just about to leave."

He took a step backward and an odd expression crossed his face. "Okay," he said. "The only other thing I have is information from Maura Presley. She's arranged for a civil lawyer to prepare briefs for a civil case against Vega, for reparations to the families of the people who died in the Sky Walk's collapse. She's also asked him to look into restoring my dad's architectural license."

"I'm glad, about all of it. So you and your dad—"

Dawson didn't speak for a minute. He walked over to the TV and examined it. "Yeah, we're doing okay. I realized I never gave him a chance."

Juliana looked at him. It obviously had been a big step for him to go to his dad and apologize. It had taken a lot of courage. Speaking of courage, if she was ever going to apologize to him, now was the time. She was afraid that once he walked out the front door she might never see him again.

She took a long breath. "I know what you mean," she said.

Dawson cocked an eyebrow at her. "What I mean about what?"

"About giving people a chance. I realized—" She'd used up all her breath, or maybe it was the tightness in her throat. She tried again. "I never gave you a chance."

He leaned against a dark wood bookcase and picked up a DVD, examining it. "Tell me more," he said without looking up.

She frowned at him. Was he mocking her? She couldn't be sure. "I should have let you explain when I—when I found out who you were—are."

"Yeah—" He took a deep breath. "I guess I should have told you who I am from the beginning."

"I understand why you didn't," she replied.

"You do?" he asked, lifting his head slightly. The odd, pensive look was still in his expression.

She nodded. "I probably would have shot you."

He nodded, but he didn't smile at her joke.

She swallowed hard. "Dawson, I want you to have—" She stopped. What had she done with it? She patted her pockets. It had been in these jeans—which she'd washed.

Oh, please, please don't be lost. She slid her fingers into the left front pocket and felt around.

There. Thank God. She slid her hand out and closed her fist around it. Her breath whooshed out in relief.

"What are you doing?"

"You know how many times I asked you not to call me Jules?"

He nodded, looking wary. "A lot."

"Well, it was because that's what my dad called me. I didn't want anyone else—I didn't want you—that close."

He looked down at the DVD.

"Here," she said, stepping closer to him. She was going

to chicken out if she didn't get it over with. "Hold out your hand."

He did, frowning.

"I want you to have this. It was my dad's. It was very special to him. He'd have liked you. He'd have—told me to get over myself." She ran the words together, afraid she might cry before she got them out.

She had no idea what he would do—she had no idea what she wanted him to do. All she knew was that for whatever reason, it seemed right that he should have her dad's wedding ring. It was little enough payment for everything he'd done for her.

"What is this?" He held it up, then brought it closer and squinted. "Do you know what's engraved on here?"

She nodded. *Here they came.* The tears. She sniffed and wiped her eyes. "I know. My mom did it. She had it engraved and gave it to Daddy on their wedding day."

He looked stunned. "What am I supposed to do with it?" he asked, his voice sounding hoarse.

"I—I don't know. Wear it? Put it in a box somewhere?" She wiped the tears away and stuck her chin out. "Pawn it if things get tough?"

His throat moved as he swallowed. He frowned, raised his brows, frowned again. Then he laughed.

"Don't—" she started, but he held up a hand.

"No, wait—" he gasped. "You're not going to believe this."

Juliana's heart wrenched, hurt by his laughter.

But the laughter stopped and he grew solemn. He drew in a long breath. "I was talking to my mom and dad last night and, well, you came up. I was telling them about your wanting to be a private investigator and how—" he cleared his throat "—how brave and determined you are."

He stopped, twirling her dad's ring on the tip of his index

finger and staring at it. "Mom, she's brave and determined, too. You'll like her."

Juliana was speechless. She'd never seen Dawson like this. He was awkward, maybe even shy.

"So my mom gives me a look and goes to her room and comes back with something. She—you'd have to know her—" he said, shaking his head. "She still treats me like I'm sixteen. She patted my cheek and said maybe it was time she gave it to me." He sucked in a breath, as if his words had used up all his air.

"Gave what to you?" Juliana's lungs felt deflated, too. She didn't dare to guess what he was talking about.

He reached into his back pocket and pulled something out—a box. Tiny. Velvet.

"Wh-what's that?" she asked, hardly able to hear herself over the pounding of her heart.

He fumbled with it for a second, then finally opened it. Inside, on a black velvet pillow, was the most beautiful ring she had ever seen. The gold setting mimicked flower petals and on each petal was a diamond or a ruby.

"Oh," she said, choking on the word. "What—what is that? Why are you showing it to me?"

"Because my mom told me to."

Her gaze snapped to his. "What?"

He smiled. "I think I already knew, but I can be a little dense sometimes. My mom told me to tell you that I love you."

"You—"

He nodded. "This was my grandmother's ring, and I'd be most honored if you'd consider wearing it. I'd like for us to be partners."

"Partners? Dawson, I don't understand what you're talking about. The ring, it's too much. It's—"

He grinned at her. "I need somebody who's as good at

paperwork and research as you are because I hate that stuff. I want you to come to work for me, as my partner."

"Your partner." Something didn't sound right. He was holding a beautiful, priceless ring and talking about *hiring* her.

"Yeah. In D&D Services. But we'll have to change that."

"Change what?" She felt like a parrot. All she could do was repeat what he said.

"The name. Not change it exactly. Just its meaning. It was Dedicated and Discreet. Now it'll be Delancey and Delancey."

"Delancey and—"

Dawson picked up her hand and slipped the ring onto her left ring finger. "And Delancey." Then he looked up at her with what looked like fear in his eyes.

"Hmm," she said, frowning at him. "If you're going to be a married man, you're going to have to say what you mean."

He laughed and shook his head. "I guess I am. Will you wear my grandmother's ring and promise to never leave me?"

Juliana stared at him until his brows drew down and his intense blue eyes darkened. She realized she hadn't answered him, so she threw herself into his arms.

He kissed her. For a long time they kissed and nuzzled and whispered and kissed some more. Then Dawson lifted his head. "Does this house have any bedrooms?" he asked.

Juliana giggled and took his hand. "Yes. This way," she said and led him to her room.

"This is yours," he said.

She nodded. "But wait. I haven't said whether I'll wear your grandmother's ring." She took a deep breath. "I will— if you'll wear my dad's ring."

"I will," he said solemnly. He handed her the ring and she slipped it onto his left ring finger. "It fits perfectly," he said.

"That's because you have perfect fingers." She kissed each

one of them. Then she raised her head and kissed him. Soon both of them were breathless.

"Don't you like this house?" he asked her as he unbuttoned her shirt.

"Yes, of course I do," she answered as she unbuttoned his. "But it's too big for me."

"Sell it to me," he said, sliding her shirt down off her shoulders and kissing her skin.

"You?" Her fingers quit working. "Why?"

He kissed the curve of her shoulder and traced it up to her neck with his lips. "I've always wanted a big house, and I have a feeling we're going to need one. Just because your dad's not right here with us doesn't mean we can't fill this house with grandchildren for him."

Juliana beamed as tears filled her eyes. "No, it doesn't. Are you suggesting we get started now? Because I think that's a great idea."

* * * * *